M. C.

I am my
Brother's Keeper

C . J .   M C S H A N E

 FriesenPress

Suite 300 - 990 Fort St
Victoria, BC, Canada, V8V 3K2
www.friesenpress.com

Copyright © 2015 by C.J. McShane
First Edition — 2015
Photographs by Don Thomas

ISBN
978-1-4602-4915-4 (Hardcover)
978-1-4602-4916-1 (Paperback)
978-1-4602-4917-8 (eBook)

1. Fiction, Crime

Distributed to the trade by The Ingram Book Company

Acknowledgements

I learned early on to seek counsel from those in my life who would care enough to give me sound and practical advice while writing this novel. I would like to say thank you to those who participated in the project beginning with Lynn Harris, a wonderful friend who first advised me on content, structure and style. Lynn told me the ending of the book was every bit as important as the opening and she advised me not to fall into the same "end all" as some authors do by hurrying the ending. I hope you are pleased, Lynn, because I listened. I would also like to thank my brother Don Thomas who advised me on content, but also provided the colors design and photography. The book simply would not be what it is without his contribution and I am grateful. A book without a cover is a book without appeal. My brother J.C. Bullard along with my old friend Paul Gonzales and his wife Valerie all provided great feedback on content but also posed for the cover. I can't say thank you enough for agreeing to put it out there, as you did. Bradley Junker and Saint Nick both contributed advice and encouragement while participating in the production of the promotional materials. Gary Moore provided direction and support with graphics and marketing and the team at FriesenPress provided editing, publishing and marketing support. Our four children and their spouses played a critical role in the writing of this book with their encouragement, love and support and to them I say thank you for not getting tired of hearing me talk about it. A special word of thanks to my wife Pam, who spent many hours proof reading, discussing ideas and for providing the initial editing of the manuscript. Without her patience and love, I simply would not have finished the project.

C. J.

*S*ome would ask, what exactly is a One-Percenter? The answer you get to that question will depend on who you ask. Law enforcement will tell you that 1%ers are outlaw motorcycle gangs, organized criminals, men whose activities center around violent intimidation and coercion. Ask the poor whose children receive gifts at Christmas, often distributed by 1%ers and carried on their motorcycles into the neighborhoods where John Q Public wouldn't dare venture, and they'll tell you that 1%ers are their heroes.

To the public at large, the 1%er is an enigma, largely unknown or unfamiliar and someone to be wary of.

Ask the man who wears the 1%er patch and he'll tell you that it represents his way of life. A life that revolves around three fundamental tenets: Love, Loyalty, and Respect. A **Love** for the freedom of the open road and for his brothers who share the road with him; **Loyalty** above ALL ELSE to his brothers, and the willingness to defend those brothers beyond the bounds of bleeding and breathing, and finally, **Respect** for all who SHOW respect and a punishing response for those <u>who do not</u>.

Jake Coleman is one such man. Come ride with him as he experiences the complexities of existence in a 1%er Motorcycle Club, and the difficulties involved in "Earning the Patch." Feel his sense of belonging as his friendships deepen, and know his heartache at the loss of those he admires and loves. Understand his determination to belong as he finds his place among those known as Los Patrons, and share in his sense of purpose, as he realizes,

"I Am My Brother's Keeper"

One man's journey in search of Brotherhood

March, 2013

Daylight was fading and the pain was crippling. I couldn't have been there more than a couple of minutes, but the smell of blood mixed with gasoline left me wanting to puke.

My right shoulder was blown to hell, my left leg was broken, and it was hard to move without hurting.

I can't believe it! That mother fucker shot me! He watched me go down and now, here I am, lying in this ditch buried in a twisted heap of spokes, chrome, and blood.

Oh man, there is so much blood and I'm so light-headed. I gotta find a way to get moving or I'm going to fuckin' bleed out, right here!

God Forgives Ө Patrons Repay

M. C.

I am my
Brother's Keeper

Chapter One

HANG AROUND

It was Saturday night in May of 2011. The Texas summer had come early and my air conditioning was broken. There was nothing on television and pussy was scarce. With no one to ride with and another lonely night in my hot apartment facing me, I decided to get on my bike and ride to the bar up near the Beltway, a place called Bikers' Haven. I'd ridden by the place many times seeing a lot of different people going in and out, but I had never stopped. I was fuckin' bored to shit and I wanted some adventure so I decided to check it out. The twenty-minute ride to the place was a great break from my boredom, and as I rode, letting the wind cool me from that sweaty existence in my apartment, I couldn't help but think of what it must be like for cagers who never get to experience the freedom of riding a motorcycle. I chuckled, thinking, *I don't even own a car.*

When I rode onto the property, I was distracted by something going on behind the bar and decided to check it out. It was a fight and not between just two men – this fight put one man against three. Now, unless you're some kind of superman, one man taking on three is pretty fucked-up odds. This fellow, however, was giving a good account of himself, and I thought for a moment that I might just watch and see how it turned out. But I knew instinctively that one man by himself simply stood no chance, and that shit just didn't sit well with me, so I decided to even things up a bit. I took the blackjack out of my saddlebag and hit the biggest of the three fuckers hard behind his right ear, which laid his ass out flat. As I turned to get a look at the others, the smallest of the trio hit me so hard that my left eye immediately swelled shut and my nose bled like an open faucet. A little blurry eyed, I could see the front of my shirt was covered in blood – MY blood. My pride was more than just a little bruised for letting that little bastard get the better of me, so I grabbed him from behind, put him in a tight choke hold, lifting him off the ground until he passed out. Seeing his body was limp, I threw him to the ground, and spat the blood in my mouth full in his face.

Now, the odds are right for a good fight.

Taking the bandana from my pocket, I began cleaning my face and stepped back to watch. The fight, however, didn't last long after that, as I watched the third man fall to the ground, knocked completely unconscious. I did get a good laugh, though, as I watched the one left standing walk around and piss on each of the fallen men. As he walked toward me, it was easy to see this guy was badly beaten. His face was opened in several places and he was bleeding profusely. His arms and shoulders were already bruising from the boot that had been put to him, and he definitely looked the worse for wear. He walked straight up to me and said, "I don't know who the fuck you are, man, but I am damn grateful you came along." Putting his hand out to me, he said, "My name is Diego Santiago and I'm the V.P. of the Los Patrons Motorcycle Club."

I took his hand in mine and said, "I'm Jake Coleman."

"Okay, Jake, c'mon in and let me buy you a beer. I want to introduce you to some of my brothers."

"You're going to need stitches," I said.

But he just laughed. "From the looks of it, your fuckin' nose is probably broken, not to mention the fact that your left eye is almost completely closed. Now, I've got someone inside that can give me stitches, but there ain't no stichin' that can fix that fucked-up nose of yours, and nothing can make ugly anything but ugly." Still laughing, he entered the bar.

You would've thought I was the devil himself from the looks I got as I followed Diego in. You could tell my life wasn't worth spit with these guys until Diego explained what had just happened. A BIG, burly, red-headed dude they called Clutch immediately took Diego into the back room. They were followed by a small, fashionably-dressed woman carrying a briefcase. Out of the same room came two near-naked, tatted-up women with some towels and a bowl of water. They set to cleaning me up, and that's when I noticed the bar customers had all left. The only people left in the place, were the Patrons, these two women, and me. The women worked quickly to clean me up, and they managed to scrounge up a clean shirt for me that actually fit. Before they went about their business taking care of the Patrons that were still in the bar, they introduced themselves as Ashley and Marti, and told me they did everything as a pair, including fucking. Ashley wrote their names and phone numbers on a napkin, put it in my shirt pocket, smiled widely and said, "Give us a call if you're ever in the mood for a party."

About twenty minutes passed before Diego, Clutch, and the woman emerged from the back room. Diego was stitched up, cleaned up, and smelled as if he had just smoked a bowl. He asked how I was and I said, "I'm ready for that cold beer."

We sat at a table in the corner and Diego said, "I appreciate your help with those assholes outside. Have you heard of the Los Patrons?"

"You can't live in Texas and not know about the club, and what I know is, you guys have a pretty rough reputation."

"People have said a lot of things about us, some true and some not. The one thing that is true is we take care of our own, and it's that truth which has given us the reputation you're talking about. Jake, there aren't many men that would get involved in a fight when they have no personal interest in it, and that makes me curious about you."

"Curious about what?"

"For starts, why?"

"Look man, I've been alone with the odds stacked against me more times than I care to remember. I hate that shit and don't take this wrong, but if it'd been the other way around, and you were one of the three on one man alone, I would've come after you."

He just smiled and said, "Well, it's good I was alone in that fight, or I might've been the one waking up with a headache from your black-jack, right?"

I just smiled as I opened a pack of cigarettes.

"What do you do for a living?"

"I drive a forklift, mostly for temp services and pretty much any-where in the southwest Houston area."

"Making a living?"

"It keeps gas in my bike and groceries on the table. I also get a small disability check from the military that covers my place."

"Military, huh, what branch?"

"Army. I served in Afghanistan from April 2004 through October 2005."

"What'd you do over there?"

Feeling a little irritated with all the questions, I sat up straight and asked, "Does that really matter?"

"Relax, man, I'm just trying to get to know you."

I leaned back in my chair, lit a cigarette and said, "Target acquisition and elimination."

"A sniper?"

"Yeah, I was a sniper.

"So, you've killed a few men?"

I looked him straight in the eyes and said, "Fifty-one confirmed kills in eighteen months."

"Well, that explains it."

"Explains what?"

"That explains why you didn't hesitate to jump in and help me out. You weren't afraid and you had the skills to handle those two fuckers without much trouble. What's the disability check for?"

"My partner, Dutch McDonald, and I were coming off a reconnais-sance mission through a remote and mountainous part of Afghanistan's

Dai Chopen district, an area the army was preparing to bomb the hell out of. Our job was two-fold, and the first was easy. Get as much intel on the enemy positions as possible, and provide coordinates to the artillery batteries responsible for bombardment. Our second mission was to eliminate a raghead named Odaubi Hossam. He was responsible for leading attacks on civilians in the area who didn't support the Taliban, and it was those same civilians who kept us fed with information regarding the Taliban's movements. He had to be eliminated if we had any hope of maintaining an open line of communication, and that task fell to my partner and me. Well, we popped that asshole good, just as planned, and were on our way back to the extract zone when we encountered a group of Taliban fighters and found ourselves in the fire-fight from hell. We were trying to make our way back down the mountain to a fortified position when Dutch's legs were shot from beneath him. Thinking I could drag him over the boulder below us, I turned to reach for his pack, when I saw he had also taken a round in the head and had been killed. Dutch and I had trained together for six months before going to that hell-hole of a country, and once there, we did everything as a team. For the next eighteen months, we got to know each other very well and he came to mean a hell of a lot more to me than just being my partner – he became family."

Man, isn't that thought original – family. I didn't have it before I went to Afghanistan and I don't have it now.

"I marked a large stone near his body, using his blood so that he could be found, and I grabbed his dog tags and kept moving. At this point, I was just trying to stay alive. It took some time and some hard moving but I was finally able to lose the bastards. But in the process of climbing down that fuckin' mountain, I fell into a shallow crevice, breaking my left leg in three places. I was hurt bad and I knew it and it was getting dark, so I activated the emergency tracking beacon I'd been supplied with and signaled, as best I could, the enemy's position. It didn't take long before that mountain lit up with US rocket fire and then came the helicopters with the Navy SEALS. Man, I had never been so glad to see someone as I was those guys. They pinned my leg and put me in the helicopter, and then I led them to Dutch. It was easy to find him because he was only a few hundred yards away and his blood showed clear under the helicopter's lights. It took only a couple of minutes for them to recover his body and we were gone. That SEAL team saved my life and recovered Dutch's body before returning to base. I was unfortunately never able to say thank you to any of them, because as soon as they dropped me, they were gone again.

"Man, you want to talk about brotherhood – there's nothing like brotherhood earned under fire. Anyway, I was taken to a M.A.S.H. unit for treatment before being transferred to Landstuhl Medical Center in Germany. It was there where they put my leg back together, and where I spent the next three months recovering. After a medical review board finished with me, I was discharged, shipped state-side, and given some basic education benefits for civilian training. That, along with my disability check, is as they say, history."

"It sounds like you've been through some really bad shit, bro, and I gotta say, you got all my respect for what you've been through."

I nodded with my approval of his statement and said, "I have a question for you."

"I'll answer if I can."

"With all the men you have in here, how is it that you are caught alone outside by those three guys you were fighting with?"

"Jake, I'm not normally alone, not ever. Usually, I have my sergeant at arms with me everywhere I go, but I got careless tonight. I went out back to get a pack of smokes from my saddlebag, and they were there going through my shit. I hadn't thought to let anyone know I was going outside because I didn't expect a problem. Believe me, lesson learned. You can bet I'll never make that mistake again."

Clutch walked up and said, "Those assholes are handled, brother."

Diego gave a quick nod of approval.

"What's that mean?" I asked.

"What would you do with them if you were me, Jake? Do you think I should call the cops?"

"Somehow I don't think the cops would be your first choice."

"You're right about that shit, Jake, fuckin' cops wouldn't be my first choice. Fact is, cops wouldn't be on my list of choices, period."

"Understood. Well then, Diego, how 'bout we just drink another beer and be glad I showed up when I did. Besides, whatever you do with them, they probably got coming anyway."

Diego smiled and yelled for a prospect to bring a bucket of Modelo. For the next hour, we sat drinking beer and just shootin' the shit.

Finally, Diego looked at his watch, "It's time for church, man, and I gotta go."

I chuckled some and said, "Church. You don't look much like the religious type."

Diego just smiled. (I was to later learn that church referred to the club's chapter meeting.) He asked for my phone number and address and told me that he was sending a couple of prospects with me to ensure I got home safely. Before I left he told me the Los Patrons were throwing a party the next night at their clubhouse and that he would make sure I knew the address. I'd like you to be there, Jake. As my guest, of course."

We shook hands and then he left. The two men he sent with me got on their bikes and we were on our way to my apartment in Rosenberg. As I rode, thoughts of my childhood came to me, and I remembered that day when my mom took me downtown to watch the "Bikers" ride through town. All I remember about them is, they were a west coast club and they were headed somewhere for a funeral. I watched them come through our small West Texas town, listening to their loud pipes and smelling the strong fumes from their exhaust, and I knew right then that someday I would own my own bike and I'd be just like those guys. Now, almost thirty years later, having ridden motorcycles for more than twenty years, I was fighting alongside of and drinking beer with a vice-president of the most notorious motorcycle club anywhere in the Southwest. The adrenalin rush was at its peak and I sat tall in the saddle as we motored down 59 South, headed for home.

𝔐.ℭ.

At the clubhouse, the mood was tense. Diego called Clutch to the side and told him to make sure the three men from the bar were brought into church at the beginning of business. "I want to know who sent them."

Clutch told Diego the men were already inside, and although he wasn't sure who all of them were, he'd found a cut in their car, which confirmed that one of them was a member of the Warriors Motorcycle Club. "Judging by the size of the cut, it probably belongs to the biggest of the three men. Diego, that cut has a sergeant at arms patch on it and I put it on the floor, out in front of that fat ass."

Walking inside, Diego immediately ordered the prospects outside, saying, "Keep the bikes and the doors secure." He turned to the big man, picked up the leather vest that was lying at the man's feet, and examined the Warrior's patch that was sewn to its back. Then he turned it around and carefully examined the patches sewn to the front.

He smiled as he held the vest up to the man and asked, "Is this your cut?"

"It's mine."

"Tell me what your name is, who sent you, and why a Warrior would want to attack a Patron."

The man looked at Diego, spat, then said, "Go fuck yourself."

Enraged by the disrespect, Diego tossed the man's cut to the side, and had his arms and shoulders firmly pinned to the floor. With the help of several other brothers, Diego pulled off the Warrior's boots, pants, and underwear, then took out his knife and said, "I'm going to cut you, man, and not gently, like I would a pet, but I am going to cut you, and when I do, you're going to scream like the fuckin', squealing pig you are."

Immediately, Diego kneeled between the man's legs and cut his scrotum from his body. The man's screams sent a chill throughout the room, and the other two men were positioned so they could watch their friend's agony.

After a few deafening moments, Diego leaned forward, spat in the man's now blood-drained face, then struck him in the throat with his knife. He stabbed him with such force that his windpipe was ripped from his throat. They all watched as the man died, his blood gushing onto the floor around him. The other two men were then forced to sit on the floor against the wall, not far from where the dead man lay. As his blood pooled around them, Diego turned to face them holding the dead man's scrotum in one hand and the bloody knife in the other. "Are you going to answer my questions?"

Both men readily agreed to tell Diego whatever he wanted to know.

They said they were chapter members of the Rebel Souls Motorcycle Club (a support club of the Warriors Motorcycle Club) and had been sent to kill Diego. They had no idea why the Warriors wanted him dead, but they both wanted to patch over to the Warriors, so they did as they were told.

"Who is the dead man who gave his balls to me?"

"He was the sergeant at arms of the San Antonio chapter of the Warriors Motorcycle Club," answered the smaller of the two men.

Diego laid the knife aside and placed the mass of flesh onto a table that stood beside him. He picked up a towel from the table and cleaned his hands as he walked over to the smaller of the two men. Looking the man directly in the eye, he pulled his pistol from inside his own cut and shot him in the forehead. The back of the man's head exploded onto the wall behind him, splattering the man sitting next to him. That man, now covered in blood and brain matter, lowered his head and began to sob.

Diego stepped over to him and asked, "Why the tears?"

The man answered, "I just wanted to ride my motorcycle and party a little. I never thought it would come to this." He sobbed harder and said, "I don't want to die."

Diego stared at the man for a brief moment, then said, "Look at me."

The man raised his eyes until they met with Diego's, then calling him a "Pussy," Diego pulled the trigger. The bullet ripped through the man's upper left cheek, blowing out his left eye. It exited through his lower right jaw, scattering teeth, pieces of his jaw bone and flesh all over the floor. Blood poured from the massive opening in his face, quickly mixing with the blood already present from the other killings. The shot hadn't killed this man and as he tried to right himself, his hand slipped in his own blood, and he fell into the lap of the dead man on his right. He reached for a mouth that had been blown away and gasped for air. It was apparent to all who watched that he was suffocating. Diego, realizing the man was still alive, kneeled and watched as the man, in sheer panic, used his one remaining eye to scour the room, presumably looking for help that wouldn't come. Diego stood, looked at the crowd around him, and said, "Punk-Ass little bitch." He looked back at the man, who had stopped moving. Everyone knew he had died.

The air was now thick with the smell of blood mixed with urine and excrement as the bodies gave up all that was left within them. The scene was unlike anything anyone there had experienced before, and no one present doubted Diego's ability to enact horrific violence on anyone he considered his enemy. Hoping to air the place out a little, the brothers moved quickly to pull the bodies toward a window that was opened, and the prospects were brought in and instructed to clean up the mess.

Picking up the vest that had belonged to the big man, Diego said, "I have no idea why a Warrior would come here looking for a fight, but his patch and his balls will be sent back to those fuckers in San Antonio with this message: *God Forgives, Patrons Repay.*"

He looked at Clutch, saying, "Make sure the prospects clean this place up right. We have to get ready for tomorrow night. Viejo will return from county and he'll want an explanation for what happened here."

M.C.

Later that evening, well after the two men that Diego sent to escort me home had left, I heard another bike drive up my street, and then as suddenly drive off again. As I walked to the door to take a look outside, my doorbell rang, and to my surprise it was the woman from the Haven, the one who had stitched up Diego. I opened the door. She introduced herself as Carmen and I invited her in. As we sat on the couch, she told me that Diego had sent her with directions to the clubhouse. She handed me a piece of paper and said, "Diego wanted me to deliver the directions to you personally, and he told me to make sure that you were made comfortable."

I looked up from reading the directions and asked, "What, exactly, does 'made comfortable' mean?"

She moved close to me on the couch and dragging her fingernails lightly across my upper forearm said, "Whatever you want it to mean."

"Tell me again what your name is and how you fit into all of this."

"My name is Carmen Santiago and Diego is my husband."

I jumped up from the couch, "You're Diego's wife? There's no fuckin' way you're doing anything to make me comfortable."

Carmen pulled the cellphone from her purse and made a call to someone she spoke to in Spanish. They had spoken for only a moment when she handed me the phone. "He wants to talk to you."

I took the phone and it was Diego. "Jake, do you think my ole' lady is ugly?"

"NO, man, but what the fuck am I supposed to do with her?"

"Today you saved my ass and if not for you, I might have left this woman a widow. Tonight she is for you as my gift. Make her comfortable and while you're at it, keep her safe."

He went on to tell me that he was leaving for the night to take care of some business for the club and said the trouble at the bar had made him uneasy about her safety. He said he would consider it a personal favor if I would do this one thing for him. "You can give me a full report on 'how it was' tomorrow night at the party, if that makes you feel better. Personally, I think she is one fine piece of ass, but I *am* partial." And with that, Diego hung up the phone.

I could hear my bathtub filling with water and as I walked in, Carmen said, "You smell of blood, cigarettes, and beer." As she began unbuckling my belt, she said, "I never sleep with a man who has the blood of another on his skin, so we have to clean you up." She finished undressing me and smiled, saying, "Get in."

I sat my ass in the water and leaned back, feeling the sting of the water on my hands, which were covered in scrapes and small cuts from the afternoon's fight. As I watched, she began to undress with the skill and artistry of a well-trained stripper and all thoughts and concerns over who she was simply disappeared. For the first time, I really looked at the woman. She had jet-black, shoulder-length hair, black-as-night eyes, and beautiful, light-brown skin. She couldn't have stood over five feet tall or weighed much more than a hundred pounds. Oh man, this woman was damn sure put together right! She climbed into the tub, sat straddling me, and immediately leaned into me, pressing her tits against my chest. Kissing me, she raked the silver ball in her tongue across my front teeth. "Now is the time for making each other comfortable."

No rooster could've had more cock in him than I had in her at that very moment. She rode me like she hadn't been fucked in months. We splashed most of the water out of the tub and fucked our way to a fast, hard finish. Lifting herself off me, she started refilling the tub and as the water rose around us, she told me the Patrons often 'loaned' their ole' ladies to visiting brothers. "The only rule is, as with all club property, what is borrowed must be returned to the owner in at least the same condition as when it was loaned."

I commented, "Property? Well, Carmen, I'm not one of Diego's brothers."

Carmen sat up on her knees and pointed to the words, "Diego's Property," which had been tattooed just above and to the left of her bush. "Jake, my husband never invites anyone to a party either as a guest or otherwise. He has his sergeant at arms make the invitation, or rather, the demand. You're the only man, brother or not, that he's ever allowed to even look at me much less touch me and I'm here, not for the moment, but for the night."

"Okay then, I never spend the night with anyone I know nothing about. Care to answer a few questions for me?"

She smiled big, "Sure, what do you want to know?"

"How long have the two of you been married?"

"Four years."

"How'd you meet?"

"When the club needed legal help, it used the law firm I worked for, and about six years ago I was assigned to defend Diego in a battery case connected with the manager of a bar the club had a financial interest in."

"Wait a minute, I thought you were a doctor or a nurse. Didn't you stitch Diego's face earlier at the Haven?"

"You know, Jake, hospitals and clinics are required by law to report injuries they suspect are connected with violence and the Los Patrons have had their fair share of cuts, bruises, and the like. Since the club wants as little to do with the police as possible, many of the women, me included, have learned some basic first aid, including how to stitch up cuts."

"Why are you a part of any of this, Carmen? I mean, you're a beautiful woman with a professional career, and I have to believe you could have just about any man you want, so why would you choose this kind of life for yourself?"

"So, you think I'm beautiful, Jake?"

"Yeah, I think you're beautiful and you know you're beautiful, too. That's why I think there's a hell of a lot more to your story."

"Jake, you're looking for what we lawyers call the smoking gun. That one thing that reveals motive, because nothing of consequence ever happens in this world without motive right?"

"Okay, call it what you want; motive, curiosity, or maybe just interest on my part."

She looked at me and said, "I've not had anyone show so much interest in me since college. Do you really want to hear all of this?"

"Carmen, we appear to have all night and yes, I'm interested. Please, go on."

"My maiden name is Carmen Ruiz Valdespino, daughter of Aaron Esteban Valdespino, the largest distributor of tea in all of Mexico. I was raised with the best of all my father could afford; all the best clothes, the best education, and the very best in isolation. My father picked my friends, he picked the college I attended, and he even picked my profession. He wanted me to be the legal counsel for his business here in the US, and in the beginning that was the plan. But after so many years of living without choices and with the isolation turning into suffocation, I simply had to break out and be on my own. I studied criminal law instead of business law and graduated top in my class. After I passed the Texas Bar, I went to work for Ramirez and Associates down on Houston's east end. The firm specialized in criminal defense and I worked the first year as a junior associate, supervising the research of the paralegals and assisting with court trials. It felt great and I knew that I was well on my way to living my own life." Reaching for a hand towel that lay on a table behind me, she moved so that her breast eased across my face and in doing so, brought immediate energy back to my libido. Grinning as she moved back into position, she went on with her story. "After some time, Adolfo Ramirez, the senior partner in the firm, called me into his office and told me that he was assigning me to my first case as lead attorney. He explained that it involved a motorcycle club whose vice-president had been charged with assault. He gave me the case file and Diego's name, saying Diego would be in the office that afternoon for consultation. Diego arrived at the appointed time and when he entered my office, I was instantly attracted to him and his bad boy image. He was so different from every man I had ever known, and though I tried to hide my interest, he must have picked up on it, because he looked at me in a way that told me, if I were to let down my guard, I could easily be devoured by him. I spent the next couple of hours just trying to put all the pieces of his battery charge together so I could properly defend him, and in doing so, I realized that his image as a bad boy was no act. Diego Santiago was one very rough character and I knew it. That realization should have been a warning to me, but instead, it only deepened my attraction for him.

"The case came to trial two weeks later and I successfully defended Diego with all charges being dropped. After court was dismissed, he invited me to dinner, and although I knew I shouldn't, I agreed to go. After that, I started going on rides and spending time with him at the Haven and a few other places the club has interests in. Jake, I had spent my whole life isolated from the real world, and suddenly I found myself in the middle of an environment where people lived their lives in a very primal way, and it was exhilarating. My attraction for Diego didn't stop with the man but extended to what he represented.

"We'd been seeing each other for only about six months when my parents were killed in a commuter plane crash, and all of a sudden I found myself with no family and with the horrible feeling of being orphaned. I know that sounds like a really stupid thing to say, especially at my age, but that's how I felt. My uncle was my father's business partner and he made it very clear to me that since I hadn't followed my father's wish to pursue business law, that I should expect nothing from my extended family. Diego was there for me during that time and believe me, it was the worst time of my adult life. He made sure I wasn't alone, and then one day he told me that I could be a part of his family and I would never be alone again. We married the very next day."

"So, he made you his wife and now you are the chapter matriarch, right?"

"Diego is my husband and I am his ole' lady."

"How is that different from being his wife?"

"An ole' lady is property, not priority. If Diego acknowledges me as his wife, he has to treat me as though I matter more than the other property he owns. Think of it this way – my husband rides a Road King and it is important property to him. He depends on it and needs it for transportation, but you would never see him go outside and caress it and ask it how it feels about being washed. I attend to his personal needs, the club's legal affairs, and I occasionally stitch up a cut. Diego is my husband, and simply put, I am his ole' lady."

"Why do you stay?"

Again, she rose to her knees and turned slightly to the right, brushing her hair to one side so I could see the letters "LPOL" tattooed on her left shoulder. "Where would I go, Jake? I have no family left and no one to care about me. The club has become my only family and I stay because I am an LPOL."

"What is an LPOL?"

"It means that I am a *Loyal Patron Ole' Lady*. Now, Diego told both of us to see to each other's comfort and we have talked all I want to talk. The water is warm and my pussy is aching. Do I need to say more?"

I was awakened that next morning by the sound of Carmen's cell phone and I watched her step away from the bed and head off to the bathroom. Once again she was speaking in Spanish and I could only assume it was Diego she was talking to. She came back to bed, kissed me deeply, and told me that Diego was sending Clutch for her. Before getting up to dress, she told me that she would not be able to "pay attention" to me at tonight's party and that I should not even look her way. She went on to say, "You and Diego are square."

I responded by saying, "Okay."

As she dressed, I watched thinking, *This won't be a night I soon forget.*

A moment later, we heard the pipes of the Fatboy Clutch was riding come up the street. Carmen looked at me, saying, "Don't be late tonight."

She left my place in a trot, met Clutch at the curb, mounted the back of the bike, and never looked back as they rode off down the street. I walked back into my house deciding I needed a shower and some breakfast. When I walked into the bathroom I had to take a second look at the mirror. On it was a perfect set of lips with a note written in lipstick below: Thank you, Jake, for all of last night. I was *VERY* comfortable.

Suddenly, I felt that all too familiar sense of ... lonely!

𝔐.ℭ.

I spent the rest of the day just trying to stay busy. I was apprehensive about attending the party, and it was all I could do not to think of Carmen. I left my place just in time to pull up in front of the clubhouse at exactly nine in the evening, the time the note had said to arrive. You could hear the music over the sound of my pipes as I backed my bike up against the curb, and I could see there was definitely a party going on.

I was met by the chapter road captain, a short and very lean guy with a heavy British accent. He put his hand out to me and said, "My name is Britt and it is great to meet you. Diego told everyone that we have a man in our company that knew how to take care of business and we were to make him feel at home, so welcome, Jake."

"Thanks, what now?"

"You meet Viejo. Jake, when you get to the door you'll be met by Crow, the sergeant at arms who is responsible for Viejo. He is going to search you and it wouldn't be good if he found a gun on you."

"You can search me if you like, but I don't own a gun."

With that, Britt walked me up the steps to the front door. There stood the biggest mother fucker I think I have ever met up close. He looked down at me and said, "I'm Crow and I gotta look inside your jacket and pockets."

I offered him a look and when he finished he whispered in my ear, "Viejo is my brother and MY responsibility. What you did for Diego was good man, so don't fuck things up with Viejo, cause if you do, it will be ME you pay the price to for your fuckup. Understood?"

"Understood."

Crow escorted me to the back of the front room and there at the bar sat an aging white guy smoking a cigar. He got up and met me halfway across the room. "My name is Marc and you're Jake, right?"

"Right, I am supposed to be meeting Viejo. At least, that's what I was told."

"Well, Jake, I'm Viejo. C'mon over and let me get you a drink."

I took a seat at the bar and all the while Crow watched me as though I might suddenly whip out a hidden UZI and take out the entire room. Marc smiled and said, "I could see by your expression when we met that I'm not what you expected."

"The truth is, man, I didn't know what to expect. In fact, these last two days have been a blur for me. Yesterday I was at home, bored, thirsty for a cold beer, and wanting a little company, and today, here I sit with the president of a motorcycle club that everyone knows you don't fuck around with. Yeah, I guess I am a little confused about what to expect and why I'm here."

Marc poured two shooters of Cuervo and we downed them, chasing them with Modelo. He puffed heavy on his cigar and told me the reason I had been invited to the party was so the club could thank me in person for what I'd done for Diego.

Diego walked up with Carmen at his side, hugged me tight and asked, "How was last night, Jake?"

I said, "It was a comfortable night, Diego, and thanks for making it so."

Diego smiled and lifted his drink in toast and I did likewise.

As Carmen walked away from the conversation, I told Marc that I was confused about one thing and he asked, "What's that?"

"With a name like "Los Patrons" most people think this club is for Mexicans but you're white and so are Britt, Crow, and Clutch."

"You know what's common about all of us here? The color of our blood, and it's all the same...red. I have spilled my blood, Diego has spilled his blood, and now you have spilled your blood, and for that you have my gratitude and that of all the Los Patrons."

Diego said, "Tell us of your family, Jake."

I responded by saying that I never really knew my father as he'd left when I was very young and that my mother had died shortly after I returned from Afghanistan.

"No brothers or sisters?" Marc asked.

"No, I live in Rosenberg with no family."

Marc asked me if it was habit on my part to involve myself in the business of others, like I had with Diego.

"Nope. It just seemed like the thing to do at the time and that's all there is to it."

"I like you, Jake, and I'd like to see you hang around with us for a while. Who knows, after a time you might find life with us more enjoyable than it seems for you right now. You cool with that, man?"

"Yeah, I'm cool with that."

Diego said, "In July we are taking a ride to a place near Big Bend to meet up with the other Texas and New Mexico chapters. It's going to be one hell of a party. The pussy will be plenty with all the booze, weed, and food you could want, and with the party being out in the desert, the cops won't fuck with us either. You interested in coming along, Jake?"

"Hell yes," I said. "I'll be there."

𝔐.ℭ.

Almost three months went by and I found myself spending most of my free time with the club. Even Crow took a liking to me. It began to feel as though I had access to whatever I wanted, that is, except church. I was never allowed behind those doors and man, I was so fuckin' curious.

The Wednesday before we were to leave on Friday for Big Bend, Diego told me the club had voted and had unanimously agreed that I should be offered a prospect patch. I was surprised by the offer as I had never expressed an interest in prospecting for the club. I told him that from what I had observed, prospecting looked like one hell of a lot of work. Diego said, "It is a lot of work, Jake, and a big commitment of time."

"How long?"

"It really depends on how well you adapt to the prospecting rules."

"Rules?"

He told me that during the prospecting period, I would have to make myself available for whatever was asked of me by whatever patched brother asked it; day or night; good weather or bad weather, it didn't matter…if a patched brother demanded my time, I had to comply.

"Jake, the Los Patrons must be assured of your loyalty and commitment, and your willingness to live by our one and only code – IAMBK."

He opened his shirt and the letters were tattooed across his upper chest.

"What do the letters mean?"

"I Am My Brother's Keeper. With the Los Patrons our blood means everything. It is our bond and we are serious about that. In fact, our brotherhood's survival depends on everyone's unyielding commitment to that bond. You asked how long, Jake. At a minimum, one year of your life, and in that year nothing else can take priority over the Los Patrons. One last thing Jake – the initiation fee is collected up front and unlike a department store, we don't make refunds if you or if we later change our minds."

"How much?"

"We will require the title to your bike."

I was astonished. "My bike?"

"You have to want to be a part of us or you won't make it through the prospect period. The title to your bike ensures you think through your decision to be a part of us very carefully, and that you are completely committed to the brothers once you put that prospect patch on. This is the only invitation to become a part of us you will ever get. So think about it, Jake. You can let me know after we return from the desert."

Chapter Two

PROSPECTING

Friday arrived and we met at the clubhouse at six-thirty in the morning. Viejo wanted to get at least halfway there before midday to avoid the heat and the toll it would take on the body as well as the bike. I was surprised to see all five Houston chapters there to make the trip with us – we totaled close to eighty bikes, along with two chase trucks for the trip. Diego told me to ride at the very back of the pack with the prospects and the chase trucks, and to be careful not to fall behind the group or get caught alone at gas stops. "You never know who follows us on rides like these, so just stay close and be watchful."

I couldn't help but think how fuckin' awesome it was to see so many people so excited to get underway, and as the thunder of eighty Harleys fired up, I swore I could feel the ground shake beneath my feet. It took almost fourteen hours to make the six hundred fifty-mile trip to the rendezvous point near Big Bend. I was surprised that we made it that quickly considering we had to stop and fuel four times along the way, and fueling eighty bikes and two trucks doesn't happen quickly. Daylight was falling as we arrived, and thankfully so was the temperature. It had been a long, hot trip and all I could think of was how good a cold beer would be right now. We pulled our bikes into a roped-off area and were directed by prospects with orange-coned flashlights on exactly where to park. The Albuquerque, Las Cruces, Carlsbad, Santa

Fe, Ruidoso, Corpus Christi, and El Paso chapters were already there when we arrived and the party was well underway.

Within an hour of our arrival, Diego introduced me to the national president, Bull "The Bull" Taylor, known as El Presidente and to each of Taylor's national board officers. The Bull thanked me for getting involved in Diego's fight and said, "I understand you've been offered a prospect patch?"

I looked first at Diego and then at The Bull saying, "Yes, I have and I'm honored by the offer."

The Bull motioned for me to come close as he extended his hand to me. "I hope to see you become a part of us, Jake."

Diego moved closer to The Bull for a private conversation, and Britt slapped me on the back and said, "C'mon Jake, let's go see what there is to see." We walked the entire compound counting fifteen compound style tents set up for sleeping (all you had to do was throw your bed roll out) and fuck if I could believe it, the tents were all set up with air conditioning. The chapters had pooled their money and rented a semi with a fifty-two foot trailer rigged with generators to fuel the lights, the coolers, the air conditioning and two ice machines attached to two five hundred-gallon water bladders. Showers and portable toilets were stationed near the slope not far from the water bladders, and the ice machines were on the opposite side of this makeshift compound. Not much had been missed to ensure this was a good party.

The party tent was at the center and was four or five times larger than the other tents. Inside was a stage, complete with three stripper poles, a sound booth with a DJ, and a row of tables lined up end-to-end, thirty foot in length and covered in food. There were four fifty-gallon water tanks iced down with beer, and about a dozen prospects in the place working their asses off trying to keep up with, who the fuck knows, how many brothers. I had no idea where they got the strippers, but there were never any less than six of them at any one time on the stage and they were all *Penthouse* beautiful! The shows they put on often involved the strippers fucking each other and the occasional fucking of a very fortunate brother chosen from the crowd for one reason or another. Other than those few occasions, the strippers were strictly 'off limits' as they were well-paid entertainment for our collective benefit. For most, the need for pussy was supplied by an ample supply of women (referred to as sheep) that regularly followed the club to such events. Each of them was more than willing to supply the needed blowjob or whatever else a brother might want.

It wasn't long before Britt was sending a prospect on a mission. He came back a few minutes later with two ice-cold beers, and Britt quickly suggested we move closer to the stage. As we stood in the crowd, watching two gorgeous strippers on the main stage getting each other naked, I heard my name called out by the DJ, who said, "Jake Coleman, FRONT and CENTER."

I looked at Britt. "What the fuck, man?"

He just smiled. "Go on, Jake, have some fun."

As I made my way toward the front, I watched a chair being lifted onto the stage and every brother in the place was chanting my name. When I got to the stage-front, the two beauties up top motioned to me with their fingers to get up on stage. I was a little nervous with a tent full of people all watching, but I climbed those steps up onto the stage. I was made to sit in the chair facing the crowd as one of the two women, completely nude, sat almost lying in my lap, and began grinding for all she was worth. The other woman was busy dancing the pole until it was her turn at my lap. This went on for a short time and before I knew it, I was completely naked and the party was on. Between the music, the weed and the booze, not to mention the pussy, I got so fucked up I had to have help finding my way back to my bedroll. I woke up the next morning wondering if one of those desert rats hadn't shit in my mouth, and all I could think of was a drink of cold water and some toothpaste. I came away from that night with something new and unexpected – a good friend in Britt. It was obvious to me that he and I would become close, and I spent the bulk of the next two days either hanging with him or Diego.

All in all, it was a great party and I was treated like a celebrity the entire three days. If this party had been intended to seal the deal, it had worked. I realized that in less than three short months I had partied like a rock star, made more friends than I had thought possible, and felt like I was among family for the first time I could remember. The loneliness that had so previously plagued my days and nights seemed now like a distant memory.

Prospect I was offered and a prospect I'd become.

It was ten on Monday morning when the chapter prepared to leave for Houston. Three days of nonstop partying had left me with one hell of a hangover, and the dread I felt looking at another fourteen-hour ride home hovered over me like the smell of gasoline on my boots. It was already eighty-five degrees and we were just getting under way when Viejo, Diego, Crow, and Clutch suddenly crowded together with The Bull.

The Bull had received a call from a friend of his with the San Antonio Police Department, telling him that a statewide alert had been issued by the Department of Public Safety Gang Task Force about potential motorcycle gang activity. It seemed that one of our clubhouses in Houston had been bombed and at least one person had been killed. After a couple of phone calls it was determined that it was the Houston Chapter clubhouse that had been bombed and it had burned to the ground. Cruz, the chapter secretary (one of the original four founders of the chapter), had died in the bombing. Along with a couple of other brothers, he had stayed behind to ensure the uninterrupted collection of money from the club's various business interests.

The news of the bombing and the brother's death passed quickly among the chapters present, as did the news that it was the Warriors who had carried out the bombing. For the next hour I witnessed every single brother present walk up to Viejo and Diego and hug them both saying, "God Forgives, Patrons Repay." Britt told me that little statement meant that each member, regardless of chapter affiliation, took personal responsibility for ensuring this debt was repaid in full. I was certain from what I had observed that the Los Patrons fully intended to repay the debt.

The trip home was a long one, and since there was no longer a Houston clubhouse to go home to, we all went to the West Houston Chapter's clubhouse in Katy. It was there I approached Diego with my decision about the prospecting offer. I said, "Diego, you offered me a prospect's patch and if it is still available to me, I will happily sign the title for my bike over to the Los Patrons."

Diego responded by saying, "Things are different now, Jake. We're at war with the Warriors and if you prospect for the Los Patrons you become a sworn enemy of those cocksuckers. You understand that your life could be endangered by that decision?"

"Diego, I have no friends and I have no family. This is my chance to have both."

"Wait here," He walked over to Viejo and the two spoke briefly before Viejo called the Houston Chapter members together along with our West Houston hosts present. He took a prospect patch and a MC cube out of his saddlebag and announced to the entire group that Houston had a new prospect.

"There ain't no time for speeches tonight, Jake, so I got only two things to say: First, I expect much from you." Then, shoving the patches into my chest, he said, "The next fuckin' time I see you, these patches had better be sewn on."

The prospect work began very quickly. I was sent to help the three prospects from West Houston unload our chase truck and secure the chapter's clubhouse for the night. It was about one-thirty in the morning when I finally got on my bike and headed home. Remembering what Viejo said about the patches, I stopped at a twenty-four hour grocery store and bought needle and thread. Fortunately for me, I had sewn many a patch in the army, and the job of sewing the prospect patch and the MC cube was an easy task for me.

It was almost four in the morning and I was just getting into bed when my cell phone rang. It was Clutch. A little over an hour earlier

Viejo and Crow had both been killed in front of Viejo's home in Pearland. Clutch told me the entire chapter was to report back to the West Houston Clubhouse in Katy as quickly as possible. When I arrived, I was told that the killings were the work of the Warriors and Diego had ordered the prospects to be armed and stationed outside the clubhouse to watch for any unusual activity. I was given a Benelli M4 combat shotgun and told to watch the street and sidewalk leading to the front of the clubhouse. I was instructed to shoot anyone that tried to enter the property who wasn't wearing a Los Patron cut or carrying a badge.

I sat in the shadow of the porch until daylight, grateful that all had been quiet and I hadn't had to act on my instructions. As the morning sunshine began to warm my face, Clutch called me inside. He took the shotgun from me and told me the "sheep" were cooking breakfast and that I should eat while the eating was available. I wasted no time getting a cup of coffee and an egg sandwich down me. Truth was, I was hungry and flat worn-out from the ride home, the stress of the killings, and the lack of sleep.

I must have nodded off because one of the women who had been cooking gently nudged me on the shoulder and woke me. She told me that she had heard someone call my name from another room. I quickly got up and went to the main room of the house where Diego had gathered the brothers together, along with the prospects. He told us we were having an emergency meeting. Of all the church gatherings I had seen called, this one was different because it had been called with the prospects in attendance. Once the sheep had been sent back to the kitchen, the prospects were instructed to guard the perimeters of the main room, the doors, and the windows. There was no roll call and no other formalities were observed. Diego opened church by saying, "God Forgives, Patrons Repay," a statement that was becoming very familiar.

I heard someone from the crowd say, "Fuckin' A, WE DO and fuckin' payback's a bitch."

Diego nodded his approval of what had just been said, then went on to tell us the Warriors had killed Viejo and the others as payback over a drug buy that had gone bad. Cops had busted several Warriors who had been at the buy and they were spreading bullshit lies that Viejo and Diego had "turned," resulting in the bust. It was here that I found out why Diego had been fighting in the parking lot of the Haven that night. The cops, he said, had fucked up everything with their lies and he couldn't understand the motivation, except for one possibility; money. Someone was benefiting somehow from what was going on between the Los Patrons and the Warriors, and we had to figure out who it was and put an end to that shit. Diego told us the killings had been perfectly timed, taking place when the brothers were most vulnerable, and he suspected a punk was among us. "As soon as we find out who the fuckin' punk is, his life is over and whoever is helping him will die with him."

I was given an S&W SD40 and told to go nowhere without being armed. The Warriors were definitely targeting the Houston chapter members and we each had to stay prepared. Diego told us that the five Houston chapter presidents were meeting the next night to plan the retaliation for the deaths of the brothers and he went on to say, "Everyone stay focused and watch your shit over the next several days. I don't want to lose anyone else because someone gets stupid or careless."

𝔐.ℭ.

Diego called the Houston chapter together the next evening to approve officer appointments. He asked the chapter to support the appointment of Clutch as the Houston V.P., Bullet as Houston Secretary and Whiskey as Sergeant at Arms. The appointments met with no resistance from the chapter membership and since there wasn't a single no vote with Diego's selection for the three roles, there would not be the need to prepare for an election. Diego felt a great deal of relief with that part of the day's business, and with the appointments settled, the hard business ahead could be accomplished without the distraction of elections.

It was ten o'clock that evening when the chapter presidents gathered to meet. The meeting was opened without the usual roll call and Diego asked that there be no official record kept. Given the nature of the meeting, everyone agreed that was a good idea. West Houston was represented by the President, Chulo; Hawkeye from Texas City; Shady from North Houston; and Broker from Baytown. They were all there and they all knew what this gathering was about. It was about payback.

Chulo was the first to stand and he spoke directly to Diego. "I know what Viejo meant to you brother, I am deeply sorry for your loss. West Houston stands with you and we'll bleed to the last drop to make this thing right."

The other chapter presidents all stood and agreed to stand with the Houston chapter and with Diego, to whatever the end of this thing looked like. Diego spoke. "It's a usual part of tradition for the six of us, when we meet, to remember and respect our brothers that have died. I was thinking today how we always include that fucker who betrayed us in the beginning, and you all know that I am speaking of Sand Man. He fucked us over when he created the Warriors and now that cockbite is bombing our homes and killing our brothers. Without Viejo, I would still be down on Houston's East End, gangbanging, maybe dead by now. Instead, HE is dead, and why? Because of Sand Man and the rest of those fuckin' Warrior cocksuckers who lack the courage to talk to us, and instead believe the cops. Now here we are, being killed by them, one by one. I owe my life to the Los Patrons and to each of you and I am grateful that you are all in agreement with me and what we have to do, but you all need to know that I will never again mention the name of that Warrior traitor at any church gathering anywhere. BLOOD is all I want from him now and I want ALL OF IT I CAN TAKE! Before this is over we will have burned all of their clubhouses, killed all of their officers, collected their patches, and gotten payment in blood for what they have taken from us. Anyone left alive will surrender their colors, bikes, jewelry, and anything else belonging to the fuckin' Warriors."

Shady spoke up. "The Bull will never approve a plan for the complete annihilation of the Warriors, Brother. Everyone here knows how he feels. He wants the Warriors to patch over and he believes we have the chance to force that to happen."

Diego spat on the floor. "We haven't even buried our dead and we're already discussing a patch-over. All that bullshit talk is a discussion we'll have at another time. The order of business here tonight is HOW and WHEN we get payback."

Quiet overcame the entire gathering as reality settled in. They would now actively hunt down and kill Warrior members. Over the next three hours, the group discussed and argued over the plan specifics and finally agreed on three principal actions. The first action would be the chapter hits. They would hit the Warriors in Dallas, Kilgore and both Houston chapters. They would ask The Bull to send the Nomads after the Lubbock chapter. Shady and Broker would take care of the Cut and Shoot chapter and Diego and Chulo would handle the Houston and San Antonio chapters. The second action involved the Austin clubhouse. It was a thing of pride for the Warriors and it was decided that Hawkeye would be responsible for acquiring the necessary munitions to destroy it and that he would oversee its destruction personally. Everyone agreed on the third action and that was the killing of Sand Man. Being the national president meant that he'd never be alone and that would make a close-up hit very difficult.

Diego stood. "I have the perfect person for the task. Hitting that son of a bitch from a distance will not be a problem."

It was agreed that Diego, Chulo, and Hawkeye would ride to Corpus Christi the first weekend in August. They would meet with The Bull and get his approval for the plan.

"Until then," Diego said, "We have three brothers to bury."

Chapter Three

SAYING GOODBYE

The day started early and seven days had passed since the bombing. Cruz had been on ice the entire time and only since the death of Viejo and Crow had his body been released to the mortuary. Now all three were together and the funeral had been fully planned. They would be buried at the same time, in plots purchased by the club. Viejo had only a living sister, but Crow and Cruz had living parents, brothers, and sisters. It was an absolute clusterfuck trying to arrange for the families to be part of the services, because they wanted things done differently than we were going to do them. Consuelo Estevez (Cruz's mother) wanted a Catholic priest and a full rosary ceremony, while Penny Morris (Crow's mother) wanted a Methodist funeral. Only Kathy Godard (Viejo's sister) understood the difficulty of what we were trying to accomplish and cooperated fully with the club's wishes. It was left up to Carmen to explain to the parents that the Los Patrons held power of attorney over the brothers and all that was theirs, including the legal right to bury the two men with or without their family's consent or presence. We would bury our brothers our way and comfort the families the best way we could. Only the brothers and family would speak over the bodies, and there would be no priests or ministers present. There would, however, be a viewing, which was scheduled for the next afternoon beginning at three o'clock.

Since I had begun prospecting, my job had included working the bar at the clubhouse, emptying trash, cleaning restrooms, doing clubhouse laundry, cleaning up vomit, washing motorcycles, making beer runs, escorting ole ladies wherever the fuck they wanted to go, and just about whatever else a person could imagine, and all that on top of working fifty hours a week driving a forklift. Between the job and prospecting, I barely knew if I was coming or going as the work went on for what seemed like endless hours and days. Today, however, my job was to ensure the families' needs were attended to, and I have to say, this job was by far the most difficult I had dealt with since becoming a prospect. I was told to make sure the families stayed out of the way, so that we could tend to the business at hand, which was to bury our dead. I arranged hotels for the families, and their transportation to and from the viewing, and to and from the funeral. Watching those two women wail over their dead sons during their private viewing times was the toughest thing I've ever done, and I had nothing but dread at the thought of what the formal viewing and funeral would be like.

It was up to Britt to communicate with local law enforcement about the expected turnout regarding the out of town chapters' arrival and the funeral procession. Britt told the local cops to expect between three and four hundred brothers on motorcycles, not to mention support clubs and affiliates that would be arriving. Local police and sheriffs' departments were bracing for the influx of around five to six hundred hardened bikers for the funeral and were preparing to shut down one of two inbound lanes on both I-45 and I-10 to allow for the bikers to make their way in. Since the funeral would be held in Katy, officials of Fort Bend County, in the hope of having some control over events, made the fairgrounds available for bikers wishing to camp. It appeared, for all intents and purposes, that we were ready to get the viewing and funeral underway.

It was about ten-thirty the next morning, and I was inside the clubhouse with the national officers, Diego, Britt, Bullet, and Clutch, when Chulo came into the room and yelled, "Prospect, turn the TV on and put the volume up so we can all hear. The other chapters are already arriving and it's on the news."

I moved behind the bar and tuned the television to channel eleven, and sure as shit the news was broadcasting. There was a helicopter flying over I-10 East and there were motorcycles riding side by side in a procession that was at least a half mile long. The same was true of I-45 North and South. Motorcycles were crowding SH59 coming from the northeast and from the southwest. It was impossible to estimate how many bikes there were, but for sure it was a damn sight more than four hundred and it was only ten-thirty in the morning. I was working my ass off trying to take care of nearly twenty-five brothers in the clubhouse when The Bull called me over. He handed me a beer while pointing at the television and said, "Take a look, Prospect, what you see there is what true brotherhood is all about."

I kept up pretty well with the brothers at the clubhouse until right after lunch when we all left for the funeral home. I had barely walked through the front door, when I got a call from Crow's dad. He asked that the family be allowed an hour of private time with the bodies before the viewing was opened to the club, stating, "My wife will not be able to tolerate such a crowd as we have been seeing on television."

I looked at my watch and it was already one thirty. The old man's request seemed doable, but only if we delayed the viewing for a few minutes. With the viewing scheduled for three, time was short, so I hurried to deliver the request to Diego. His response was firm, "The bodies are being delivered in thirty minutes. Tell them they can view from two until three o'clock, but we aren't changing the viewing times."

Knowing it would be impossible for the family to get to the funeral home by two, I braced for what I expected to be an uncomfortable call. When I delivered the message to the old man, he said, "Go tell your boss I said he's a prick. You can also tell him we'll arrive at two-thirty and we'll take a taxi. You don't need to help us any more."

It was obvious both sets of parents didn't like us, however Viejo's sister remained cooperative. I delivered the message to Diego exactly as the old man had said it. Shit, I was concerned the old man might make a scene and I wanted Diego prepared. I was surprised when he said, "I've arranged for the bodies to be placed in the study behind the chapel and they'll remain there until four-thirty. I want you to meet the taxi and personally escort the family members into the study, the back way in, and then make sure they are all safely at the hotel when they're finished. We're going to give the family their time and our respect."

The families arrived by taxi about fifteen minutes after two and I directed the taxi around to the service entrance at the back of the chapel. I met Crow's father as he stepped out of the taxi and told him that Diego had made arrangements for over two hours of privacy with their sons, and he wanted them to know the club offered its condolences. The old man leaned heavily on the hood of the taxi and wept. Viejo's sister put her arms around my neck, and with a strong hug whispered, "Thank you."

I stayed with the family the entire time and I had taxis waiting for them at four-thirty sharp, as I had been instructed. Before they all left for their hotel, Crow's father offered a shaky hand to me and said, "Please tell your boss that I am grateful." He then bowed into the taxi and wept even more.

From four-thirty until seven o'clock, as sergeants at arms from several chapters kept a watchful eye, the brothers and their ole' ladies all passed by the coffins offering condolences to the families that were present. As each man passed the coffins you would hear them say, "God Forgives, Patrons Repay." It was becoming very obvious to me that these men all felt the loss and were all equally willing, yes even eager, to repay the debt.

The viewing ended exactly on time with sergeants at arms lining up the motorcycles by chapters then by officer, rank and file. Highway 59 South had been closed to all traffic by the Department of Public Safety except for the motorcycles. The motor deputies provided by the county escorted an untold number of bikers to the fairgrounds. It was a fuckin' sight to see for sure.

It was close to midnight when Britt and I rode to the fairgrounds, and there were about a dozen deputies on site with at least a thousand bikers in makeshift tents and campsites. The place appeared to be fairly quiet, although bikers are not priests so there was plenty going on that kept the cops on close watch. Fortunately, there weren't any big issues that required intervention, just a lot of weed and women running around showing some tits and ass. I followed Britt through the fairgrounds and made sure all was in order for the morning before heading back to the clubhouse for some sleep.

The morning came early and I had only a few hours sleep before I had to get over to the hotel and work out the final details with the families. They would arrive at the chapel via the mortuary drivers and would be seated in the family section at the side of the chapel, just out of sight of those attending the funeral. Diego would be the first speaker, followed by The Bull and four others who had known Viejo. The eulogies for Cruz and Crow would come after Viejo's. There wasn't a single family member who wanted to speak, which kept things really simple. The family being prepared, I left for the funeral home.

By nine o'clock every seat in the chapel was filled with brothers and their friends. There were so many in attendance that the chapel parking lot, along with six blocks around it, was packed with bikes and people. The families arrived and were seated when Diego approached the front of the chapel. He opened with a brief but heart-wrenching story of how Viejo had rescued him from the street gangs of Houston's east side and how much he loved the man he called brother, the man who in truth was much more a father to him than anything. Diego's voice broke often as he described the encounter of his first meeting with Viejo, and the entire room felt his sorrow. He spoke next to the sister of his longtime friend and said, "Kathy, Marc often spoke to me of you, and he told me that as children you were always looking out for him. He told me of a time when your stepfather gave you a beating that was intended for him and that you took it because you were his only real protector. I can tell you that he loved you, and your safety and well-being were important to him. You have a home among the Los Patrons if you want it, and we are ready to be family for you, if you will accept it." Kathy looked away as if in deep thought.

The Bull spoke next of the contributions to the club that had been made by Viejo. He spoke of the many occasions the two had toasted the sunrise with Cuervo and Modelo (Viejo's favorite) and he offered condolences to the families of those being buried. The eulogies for the other two men were delivered by those within the club who had been close to the dead brothers. It was a sad time and the air was heavy with emotion.

The five Houston chapter presidents were selected as pallbearers for Viejo and it had been decided there wouldn't be a sixth as these five men were his closest brothers. Pallbearers for Cruz and Crow were selected from the many brothers throughout the club that were closest to the two.

Viejo's body was the first carried out, followed by Cruz's and then Crow's. Then came a funeral procession that could only be described as unforgettable. There were three hearses with five family cars followed closely by The Bull and his national officers, the five Houston chapter presidents and their respective sergeants at arms, and motorcycles (riding peg to peg and in tight formation) for more than a mile. The cemetery was a five-mile drive that took about forty-five minutes to complete. There simply wasn't enough room for all the motorcycles at the cemetery, so many parked roadside and made their way by foot to the burial. As the bodies were being lowered into the ground, The Bull made one very brief statement saying, *"God Forgives, Patrons Repay!"* With that each family member tossed a handful of dirt on the coffins and the brothers selected as pallbearers shoveled the remaining dirt into the graves.

After the bodies were interred, I escorted the family members back to their hotel and they all said their goodbyes and left, save one. Kathy and I were heading to Viejo's home to go through his personal things, and she asked that Diego meet us there.

When Kathy and I arrived at Viejo's home in Pearland, Diego and Bullet were already inside. Kathy went straight to Diego and asked, "Do you know who is responsible for my brother's murder?"

Diego responded, "We know who is responsible, Kathy, and they will pay with their lives for what they have done."

Until now Kathy's demeanor had been calm and deliberate, but that changed in an instant as I watched her lose complete control of her emotions. She fell into Diego's arms sobbing hysterically and said, "I have lost all that I have. He was all I have ever had." She sat on the couch crying uncontrollably for what must have been at least twenty minutes, while Diego did all he could to console her.

Kathy suddenly sprung up from the couch and threw her arms around Diego's neck whispering so low that only Diego could hear. You could see from the expression on his face that he was troubled by what she had said, and as he pulled her arms down he said in a very stern voice, "Kathy, you have no idea what you are asking of me."

"Promise me, Diego. I WANT to hear you promise."

Diego replied, "You'll have what you've asked for." He looked at me and said, "Make sure she has everything she needs before you leave here." He then motioned to Bullet, and they both left without saying another word.

Chapter Four

SAN ANTONIO

It was now August and the Texas heat was at its peak. The temperature had been over one hundred degrees for ten days straight and it was already nearing that mark at nine o'clock in the morning. The meeting with the national board had been scheduled and time had been set aside for Diego to present the retaliation plan, so Diego, Chulo and Hawkeye, along with Sergeants at Arms Whiskey from Houston, and Pusher from West Houston began the three-hour ride to Corpus Christi. They got there a little before noon and pulled into the clubhouse parking lot where National Sergeant at Arms, Rico, met them and promptly escorted them in. After two hours of discussion, The Bull green-lighted the entire plan, with one condition. The killing of Sand Man must not involve any other national officers. The Bull said, "I want them ready and willing to discuss a patch-over."

Diego, pissed off at The Bull's statement said, "Fuck them mother fuckers and while we're at it, explain to me WHY we would want that shit back in our house?"

The Bull stood from his seat. "Diego, I understand your hate and where it comes from, but there are too fuckin' many of them for us to drive them all out of Texas and if we try to do that, we'll have every fuckin' fed in the country up our asses with their RICO prosecutors. Now, you listen to me! We can be smart and grow our influence and our business, or we can be stupid and let a war cost us everything we have. The Warriors have significant business connections, and if we allow those connections to falter we will have another club or some fuckin' street gang looking to score their deal, and I WILL NOT allow that to happen. Now, I want your fuckin' commitment on this – Sand Man is the ONLY national officer to die."

Diego finally agreed to all of The Bull's requirements, then The Bull asked, "When is this all going to happen?"

"We hit the chapters and the Austin clubhouse the first week of October. That gives us time to make sure we have all the details of the plan worked out. Can we depend on the Nomads to handle their Lubbock chapter?"

"They'll handle that and anything else you need of them. What about Sand Man?"

"We still have to plan that, but I'm thinking late October, early November."

"The prick goes to this shit-hole of a club in south San Antonio every Thursday night at five o'clock. He has his sergeant at arms and his ole' lady with him, but he'll be there. The place is called Slim Jim's."

Diego nodded. "We'll get up there and check it out."

Chapter Five
RETALIATION

It was October and two months had passed since the funerals. There had been no more violence and things had settled down a bit. Diego was at his kitchen table staring out in space as Carmen made coffee.

"Carmen, this thing with the Warriors is about to happen and I'm going to send you to Jake for a few days."

"What are you going to do?"

He sat as if he hadn't heard the question and Carmen said, "Diego, I'm afraid, and not just for me, but I am also afraid for you." He looked at her with obvious pain in his eyes, and without saying another word, put on his cut and headed toward the door.

Carmen, hurt by his blatant disregard for her feelings, yelled, "You can't just leave without telling me what's going on, Diego."

"Carmen, it's hard doing what I'm about to do, knowing we're going to accept those fuckers back into our lives when this thing is done. I hate that fucking Sand Man and I hate everything he represents. Now, I have some business to attend to and I'll be gone for a few hours. I've already called Jake and he's going to meet me here at nine-thirty tonight. You need to be ready to go when he gets here."

Diego left the door open as he walked to his bike, started it, and as Whiskey arrived, they both rode off.

It was nine-fifteen when I pulled into Carmen's driveway. She walked out to meet me and had barely gotten off the porch when Diego and Whiskey rolled up. I walked over to greet him and said, "Diego, you know I should be going with you."

Diego's reply was direct. "What I fuckin' know, Prospect, is I'm leaving you here with my ole' lady and you have a job to do. That job is to make sure she's safe. You fucking got that?"

"I got it, Diego."

He looked at Carmen. "Give us some space, woman."

Carmen walked back to the porch as instructed, and when Diego was satisfied she was far enough away to be out of hearing range he said, "I'm sending her with you for two reasons, Jake. One, because I can't be distracted worrying about her and two, because I know she likes you."

He looked hard at me. "You'll get your opportunity to be in this fight before it's over. But for now, I need you to take care of Carmen." He hugged me hard. "I'll see you in a couple of days." Having said that, he and Whiskey went inside.

Carmen looked at me as Diego walked past her. "He hugs you goodbye and acts as though I'm not even here?"

We stood motionless for a few moments just looking at each other before Carmen opened her car door and got inside. I fired the engine on my bike and pulled into traffic, watching closely to make sure Carmen followed.

We arrived at my apartment in about twenty minutes. I parked my bike, quickly grabbed her bags, and went inside. Once inside, she asked, "Do you have any wine, Jake?"

"No, Carmen, I'm sorry, I don't. I'll run to the liquor store and get a bottle. It's not a problem."

"That's sweet of you, Jake, but truth is, I'm tired and I just want to go to bed."

I picked up her bags and took them into my bedroom. Turning the light on, I realized the room was a fuckin' mess. "Shit, I'm sorry

Carmen, the room's a mess, I know, but the bed's comfortable, so you should sleep well."

She looked at me with very tired eyes. "I remember your bed, Jake, and I'm sure I'll be fine."

Before she could say anything else, I said, "I'll sleep on the couch, but if you need anything, just yell out."

She smiled, then kissed me. "Good-night, Jake."

Sleep wasn't coming easy as I lay on the couch, thinking of her, still able to taste the lipstick from her kiss. *What the fuck is wrong with me? I feel like some high school kid in a dream-world, worshiping some damn cheerleader. No, this is different. I'm no kid and she's no cheerleader. I'm a prospect and she's the wife of our chapter president – I gotta stay focused.*

I awoke the next morning to the smell of coffee and the sound of bacon sizzling. I got dressed and walked to the kitchen where Carmen was at the stove, cooking. I watched her for a moment, and once again found myself wondering how it would have been to share my bed with her. It hadn't happened, and not because Diego had forbidden it, because he hadn't. It hadn't happened because neither of us were sure about the outcome of the next few days, and we both needed to be able to think and reason without the weight of guilt that would surely have come from such a decision. I admired her for a moment longer before sitting down at the kitchen table.

She poured a cup of coffee, set it on the table in front of me, then leaned over and kissed me.

"Breakfast will be ready in a few minutes, Jake. Would you like to watch the news while you wait?"

"Sure, Carmen, that'd be great."

She tuned the television to the local news just in time to hear the reporter say, "Nine members from the Houston outlaw biker gang, Warriors Motorcycle Club have been shot down in a bloody massacre by unknown assailants."

Carmen turned up the volume, then sat in the chair next to me, as the broadcast continued. "An unidentified source on the scene reported that each of the dead men had his left ear removed, which is evidently intended to send a message of some kind." The story ended with the words, "*So Much Carnage!*"

It was very apparent the retaliation was well underway. The next day went by quickly with the news twice more reporting on MC violence. There were the killings of two Warriors in Dallas, along with five members of the Rebel Souls Motorcycle Club just outside of Kilgore, and still three more Warriors members in Lubbock.

The reporters were now broadcasting on all the local and national networks that Texas was embroiled in a biker war similar to the Canadian biker war of the nineties, and the Los Patrons were suspected of being at the center of the violence. By Friday it had been four days since the Los Patrons began retaliating against the Warriors and there had been additional attacks in Houston as well. The news broadcasts reported on the explosion and total destruction of the Warrior's clubhouse in Austin, and the body count continued to grow. The dead now stood at three Los Patrons, twenty-three Warriors, and nine Rebel Souls.

About nine o'clock that evening Diego called me on the phone and told me to come to a place called "The Den" just outside of downtown on Navigation. He said that Whiskey would be at my place soon to pick up Carmen, and that I should haul my ass there as soon as I could.

I got to the place in about forty-five minutes and was immediately escorted to the office by the bar manager. There sat Diego with a member of the Warriors gagged, bleeding, and barely alive.

Diego rose from his chair, hugged me, and said, "Okay, Prospect, it's time for you to get involved."

He showed me pictures of a Warrior receiving a package from a Patron and the exchange of cash between the two. I asked Diego where he'd gotten the information and he said that a paid friend of the club, a detective from the Gang Task Force of the Port of Toller PD, had provided it.

I asked who the men in the picture were and Diego said, "The Warrior is this dying fuck sitting here, and he is the one who was working with that fuckin' punk we've been looking for."

When I asked about the Patron, Diego spat on the floor. "There is our punk! You'll never believe this, but that fucker has eaten at my table many times and we've shared many good times together. All the while, he planned to betray his brothers and me. The son of a bitch has known the whereabouts of our brothers and has been feeding information to the Warriors since before the trip to the desert."

I looked at the picture again, and my heart sank as I stared in disbelief. Of all the brothers I'd met, I would never have guessed it to be him.

"I called him about twenty minutes after I called you and he'll be here any minute. When he gets here he'll be brought back here just like you were, and when he sees this mother fucker lying here, he'll know why he's here. Tonight, you earn your top rocker."

"What do you want me to do, Diego?"

"Kill him! Do it quickly and do it quietly, and after he is dead, kill the other mother fucker, too. Then, I'll need you to get rid of both bodies."

No quicker had Diego told me what he wanted when we heard a bike roll into the parking lot. I moved into the shadow behind the door just before Britt came walking into the room. He saw the Warrior lying in the corner, pulled his pistol from his cut and said, "What the fuck?"

I moved quickly, shoving my knife into his back.

I stabbed him low enough to ensure the knife penetrated his lung and far enough toward the center of his back so the blade would cut into his spinal cord as I pulled it out. He tried to scream as he sank to one knee, but there was no air in his lungs and all he could manage was a soft gurgle. As he fell to the floor, I quickly rolled him onto his back, stabbing him deep in the chest. He reached for me as if to plead for his life and I said, "Fuck you," and stabbed him again.

With Britt now dead, I walked straight over to the Warrior and grabbing a handful of hair, I pulled his head toward his knees and stabbed him once in the back of the neck, right at the base of his skull, severing his brain stem. His body immediately began convulsing and his thrashing was so violent, the blood vessels in his eyes burst, completely engorging his eye sockets, and blood flowed heavily from both ears. It took a little longer for this one to die and as we watched, Diego said, "Damn, that's a nasty fuckin' way to die!" He looked at me and smiled. "And two more make fifty-three, right?"

"Yeah, right."

Diego walked first to Britt and sliced off his left ear, then immediately did the same thing to the dead Warrior. I stood there watching Diego place the ears in a zip lock bag when he looked up at me and said, "I have the ears of every Warrior and Rebel Soul that we've killed. They're in the freezer at the club house."

"What are you going to do with them?"

"Remember that night at Viejo's when Kathy lost it? She asked for proof that those responsible for her brother's death had been killed. This is what she wanted. I'll get rid of them after she's seen them."

"You're fucked beyond imagination if you get caught with them, Diego. You know that, right?"

"I'm not going to get caught with them."

"Where do I take the bodies?"

"There's a place on SH-290 just off FM-1560, a rendering plant called Disposal Rendering, Inc. The owner is a friend of the club and he'll be expecting you." Diego laughed. "These fuckers are going to become dog food."

After we loaded the bodies into a borrowed truck, Diego said, "This business with the Warriors will soon be over, and, hopefully, we can get back to business with relative peace, but I'm going to need your help with one last detail."

"What?"

"We'll discuss that after church on Tuesday. Be careful tonight, Prospect."

He gave me a big hug and we went our separate ways. The night's cool air helped me settle down a little as I drove to the rendering plant.

I'm in a borrowed truck with two dead bodies in the back, covered by a tarp. Man, wouldn't that make the news if I got pulled over and arrested. Fuck! What if Diego got caught with those ears? Now that would damn sure make the news. Drive carefully, I reminded myself. *Drive carefully.*

As I arrived at the rendering plant, I recognized a stench I hadn't smelled since Afghanistan, the smell of rotting flesh. (It was a common smell in a country where so many had died and were often left to rot.) The smell almost turned my stomach when I stepped out of the truck.

This gangly-looking fucker eating a sandwich and drinking a Coke met me. I asked him, "How in hell do you eat food in this place? The stink is so bad."

He pointed to a truck about fifty feet to the west. "You smell the animals from today's ranch run. They sometimes lay by the roadside for a week before we're notified to pick them up. That truck arrived here about an hour before we closed. It's bad, I know, but you get used to it after a while."

I asked him if he knew why I was here and he said, "Yep," then pointed toward a dock about a hundred feet up the road. "Back your truck into that unloading dock and I'll be there in a minute."

I was in place for only a couple of minutes when the guy walked up and removed the tarp. He told me he was going to need my help, and I said that I would do whatever was needed. Together we unloaded the bodies and I helped him undress and shave both men, throwing their clothing and hair into a furnace going full blast. We lifted the bodies onto a stainless steel table near a conveyor belt and he said, "Ok, I got it from here. There's a hose you can wash the bed of your truck with hanging next to the dock and you need to throw that tarp in the furnace." I did as I was told and got the fuck out of there.

It was three in the morning before I got back to my place, and I didn't think I would ever get the stink of that place off my clothes and skin. *A fuckin' rendering plant! How the hell do we make the kind of friends who are willing to do that kind of shit? And the ears, what the fuck? I saw some crazy shit in the army but I would never have dreamed about things like this happening here in the US...*

Before drifting off to sleep, I lay and wondered about what would come of Tuesday's church and what Diego would ask of me next.

Chapter Six

THE PATCH

I arrived at church earlier than normal, hoping to see Diego before anyone else arrived. I hadn't seen him since Wednesday night, and I had only talked to him briefly during the weekend. To my very pleasant surprise, it was Carmen who next arrived. She was dressed in a pair of tight jeans, a Harley shirt, and boots, looking and smelling sexy as hell. I commented on this being the third time I had been alone with her since that first night at my place.

She smiled and said, "You think of that night often, do you, Jake?"

"I didn't say that. I was just saying it's nice to see you without feeling the need to look the other way."

"I do think of that night, Jake, and I have often wished for another opportunity to…make you comfortable."

As I stood there trying to think of how to respond to what she had just said, we heard the roar of Diego's Road King as he and Whiskey rode up to the two of us. Diego got off his bike and said, "My prospect and my ole' lady just, uh, shootin' the shit. Hmmm, what the fuck should I suppose you were talking about?"

I just about shit my pants when Carmen said, "The comforts of life, my husband, that's what we were talking about." They smiled at each other and at me before kissing and walking into the clubhouse.

As Diego entered the clubhouse, he put his hand on my chest. "I'll call you when you're needed, *Prospect*," and closed the door behind him.

I was a little bewildered, not to mention totally pissed off by Diego's treatment of me. I was left to stand guard at the door as, one by one, each of the chapter brothers walked by me sneering, cursing and acting as though I was suddenly dog shit. After almost an hour and a half of waiting, I was finally summoned inside. There was a row of tables arranged at the front of the room with a single chair in the center facing the group. *Fuck, I'm facing an inquisition.*

Diego sat at the center of the table, directly facing me, with the brothers surrounding him in a semi-circle. Whiskey frisked me, took my pistol and knife from me, and sat me in the center chair.

Diego was the first to speak. "This prospect has killed a Patron and I was witness to it and we are here to decide what we want to do with him."

Shocked by what Diego said, I tried to stand and speak, but Whiskey put a strong hand on my shoulder. "Sit down and shut the fuck up."

Diego spoke, "Is there a brother in the room who wants to speak?"

Bullet stood. "I got nothing but respect for what Jake did, and if I'd known about that mother fucker, I would've killed him myself."

Diego took a pistol out of his cut and laid it on the table in front of him. He looked at me. "A few nights ago, I watched you kill two men, and you did it as if it were nothing more than shooting a mad dog or stepping on a cockroach. It was fuckin' cold the way you did it; no emotion, no anger, and no remorse. You got rid of the bodies by yourself and kept the club clean of the whole issue. You're one bad mother fucker, Prospect – ain't no question about that. More importantly, you've shown me and every brother in this room that you're someone we can trust and depend on."

He stood from his chair, and speaking to the brothers, asked, "How do we reward this prospect for what he's done?"

Bullet spoke again, "Give him the bastard's gun!"

Diego picked up the pistol he had previously laid before him, walked over to me, and handed me the nickel-plated, Colt 45 semi-auto. "It has ivory grips engraved with the club patch. This gun belonged to that cocksucker, Britt, and since you're the one who killed him, it is only right that you should have it."

Clutch spoke up and said, "That fucker also rode a Heritage Classic Custom with the patch painted on the tank and fenders."

Diego said to me, "The bike is yours, also."

I wanted to speak, but Diego placed a finger over his lips in the motion meaning "Quiet."

"Brothers," Diego said, "we've got a problem. We all know that a prospect may not possess anything displaying El Patron."

It was at this point that The Bull walked into the room, carrying a cut fully patched front and back. He walked straight up to me and said, "On your feet, Prospect!" I stood as Whiskey removed the prospect cut I was wearing. The Bull placed the new cut on me and proceeded to lecture me on the responsibilities of a patched bother. I was completely stunned. I believed I was about to get fucked and instead, I had been patched! Not in the year I had been told, but in seven months. It was obvious to me now the entire night had been staged and was all part of the patch-in ceremony.

When Carmen walked into the room followed by two women, I figured out quickly there was going to be one hell of a party that night. Smiling at me, she said, "Your comfort *tonight* will be attended to by Ashley and Marti." She kissed me gently, high on my cheek and whispered in my ear, "*Enjoy.*"

Diego walked up and placed his arm around me saying, "We'll talk tomorrow, but for now, the night is yours, Brother!"

For the first time in my life, I felt a sense of belonging. I had friends, I had family, I had a tomorrow and I had purpose.

I Am My Brother's Keeper!

Chapter Seven

SAND MAN

I awoke about seven the next morning with Ashley on my right and Marti on my left. The sheets were wet from what could only be described as a night filled with wild-ass sex, and though it had been fuckin' great, that was last night's pleasure. Right now, I could think of nothing else but that I needed to piss. It took a moment or two before I realized I wasn't at home. I slipped on my jeans and stumbled my way down the hall to the shitter and pissed for what seemed like a fuckin' hour. After finishing up in the bathroom, I walked to the end of the hall where I heard voices. Opening the door, I realized I was in the clubhouse.

Diego and Clutch were standing at the bar and started laughing when they saw me. I asked them what the fuck was so funny and Clutch replied, "Bro, you look like you've been playing dress-up, with all that lipstick…If I had a camera, I'd take a picture of you. Looking at Diego, he said, "Hey, Jake here doesn't have a road name and I think Lipstick sounds perfect for him. What 'ya think, Diego?"

By now, they were both getting a good laugh, so I gave them the finger, showed them the white side of the moon, and went back to my room only to find Ashley and Marti snuggled up and spooning, still very much asleep. Rather than wake them, I gathered my things and headed off to the shower, and got dressed. Feeling hungry and needing a cup of coffee, I went back to the bar where Diego and Clutch were and poured myself a cup.

Clutch asked, "How does it feel wearing those colors?"

"It feels great, Brother."

"Are you sober enough for the three of us to talk some?"

"Of course,"

Diego and Clutch both walked to the chapel and I followed, closing the door behind me. We all sat down at the table and Clutch pushed a sergeant at arms patch over to me.

Diego said, "Jake, I'm asking you to accept this patch and the responsibilities that go with it."

"What about Whiskey?"

"Whiskey's main responsibility will be the clubhouse, rides, and safeguarding Clutch. Your responsibility will be to safeguard the business dealings and you'll also be responsible for my security. When and where I go, I'll want you at my side. Oh, by the way, Jake, you can tell those temp agency bitches you are working for to shove their forklifts up their pretty white asses. You don't have time for a job any more."

"What am I supposed to do for money?"

Diego passed an envelope over to me. "The Los Patrons take care of their own, Jake."

I opened the envelope and counted out ten thousand dollars. "Ok, this is a lot of money so, what I mean is how…"

Diego waived away my questions. "Jake, you'll be responsible for the collection of payments from our various business interests. For your responsibilities you take fifteen percent and your collectors take five percent. The chapter board receives forty-five percent with fifteen percent going to the national board. The remaining twenty percent is placed in the safe for legal fees, parties, cops, funerals, and emergencies. Once a quarter, you meet with our nine support clubs and collect fifteen dollars per member. With what we take in monthly, you should be able to bank eighty or ninety grand a year, easy. Money for you isn't going to be an issue. Got it?"

"I got it!"

Clutch pushed another patch over to me. This one had the number 13 embroidered inside a diamond.

Diego said, "The letter M is the thirteenth letter of the alphabet and with some clubs, the patch is intended to identify the man wearing the patch with the motorcycle. Think about it, he's in a motorcycle club, right? Then you have other clubs that fuck with the cops over the patch, and say that it stands for marijuana, or methamphetamine, or who knows what the fuck else. In those clubs, you see a LOT of men wearing the patch and usually, it will be sewn high on the vest, almost always straight across from the 1% diamond. With the Los Patrons, there are only a few who wear this patch, and that's because not many have done what's necessary to earn it."

"What'd I do to earn the patch?"

"Listen close, Brother. For us, the patch has absolutely nothing to do with the alphabet or motorcycles or marijuana or anything else beginning with the letter M. Instead, it has everything to do with people or better yet, a certain number of people. In a citizen's court of law, there is always a jury of your peers and that jury is normally made up of twelve people, right?

"Right."

"Those same twelve people are responsible for determining a person's innocence or guilt. But the process for imposing the penalty for a guilty verdict is the responsibility of one person, the judge. We bring these two numbers together on a 'Diamond 13' patch and award it to the brother who has acted as both judge and jury. Jake, the *few* brothers within the Los Patrons who wear this patch are brothers who have killed on behalf of our club. We sew this patch to the lowest point possible on our cut, nearest to the closure on the right side. We put the patch close to your gut and as far as possible from your heart, because we know, as you know, a man who allows his heart to get in the way of killing will never have the guts to complete the task. Now, the fuckin' cops would love to hear someone admit to the true meaning of that patch and then every brother wearing the patch would be on their way to jail. So, if anyone ever asks you what it means, your answer is, 'motorcycle,' understood?"

"Understood."

"Remember when I told you that I would need your help with just one more detail?"

"Yeah, tell me what you want me to do."

Diego went on to explain. "We are ready to finish this war with the Warriors and when it is over we intend to force a patch-over. We will take control of their business interests and clubhouses, and accept them into our lives as brothers. We will accept all but one and his name is Sand Man."

"He is the one who led the break away from the Los Patrons in the beginning, right?"

"Right."

"What happens with him?"

"He dies!"

"I see. I assume that is where I, and the one last detail you spoke of, come into the picture, right?"

"We can't get near enough to him to kill him close up and The Bull has insisted that he be the last to die. We'll have to take him from a distance and that, Jake, is where I need your help. I want you to snipe the fucker."

"Brother, I'm willing to do whatever I need to do. Just give me the details,"

"We need to make a trip to San Antonio and figure out how we're going to handle it. The Bull gave me some information I want to check on up there and I want to get an early start, so meet me here at nine in the morning and we'll leave from here."

Butterflies! Shit, I haven't experienced butterflies since Afghanistan, but I sure the fuck got them now!

The next morning arrived and as planned we were in a borrowed car and on our way by nine o'clock sharp. We took I-10 all the way to San Antonio then made our way to the corner of South Presa and Pereida streets on the south side. Exactly as The Bull had said, there was a rundown old bar called Slim Jim's. Diego circled the place a couple of times, and after a few moments I had my bearings. The bar parking lot and front entrance faced the west and across from the place was an empty field. At the far end of that field was an old building that appeared to have once been some kind of old church or perhaps a street mission. I suggested to Diego that we check it out. Diego drove to the front of the place, and found an entrance where the gate once stood, so we drove on in. We followed the driveway all the way around the back of the building where the garage and trees completely concealed us and the car. It had a chain link fence that covered the back of the property with a bunch of old boards tied into it for who knows what reason. The whole place was covered in graffiti and generally looked as though it had been the home of street people. We got out and peeked through gaps in the boards, revealing a completely un-obstructed view of the parking lot at Slim Jim's.

"This place is perfect!" I said. "What time does Sand Man usually arrive?"

"According to The Bull he gets here about five o'clock every Thursday evening."

I took a quick look around. "The sun will be at our back which will help conceal our presence, and it will make it much easier to get away once we finish him. Of course, if he's late and the sun is too far down, our movements will be that much easier to detect."

Diego looked at me. "Let's hope he isn't late."

"Diego, when I was in Afghanistan, I would sometimes be ordered to make a mess out of my target because doing so scares the shit out of the enemy. A frightened enemy capitulates much faster than an enemy pissed. How big a mess do you want me to make?"

"I want him dead, and I want to send a very strong message that will bring the rest of those fuckers to the table to discuss the patch-over."

"Ok, then. I'll need a very special rifle with a certain kind of ammo, and I'll need someone to spot for me."

"Get a list put together and I'll give it to Hawkeye. He'll be able to get whatever you need."

The two and half hours back to Katy went by quickly and while Diego drove, I compiled the list of what I needed. As we pulled up to my apartment, I asked him when he wanted to hit Sand Man.

"As soon as we can get together whatever you need to get it done."

"I'll need a couple of days to practice with whoever is going to spot for me, and that person is as important as the equipment. Give me Whiskey as my spotter."

"Done."

I handed him the list. "The rifle will cost around $3,500 with the ammo costing another $200 at least and the spotting scope will cost another $1,800."

Diego read the list. "Will we send the message I want with this set up?"

"At 150 yards, his head will simply disappear and the round will lodge into that brick wall behind him."

"Not a problem – a worthwhile spend," Diego replied.

The paper read like no grocery list Diego had ever seen:

1- AAC Micro 7 Bolt Action Rifle fitted with AAC Suppressor

1- Leopold Illuminated Optic 1.5 x 5 scope with 300 Blackout dedicated reticle

1-box of .300 Blackout 220 grain subsonic explosive tip ammo

1 – Mark IV 12 – 40 x 60 Spotting Scope

It took about a week for Hawkeye to deliver the equipment. Whiskey and I practiced at 100, 150, and 200 yards and we were dispatching apples with ease. Two days later, we were on our way to San Antonio and were both feeling a bit anxious. We were in a borrowed, beat up, old truck so as not to look suspicious when we arrived at the old mission or whatever that place was. By now we were sure our phones were tapped, so Diego supplied us with a pre-paid cell phone to call him with once the job was finished. We stopped for gas only once on the trip and arrived about two-thirty that afternoon. The place was as it was when Diego and I had left it, except for one old bum who was sleeping just inside the back door of the place.

The old man awoke and spotted us, but Whiskey quickly had him shoved into a corner and killed him with a strong blow to the throat. It took a bit of work on both our parts to hide the old man, but after looking around we found a narrow shaft near the cornerstone of the building that was probably twenty-five or thirty foot deep, and we just shoved his body into it. We knew it was well hidden when we heard it thump as it landed somewhere in the darkness. I hadn't counted on anyone being there and I sure as hell didn't feel good about killing the old man, but we could ill afford a witness to finger either of us as having been there. We unloaded the equipment and got everything in place, taking care not to leave ourselves exposed. Having concealed ourselves with a bunch of old boards and tin that had blown off the roof of the building, we made ourselves as comfortable as possible and waited.

We had more than two hours to go, and because it was so important to remain still and quiet, Whiskey and I did very little talking. With nothing much else to do but wait, my mind drifted back to my first mission back in Afghanistan. I remembered how nervous I had been and how many times I'd checked and re-checked my equipment, making sure there was no room for a miss. I knew then, back in Afghanistan, just as I knew in San Antonio, that a miss could be disastrous, not only for our objective, but also for our ability to escape the scene without detection. Our only hope in getting out of San Antonio without getting caught was to cause so much panic and fear that our movements wouldn't be seen due to the sheer terror experienced inside that bar. I had to get it right, so as I had done before each successive mission in Afghanistan, I re-checked my equipment and took one last inventory of my own movements to ensure this thing went off without a miss.

Whiskey and I had remained motionless for more than an hour and a half and were both soaked with sweat and fatigued from the lack of movement. We had a clear view of the parking lot at Slim Jim's and we had parked the truck just inside the old garage completely out of sight so we could drive straight out within seconds of the shooting. Knowing that we would soon be faced with the reality of why we were there, we looked at each other and gave the thumbs up, meaning that we both knew we would soon be very busy.

It was a little after five and the sun was setting. We heard the roar of motorcycles as they approached the old bar and watched as five bikes pulled into the parking lot. Sand Man and his ole' lady were in the middle of two other bikes; one in front and one behind, ridden by, we assumed, his sergeants at arms. There were two bikers that followed just a couple of moments behind the three and those two men were easily identified as prospects. We waited until they were all off their bikes, hoping that Sand Man would move into the clear, and he did just that. He was talking to his ole' lady and facing directly into my scope when Whiskey began to call out wind, distance, and elevation. As he called the adjustments out to me, I adjusted my scope until we were both perfectly in sync.

Whiskey spoke softly and said, "Target's right," and I pulled the trigger.

Whiskey reacted quickly to what he saw, saying, "Ah, fuck man, you made a mess out of that fucker! His head exploded, and I swear I saw a piece of his skull fly out into the parking lot."

We watched as the other men panicked. They quickly ran for a place to hide, but after a moment, and to my surprise, one of them came back into the parking lot and for a brief moment, in a defiant posture, just looked around. I watched him and wondered, *What the fuck is he doing*? My question was answered quickly as I watched him reach down and drag the woman into hiding. With all of the commotion, I hadn't noticed that she had fallen. As he dragged her away, I could see that her head was completely covered in blood.

"Whiskey," I said. "We've gotta get the fuck out of here, Brother!"

We quickly loaded the rifle and the spotting scope into the truck, got moving, and were soon heading down I-10 back toward Katy. Using the phone Diego had given me, I called and reported, "Two down."

Diego replied, "You can explain that when you get home – just get home."

The drive home went exactly as planned. We stopped at a little, out-of-the-way place in Flatonia, which was about halfway home, and handed off the rifle, ammo, and spotting scope to a club contact who would turn the equipment back into cash. We had neither the need to keep such a weapon around nor did we want to have anything incriminating on us should the cops get nosey. We grabbed a little dinner at a local diner and cleaned up good before finishing the trip. It was about ten-thirty that night when we pulled into the parking lot of the clubhouse.

Diego met us and immediately grabbed me and hugged me tightly saying, "It went off clean, Brother. Pallbearer (Warrior National V.P.) has already called The Bull asking for a sit down. It appears we'll reach an end to the violence without any concessions on our part."

"That didn't take long."

"Well, you made quite a mess of Sand Man, and it had the desired effect. The Warriors want this thing over and are willing to do whatever it takes to make peace."

"What about the woman, is she dead?"

"No, she had a bump on her head and her hair was covered in Sand Man's blood. She was quite a mess as I hear it, but completely unharmed."

"What now?"

"We wait. The Bull will call us together soon and that's when the future will be determined."

Chapter Eight

THE BUST

Whiskey and I stayed long enough to have a couple of beers, and with the job done, we just sort of breathed easy. It was about eleven-fifteen when I left for home and I was in bed by eleven-forty-five. The sleep was well needed but soon interrupted as I was awakened by the sound of a thundering crash. Before I knew it, I had been grabbed from my bed and thrown hard to the floor. I was given my Miranda Rights as I watched my apartment being trashed by cops who looked like the soldiers I'd served with in Afghanistan. As I sat on the floor in my underwear watching these guys tear my shit up, one of the assholes walked over to me with my bag of cash and asked me what I was doing with such a sum of money.

I responded, "It's not unlawful to keep cash, is it?"

"No, it's not, but owning this might be." He showed me the pistol that had been given to me by the club when they patched me in, Britt's gun with the patch grips. "Where did you get this?"

"It was a gift from a brother in the club, and there's no fuckin' law against that, either."

The cop jerked me to my feet, looked me straight in the eye, and said, "You ain't nothing but biker trash," and spat at my feet.

I was taken to the prisoner transport vehicle (PTV), shoved inside and shackled to the floor and wall of the truck by my feet and hands. There were seven other brothers in the PTV with me, including Diego,

Clutch, and Whiskey. Diego looked up at me smiling and asked, "Where are your pants?"

I just shook my head.

He said, "They took down the clubhouse, too, Brother, and the last thing I saw before being put in here was an ice chest being brought in." He and I looked at each other knowing exactly what that meant. "No worries. We all need to keep quiet until we have Carmen in the room with us."

The cop stuck his head in and yelled, "Quiet! Absolutely no talking!"

Diego yelled back at the cop saying, "Fuck you, mother fucker," which resulted in his being gagged.

An hour later we were all being booked into the county jail. It was nearly ten in the morning before any of us were given the opportunity to make our one telephone call. Diego made his call to Carmen and the others made various calls to wives or girlfriends, and one brother actually called his grandmother. I had no one to call and waived my right. I knew that Carmen would arrive soon and that was all I needed to know. Diego, Whiskey, Clutch, and I were moved to isolated cells, while I had no idea what happened with the remaining four brothers. It was about three in the afternoon when Carmen finally arrived. She was dressed in a dark business suit with a skirt cut just above her knees and high heels. Her hair was pulled up in a French twist, and she looked like she could take on the world. The fact is, I don't think I ever found her more beautiful than I did sitting there in my orange "Halloween" suit, standard issue for prisoners of the county.

She was waiting in the prisoner/attorney conference area with a big deputy not far in the distance when I was brought into the room, shackled hands to waist and waist to ankles. I was made to sit in a chair across from her and my hand shackles were locked to a ring at the center of the table. Once the deputy was back behind the sound-proof barrier, she asked how I was doing. I told her that I was hungry, but other than that, I was fine. She asked if I had said anything during the arrest and I repeated my exchange with the cop that jerked me out of bed, including the fact that he'd called me biker trash. She told me that I had handled myself well and that she thought I'd be out before nightfall. I asked about Diego and she said he was being held pending charges under RICO statutes. Knowing enough about the statutes to realize a conviction could mean life behind bars, I asked what they were basing those charges on.

"They claim to have evidence that Diego ordered the bombing of the Warrior clubhouse and the killing of Sand Man."

"That's not possible," I told her. "There were only a few people who knew of that plan: Diego, me, Whiskey, the Houston chapter presidents and the National Board."

"Go back to your cell and stay quiet. I still have to interview the others. I'll be back later this afternoon to post bail."

With that she squeezed my hand, smiled, and left the room.

About nine o'clock that night, I was brought in to process out. They gave me clothing that Carmen had supplied and allowed me to change. My cut was returned and I was advised to ask my attorney about the confiscated cash and gun. Carmen was waiting for me in the lobby and hugged me tightly when she saw me.

I asked about the cash and the gun and she said, "It can only be released if the grand jury refuses to find cause. If that happens, it will all be returned to you."

"What happens if they find cause?"

"It will be held as evidence to be used by the prosecution when you go to trial."

"Ok, what do you think?"

"It's not good, Jake! Let's go home because we have a lot to talk about. You have to fill in all the gaps for me."

"Home?"

"As an officer of the court, my home can't be wired or watched unless I request protection. We'll have complete privacy there."

We got to Carmen's home a little after ten-thirty and Carmen asked me to pour her a Chardonnay. I helped myself to a Jack and water, and sat on the couch next to her fireplace. While sitting, I looked around and thought, *I can see her everywhere and this place even smells of her.* She startled me as she came into the room, having changed into an old comfortably worn pair of jeans and a loose top.

She asked me what I was in such a trance about and I responded, "Trance?"

"What were you thinking so intently about?"

"Your home, it reminds me of you." I looked up from the couch. "This place is beautiful."

She smiled as she sat beside me and lightly touched the hair of my brow. "I'm sure by now you could use some relaxation, so I've drawn you a bath."

"Am I bathing alone?"

"Is that what you want, Jake?"

Leaning forward, I gently pushed her down on the couch, kissing her while breathing in the smell of her fragrance. Her scent overpowered my senses, as I slowly undressed her. The shape of her form was unlike any I'd ever known and as I brushed across her nipples, her breasts became flushed and perked with her passion. As I moved down her body and tasted her for the first time, she arched her back, biting her bottom lip and whispered, "Jake, please don't stop." Her orgasm was strong and the look in her eyes was one of complete contentment. As the night turned into dawn we made love several more times, but it wasn't like that first night. This time, there had been no permission given, no ole' ladies loaned, and no going back. We both knew we had crossed the line. Call it circumstance, call it karma, or call it whatever the fuck you want, but things were definitely different with the morning's light. I wanted her now more than anything I could imagine and I couldn't imagine how that could ever be.

Chapter Nine

RICO

round nine in the morning Carmen was notified that charges were being dropped against me and all of my brothers, except for one. Diego was being held pending a RICO investigation. She was told that federal authorities would soon take custody of Diego and to expect him to be moved to a federal detention facility. As for me and the rest of my brothers, we would be returned our property, simply by signing for it. Carmen called each of the brothers and told them to meet us at the sheriff's office at ten thirty.

Before we left, Carmen moved close and said, "Jake, I've always been a loyal wife and I've never dishonored my husband. Though I've known his touch many times, I've never felt loved by him. I'm not sure how our tomorrow will look, but you need to know, I'm in love with you and I have been from that very first night." She moved to kiss me and as I started to speak, she placed her finger over my lips. "Just kiss me."

When we arrived at the jail, my brothers were there waiting for us and Carmen watched as each of us collected our property. As the evidence officer was about to hand me my gun, that prick cop, the same one who'd arrested me, took it and threw the ammo onto the floor. Handing my gun to Carmen, he looked at me and said, "You can pick your ammo up off the floor where it and you belong, biker trash."

Carmen witnessed the stare-down between me and that idiot fucking cop, moved between us, and said, "Officer, this man is not being charged with any crime and I'm his attorney. I'm also an officer of the court and I've just witnessed your harassment, so I have some advice for you. Go on about your duties and leave my client alone, or I will have YOU brought up on charges. Understood?"

That fucker just smirked, turned, and walked away.

I said, "He doesn't like me, now, does he?"

As she gathered my ammo from the floor she said, "Fuck him, he's not your problem."

Clutch, now acting as president, ordered the brothers back to the West Houston Clubhouse where a decision would be made about what to do next. Carmen dropped me at my apartment so I could get my bike, but before leaving she kissed me and said, "Call me when you're able."

When I got to the clubhouse, Clutch was at the bar opening a beer and called me over to join him. I swallowed a shot of Cuervo, followed that with a long drink of Modelo, and sat down to listen to what he had to say.

"A woman has snitched to the fuckin' cops about the Warrior club-house, the ears and about Sand Man. I am pretty sure who she is and that cunt's gotta disappear."

I asked, "You know who she is?"

"Yeah, it's fuckin' Kathy, bro."

"What?! No fuckin' way, man, that's Viejo's sister. She would never give up the club and she would sure as hell never give up Diego. He's like family to her."

"Jake, nothing is at it appears. She HATES the Los Patrons and always has. In the beginning, after Viejo first joined the club, she suddenly found herself an outsider and she's always kept her distance because Viejo placed more importance on the club than he did on her. I'm telling you, bro, if she disappears then so does the charge against Diego."

"What do we do?"

"We have to get rid of her."

"What exactly are you suggesting, Brother?"

Clutch's response was coarse. "Bro, what the fuck do you think I am suggesting? We have to silence that fuckin' bitch or Diego will spend the rest of his life in jail. We have to kill her, man, and we have to get it done before the Feds get her into protective custody."

The whole conversation shocked me to the core. I simply couldn't believe what Clutch was suggesting. This wasn't just any fucking street whore we were talking about. This was the only living family member of Viejo. To kill her would take a sanction from higher up, but from who? The Bull? There's no fucking way he would ever endorse an action like that and that left only the National V.P., Digger. He was actually responsible for the overall security of the club and could order the hit using anyone he wanted, even a Nomad, if he chose to.

It didn't take long for Clutch to arrange the meeting with Digger, and the men agreed to meet the following afternoon in Victoria, at the Adobe Motel just off Highway 59. Victoria was about halfway between Houston and Corpus Christi and would be the perfect meeting place since Digger was there visiting family.

Before we split up, Clutch took off his cut, removed the V.P. patch, handed it to me, and said, "Diego told me to give this to you if things were to go bad with him, so make sure you have this sewn on before we leave for Victoria tomorrow."

"What about Bullet?"

"Bullet balances the books and he's very good at that, but no one would ever follow him. Diego knows that and so do I. I ain't saying I want something to happen to me, but if it does, this chapter will fall to you and not to Bullet. You got that, bro?" he asked.

I nodded. "Okay, Brother."

Clutch and I arrived at the motel right at two-thirty the next afternoon and went directly to room eleven on the east side of the place. Digger was waiting at the door. The three of us exchanged hugs and

I asked with some surprise, "Are you alone here, Brother? Where's Dillon?" (Dillon was the national sergeant at arms responsible for his personal security.)

"What the fuck?" he said. "Given the nature of what this meeting's about, you thought I would bring someone to witness it? You gotta be out of your fuckin' skull, bro. Now get on inside, I don't want to have this conversation out in the open."

Clutch started the conversation saying, "We know who gave up Diego."

Digger responded quickly saying, "No, you don't. You think Kathy Goddard gave him, but you're wrong."

Clutch and I looked at each other, surprised by Digger's statement.

Clutch asked, "Who then?"

Digger responded, "Diego gave up Diego."

"What does that fuckin' mean?" I asked.

"It means, Jake, Diego let his hate get the better of his judgment and on the night of the bombing of the Warrior clubhouse, Diego phoned Sand Man. He told him that he had ordered the destruction of their clubhouse and bragged that he would personally ensure that Sand Man would share space in hell with Viejo where he and the devil would take turns fuckin' him in the ass for all of eternity. That fuckin' Sand Man had his phone set to record the whole conversation. Now, what the fuck do you think Sand Man did with that recording? Well, let me tell you. He gave it to one of his paid cops there in San Antonio, who put the rest of this bullshit into motion the moment the news about Sand Man was released."

Clutch asked, "How did Kathy's name come into play?"

Digger said, "Fuck if I know and fuck if I care. That bitch is partially responsible for getting Diego fired up. The fuckin' ears man – the Feds have them and because of those fuckin' ears they have all the evidence they need to put him away. Diego is completely fucked."

"What happens to him now?" Clutch asked.

Digger looked hard at both of us as he lit a cigarette and said, "Diego dug the hole he is about to be buried in. The Bull is about to release a statement disavowing Diego's actions as purely personal, and completely denying any knowledge of any part of it." He looked at me. "We've taken steps to make sure that Diego is the only brother to fall and you can thank your soon-to-be "Warrior brothers" for that."

I asked, "How's that?"

"Pallbearer has agreed to testify that both you and Whiskey were at the unification meeting between the Los Patrons and the Warriors that took place the afternoon Sand Man was killed, and if there are any other Patrons charged for any of the killings, they will be given alibis from the Warriors as well."

"What happens to Kathy?" Clutch asked.

"Kathy took a long boat trip off the coast of Corpus Christi earlier this morning and I don't think she had any plans of returning. The Bull and Pallbearer are there now working on plans for a patch-over. Now, I suggest the two of you go back to Houston and take whatever steps are necessary to ensure the Houston chapter has a solid board and is able to move forward with business. I'll let you know when and where to plan for the Houston patch-over party."

Clutch and I returned to Houston with many questions still unanswered, but we also returned knowing the questions we wanted answered, we couldn't ask. We had a party to plan and I had to go home and explain to Carmen as best I could that her husband alone was going to fall for all that had happened. I hoped the news would not leave me without what I wanted most…which was her.

It was almost midnight when I got back to my apartment. I realized when I stepped through the door that I hadn't been home since first being arrested. The place was a fucking wreck and all I could think of was how badly I wanted to call Carmen. The truth was, for the first time in a very long time, I felt fear. Not the fear you experience knowing you are about to risk life and limb, but the fear of losing something you just can't imagine living without. She told me that she was in love with me but she'd also told me that she was a loyal wife and a loyal Patron Ole' Lady. Both of those circumstances were in place long before she and I first met.

I dialed her number and she answered. "I have been sitting by this damn phone all evening worried sick and wanting to call. Please tell me you're on your way here."

"I'm at the apartment, Carmen. I'll come in the morning."

There was a pause before she asked, "What's wrong?"

"Carmen, I'm tired and I need sleep. We can talk in the morning."

"We can talk tonight! You can have all the sleep and anything else you want, just please come here. I need to know what's going on and you can't leave me alone."

Finally I agreed to come to her place, but I did so with a lot of reservation. With all that I had learned that day about Diego, the feelings of guilt had just about consumed me. The big question for me now had little to do with the club or Diego, but it had everything to do with Carmen. How would she respond when I explained to her what she was never supposed to know, and how would she feel about me knowing Diego was going to take the fall alone, and that I was powerless to do anything about it?

I pulled up in front of Carmen's home at one-fifteen in the morning and my heart was pounding so hard it made it hard to breath. I couldn't fucking believe that my feelings were governing my actions so that I couldn't think clearly. I had barely shut down the engine on my bike when the door of Carmen's home opened. She stood in the doorway dressed in nothing but panties and a very light negligée.

I walked up the sidewalk as she met me on the porch. "Jake, I have been waiting all day for just a call, just the sound of your voice, and when you finally call you tell me that you are at your apartment and you will see me tomorrow?"

"Carmen," I said, "I have bad news about Diego. Let's go inside."

Chapter Ten

THE PATCH-OVER

$\mathcal{A}$ngrily, Diego yelled at the interrogating officers, "Fuck you! I ain't fuckin' telling you asshats jack shit!"

Special Agent Bernard Ross of the FBI's North Texas District Office, assigned to the Outlaw Motorcycle Gang Task Force, and Shannon O'Hare of the Department of Justice Organized Crime and Drug Enforcement Unit both walked into the room and excused the interrogating officers of the Fort Bend County Sheriff's Office. Ross sat in a chair directly opposite of Diego and said, "Mr. Santiago, my name is Special Agent Ross Bernard with the FBI and this is Agent Shannon O'Hare of the Department of Justice. We are here to inform you that you are being held under RICO statutes and the Federal Bureau of Investigation will be taking charge of investigating the crimes you are charged with. You have been given your Miranda Rights and so I will ask, are you willing to cooperate with the Federal Government's investigation?"

"Fuck you," Diego responded.

Ross answered quickly by saying, "The Federal Marshal's office will take custody of you momentarily and you will be transported to the Federal Detention Center in Seagoville, Texas, where you will remain until the investigation is complete. The Sheriff's Office has provided us with your lawyer's contact information and she was notified earlier that you are being moved. She will be given the information on your location as soon as we have you moved and secured. Until that time, I would suggest that you remain calm. Are you in need of anything? Are you hungry?"

Diego responded in a calm tone. "Yeah, how about a fuckin' blow job, ass wipe?"

Ross smiled at Diego. "It's going to be fun working with you, Mr. Santiago."

As the two officers prepared to leave the room, O'Hare told the deputy federal marshal who was there to transport Diego, "I recommend you bag and gag this one for transport."

It was close to dark when the deputy marshal and Diego boarded the private plane headed for Seagoville Airport. Diego was in a strait-jacket and gagged, with a waist chain and ankle shackles. After being seated, he was chained by his ankles to the floor of the plane, and his waist chain was secured to the floor behind the seat. The deputy marshal sat in the seat facing him in the adjacent aisle and stared at Diego with an expression lacking emotion. As the plane began its taxi, the deputy marshal leaned forward and whispered, "You can become a state's witness and enter the witness protection program or you can spend the rest of your life in a federal maximum security prison. Why don't you take this 'quiet time' and think about what that means."

Diego looked at the deputy marshal for only a moment, winked, and as best he could, smiled.

𝔐.𝔈.

Carmen sat on the couch and lit a joint while I poured a Jack and water. The smell of weed took me back to the day when I first got laid as a teenager. She and I had been smoking weed that day too and it lowered our inhibitions, which made sex that much better for both of us. I hoped getting high would make what I had to tell Carmen easier for her to accept.

As I sat next to her she said, "Okay, I'm ready for the bad news."

I detailed the information exactly as I had received it from Digger with her paying close attention to every word. After a few moments she took a hard hit off the joint, then passed it to me. "On the night before the retaliation began, Diego told me he was sending me to you, and that you would keep me safe. He did that, I think, because he knew at some point in all of this he wouldn't be coming home. He was so angry, Jake, he told me that the Warriors owed blood for what they had done, and he would never be able to call them brothers."

She sort of drifted for a moment and then abruptly said, "Jake, I received a call from the Department of Justice earlier this afternoon and I was told Diego was being moved to the Dallas area. I'll be receiving a confidential dispatch via federal courier tomorrow with his exact location and once I know where he is, I'll go there and do my job as his attorney, which is to represent him and his legal interests. I'll fight to defend all that can be defended, and hopefully keep him away from the reaper's needle."

She looked at my cut. "By the way, I see you're wearing a new patch."

"Yeah, Clutch appointed me to the job. He said it was what Diego wanted."

"Give me your knife, Jake."

"Why?"

"Give it to me, Jake, please!"

I handed her my knife and she immediately cut the palm of her hand and then asked for my hand. I reluctantly placed my hand in her lap and she quickly sliced into it. She then took her hand in mine, allowed the blood to mingle, and said, "I love you, Jake. Diego left me and told me that you would care for me, and now, I'll care for you. I'm your Ole' Lady now!"

𝔐.𝕮.

It was nearly ten the next morning when I rode to the West Houston Club House and I thought as I arrived how much my life had changed over the last year. It was December and I realized that Thanksgiving had come and gone. I had much to be thankful for, but most of all, I was thankful that I was no longer alone.

When I pulled into the parking lot, I was surprised to see six Warriors standing with Clutch and Bullet. They were all laughing and acting as though they had been friends for a lifetime. I had learned through my years in the military that a man's commitment to a brother would show through best in a fight. Somehow I knew, sooner or later, that commitment would be tested. *Until then, I'll walk on the side of caution with these new brothers.*

Bullet was the first to greet me. He hugged me tight and said, "Congratulations, Brother. No one is a better fit for the job than you." He smiled big and introduced me to the Warriors saying, "Jake is our new V.P."

It was then I encountered Warrior Buck.

He stepped up and like a cocky rooster said, "I've heard of you. You're supposed to be some kinda sharpshooter with a rifle, from the Army or some shit like that, right?" He grinned big and spat on the ground. I stepped up and kicked that cock sucker in the balls so hard he threw up his lunch. Then I ripped his cut off and threw it to Clutch. As he tried to get to his feet, I kicked him again, hard, on the outside of his right knee and everyone there heard bone break.

I looked at the astonished Warrior crew and said, "Get that mouthy mother fucker out of my sight."

The Warrior crew hastily hoisted that big-mouth prick up into the back of a pickup and as they drove away with Buck in the back, Clutch looked at me and said, "I guess you're not open to talking shit out?"

"That wasn't the time for talking, bro, that cockbite was showing nothing but disrespect. With Diego facing prison and the rest of us left here to make this shit work, I'm sure as fuck not about to let some tough-talking prick get away with running his mouth, not about Diego, not about you, and not about me. God Forgives and Patrons Repay, ain't that right? Well, I ain't about forgiving the disrespect of a brother."

Clutch and Bullet stood motionless for a moment just looking at each other until the silence was broken by a Fort Bend County Sheriff's patrol unit pulling in behind us. *Fuck, here we go again.* It was the same fuckin' cop that had first arrested me – the same one who had given me all that shit over my gun at the jail, and the same prick who kept calling me biker trash.

He walked up to the three of us and said, "Where's that lady lawyer you biker trash keep around? Is she not here today to defend your sorry asses?"

I stepped up and took close notice of his name. "Pearsall, you sure run that mouth a lot and man, you do some real tough talking. I wonder how much tough talking you'd be doing without that badge?"

He smiled. "I don't need a badge to deal with the likes of you three pieces of shit. But since I have it, I'll just go ahead and use it. Is that okay with you, biker trash?"

"What do you want?" Clutch asked.

"Want? I don't want anything. I am here to protect and to serve, so I'll protect and serve every chance I get. Now, there've been complaints about loud pipes from your neighbors, and I would just hate to come back here and impound one or more of these beautiful Harleys you ride. So, let's work on keeping the noise down, boys, because you really don't want me fielding complaints here." He grinned wide as he got into his car and gave us a two-fingered salute while driving away. I returned his salute with one of my own.

"Brother, that man does NOT like you," Clutch said. "Where the fuck do you know him from?"

I looked at Clutch. "I don't know that fucker from anywhere, but I am betting I'll get to know him much better as time moves on. Okay, we're supposed to discuss the patch-over party, right?"

"Jake, that guy you just kicked the fuck out of is Pallbearer's cousin, and just before you got here he told us the sign on the Warrior's clubhouse is being removed to make room for our sign. The patch-over party for Houston is supposed to take place this Friday – there, at what used to be their clubhouse. Hopefully, the ass kicking you just gave Buck won't get in the way of that."

"Okay, Brother, I get it. You're pissed and you think I just made things difficult."

"You didn't cause any of that – Buck did. Thing is, there is so much tension right now between the Los Patrons and the Warriors and we have to remember, after Friday night there will no longer be any Warriors, only Los Patrons. These men will be, fuck bro, these men ARE our brothers and we have to start thinking that way."

"As I said, Brother, I get it."

Looking at the bandage on my hand, Clutch asked, "What's up with the hand?"

"Something between Carmen and me. It's no big deal."

"Okay, Jake, now is a good time to talk about this thing with you and Carmen. The whole chapter is talking about you two. Care to tell me what the fuck is going on between you and Diego's ole' lady?"

"She's not Diego's ole' lady any more. She belongs to me now!"

"Are you fuckin' kidding me, man? Your brother, OUR brother, is locked up and not able to defend his position and you're moving in on his ole' lady? That's fuckin' bullshit, asshole."

"Really? First, fuck you and second, fuck you again. Diego lined this shit up between me and her months ago. He ensured she had a place to go because he knew she would need a place to go. Knowing what we know about what he said to Sand Man, it's pretty fuckin' clear he wasn't intending to be part of this unified club, and now he won't be. So if you or any other brother has any questions about Carmen, let me make this clear, I Am My Brother's Keeper and in this case, I am also keeper of my brother's wife. When and if you are able to talk with Diego, you can ask him what his wishes are. If you find him to be unhappy about any part of this, we'll talk about it then. But until then, my relationship with Carmen is the business of Diego, Carmen, and me, and not open for debate with you or anyone else."

Clutch tossed the Warrior cut back to me. "You know you have to return this cut to Buck, right?"

"Yeah, I figured that shit out, alright."

Clutch looked hard at me. "Tonight, Brother."

Friday night rolled around quickly and the officers and crew of the Houston Warriors rolled into the parking lot of the clubhouse at straight up eight. Our entire chapter was already there waiting and the doors were quickly opened. As we all went inside, Buck hobbled over on his crutches, and said, "If you think giving me my cut back settles things, you're wrong. As soon as I am off these crutches, soldier boy, you and I are going to settle this shit."

I grinned and said, "If you feel the need to get the other leg broken, asshole, you just come on back for some more. I'll happily take care of that shit for you."

Clutch walked over to Buck and said, "If you have any intention of patching over tonight, I suggest you bag that conversation. Furthermore, if you want to live to see your next birthday, you should stay clear of Jake. Believe me when I say, you're outmatched, Buck."

Buck turned without saying anything and made his way to the bar where he sat on a stool. It was pretty clear from the hate I saw in his eyes that this thing between him and me would sooner or later get settled.

As planned, Clutch walked to the front of the clubhouse and called for everyone to head outside where the prospects had a bonfire roaring full. Bullet, pulling a rail on wheels with him, followed the group out to the fire. On that rail were eleven brand-new cuts fully patched with Los Patron patches and each of the Warriors, led by their chapter president, Scot, lined up for the "Burning of the Rags." In keeping with Los Patron tradition, Scot handed his president's cut over to Clutch, in show of respect for the new leadership and Clutch tossed it into the fire. Clutch then put the Los Patron cut onto Scot and they hugged briefly before Scot made his way into the crowd. After Scot, each Warrior, one by one, took off his cut and threw it into the fire then received his new cut from Bullet. The ceremony now complete, we made our way to the parking lot for the unveiling of the new "El Patron" sign that had been installed earlier in the afternoon. The prospects were ordered to make sure every brother received a shot glass filled with Cuervo. Once everyone was served, Clutch motioned for the sign to be lit, lifted his shot glass in salute, and said, "I am my brother's keeper," he took his shot, followed by everyone else.

That was it! There was no more war and there were no more Warriors. This very same party had taken place at the same time with every single chapter in the club, including the national chapter. Inside of one hour, the Los Patrons Motorcycle Club had grown by more than 400 brothers and was now one of the largest and most powerful motorcycle clubs in the southwest United States.

It was a night for celebration and all would've been perfect, but for one thing, *Diego Santiago*.

Chapter Eleven
SEAGOVILLE

At just before nine the next morning, Carmen was preparing to leave for Dallas. Arrangements had been made for her to participate in the evidence disclosure with the Federal Prosecutor at the North Texas Federal Court House at three that afternoon. She would be meeting with Diego at ten the next morning, at the Federal Detention Center located in Seagoville, Texas. Only after being briefed by the federal prosecutor on the evidence the federal government held could she begin the process of building his defense. We spoke about the risks that Diego would face and the potential ramifications to everyone involved, including us, when Carmen said, "Jake, there is something I have to tell you and the timing isn't good. I'd wait until I return, but I have to tell Diego the same thing while I'm with him."

Taking a tissue from her purse, she looked away from me as she dabbed a tear from the corner of her eye.

"Carmen, what is it?"

"I'm pregnant, Jake." She looked at me. "I'm pregnant with Diego's child."

I could see she was concerned at how I would react. "How long have you known?"

"I suspected it for a couple of days, but I confirmed it this morning. I've traced the time back so I could be sure, and Jake, I'm sorry, but you couldn't possibly be the father."

I was trying to gather my thoughts when Carmen reached out and softly touched my arm, saying, "I'm telling Diego that I'm pregnant and I'm also going tell him that I'm in love with you."

"This doesn't change things for you?" I asked.

"No, it doesn't, Jake. What about you? Do you still want me after what I've just told you?"

"Want you? For a moment, I thought you were going to tell me that... Well, I didn't know what you were going to tell me." I put my arms around her and said, "I love you, and yes, Carmen, I still want you."

"What about Diego's child? Will you want the child as well?"

I looked at her with as gentle an expression as I could muster and said, "His child, my child, your child, that kid will never know the difference unless you want it so. I'll love that baby as my own, as I love you. I just hope Diego reacts well to the news."

"Jake, other than Viejo, I have never known Diego to show affection for a brother as he has for you. I can't explain it, but I suspect it has everything to do with how you met. The fact is, those three men were there to kill Diego and probably would have, if not for you. I really don't think either of us needs to worry about his reaction."

She stood and put her arms around me and for a moment we both just held each other.

"Jake, what do you want me to tell him if he asks about the club's reaction to us?"

"Tell him the truth."

I loaded her bags into the car, kissed her good bye, and watched her drive away. *I hope my brother is as receptive to all of this as she thinks he'll be.*

𝔐.ℭ.

Agent Ross walked into the interrogation room at the Seagoville facility and sat across from Diego. He lit a cigarette and handed it to Diego, then lit another for himself. "Mr. Santiago," he said, "the federal government is willing to make certain concessions regarding the crimes you are charged with. Those concessions could prevent you from serving any prison time and could ensure your successful placement into the federal government's witness protection program. Are you interested in speaking with me concerning the concessions and what would be required of you in exchange for them?"

"Is my attorney here?" Diego asked.

"She is at the federal courthouse in Dallas, reviewing the government's evidence with the prosecutor. She is scheduled to see you tomorrow morning at ten o'clock."

Diego's response was direct and to the point. "My attorney knows what my response to that offer will be, and I'm sure by now she has already told your prosecutor to go fuck himself, and as for me, I have nothing more whatsoever to say to you." Diego then lowered his head, stared at the table, and remained quiet. Without speaking another word, he was eventually returned to his cell.

Ross walked out of the interrogation room and met O'Hare as he was leaving the observation room. "It's as though he wants to die!" O'Hare said.

Ross said, "With that kind of attitude, he may just get his wish."

𝔐.ℭ.

It was three-thirty in the afternoon and Carmen sat waiting. *One more in the many games these prosecutors play while preparing for trial. He thinks by making me sit here for thirty minutes waiting like some schoolgirl in fear of the principal that he will somehow gain the advantage.* Deep in thought and growing impatient, Carmen was startled as the door to the conference room finally opened and in walked the prosecutor.

"My name is Bill Tomlinson and I represent the government in its case against your client and husband, Diego Santiago. Before we start, you should know that I strongly disapprove of you representing your husband given your own involvement and potential incrimination in this case. Additionally, if I find one shred of evidence that would support an indictment, I will immediately move to have you removed from this trial and request a warrant be issued for your arrest. Now are the game rules clear to you?"

"Are you through shaking your 'willie' at me, Mr. Tomlinson? Because I am totally unimpressed with your bully tactics. Just so you know, the game rules you speak of are the laws of the United States as set forth and enforced constitutionally. As for me, the rule of professional conduct will govern my actions going forward, and I would strongly suggest you take an inward look at your own conduct before you address me again."

The prosecutor sat at the conference table across from Carmen and handed her a single file containing the charges supported by the evidence. Premeditated Murder - One Count, Conspiracy to Commit Murder – twenty-eight counts and Possession with Intent to Distribute. The evidence disclosure included a transcript of a telephone conversation between Diego and Jarret McDaniel (Sand Man) dated Tuesday, October 9, 2012, detailing Diego's threat against Sand Man's life. It also contained evidence of the ears that were taken from the clubhouse freezer during the raid. The ears were being checked against the DNA from each of the murdered men and Diego.

"Given the government's desire to prove that your client didn't act alone, we will allow your client one option. If your client will fully disclose his involvement and the involvement of all parties connected with the murders, the government will place your client, and you with him, into protective custody while it prosecutes the case. In addition, his and your placement into the federal witness protection program will be guaranteed. Counselor, this offer is good for twenty-four hours, at which time the government will prosecute its case under RICO statutes while it continues to investigate the involvement of others who may otherwise be implicated. Do you have any questions?"

"The ears? What evidence is there connecting my client to the ears?"

"As you very well know, counselor, for prosecution RICO statutes require proof that criminal activity occurred at the direction of the leader of a criminal organization, and there is no requirement that proof be presented identifying the leader as having had direct involvement in the crime. The ears were discovered in the freezer located inside the clubhouse over which your client had direct control. The government will prosecute at a minimum that he ordered the killings of those twenty-eight men. If your client's DNA is found, as I suspect it will be, on that ziplock bag, or the ears themselves, it will prove that he not only ordered the murders but participated in them. With that evidence in hand, the federal government will prove its case against your client and seek the death penalty for his crimes. I understand that you're meeting with your client at ten o'clock tomorrow morning and I suggest you advise him well."

Tomlinson stood abruptly to leave the room, but before he closed the door behind him he looked hard at Carmen. "Remember what I said, counselor, advise your client well."

As Carmen prepared to leave the conference room, she once again felt the nausea that had plagued her so for the last several days, a gentle reminder that no matter the outcome of the trial, Diego's presence in her life would continue to play a part in her decisions now and for a very long time into the future.

At nine-thirty the next morning, Carmen arrived at the Seagoville Correctional Facility. Because of the circumstances surrounding Diego's removal from Fort Bend County and his placement into federal custody, Carmen's credentials for entry into the detention facility had been pre-approved. She was moved quickly through the check in procedure, briefed on the prison security procedures, and then badged for visitation. She was taken to the prison conference area and met there by FBI Special Agent Ross.

When Carmen entered the area, Ross moved forward, extended his hand and introduced himself.

"Mrs. Santiago," he said.

Carmen responded bluntly. "I prefer counselor, Agent Ross."

"Fine, your client has been briefed on what the government is prepared to offer, and the clock is ticking as you have only five hours from now to obtain a signature from him accepting the offer. I will say that he has been less than cooperative."

"I see. Agent Ross, is it standard protocol for the FBI to interrogate a witness who has not agreed to speak without his or her attorney present?"

"Counselor, I did not interrogate your client. I simply presented the offer to him that was presented to you last afternoon."

"How did my client respond to your presentation of the government's proposal?"

"I won't repeat the vernacular he chose to use, but I believe I can say he'll have no interest in cooperating. Is my thinking correct, counselor?"

"I haven't spoken to my client since before he was moved from Fort Bend County, but I believe you are likely correct, Agent Ross."

"As I expected. May I speak candidly with you, and not as his counselor, but as his wife?"

"No, you may not, Agent Ross."

"Fine. Then I'll speak to you as a possible co-defendant. Please sit down."

Carmen exploded. "I have already been through this with the prosecutor and I have no intention of sitting through this with you."

"Mrs. Santiago, you should understand this – it is Prosecutor Tomlinson's responsibility to prosecute evidence and it is my responsibly to gather it. You're considered a person of interest in this investigation and you'll take a seat voluntarily, or I'll have you detained until such a time as you are willing to speak with me. Now, won't you please have a seat?"

Carmen sat and pulled a tape recorder out of her brief case and set it out to record. Agent Ross picked it up and turned it off. "Unless your husband cooperates, he will be found guilty and the government intends to sue for the death penalty."

"The prosecutor has already informed me of his intentions, Agent Ross, and I see no need for us to discuss this again."

"Listen, your involvement or even your knowledge of decisions made by your husband can put you at risk of prosecution. You do understand that, don't you?"

"I understand that you are detaining an officer of the court without due process and that, sir, is what I understand. If you have evidence incriminating me in any way, I suggest you present it to your prosecutor and issue a goddamn warrant for my arrest. Otherwise, you need to release me to see my client so I can do my job. Now give me my fucking recorder."

Ross slid the recorder across the table to Carmen. "You can expect to be deposed soon."

"Agent Ross, if you are through, I would like to interview my client. Now, will you have someone escort me to him?"

Ross motioned for the guard to take Carmen to the visiting area. He looked at her across the table. "Have a nice day, counselor."

As Carmen entered the visiting room and sat down, the guard handling Diego brought him in free of chains and wearing prison-issued scrubs with socks and sandals. He smiled as he walked in, was instructed to sit in his chair, and told not to rise without alerting the guard that he was ready to leave. There was to be no touching, other than what was necessary in the reviewing of material. Smoking was permitted and drinks purchased from the prison commissary would be provided upon request. With the rules laid out, the guard stepped into a soundproof observation room and sat down.

Seeing the room was free from federal ears, Carmen said, "The prosecutor intends to seek the death penalty."

Diego shrugged his shoulders. "It'll take the fuckers a few years before they get a needle in my vein."

"I don't suppose it would do me any good to encourage you to take the deal offered by the government, would it?"

"Carmen, you know better than to ask me that bullshit, so don't bring it up again. What I want and need now is a little commissary money and a few comforts of home. I need a radio, cigarettes, and maybe something to read."

"Will you at least cooperate with some type of plea bargain?" she asked.

"What will that get me, Carmen?"

"It might save your life, Diego."

He grinned. "Sure, I will give them a full confession on my part, but I won't give up my brothers. If you can work a deal with that, I'm good with it."

"Diego, The Bull released a statement disavowing all knowledge of what has happened. He said you acted alone in an effort to undermine the reunification of the two clubs and no one is going to testify on your behalf. You won't turn on your brothers, but not one of them is going to step up to support you."

"So, is that supposed to fuckin' piss me off, Carmen? Do you think I would act differently? I was opposed from the very beginning to bringing those fuckers back into the club and if I could've stopped it, I would've. It was and is personal for me. The Bull is doing the right thing and I would do the same."

Carmen looked away for a moment to gather her thoughts and Diego said, "Something else has happened. Tell me, woman."

"I'm pregnant, Diego."

"Pregnant? Who's the father – me or Jake?"

"You are."

"Like hell I am! How the fuck am I supposed to father a child from this fuckin' place or better yet, how the hell do you explain to a kid that he or she has a *daddy* that is a convicted murderer? Fuck that shit! Bring me divorce papers and go marry Jake. He's one hell of a lot better example of what a husband and a father should be than I could've ever been. How do you feel about him? Are you in love with him?"

Carmen paused and Diego raised up in his chair, which alerted the guard who hastily stepped in and told Diego to remain seated. Diego relaxed his posture. "I fuckin' asked you a question, Carmen!"

"Yes, I'm in love with him."

Diego grinned. "And you didn't think I knew that? It's okay, Carmen, he's my friend and more than that, he's my brother and he should step up. Fuck, he owes me that. Next time you come here bring the papers, and I'll sign them, understood?"

"I understand."

"How are my brothers accepting it?" Diego asked.

"Not good. They think Jake is trying to move in on what belongs to you, and I have no idea what they are saying about me."

"Is Jake wearing the V.P. patch as I instructed?" Diego asked.

"Yes, but there is a lot of tension between Jake and Clutch and it's showing."

"Okay, Carmen. I need to see Clutch in person. Can you arrange for him to visit?"

"Yes, I can arrange it for Wednesday morning. It's the first time you're allowed visitors other than me."

"Okay, what do we do about this plea shit you're talking about?"

"I'll have to meet with the federal prosecutor to work that out. As it stands right now, he claims he will not bargain. We'll see how that works out when we review the discovery facts with the federal judge."

"Carmen, I want this shit done quickly. Whatever my life is going to look like, I want to get on with it!"

"Diego, this process isn't going to be fast, but I'll do everything I can to keep it moving."

Diego motioned for the guard, and stood. "Get Clutch up here and bring me the divorce papers."

He walked from the room without saying another word.

As she stood to leave, Carmen braced herself on the table feeling faint. *I have to see a doctor as soon as I get home because something isn't right. The nausea is almost non-stop and these moments of feeling faint are happening way too often.* As she walked toward the visitor exit, Carmen's balance became uneven, and then everything suddenly went dark.

It was noon by the time Carmen awoke. She was in an ambulance being transported to Presbyterian Hospital in Kaufman, some fifteen miles away. She tried to rise but the EMT attending to her gently held her down and calmed her by telling her she was safe and why she was being transported.

She had fallen about ten feet short of the visitor's exit, unconscious and blood running down both legs. The prison staff had immediately moved her to the infirmary where doctors had determined she had suffered a miscarriage. The EMT explained that prison officials had called for the ambulance so she could be moved to an appropriate place for treatment. He asked all the necessary medical questions and as she answered, tears swelled up in both eyes. All she could think about was her parents. She suddenly felt overwhelming sadness and a sense of loss not experienced since their deaths. She was so sad that she barely heard the EMT ask who should be notified.

Instinctively she said, "My husband's name is..." Then after a pause she asked, "Do you have a piece of paper?" The EMT took a pen and paper and she gave him the telephone number. "His name is Jake Coleman. Please call him and tell him where I am." Carmen asked for a towel, and wiping the tears from her face, she held it like it might have been her favorite blanket from early childhood.

Within twenty minutes, she had been delivered to the emergency room and was hastily moved to an examination room designed for OB patients. The doctor at her side was a female who spoke quickly, saying, "Mrs. Coleman, my name is Dr. Phillips and I need to ask you a few questions."

"My name is Carmen Santiago. My identification and my insurance information is in my briefcase."

"I am sorry Mrs. Santiago, I was misinformed concerning your name."

The tears were flowing heavily now as she said, "Please call me Carmen."

"Okay, Carmen, as you've been told, you suffered a miscarriage. You're still bleeding and it is important that we move immediately to perform what is referred to as a D&C. The procedure will take about thirty minutes and is necessary for us to be certain that all the matter related to your pregnancy is removed from your uterus. You'll be awake during the procedure, but you won't feel anything in the area below your waist. While there, I will examine you to make sure there are no other conditions that may need follow-up treatment once you return home."

"Has anyone called Jake?"

"Yes, Mr. Coleman has been notified and it's my understanding that he's en route from Houston. Do you understand everything I've explained to you?"

"Yes."

"Good, one of the nurses will be in to have you sign the authorization for treatment and we will begin preparing you for the procedure." Phillips reached down, took Carmen's hand in her own and smiled. "Everything will be okay, Carmen. Just relax and this will all be over soon."

As the doctor walked away and the nurse began the process of having Carmen sign the releases and authorizations, Carmen's mind drifted to something Diego had said. *How the hell do you explain to a child that he or she has a daddy that is a convicted murderer?* At almost the same instant she thought to herself, *How could I ever bring a child into the world I live in? I'm as guilty as Diego.* She sat up in bed and said, "Bring that doctor back in here. I want to ask her something."

It took only a couple of minutes for the doctor to be at Carmen's bedside. "Is something wrong?"

"Can you perform a tubal on me while I am here?"

"Why would you ask for such a thing? This isn't the time for a decision like that."

Carmen exploded. "I'm a defense attorney, licensed to practice in Texas, and you can believe me, bitch, I know fucking good and well what I'm asking for. Now I don't need you sitting in judgment over any decision I make, I just want to know, can you do it?"

Phillips looked sternly at Carmen. "No, Carmen, I can't do that here. We are not staffed for it and it is not procedurally necessary under emergency treatment protocols. That's a procedure that you'll need to discuss with your doctor once you've returned to Houston."

Leaning back on the gurney, Carmen looked at the ceiling, her eyes blurry with tears. "Let's just get this over with."

𝔐.𝕮.

Jake hurried to get his saddlebags packed while explaining to Clutch what had happened. Both men had agreed that Whiskey, along with the two most senior prospects, Cappie and Patch, would ride at his side and be at his disposal during the trip. The Dallas Chapter president had also been informed of the situation and was having a few brothers from his chapter meet them at the hospital. He had arranged for Jake, Whiskey, and the prospects to stay at the Dallas clubhouse while in the area, and the Dallas brothers would be there to help them find their way and get settled in.

By four o'clock Jake stood in the drive of his apartment talking to Clutch, saying, "I don't know what happened up there, Brother, but I gotta get up there quick as I can."

Clutch looked at Whiskey, then looked back at Jake and said, "You move carefully, Brother, and go do whatever it is you have to. We'll still be here when you get back." He put his arms around Jake and hugged him hard. "Ride safe." Looking at the prospects, he continued, "I don't give a fuck if he is in the head taking a shit, you fuckers better be available to wipe his ass if he needs you to."

Whiskey pulled to the center of the road, allowing the prospects to roll in behind Jake, and together they headed north on Highway 59.

Chapter Twelve

A TIME OF ANGUISH

Our trip to Dallas wasn't five minutes underway when the red and blue lights of a Fort Bend County Sheriff's cruiser pulled us to the side of the highway. We all pulled over and got off our bikes, and as the cop got out of his car, he pointed and yelled, "Get over against the road barrier!" As we all moved to accommodate his instructions, I heard that familiar voice saying, "All but you, biker trash. You get back to your motorcycle."

I couldn't fuckin' believe it, this dipshit, Barney the bozo cop, had pulled me over at the worst fuckin' possible moment, and I knew he was going to do his best to provoke me.

Keep cool and don't give this fucker reason to jail me – not tonight.

As he approached my bike, I said, "I ain't got time for your shit, Pearsall, so write us whatever tickets you need to, so we can get on our way."

"You haven't figured out who I am, have you, mother fucker?"

"I could care less who you are, you fuckin' cockbite, but I'll tell you this much, I'm getting goddamn tired of your bullshit and your fuckin' harassment. If you got some kind of hate complex with me or some kind of score you want to settle, it'll fuckin' have to wait."

He just grinned. "What's your hurry, Jake? I thought we might just spend a little time getting to know each other."

"FUCK YOU MAN! Get on with whatever you're gonna do or let us the fuck go."

Whiskey and the prospects moved off the wall, sensing the situation was getting ugly. Pearsall pointed his finger at them, and said, "Stay on the wall, we're almost done here."

He took a picture from his pocket and handed it to me. "Look it over, Jake, my telephone number is on the back. Call me when you get back from wherever you're going."

I looked at the picture, one I had never seen before, and saw my mother with me holding her right hand and an older boy holding her left.

I stared after him as he got back in his cruiser and drove off. Again I looked at the picture and couldn't help feeling all mixed up inside. Mom had been gone for a while now and here comes this fucker with a picture of her. Feeling angry, I shoved the picture into the pocket of my cut. *Okay, so now this fucker calls me Jake instead of calling me biker trash. He has a picture of my mother – one I have never seen. Who the fuck is this asshole, and what's he doing with a picture of my mother? I ain't got the time for this shit tonight.*

Whiskey, seeing I was disturbed, walked up. "You'll have to deal with that son of a bitch sooner or later, Brother, but if you'd rather, I'll happily deal with him for you."

I just looked at him, shook my head. "Let's roll."

The four-hour trip to Kaufman went by without further incident. When we arrived at the hospital, there were five of our Dallas brothers parked outside the emergency room. We all exchanged the customary hugs and I asked the sergeant at arms, a brother known as Braid, if they had been inside yet. "Yeah, we went in and I think we scared the shit out of everyone in the place, because before we knew it, there were three of their rent-a-cops watching us with their hands near their guns. Bro, they wouldn't tell us shit so we decided to wait out here for you."

"That's cool, Brother, and I really appreciate you coming."

Whiskey and Braid followed me in while the other brothers and prospects waited outside. As I approached the desk, I saw the security cop Braid had told me about walk up behind the woman at the registration desk. She looked at me and said, "I've already told you people, I can't release any information to you."

"I'm Jake Coleman."

The security cop stepped forward. "I need to see some identification," so I handed him my driver's license.

He looked at my license, looked at the registration clerk, and then handed me back my license. "Follow me."

We all fell in behind him, but he turned and looked at me. "Only you."

Whiskey and Braid turned and went back outside as I was taken to Carmen's bedside.

When I walked into the room, Carmen immediately began to cry. I sat on the edge of her bed, held her close, and whispered, "Everything will be okay."

She looked up at me. "I lost the baby, Jake."

"I know, I was told. You're young and there's still plenty of time for children."

"No, Jake, we can't. I can't."

Surprised by her statement, I instinctively pulled away. "Carmen, what are you saying? I thought you wanted children."

"If we have children, I'll always be making choices, Jake. Choices regarding their welfare, choices that could impact my place in your life. Jake, you know as well as I do, the life we live is not a place for children." Carmen reached up, put her arms around me. "I'm glad you're here."

Dr. Phillips walked into the room and introduced herself. "Can we have a word, Mr. Coleman?"

"Sure." I stood and told Carmen that I'd return soon.

Phillips walked out the door and I followed her to a small conference room just down the hall. We walked in and she closed the door behind me. "Please, have a seat."

I sat down and she asked me if I needed anything, coffee or water. "No, I'm fine."

"Mr. Coleman, it's none of my business what your relationship with Carmen is, but she identified you as her guarantor, so I want to make sure you understand what's happened here."

"Okay, let's hear it."

"Carmen suffered a miscarriage and was bleeding badly when she arrived. We performed a procedure to remove all matter connected with the pregnancy from her uterus, which is necessary to avoid infection. During our explanation of the procedure, Carmen became very insistent that I perform a procedure preventing further pregnancies, a procedure referred to as a tubal ligation. This surgery requires a hospital recovery greater than I am authorized to perform, given her condition. I advised Carmen that we could only treat the emergency at hand and I recommended that she discuss those options with her primary physician once she's returned to Houston."

"I'm not accustomed to seeing her in such a fragile condition."

"However early in the pregnancy she was, Carmen's just lost a child. She's experiencing emotions that you'll never be able to fully understand. I would encourage you to be as gentle with her feelings as you can be, and get her in front of her primary physician as soon as possible, once you're back in Houston."

"How long before I can take her back to Houston?"

"She'll be moved to a private room within the next hour and will be kept overnight for observation. If everything goes well through the night, you can take her home tomorrow afternoon. I assume it goes without saying, Mr. Coleman, that she will not be riding a motorcycle as her means of transportation back to Houston."

I looked at the doctor. "Do I look like a complete asshole?"

Phillips smiled. "Do you have any questions for me?"

"Not at the moment."

"Carmen needs her rest, so I suggest you go say goodbye and come back in the morning. Do you need a recommendation for a place to stay in the area?"

"No, my brothers have arranged a place for me to stay."

"I see. Well, here is my card. Please don't hesitate to call me if you need to."

Before the nursing staff came and moved Carmen to her room she told me that Diego had said he wanted Clutch to visit him on Wednesday. I asked why and she said, "To explain things with us. He also told me to work out whatever plea deal I can get him without incriminating anyone else in the club, and then he told me to bring divorce papers."

"Divorce papers? Just like that, he asked for divorce papers?"

"He doesn't love me, Jake, but he cares enough to want me safe. I think that's what he's wanted from the beginning."

Sensing that Carmen was getting her facts a little out of order, I said, "Okay, Carmen, we'll talk about this tomorrow. You get some rest." I kissed her and as I left the room, she appeared to have already fallen asleep.

Walking into the parking lot, Whiskey, Braid, and the others all expressed concern for Carmen and then Braid said, "The clubhouse is about twenty miles north of here, off I-45 and Texas. Traffic in that part of town is a real bitch right now, so if you're up to it, there's a club-friendly tavern not far from here where we can go get a couple of beers."

"I could sure the fuck use a drink after this night," I said.

We all mounted up and motored over to a place called The Whiskey Baron. I was relieved to see the place almost empty and the few that were there left quickly after we arrived. The brothers and I picked a table to the right of the entrance about halfway back so we could watch who came and went while we were there. I took the opportunity to call Clutch and moved to a small table a couple of feet away so we could speak privately. Clutch answered and immediately asked how Carmen was.

I gave him the rundown on her condition.

"Diego told Carmen that he wanted you to make the trip to see him and he wants you here early Wednesday morning."

"Did he say why he wanted me to come?"

"According to Carmen, he has a list of issues to speak with you about, including my relationship with Carmen."

"I see. Why not tomorrow instead of Wednesday?"

"Mondays, Wednesdays, and Fridays are the only days available for visitation. You can't get registered for visitation until tomorrow and that makes Wednesday the earliest you can visit. You'll have to call and find out what kind of information they'll need from you to register before coming, so I'd try to get that done tomorrow if I were you."

"Okay, no problem. When are you coming home?"

"I'm staying at the clubhouse tonight and Carmen is being released tomorrow, so I'm getting a room close to the hospital, and I'll stay there through Wednesday. That should give Carmen some time to rest before making the trip back to Houston, and you and I can talk after you meet with Diego."

"Are you planning to see Diego?"

"Depends on whether or not I can get registered. I'm not sure I have everything I'll need for that."

"Are there any surprises I need to be prepared for when I see him?"

"Remember, Brother, I've neither seen nor talked to him. In fact, I'm repeating what Carmen told me were his instructions. To put it best, she's doing good right now to remember what Diego told her, so if there's some kind of surprise waiting for you, I wouldn't know what it was."

"I take it that Diego doesn't know Carmen lost the baby?"

"There isn't a way for him to know that, unless the prison officials told him and that's doubtful."

"Okay, Brother, I'll get up there Tuesday night. So let me know where you and Carmen are staying and I'll get a room there as well."

After hanging up with Clutch, I sat with the Dallas crew for about an hour just drinking beer and shooting the shit. I reached inside the pocket of my cut for my smokes and something fell onto the floor. It was the picture Pearsall had given me back in Rosenberg. When I picked it up and looked closely at it, I experienced a very vague memory of the time when the picture was taken. Shit, I couldn't have been more than four or five years old at the time, but there was a memory. As I looked at the older boy in the picture, I couldn't help but wonder who he was and why Pearsall had the picture. *I guess I'll know soon enough cause this stupid fucker put his personal telephone number on the back of the picture and told me to call.* I wrote the number on a napkin, handed it to Whiskey and said, "This is the telephone number for that idiot cop. He wants me to call him when I get back, but I think I'll pay him a surprise visit instead. Get me that asshole's address."

Whiskey grinned wide. "It'll be my fuckin' pleasure, V.P."

The night air was cool and it had started misting by the time we left for Dallas. The traffic had died down, but, man, those twenty miles to the clubhouse were about all I could manage after the day I'd had. We got there about one in the morning, pulled the bikes behind the fence, and went inside. I was impressed with the place – it was complete with a couch, a pair of overstuffed chairs, a recliner and a sixty-inch, big screen TV. The place looked like the living room in anyone's home - that is until you saw the bar, complete with a stripper stage and two poles. There were two pool tables between the stripper stage and the living room, and a kitchen with a dining table that would seat about eight people. The chapel was off to the side of the building, behind see-through plate-glass windows and behind it, in the back, were two separate bedrooms and a bunkroom with a shower and bathroom just down the hall.

Braid unlocked the VIP bedroom and told me to get some rest. "Whiskey will be in the room next to you and the rest of us will bunk down the hall."

Yep, this place had it all, but all I really cared about was a shower and some sleep.

As I lay in bed watching a light flickering outside the window, my mind drifted back to the picture and it dawned on me who Pearsall was. *I don't how I missed it before. I guess I was so caught up in the events of the day that I just didn't see it. He's the boy in the picture, but that still leaves a lot of questions. Who is he, why is he in the picture holding my mother's hand, and why the fuck does he hate me so much? I will know soon enough, but for now, I just want to sleep.*

The night passed into day and I woke at the sound of a siren passing in the distance. I got out of bed thinking of Diego and wondering what my friend and brother would be doing about this time of the morning. It was important for me that I get over to Seagoville myself and see him. I would go on Wednesday maybe, and as early in the morning as I could.

My thoughts were interrupted by voices outside. There was the sound of a small boy and that of an adult male, which made me decide to walk outside and see for myself what was going on. At the gate to the entrance of the parking yard was a little boy with his father. The boy was giving his dad a lot of grief about wanting to see something.

I walked up to the man and asked him what it was the boy wanted to see.

"I'm sorry," he said in broken English. "My son saw the motorcycles and was begging me to let him come closer. I'm sorry, I don't want any trouble and we are leaving."

"It's okay, bring him in, he can look."

As the two came inside I asked, "What's his name?"

"His name is Antonio."

I knelt down so that I could make eye contact with the kid. "Hello Antonio, my name is Jake." I put my hand out to the boy and he took hold and gave it a hard shake. Then he asked, "Can I go for a ride?"

I looked at the boy's father. "Can he ride with me around the block?"

The man looked at his son, then smiled and nodded his approval.

I didn't have a helmet that would fit the boy, so I just picked him up and set him on the back seat, giving him instructions on how to sit and how to hold on. I mounted up, fired the engine, pulled out of the parking yard, and around the block we went. I took him three times with him begging for a fourth and then a fifth and finally, I pulled back into the yard, which by now was full of my crew and all my Dallas brothers.

We got off the bike and I asked the little boy how old he was.

"I'm nine years old!"

"Wow, you are almost a man, aren't you?"

He said with great enthusiasm, "I AM a man."

I went to my saddlebag and took out a Los Patron bandana, fashioned it so the El Patron logo would be clearly visible, and wrapped it tightly around his little bald head. From out of my bag I took a Los Patron patch and handed it to him. "Antonio, today and from now on, you're my little brother." The little boy was so happy he jumped up and hugged my neck so hard that my necklace with the Patron pendant came out from underneath my tee shirt.

When he saw the pendent he reached to touch it but his father said, "No Antonio."

The boy instinctively pulled his hand back.

I looked up at his father and then back down at the boy. Smiling, I took off the necklace and put it around the child's neck. Then I asked him, "Do you remember my name?"

"Your name is Jake and I'm your little brother."

"That's right, little brother!"

After some discussion with the man, we discovered the boy had been diagnosed with an inoperable brain tumor and that at best, he would live only another six or eight months. The boy's father had already sold all he had trying to provide for his son's treatment and was now penniless and homeless. Both father and son were living at Our Lady of Guadalupe, a Catholic Mission a few blocks away and the future for both looked daunting. I pulled two hundred dollars from my pocket and gave it to the boy's father, and my brothers who had witnessed the moment all scrambled to gather cash that they could give as well. All together, we handed the man a total of six hundred dollars. We all knew the money would have zero impact on the future but would ease some of the miseries of the present.

After some discussions with the Dallas brothers, Braid assured me the Dallas crew would put together a benefit and get as many of the locals and supporters out to help this little boy and his father as possible. I told Braid that I wanted to know when and where the benefit would be held because I wanted to be involved. As I watched, the little boy waved goodbye, and he and his father walked down the sidewalk. Watching them leave, a large lump grew in my throat as I thought of all they were faced with. I swallowed hard, turned, and went inside.

𝔐.ℭ.

Bill Tomlinson entered his office to find a court order on his desk granting a Motion for Continuance in the case of The United States – vs - Diego Santiago. The reason noted on the continuance was, Council's Inability to Appear, Due to a Medical Emergency.

"I'll be god-damned!" Tomlinson shouted out loud. His voice was so loud that his administrative assistant came running into the room wanting to know if something had happened.

He shouted, "Get me Agent Ross on the phone, NOW!"

The assistant hurried out of the room and within five minutes, Tomlinson's phone rang through. It was Special Agent Bernard Ross of the Federal Bureau of Investigation.

"Good morning, Bill."

"Well, good morning to you, Bernie. How the hell are you this fine Monday morning?"

"How can I help you, Bill?"

"Well, Bernie, you can start by explaining to me how the fuck that bitch managed to secure a continuance and have it on my desk before

I got to work this morning. Do you realize that she has completely tied my hands and I can't even charge the son of a bitch until she is able to appear? I was expecting to level RICO charges against him this very fucking morning! God-dammit, Bernie!"

"Bill, the woman had a miscarriage shortly after she finished interviewing Santiago. She collapsed in the prison hallway and had to be transported to Presbyterian over in Kaufman. Her petition was heard and granted via dispatch at seven-thirty this morning. Shit man, she couldn't even get it done in person because she was still in the hospital."

"Are you kidding me, Bernie? You tell me, how in Christ's name did she pull that shit off?"

"Look, Bill, all I know is, I received a courier at eight-thirty this morning from the court clerk of the US District Court, ordering the prisoner to be held in transit until his attorney is available to represent him. He is officially detained and can't be moved out of the detention area until she resumes his representation. You know what I would do if I was you, Bill?"

"Why don't you tell me what you would do, Bernie."

"Bill, I would show some professional compassion and send flowers, or better yet, go see her in person."

Before slamming the phone in Agent Ross's ear, Tomlinson very quietly said, "I'll tell you what, Bernie, why don't you go fuck yourself."

𝕸.𝕮.

It was close to ten in the morning when we rolled into the parking lot at Presbyterian hospital. The twenty-mile trip from the clubhouse to Kaufman had only taken thirty minutes. *I'll never bitch about Houston traffic again. Traffic in Dallas is as bad, if not worse, than anything I've dealt with at home.*

Whiskey and I walked into the hospital and once again we were met by hospital security. The security cop was not the same guy as before, but like the other, he wanted to see identification. I handed him my driver's license and motioned for Whiskey to do the same when the security cop said, "I don't need his I.D., only yours."

I looked at Whiskey. "Well, Brother, it looks like they trust you more than me. You are going back without having to show your I.D."

The security cop immediately said, "He's not going back with you."

I looked at the guy. "He goes with me. Now, you can choose to look at his I.D. or not and I don't give a shit, but believe me when I say it, he's going with me. Now, do you want to record his I.D. or not?"

The security cop looked at Whiskey and took the I.D.

When Whiskey and I entered Carmen's room, I was surprised to see her with her cell phone in hand and her laptop on the tray table. I walked up to her and kissed her. "It looks like you've been busy."

"I had to file a motion for continuance before that jerk prosecutor filed charges against Diego. If I'd waited beyond this morning, Diego would have been facing a grand jury with a court-appointed attorney representing him. I bought him a little time and some time for me to approach the prosecutor with a plea."

"Sounds complicated. How did you manage to get all that done? Don't you have to file those motions in person?"

"You're supposed to but there are ways to get around some of that, if there are extenuating circumstances. The fact that I'm in the hospital and not physically able to represent Diego in person is certainly an extenuating circumstance."

"Okay, well, how'd you get the motion filed so early in the morning when you weren't able to leave the hospital?"

"I called the court clerk this morning and explained my situation to her. She was very understanding, having recently experienced a miscarriage herself. I had the hospital staff fax my petition directly to her, and she walked it into the judge and he signed the order."

"I see, so what now?"

"I'm working on the plea deal. Once I'm finished, I have to get it in front of Diego for his signature and then I go see the prosecutor. I'm hoping to get it all wrapped up by Wednesday afternoon."

"What kind of deal are you trying to work out?" I asked.

"I'm trying to negotiate a life sentence."

Whiskey looked at me, then at Carmen. "Life? Is that the best you can do for him?"

Carmen responded before I had the chance to react. "Diego is sacrificing his freedom for both of you, and for the rest of the club as well. He isn't willing to incriminate anyone, and has told me that under no conditions will he negotiate the implication of his brothers. Since he has no intention of giving the prosecutor anything, outside of his own confession, the only hope I have for him is to make sure the United Sates government does not prosecute for the death penalty, which by the way, is exactly what the prosecutor intends to do."

Whiskey spoke quickly. "Carmen, I'm sorry. I didn't intend to react that way, but I wasn't prepared to hear that we were going to agree to a life sentence without trying to get something better."

"Whiskey, I am trying to keep Diego alive, and right now I'm not even sure I can accomplish that. Jake, have you rented a room yet?"

"Not yet, but I will as soon as I leave here."

"Okay, I've arranged for you to see Diego today at two o'clock. You'll need to carry your I.D. and wear a short-sleeve shirt. Make sure you do something with your cut because you won't be allowed to wear it while you're inside the detention facility."

"You've been busy."

Carmen's eyes became wet with tears as she looked up at me. "I have to keep my mind busy, Jake, otherwise I will spend the entire day crying."

I leaned over and kissed her gently. "I made a new friend this morning."

"Really? Tell me about this new friend."

I told her everything about Antonio, and how hard it was for me to watch him walk away, knowing he would never experience all that life had to offer. I found myself sort of rambling about the whole thing, when I noticed Carmen was smiling.

I turned to ask Whiskey to get me a cup of coffee and realized that he had left the room. I looked back at Carmen. "I would have loved that baby, Carmen, I really would have."

Carmen placed her phone on the bed and put her arms around my neck, hugging me tightly. "I know that, Jake, and I have no doubt the baby would have loved you as well."

We sat there just kind of holding each other for a moment when I looked at my watch. "Okay, if I am going to see Diego at two, I gotta get going." I kissed Carmen goodbye and headed straight for the parking lot.

Whiskey was sitting on his bike smoking a cigarette, but stood as I walked toward him. "Brother, the two of you look natural together and for what it is worth, I think this thing between you and Carmen is a good thing. Also, Brother, I'm sorry if I came off hard about the life sentence thing."

"Whiskey, I appreciate what you said about Carmen and me. It means a lot, Brother. You also need to know that you don't owe an apology for what you said. Diego is our brother and believe me, I'm no happier with what she said than you are. It's unfortunate, but I don't think there's a damn thing we can do to change it. Hopefully, Diego will help me understand what he wants us to do when I see him this afternoon."

It was one-thirty when Whiskey and I arrived at the security check-in at Seagoville. I gave my cut to Whiskey and as Carmen instructed, I wore a plain, white tee shirt into the security building, handing the guard my driver's license. I was taken to a room off the main entrance, searched, and removed of all my belongings, including my sun glasses, wallet, rings and my bracelet. I was given instructions on the prison rules for visitation, badged and then escorted to the visitation area, which contained a single table. No sooner had I sat on the bench than Diego was brought in. He was shackled feet to waist, and led by handcuffs. The guard helped him get seated then locked the chain of his handcuffs to the ring at the center of the table, further restricting his movement. Before moving into the soundproof observation room, the guard once again reviewed the rules of visitation, and warned that any violation of those rules would result in the immediate termination of the visit. He then moved into the observation room and sat down.

I spoke first. "Brother."

"Brother, it's damn good to see you and we got a lot to talk about."

"Tell me what you want me to do, Diego."

"Be yourself, Jake, and learn all you can from Clutch and the others. You will someday be president of the Houston chapter and you gotta have your shit together if you're going to grow the business and the Los Patron influence in Houston. First thing, make damn sure you get out and meet every single business contact we have. You've got to let them know the Los Patrons will continue to press our business interests no different than if I were still there. Get with Bullet and have him go with you. He knows everyone and will introduce you the right way. Did Carmen get it arranged for Clutch to come here?"

"Yeah, he's coming Wednesday."

"Okay, good. Now before we talk about anything else, Carmen told me that she was pregnant, and she also told me that she was in love with you. Do you feel the same?"

"Brother, I do, but I somehow feel out of place with those feelings."

"I have known from the very beginning that the two of you were good for each other, and there's no reason for you to feel out of place with anything. So, I have to ask you if you will take care of Carmen and raise her child. Will you do that for me, Jake?"

"Diego, Carmen lost the baby."

Diego looked at me as though he had suddenly been knocked out of his chair. "What the fuck happened, Jake?"

"Brother, she collapsed in the hallway as she was leaving her visit with you. She was treated here only long enough for the ambulance to transfer her to Kaufman, where she is now."

"Is she okay?"

"She was back at work before I got there this morning. She was able to secure you a continuance, which buys a little time for her to plan the plea deal she intends to present to the prosecutor. So, I guess I would say that she is doing okay."

"It's best, Jake. Neither of you have any business trying to raise a kid right now. Look, man, I told Carmen that I needed commissary money. I can't even buy a pack of smokes in this fuckin' place because I have no commissary credit."

"No problem, Brother, I'll handle that for you on my way out. What else can I do?"

"I told Carmen to bring me divorce papers and as soon as that is done, you need to marry her."

"Right now, that's a problem. The entire chapter thinks I'm some kind of shit-hole because of our relationship. They think I'm fuckin' you over, taking her for my own."

"That's not going to be an issue after I see Clutch. You just make sure the woman is well cared for, Brother, she's my gift to you."

The guard buzzed into the room and said, "Five minutes."

"Diego, is there anything we or I can do outside to help? There's got to be something one of us can do."

"Jake, I wouldn't have a clue what it might be. I fucked this thing up myself and now I have to deal with the consequences. If only I hadn't made that telephone call and if only I hadn't collected the ears." He looked straight at me. "If, if, if. Fact is, Jake, I did made that call and I did collect the ears and the feds know it."

The guard buzzed again and walked into the room, unlocked the chain from the center ring and helped Diego to his feet. As Diego was escorted from the room, he looked back at me and said, "Take care of Carmen, Brother, and take care of yourself. I love you, Brother."

"I love you, my brother," I said as he was escorted away.

I put two hundred dollars into Diego's commissary account and left the detention center feeling a deep sense of anguish. Since I'd begun prospecting for the club, Viejo, Crow and Britt, not to mention a couple dozen Warriors and Rebel Souls, were all dead. Now Diego, my closest friend and brother, was staring at a conviction, with at best, a life sentence and at worst, the possibility of death. Carmen had just lost her baby and was thinking she may never want children again, and now, there was Antonio. That little boy had so few years to experience life and he had only a few tomorrows left.

I gotta get the fuck out of here and I need to ride. That should help me clear my mind.

Chapter Thirteen
THE DEAL

The security officer handed me a clipboard with a document for me to sign, as one by one he checked off each of the things that had been taken from me when I entered the facility. The process was numbingly slow when all the fuck I wanted was to get the hell out of that place and get on my scoot. I was in such a hurry to get out of there that after signing for my things, I turned to walk away without retrieving my license.

The guard stood. "Mister, you'll need your license."

He was holding it between his index and middle finger and I reached out, took it, and almost ran out the door.

Whiskey was waiting at his bike. He handed me my cut, and asked, "How is he?"

I looked at him, feeling pissed that he'd even asked the question. "Well, how the fuck do you think he is? He's wearing a chain around his waist, cuffed to it with his hands and feet. He's fuckin' alone and there ain't a god-damn thing I can do to help him. Let's go, man, I just fuckin' want to ride."

We got on our scoots and motored out of the place, being careful not to break the prison's posted speed limits. As soon as we hit State Highway 175, I buried the throttle and we were soon moving south hitting speeds of ninety and a hundred miles per hour. It didn't take long for that shit to attract attention and I soon saw the blue lights of a Texas DPS traffic unit quickly gaining on us. I thought for a moment that I might try giving this prick the slip but I knew that evading an officer would land Whiskey and me in the county jail, and I could ill afford that kind of trouble right now. After pulling over, the trooper approached us slowly and at one point stopped as he was receiving instructions via his radio. He put his hand on his gun, called me by name, and motioned for me to approach him, which I did with a great deal of caution. We went to the backside of his squad car, where he ordered me into a spread-eagle position and searched me.

He quickly found my gun, took it, and placed it out of reach. "Do you have a license for that weapon?"

"It's in my wallet."

He went through my wallet, found the license. "You are required by law to inform me that you are armed."

"I followed your instructions as you gave them and I made no attempt to resist."

He cuffed me, instructed me to sit roadside, and then repeated the process with Whiskey. While he was searching Whiskey, a Dallas County Deputy Sheriff pulled up and assisted with the process, cuffing Whiskey and placing him in the back seat of the county vehicle.

The deputy approached me, and before he could speak, I asked, "Are you arresting us?"

He responded, "You were clocked at ninety-five miles per hour, and that's twenty-five miles per hour above the posted speed limit. Would you care to explain why you were moving at such a high rate of speed?"

"Look, I was trying to get some air and relieve a little stress. It hasn't been one of my better days."

The trooper rejoined us and asked, "May we have your permission to search your motorcycle?"

I laughed. "Is that what this is about? You want to search my bike? Yeah, fuck yeah, go ahead and search both our bikes. There ain't shit there, but my dirty shorts from last night, but go ahead, give a look."

That fuckin' cop went back to his squad car, put on a pair of medical gloves, and got busy going through my shit. He emptied the saddle-bags, leaving my dirty clothes out on the roadway, then did the same to Whiskey's bike. He opened the gas tank on both bikes and looked inside with a flashlight before walking off and leaving everything lying on the ground. Coming back to me, he reached down and helped me to my feet while the deputy released Whiskey.

Uncuffing me and giving me my gun back, the trooper said, "You were visiting your friend a while ago in Seagoville."

"Yeah, so what?"

The trooper was very matter of fact with his response. "Deputy Martinez here would be more than happy to introduce both of you to the county's correctional center in Dallas, and we could do just that with the guns and all your reckless driving here today. This is, however, your lucky day because we've been instructed to let you go, with this warning. If you break another traffic law or if you get into any other kind of trouble, like threatening the receptionist or the security at the hospital where your friend's wife is being treated, you'll be arrested and incarcerated for as long as the county can hold you, and then you'll be prosecuted to the full extent of whatever law you may have broken. Hopefully, you both get the message."

Both cops started walking away, but before the trooper got into his car, he turned and looking at our bikes said, "You need to get that shit up off the road before we arrest you two for littering Texas highways."

As we watched them drive off, Whiskey and I just looked at each other. Smiling, he shook his head and said, "Damn it all, Jake, I feel pretty fuckin' important considering all the attention we're getting today."

That broke the ice for me and I laughed. "C'mon, Brother, let's get our shit together and move on to the hospital. I'm hoping I'll be able to take Carmen back to the hotel when we get back."

It took only a couple of minutes to get our stuff packed up and we were back on our bikes. We motored to the next exit, where they sat

- those two brave cops who'd just rousted us. We slowed to the posted speed as we made our exit, and we both used our middle finger to signal our turn. I laughed watching those two fuckers nearly break their necks as they watched us turn around and head back toward I-45.

When we got to the hospital, Carmen's room was empty and she was nowhere to be found. I asked the nurse who had been attending to her where she was. She said that Carmen had been discharged two hours earlier and had left in a taxi.

Whiskey asked, "You got your phone, Brother?"

"It's in my saddlebag."

We both took off to the parking lot in one big damn hurry and just about the time we got to the bikes Carmen drove up beside us in her car.

"Carmen, where the fuck did you go? You just about gave me a god-damn heart attack."

"I went to Seagoville."

"To see Diego?"

"No, Jake, I didn't go to see Diego. I went to get my car."

"Your car?" I asked, puzzled.

"Yes, Jake, my car. Remember, I had it when I arrived at the deten-tion center, but I was taken away in an ambulance. It's been in their parking lot this entire time. Now, I didn't think either one of you would be willing to ride bitch on the back of the other's motorcycle to go get my car, so I decided to go get it myself. Would the two of you like to show me the way to the hotel? I am feeling a bit tired and I'd like to rest before we have dinner."

I looked at Whiskey, feeling stupid and said, "Is anything going to make sense today, Brother?"

We fired up the bikes and pulled out of the parking lot with Carmen close behind. The hotel was only a couple of blocks away and we were there within five minutes. Whiskey and I carried Carmen's things into the room and she was soon lounging on the bed with a glass of wine in her hand.

She looked at me and asked, "How is he?"

I glanced up at Whiskey who had the appearance of someone who had just been punched in the stomach, and he said, "You know, Carmen, I asked that same question when Jake came out of the security office at that place, and the next thing I knew he was cuffed and sitting on the side of the road and I was locked up inside a Dallas County cruiser."

Carmen looked at me in disbelief. "I have enough on my plate trying to keep Diego from dying in that place and I sure don't need the two of you locked up for…whatever it was you were doing."

"We were speeding," I said.

"Speeding? That's it? Speeding?"

I explained the whole thing to her and she said, "You both need to get back to Houston. It's apparent the local police are keeping a close eye on your activities here."

"Yeah, I think you're right about that. Clutch will be here tomorrow night and he's seeing Diego Wednesday morning. I was planning to head back Wednesday after Clutch and I have a chance to talk about his visit with Diego."

"Did you tell Diego that I lost the baby?"

"Yeah, I did. He was taken aback with the news at first, but quickly rebounded, saying it was best because neither of us had any business with kids. He told me to make sure you get divorce papers to him quickly, and then he told me to marry you."

"Well, that's Diego, always in control and always giving orders. Are you going to do what he told you?"

"What? Marry you?"

Whiskey spoke up. "I'm headed to the liquor store to get some beer, either of you need anything?"

"I need a pack of cigarettes, Brother."

"You got it," he said and left quickly.

Carmen was looking hard at me, as though she was hoping for good news and all the while expecting bad. "Yes, are you going to marry me?"

"Well, I don't know Carmen. Is that a proposal?" I said with a big grin on my face.

Carmen put down her wine glass, slid off the bed, and kneeled before me on the floor, saying, "Since childhood I've never loved anyone as much as I love you, Jake. If you will have me, I'll never disrespect you, I'll never challenge your direction with your brothers, and I promise, I will love you for the balance of my life."

I reached down and helped her to her feet. "Woman, never again feel that you have to kneel before me. You aren't my property and you never will be. Now, I have never been proposed to and the fact is, I thought that was my job, but since we are talking about it, you have to know that you have confused my whole world, to the point that the only time things seem in balance for me is when I'm with you. Will I marry you? Oh fuck, yeah, I'll marry you and I don't give a shit what anyone thinks or says. You'll make a fine mother and I absolutely want to father children with you."

For a moment, we stood holding each other. Then she said, "I am really tired."

I helped her get back on the bed and I as I kissed her, I could see tears welling up in her eyes. I knew she needed to be alone and I suspected we would experience more days like this one for a while yet. I left her to her privacy, feeling a new sense of responsibility and knowing that I had to make sure she was never without a husband again. Diego had made a lot of mistakes with this woman – mistakes I had no intention of repeating.

Tuesday came and went, with Carmen making a trip to the see the prosecutor, a trip to see Diego, and a final trip to meet the prosecutor and the US District Court Judge who was to bench the case.

In the meeting with the prosecutor and the judge, Carmen was told the ziplock bag containing the human ears had been returned from forensics without Diego's DNA and without identifiable fingerprints that could be tied back to him.

With that knowledge in hand, Carmen said, "Without my client's DNA or fingerprints on that bag, there is no evidence tying him to the killing of those twenty-eight men."

Prosecutor Tomlinson spoke quickly. "As you well know, counselor, it isn't necessary to prove direct involvement in the crime for a RICO charge. We only have to prove that your client was instrumental in its planning. As president of that chapter, your client had direct control of the clubhouse, its personnel, and its contents. It is very clear to the government, and we will prove based on those facts, that your client indeed was involved and ordered the killings himself."

Carmen stunned the prosecutor when she looked to the judge and said, "Your Honor, the prosecutor has charged my client, as you yourself heard, with the killings of the twenty-eight men based on his direct control over the clubhouse, its people, and its contents. The prosecutor has, however, made one very critical error with his discovery. Diego Santiago is the President of the Houston Chapter of the Los Patrons MC, not the West Houston Chapter. The clubhouse in question is the sole property of the West Houston Chapter of the Los Patrons MC and under the direct control of that chapter's president. My client, along with his Houston brothers, are all guests in that clubhouse and have control over nothing. I respectfully request the court dismiss the charges against my client for the murders of those twenty-eight men. Further, there is no physical evidence that puts my client in San Antonio at the time Jarret McDaniel was killed, and there is no witness, gun, or DNA tying him to that killing."

Tomlinson stood up from his chair and was about to speak when the judge instructed him to remain seated and quiet. He then looked back at Carmen and said, "Go ahead, counselor, finish your statement."

"Your Honor, the Los Patrons have a strict code of silence when speaking to the authorities and since my client was first arrested, the Warriors Motorcycle Club merged with the Los Patrons. That means Prosecutor Tomlinson and all of his investigators will not be able to find a single Warrior to testify against my client, because, Your Honor, there are no longer any Warriors to speak with – only Los Patrons. You can try my client, at a great expense to the taxpayers, and have this whole affair before the public, but you will not get a conviction."

The judge looked to Tomlinson for his rebuttal, and standing, Tomlinson said, "We have the telephone call, which is tantamount to a confession."

Carmen responded with, "You have a telephone call between two very old enemies where my client used poor judgment in the use of his words, but you do not have a confession and my client steadfastly denies any involvement in the killing. We can, if necessary, produce witnesses that will testify that Sand Man *green-lighted*, or put out a hit on Diego, offering as much as $10,000 for his death. There is no confession in that, but we can and will produce witnesses who will testify to that fact and with that testimony, all credibility connected with your case against my client will be completely destroyed.

"Your Honor, when my client was arrested, he was found in the possession of cocaine and was subsequently charged with Possession with Intent to Distribute. My client is willing to plead no contest to that charge, provided, of course, there is a reduced sentence in exchange for the plea."

"Prosecutor Tomlinson," the judge said, "It appears to me, the accused had no more control over the surroundings or the comings and goings of anyone in that clubhouse than you did over the investigation of the facts. Do you have an explanation that could possibly explain how your office overlooked such an important piece of information regarding the accused's responsibility in this case?"

"No, Your Honor, I don't."

"Given the facts as they have been presented here and the absence of a rebuttal of the facts on your part, I am dismissing the conspiracy to commit murder and the murder charge itself. In addition, Prosecutor Tomlinson, you are hereby instructed to work out an agreement with Counselor Santiago on a charge of trafficking, and to have that arrangement before me within the hour for my signature. Further, you have wasted an inordinate amount of taxpayer resources in the sloppy investigation of this case and I warn you sir, not to waste any more of my time. I expect that arrangement within the hour, understood?"

Tomlinson's reply was simply, "Yes, sir."

Carmen walked out of that meeting with an agreement for Diego to serve a five-year prison sentence on a charge of trafficking. The deal included the possibility of parole after two years of time served without a reportable incident. The plea deal included one more major concession. During his incarceration, upon release from federal custody, and for a period of fifteen years after time served and time credited for parole, Diego Santiago would not associate with persons of the Los Patrons Motorcycle Club or be found in the possession of articles or paraphernalia connected to it. Failure to abide by this portion of the agreement meant immediate incarceration and transfer back to federal custody to serve out the balance of unserved time as stated in the agreement. All that was needed now was Diego's signature on the plea deal and he would be credited for time served and then transferred to the Federal Maximum Security facility in Beaumont to serve the balance of his sentence.

It was late and although Carmen had won a major victory for Diego, she was saddened at having to break the news to him. The Los Patrons represented the only family he had known for most of his life, and that life, the very way of life he had become so accustomed to living, would be no more. She decided to wait until the next day to take the agreement to him and instead called Jake to meet her for dinner somewhere quiet.

Whiskey and I, followed by Prospects Patch and Cappie, met Carmen at the Village Steakhouse in Kaufman just before seven o'clock, as she had asked. When the five of us walked in, the hostess took one look at Whiskey, me, and the prospects and nervously asked if there would be five for dinner. I answered that there would be two for dinner as Whiskey and the prospects made their way to the bar where we had agreed they would eat while waiting for Clutch to arrive.

The restaurant was an upscale place and we were the object of many staring eyes as we followed our hostess to the table. I was dressed in my cut, jeans, and boots while Carmen was in a fashionable black dress with just a hint of red that would occasionally show from beneath her hem as she moved. The wait staff were all dressed in black slacks, black shoes, white shirts, and black bow ties. It wasn't long before a young man came to wait on our table. He was very polite and took care to address all questions concerning our drinks and the meal to me. It was easy to see he knew enough about who I was to be careful not to offend me. He was very attentive with Carmen, making sure her meal order and mine was taken and correctly understood. We sat for only a few minutes until our waiter brought Carmen's Chardonnay and my Jack and water.

After ordering, I asked Carmen how the proceedings had gone and she said, "Diego will serve five years at the federal prison in Beaumont for trafficking. All other charges have been dropped."

"Carmen, that's terrific, how did you pull that off?"

She explained the terms of the deal to me, including the non-affiliation clause and I asked, "What happens if he doesn't take the plea deal?"

"Twenty years with the possibility of parole after ten, but Jake, the government will make sure he does all the time which means he will be nearly sixty when he's released."

"What about the divorce?"

"I am taking the divorce decree with the plea deal. That's also part of the deal. Once he signs the plea deal and it is filed, our professional relationship will terminate. Since we'll be divorcing, he can't have any further contact with me."

We sat in silence for a few moments. "I see why you wanted to eat alone."

"That's only partially true, Jake. I could've saved myself the trouble of repeating this if Whiskey and Clutch had been here. The truth is, I needed and wanted to have dinner with my soon-to-be husband and

I also needed to feel that you understood I did the very best I could for him."

"Carmen, he's not going to face death and he owes that fact to you. His life will be different and though it may not be the life he's been living, he'll have the opportunity to start over. Somehow, I believe he'll find a new direction in life, in fact, I'm sure of it. As far as I'm concerned, you saved his life and I am grateful for the things you've done. I picked her hand up and gently squeezed it. "Regarding Clutch, he'll need to see Diego tomorrow before you do, right?"

"Yes, and I can't tell either of them anything about the plea until after I see Diego and get the appropriate signatures. This deal could still go bad if Diego hears about it the wrong way. For tonight, Jake, you're the only one to know."

"Speaking of Clutch," she said, "he just walked in the front door and is talking to Whiskey." I waved him over, but he shook his head, pointed at the bar, and went and sat with Whiskey.

Carmen said, "He's showing us some privacy, I see."

We sat for the next hour enjoying our meal and each other's company for we both knew tomorrow would bring its own stressful, sad moments. It was close to eight-thirty when we left our table and met Clutch and Whiskey at the bar. Clutch stood and put his arms around me with a bear hug like he hadn't seen me in months. He reached over and gave Carmen the customary kiss of a brother's ole' lady and then said, "Carmen, I am sorry to hear about the baby."

Carmen took a step back and looked at me with a face so suddenly pale, I thought she might pass out.

I reached to steady her and asked, "What's wrong, Carmen?"

"I hadn't thought of the baby all day long, until just now and all of a sudden, that sadness just overwhelmed me."

"Oh, Carmen," Clutch said, "I didn't mean to stir up a bunch of sad feelings for you, I'm really sorry."

"It's okay, Clutch, I'm okay. It isn't your fault and you don't need to apologize. I'm going to the room, Jake. Take your time, I know you have a lot to talk about."

She kissed me very softly and whispered, "I'm tired." She hugged Whiskey and Clutch and said, "I am glad you're here, Clutch. You may be surprised at how he looks tomorrow, but I know he'll be glad to see you. You need to check in with security at nine in the morning, and your V.P. can fill you in on how to dress and what to say and not say. It's important you not be late. These people have no tolerance for such and they really don't like any of us."

"I'll be on time, Carmen."

Carmen said goodnight and I walked her to her car. As she was driving off, Whiskey walked up to me and handed me a piece of paper, saying, "This might not be the best time for me to give you this, but here is that fucker's address."

Not connecting the dots, I asked, "Who the fuck are you talking about?"

"I'm sorry V.P., shit, I should have just said here's Pearsall's address."

I looked at the paper and then looked at Whiskey. "You gotta fuckin' be kidding me. This asshole lives right down the street from me?"

"That's right, V.P. He's in walking distance and has probably walked over to your place a number of times."

Clutch spoke up. "What do you need his address for?"

I showed him the picture Pearsall had given me, and told him the whole story of what happened as we were leaving for Dallas.

"I can't have that son of a bitch continually showing up and fuckin' with me. It's plain to see he doesn't like me and I want to know why, and I want to know what his connection with my mother and me is. So I'll be paying him a surprise visit once I'm back in Houston."

"You know the rule," Clutch said. "Make damn sure you don't dirty your colors."

"Yeah, I know the rule, Brother. I don't intend to hurt him, but I do intend to find out why the fuck he's up my ass every time I stop short.

But just as a precaution, I'll leave my cut at home. I saw Diego yesterday," I said.

"How was he?" Clutch asked.

I looked at Whiskey. "Here we go with that same fuckin' question."

Whiskey just raised his eyebrows and looked down at his boots, and Clutch, being clueless asked, "Okay, you two fuckers, either of you want to clue me into this private conversation?"

"It's a long story, Brother." I said.

Clutch looked at Whiskey. "Give us some space."

Whiskey said, "Sure thing," and quickly moved over near the prospects, who were out of hearing distance.

"Jake, I can see this thing with you and Carmen is going to be permanent, but you gotta know, man, you ain't got one brother that either understands or approves. I hope the fuck I have a better understanding soon of what's happening here, Brother."

"Clutch, I've made my peace with Diego and after you speak with him, I think all your questions will be answered. For now, I want to have a few beers and if possible, a few laughs. Believe me, Brother, tonight's the night to relax because tomorrow is not going to be enjoyable for you."

We all got on our bikes and motored back over to the Whiskey Baron, but the place was not nearly as empty as it had been when Whiskey and I were there with the Dallas crew. We left the prospects with the bikes, walked in and were immediately approached by a couple of women wanting our attention. Whiskey got between the two of them, putting his arms around each and walked them over to the bar. He positioned himself so that he could see Clutch and me while he attended to their curiosity. After a few minutes, he rejoined us and the two women sat on bar stools just watching and waiting.

I looked at Whiskey. "They look like they're waiting."

"They are," he said.

Clutch grinned. "Okay, Whiskey, what are they waiting for?"

Whiskey smiled wide. "Well, Clutch, the girls are looking for a party, and the way I see it, Jake here is the only one of us that has an ole' lady, right?"

Clutch looked at me. "That appears to be the case."

We shot the shit for a few minutes longer before I said, 'I'm tired, Carmen's alone, and I'm going to the hotel."

I told Whiskey to make sure that Clutch was up and out of bed in plenty of time to make his appointment at the detention center. He assured me Clutch would be there, on time and coherent. We all hugged goodbye and I left my brothers to their party. Before I left, I told Prospect Patch to stay with them through the night. Prospect Cappie rode out with me.

Carmen was rolling a joint when I walked into the room. "You're back early, how come?"

"Whiskey and Clutch were getting fired up and had a couple of women lined up for the evening. It's been a long day, I'm tired, and I wanted some time with you."

"Well, that's good for me," she said as she lit the joint, taking a long draw before passing it to me.

I hit the joint deep and immediately felt that sensation you only get from good weed. I put the joint out, laid it aside, and watched as she slid her hand inside her panties. "You can't fuck me, Jake, I'm too stitched up."

"I don't need to fuck you, woman, but you can bet that I will make damn sure you get what you need tonight."

It turned out to be a hot, sexual night for both of us. We laughed, we played, and we got totally fucked up smoking that fatty she had rolled earlier. I think we both needed something and we both got what we needed because at seven o'clock the next morning, she woke me telling me she was hungry and wanted to go somewhere for breakfast. By seven forty-five, we were showered and sitting in the local restaurant drinking coffee and waiting on our meals.

Carmen smiled at me. "I'll see Diego at ten this morning and by one-thirty, the prosecutor and I will sign the plea deal before the judge in Dallas. It'll be recorded by two o'clock and Diego's future will be set. All that'll be left will be to file the divorce papers back in Harris County and I'll do that tomorrow."

"You're going home tonight?"

"Yes, Jake. Since we're not filing an appeal, my obligation as his attorney ends as soon as I deliver the documents to the court. After that, I'll be part of the club he can no longer have contact with."

After we finished eating, I looked at my watch. "It's nearly eight-fifteen and I'm headed back to the hotel just to make sure Clutch is up and at it. I also have to make sure he understands the rules of visitation."

We got up to pay the ticket and she kissed me. "Call me if there's a problem."

"There won't be a problem. I'll see you back in Houston tonight."

Carmen got in her car and left for the courthouse as I left for the hotel. I got back there just as Whiskey, Clutch, and the prospects were packing their bikes for the trip home. I said, "I'm going to ride over to the detention center with you, and I thought we'd all leave for Houston together."

Clutch said, "Sounds like a plan, Brother. So, what are the dos and don'ts of this visit?"

I filled him in on the rules and told him to leave his jewelry and cut behind and then I said, "Okay, I guess that's it. Let's haul ass."

We mounted up and in thirty minutes we were in Seagoville, pulling into the parking lot of the detention center. Clutch looked at the place, then back at us, and shook his head as he walked up the steps to the security office.

𝔐.𝕮.

Clutch was checked in exactly as I had described it and within a few short minutes he was seated in the visiting area where a single table sat with a ring at the center. Diego was brought in and helped to sit at the table, and his handcuffs were once again locked to the ring at the center of the table. The guard explained the rules and then stepped behind the soundproof barrier.

Clutch was about to speak when Diego said, "How long have we known each other, Brother?"

"Ten years, Diego."

"Well, we don't have ten years to talk, so you need to listen up. You're the president now. The chapter and all that goes with it is yours – the business, the new clubhouse, the reputation, and the responsibilities. It's all yours, everything except for Carmen. She belongs to Jake. I know there have been many questions about their relationship, and I appreciate the fact that all of you have been looking out for me, but in this situation, there's nothing to look out for. When you go home, make sure all of my brothers know that I gave her to Jake, and he agreed to take care of her. I told him to marry her, and he agreed to do that for me as well. Do you have any question about any part of that, Brother?"

"Diego, if you tell me it's so, then it's so and it helps me to know that you're good with it."

Diego smiled. "I'm good with it."

He handed Clutch an envelope. "The fuckin' guards made me re-write this letter three fuckin' times before I was finally given permission to give it to you. Read it when you leave here, Brother. One last thing, Clutch. Jake is a natural leader and he will be for you what I was for Viejo, only better and smarter. I told him that it's his responsibility to go meet our business contacts and to press the relationships, as I have done. It's important that you continue with that arrangement and that you not get too close to the street. You don't want to be found giving the fuckin' orders when those asshats from the ATF and FBI come looking for a RICO."

"I got it, Brother. I'll follow exactly as you have taught me."

"Things will change, Clutch. As soon as you walk out of here, one thing for sure will have changed, it will be you making the rules, not me. You'll need to adjust your thinking and try to make sure you take advantage of the talent each of your brothers have. Be especially smart about who you trust. Believe me, you don't want another Britt in your crew."

The two men sat for the next twenty-five minutes and talked about the past, remembering the good times and not so good times. It seemed that time sort of stood still for a while, and then as Jake had warned, the first buzzer sounded that twenty-five minutes had passed. In what seemed like only a few moments, the guard came in and took Diego back to his cell. Clutch walked down the hall feeling sad about seeing his friend chained up as he was, but also feeling a sense of relief about Jake. After retrieving his driver's license from the guard, he walked out of the building and straight to Jake. He placed his arms around him. "I was wrong to feel the way I did about you and Carmen. Brother, I can assure you of one thing, this chapter will have no further questions about the two of you."

"Thank you, Brother. Carmen is on her way here to get Diego's signature on the plea deal and she'll be a few more hours getting it all filed with the court."

Clutch asked, "Plea Deal?"

I explained the arrangement to both Clutch and Whiskey and when I was finished, Whiskey commented, "Brother, I was way wrong with what I said to Carmen yesterday, she really saved his ass."

"Whiskey, Carmen's good at what she does and she found a way to make it happen for Diego, but you weren't wrong to say what you did. He's our brother and she understood your feelings."

"I don't know what you said Whiskey, but I feel one hell of a lot better about his situation knowing he can be out in two years. Jake, I'm real pleased with how you and Carmen have handled all of this."

"Clutch, it was all Carmen's work. I was just as frustrated as Whiskey here, but she stayed after it, even with the miscarriage and got him the deal. She's a good woman."

"Yes she is Jake." Clutch said. "Does she know your leaving with us?"

"Yeah, she knows, and I'm ready when you are."

𝔐.𝔠.

It was ten o'clock when Carmen checked her brief case in with security. Diego was already waiting in a private visiting area where Carmen would deliver the terms of his plea deal. He wasn't in chains, but additional guards had been placed in the observation area because Diego was without restraint.

Carmen was wearing a dark business suit with high heels and her hair was tied back into a bun on her head. As she was escorted into the visitor's area, she reached for Diego and they hugged while the guards watched intently.

Carmen spoke first. "How was your visit with Jake and Clutch?"

"Did you bring the divorce papers, Carmen?"

"Yes, I brought them."

"Give me a pen and let me sign them."

Carmen asked the guard for a pen and he stood at Diego's back while he signed in the required sections. Once the pen had been confiscated, the guard moved behind the soundproof barrier and Diego spoke, saying, "My brothers are both well instructed as to your care, and you'll never have to deal with any bullshit because of your relationship with Jake again."

"Thank you, Diego!"

"So, when do I die?"

"You don't. The conspiracy to commit murder and the murder charges have been dropped."

Diego grinned wide and leaning back in his chair with his arms crossed, and asked, "How the fuck did you manage that?"

"The prosecutor based his entire RICO case around you having control over the clubhouse, its contents and the movement of people in it. The fact that you aren't the West Houston Chapter President was overlooked by the prosecutor. Diego, the ears had no DNA, neither did the bag and there were no fingerprints either that could be tied back to you. The prosecutor's case fell completely apart and the judge dismissed the charges."

Diego chuckled. "That fuckin' Jake was right!"

"About what?"

"That night with Britt. Jake told me to dip all the ears in a bowl of peroxide and with a pair of gloves to put them in a clean ziplock before putting them back in the freezer. He's one smart mother fucker. Okay, so what now?"

Carmen laid out the documents that would set the next twenty years of his life into motion and said all that was required was his signature. As she explained the charge and his plea deal, his expression changed from that of someone who had had just found his freedom to that of someone full of determination.

Diego looked at Carmen with a smile. "Two years is not long and I can do that standing on my head. You've handled yourself well, Carmen, and I'm grateful."

He motioned to the guard his need for a pen then quickly signed the documents. After the guard stepped behind the barrier, Diego asked, "Is there anything else we need to talk about?"

"No, Diego, there isn't."

"Okay then, I have one thing left to say. There ain't no government capable of keeping me from my family. You tell my brothers I will see them all as soon as this is done."

He motioned to the guard and winked as he was escorted back to his cell.

Chapter Fourteen
BROTHERS RECONCILED

Except for stopping twice to fuel and once to eat, the ride back to Houston went without a single delay. It was almost four-thirty when I split off from Clutch and Whiskey to head back to my place in Rosenberg. Patch went with Clutch and Whiskey while Cappie stayed with me all the way into town. We stopped in Richmond to fill up with gas, and all the while I was busy thinking about Pearsall. I decided I wouldn't put off another night figuring out who this guy was and what his issues with me were. I picked up a six-pack of beer, sent Cappie on his way, and decided I would pay the prick a visit. Now that I knew where he lived, I made a quick detour by his place to see if his duty vehicle was parked out front and sure enough, it was. I rode on home and called Carmen to make sure she had finished her business in Dallas and was on her way back. She sounded good and was expecting to be home sometime around eight that night. I told her I was going to clean the place up and take care of some business before coming over. I changed into a pair of clean jeans, put on my favorite tee shirt, and put that six-pack of beer into a small ice chest. After taking one final look at that picture, I put it in my back pocket, and walked out my front door.

Pearsall's place was around the corner about a block and a half from my front door, which was a five-minute walk. As I started up his drive-way, he came walking around the side of his house, startled when he saw me, saying, "You got balls coming to my home!!"

"Really? It's not like you've never been to my home, asshole." I held up the ice chest. "I figured we could drink a beer together and you could explain this," and I held up the picture he'd given me.

He looked around as if I might have masked desperados hidden behind the trees and under the bushes.

That made me laugh. "If I wanted to hurt you, Pearsall, I wouldn't have come in broad daylight so that everyone on this street could witness it. Now you gave me this picture four fuckin' days ago and told me to call, so here I am and I got beer. How much more of a peace offering do you fuckin' want, man?"

He motioned to me to come in as he walked up his porch and opened the door.

I walked in ahead of him, but stopped quickly as I saw on the corner hutch a picture of my mother with a man I didn't recognize, along with Pearsall and me standing in front of the San Jacinto Monument. We were pretty young, but it was easy to see it was us.

He walked over, picked up the picture, and handed it to me. "We have a lot to talk about. That's Mom with my father, along with you and me the year you and Mom left."

I sat on the couch holding both pictures and he sat in an easy chair a little to the left of where I sat. I was staring at the pictures just trying get my head around all of it when he said, "Correct me if I am wrong, but I believe the Los Patrons have a saying that goes like this: 'We're brothers from different mothers.' Right?"

"That's right."

"Well, Jake, we're brothers from different fathers."

I looked hard at him. "You had better be able to prove what you just said, otherwise this visit is not going to end well."

He got up, walked over to the corner hutch, and came back with a photo album. Handing it to me, he said, "Mom gave this to me the year you were sent to Afghanistan. She put it together for you and asked me to give it to you when I felt the time was right. All the proof you'll need is right there on the first page."

I opened the photo album. There was a letter written to me from my mother.

My Darling Son,

In this photo album are pictures of you, your brother and our family when we were all together. There are also copies of the marriage licenses from my marriage to your father and to Nate's father. I included both of your birth certificates and a few other little things I thought you might enjoy. I can only assume that you have just met Nate, and I can't explain why I never told you about your brother. Though the reasons are meaningless at this point, I did have my reasons for keeping the two of you apart. I hope and pray you can both find a way to make up for lost time.

I love you son,
Mom

A letter from the grave! I was so moved by what I read, it was impossible to hold back the tears. I looked up from the book, wiped my eyes with the back of my hand, and looked over at Pearsall. "Nate, huh?"

"That's my name."

"Well, Nate, can you get me one of those beers from the cooler?"

"Sure, Jake."

He handed me the beer and opened one for himself. I lit a cigarette. "You got an ashtray?"

"I don't smoke."

I laid the album aside, walked out the front door, and leaned against the post supporting the porch's awning. He followed me and stood there for a couple of minutes with neither of us speaking.

After a long period of silence, I took a long swallow of beer. "I don't remember you, and Mom never spoke of you or your dad."

"You were only four years old when you and Mom left. I am not surprised that you have no memory of any of that. You're the lucky one. I wish I could forget those years. They sure the fuck weren't happy ones for me."

"What happened?" I asked.

"Mom divorced Dad when I was five years old, and married your dad. You were born seven months later. Three months after you were born, your dad took off. Mom being Mom and my dad, being who he is, took both of you in. That picture of us standing in front of the San Jacinto Monument was taken two weeks before your dad showed back up. I came home from school one afternoon and my dad was lying on the couch, passed out drunk. On the floor next to his bottle was a Dear John letter from Mom and both of you were gone. I took the letter and hid it away and Dad never asked about it. I guess he figured he'd destroyed it in his drunken stupor. Anyway, I put it on the back cover of the album. I thought you had the right to know the whole truth."

"I'm a little confused about how you and Mom managed a relationship through the years."

"We didn't. Mom discovered a clipping in some old newspaper of my graduation from the county's police academy. She made contact with me after you shipped out. She was already sick and told me she knew she didn't have long. She and I saw each other often over the next fifteen months and although I can't say that we re-established that mother-son relationship, we did at least reconnect. Toward the end, about the time you came home, was when she gave me the photo album."

"Were you at the funeral?"

"I was there, Jake. I watched you closely but decided it wasn't the right time for a reunion."

"I get that. You were right. It wouldn't have been a good time to surprise me with all of this."

I went back inside for another beer before lighting another cigarette. "Now would be a good time for you to explain why you hate me so. Is it because Mom took me and left you behind? Do we need to just beat the shit out of each other or what? Tell me, what the fuck do you want from me?"

Nate looked at me. "Dad was single for three years before remarrying, but he did remarry and they're still married. Both of them enjoying life and enjoying their grandchildren."

"I see, so you have children, which means that I'm not only a brother, but I'm an uncle as well."

"No, Jake, I have no children and you are not an uncle. My sister has a four-year-old son and a two-year-old daughter. Dad had another child with this wife, my sister Samantha."

"I see."

"Sam owns a small bar down on Canal, just off the ship channel, a place called Parrot's Cove. Are you familiar with the place?"

"No, I'm not. Should I be?"

He looked down at the porch and kicked at a tree branch that had somehow found its way next to the steps. "Three years ago, my brother-in-law disappeared on his way to make a deposit for the bar. He was never seen again and neither was his car. About a month after his disappearance, Diego Santiago, along with his lawyer wife and a couple of his club brothers, showed up at the Cove and presented documents signed by Sam's missing husband, deeding over twenty-five percent ownership in the business to the Los Patrons Motorcycle Club. Your club, or more specifically your chapter's president, has been draining my sister's business of its profit to the point she will soon be unable to make payroll, much less keep the place supplied with liquor. She's at the point of losing everything unless something changes soon. Although it was never proved, I know the Los Patrons killed her husband, and I'm not going to stand by and watch her lose everything she has because of that fuckin' bunch of thugs! You wanted to know where the hate comes from, now you know!"

We went back inside and sat back down. I said, "First, I had nothing to do with your brother-in-law's disappearance. Second, I'm not a thug and neither are any of my brothers and YOU need to get beyond that horseshit or there won't be anything else for us to talk about." I picked up the photo album. "Can I take this home with me?"

"She made it for you and it's yours."

"Thank you."

I stood to leave and Nate said, "What are you going to do about Sam?"

"I have no idea, Nate. I can tell you this much – if the Los Patrons own twenty-five percent of that club, there will be no walking away without something in exchange. Maybe you should ask yourself this question: What are you willing to do to help your sister?"

He looked hard at me. "I'd kill for my family."

"Okay, then. You have more in common with me than you think. I'll look into the Parrot's Cove and find out what I can. I assume all the fuckin' harassment stops here, right?"

"I don't hate you, Jake, but I hate what you represent, and I want this bullshit with the Parrot fixed."

"Nate, nothing happens in this world for free. Remember what I said, if something can be done, it won't happen without a tradeoff of some kind."

Nate put his hand out to me and said, "I'm glad you came, Jake."

I took his hand in mine, "This is all new, man, and completely unexpected. If anyone out there had told me I had family, I would've said they were full of shit. I'm glad to know the truth and I'm glad I came, too. If I can help Sam, I will."

I walked away from that house with my head swimming and my stomach feeling sick. *All these years thinking I was alone, and now to find out I really do have family. Such fuckin' bullshit to keep something so important from your own kid.*

I had to talk to Carmen and find out what she knew. Had she actually met Sam? Could we fix this thing? What would Clutch say?

I looked at my watch and it was almost nine. *Carmen should be home by now.* All I had to do was put on my boots and my cut, get on my scoot and go.

Chapter Fifteen
IT'S JUST BUSINESS

I strapped the photo album to my sissy bar and left for Carmen's house in Sugar Land. She hadn't been home long when I pulled into her drive, and hearing my bike, she hurried out to see me. I thought to myself how she looked more relaxed and happier than I had seen her in months.

She came straight to me as I was getting off my bike, kissed me, and then whispered, "I have a BIG surprise for you later," as she reached down and rubbed my crotch, grinning from ear to ear.

"Really! Well, I have some news to share with you and believe me, you'll be very surprised by what I have to tell you."

As I started getting my stuff out of my saddlebags, she looked at the photo album and asked, "What's that?"

"Part of the surprise."

I grabbed the album and together we walked inside.

"Want a drink?" she asked.

"Yeah, a drink would be great!"

It took only a couple of minutes for her to pour me a Jack and water while pouring a Chardonnay for herself. I took my bag, which had nothing in it but four days of dirty clothes, to the bedroom. The stuff somehow had gotten wet and stunk like shit, so I took it all straight to the laundry room and dumped it into the washer before coming back to the living room. When I got there, Carmen was sitting on the couch with a pipe already loaded, and she handed it to me with a lighter. I took hold of that pipe, pressed the carburetor, lit the weed, and took in the hardest draw I could. My head immediately got light and I leaned back on the couch as Carmen began giving me the best damn blowjob I had received in probably _forever_. For the next hour we had some of the best sex we had ever experienced, even with her stitched as she was. She laughed, I laughed, we listened to seventies rock, we smoked another bowl and got so stoned, I think we ate the cupboard empty of all the snacks she had. It got late and before I knew it, I was smelling bacon frying and the sun was up.

I walked into the kitchen, going straight up to her. "Last night was a great surprise for me. I needed to laugh and I needed to get laid. How is it that you always seem to know exactly when to 'get sexy' with me?"

"Oh, Jake," she said with a broad smile on her face. "You haven't begun to experience the kind of sexy surprises I have in store for you."

I smiled and hugged her tight as she whispered, "I love you."

After pouring a cup of coffee, I sat down, noticing the photo album sitting on the kitchen table.

She sat next to me and pointed at the album saying, "Yesterday was full of surprises for you, I see."

"Yes, it was."

"Have I got this right? The cop that has harassed you so much over the past few months is your brother?"

"Yes, he is, Carmen. We spent a couple of hours together at his house last night, and that's when he gave me the album."

"You went to his house, alone?"

"I know, I know. It wasn't smart on my part, but somehow I knew it wouldn't turn out bad."

"It's not my place to tell you what to do, Jake, but as your lawyer, I should be able to give advice, and my advice is never meet a police officer or anyone else by yourself. That is a good way to end up in jail, or worse, dead! Please promise me you won't be so careless in the future."

"Carmen, he's my brother and we have a lot of catching up to do. I'm safe with him, I'm sure of it."

"Jake, it wasn't so long ago, he pulled you out of your bed in your underwear, and then later threatened you in front of me at the courthouse. You wanted to put the man in his grave, and now suddenly you're telling me you trust him."

Wanting to re-focus the conversation I said, "Carmen, tell me about the Parrot's Cove."

"It's a bar, Jake, one of several the Los Patrons own an interest in. What's that place got to do with this conversation?'"

"Nate's sister owns the place."

"Jake, are you telling me that you have a brother and a sister?"

"No, I don't have a sister, but Nate does and she owns the Parrot's Cove. What do you know about the bar and how did we gain an ownership interest in the place?"

"Jake, this woman's husband and Diego grew up together and believe me, he was no saint. Now, he looked the part, a real handsome guy, and he came across as a really nice guy, but underneath that nice-guy appearance was a different person. Believe me when I say the guy was capable of dishing out a great deal of his own style of bullshit. The Parrot's Cove was not much more than a rundown, old icehouse where men from the ship channel would come after work. The place was a regular old shit-hole for regular old shit-heads. Tommy, this woman's husband, called Diego and told him that he wanted to give the place a facelift with a remodel, but couldn't qualify for a loan. He knew enough about Diego's lifestyle to know he could put together the money, so he asked Diego for a loan of $50,000. Diego took the request to the chapter and it was a unanimous vote to give the guy the money, conditional upon two things: One, Tommy had to agree to use club friendly contractors and two, he had to put up 25% of the business which would be held against repayment of the loan with interest. Diego really liked the guy and made him a straight-up loan with standard interest rates, which as you well know, is not the way the Los Patrons typically do business. Diego set up a meeting at the clubhouse and he and I met with Tommy and got all the required signatures for the loan. Diego handed Tommy an envelope with the money and a list of contractors Tommy was to use, they shook hands, and the deal was done. Things went well at first. Our contractors did the work, each of course paying the expected tribute to the Los Patrons with the entire project being completed in just three months. The place looked great and Tommy planned a grand opening designed to give the place a real kick-start. He hired a band for opening night, the kind you hire when you want to draw a crowd, and the crowd was large indeed. Diego and several brothers went to get a look at the new club they had helped build and were met by off-duty police officers that Tommy had hired to provide security. You can imagine Diego's surprise when he went inside and was immediately stopped and questioned by one of these off-duty cops.

"Tommy had hired three of these guys to provide security without talking to Diego and Diego was pissed. He pulled Tommy to the side and told him if security was needed it would be provided by the Los Patrons and not by cops for hire. After a brief but heated exchange with Tommy, Diego and the brothers were escorted out by the cops. They got on their motorcycles and left. Diego was embarrassed and very angry. He felt he had done something good for an old school buddy, only to be shit on for his efforts. The next day, Diego and Clutch rode to the bar and sat down with Tommy. It got ugly quick and before you know it, Tommy pulled a gun and pointing it at Diego, ordered him out of the building. Things couldn't have gotten any worse when Tommy stood at the door as Diego and Clutch were leaving, taunting them with his gun. Diego had the place watched for several days until he was certain he knew Tommy's routine. Then the next Saturday night, as Tommy was leaving to make a night drop, he got into his car and found himself with Diego's nine-millimeter stuck in his ear. I can't tell you much more than that, except his car wound up in one of the club's chop shops and Tommy, Diego told me, became dog food."

"Okay, with Tommy gone, do you have any idea what is owed to clear the place?"

Leaning forward and looking puzzled, Carmen asked, "What are you thinking of doing, Jake?"

"I have no idea, Carmen, but if there is a chance I can square it with the club and give complete ownership back to Nate's sister, I want to try."

"You'll have to talk with Clutch and Bullet, Jake. I'm not in the loop on the club's finances."

I smiled at her. "The bacon smells good. Are you going to get up every morning from now on and cook me breakfast?"

"How am I supposed to do that, Jake? You insist on keeping your apartment."

"I've changed my mind about keeping the place, Carmen. Now that you and I have been fully explained, there's no reason why we can't get on with our lives. When will the divorce be final?"

"I'll file the divorce decree this afternoon at the courthouse and there is a mandatory sixty-day waiting period before the divorce is granted. We have to wait an additional thirty days after that before we can apply for a marriage license."

"Okay, no problem with that. I'll call the prospects and have them meet me at the apartment. I don't have much and it won't take long to pack. They can load my shit and have it all here by this evening. That gives us ninety days to figure out where to go for the honeymoon."

Carmen smiled. "Are you really going to take me on a honeymoon?"

"Isn't that what newlyweds do – go on a honeymoon? I bet we could rent a cabin up at Lake Livingston for the weekend or something like that, don't you think?'

She jumped up. "Jake Coleman, I'm not spending a weekend at some shabby-assed old cabin at the lake for my honeymoon."

I just smiled. "I wouldn't really take you somewhere like that, woman. Wherever you want to go, I want to go."

I hugged her up close and kissed her. "For now, I gotta go pack that apartment."

I put on my boots and my cut and headed out the door.

I called Cappie and told him to get a hold of Patch and meet me at my apartment. It wasn't long before we had everything packed and in the back of Cappie's truck. As I was getting ready to get on my bike and head back to Carmen's, my phone rang.

It was Clutch.

"Brother, I know you're in the process of moving, but I've called church tonight at eight o'clock. I have some things I need to share with the chapter, things that Diego wanted everyone to know, so get what you need to do finished and try to meet me there at seven-thirty. I want to make sure you and I are on the same page with all of this, okay?"

"Sure thing, Brother, I'll see you at seven thirty."

It took Cappie and Patch about thirty minutes to haul my shit over to Carmen's house in Sugar Land. We just put everything in the garage and closed the door on it. Carmen wasn't home and we had a little time, so the three of us sat down and drank a couple of beers. Afterward, we mounted up and rode to the clubhouse, getting there at almost exactly seven-thirty. Clutch was inside and I stationed the prospects outside to make sure no one came in unexpectedly.

Clutch met me halfway across the room, and hugged me hard. "Hello, Brother."

I smiled big. "Hello, Brother."

Clutch handed me a cold Bud and a shot of Jack. "It was tradition with Viejo to shoot Cuervo and chase it with Modelo, but I like Jack Daniels and Budweiser and I thought tonight, we would start our own tradition."

He lifted his glass in salute. "Here's to the future."

We downed the Jack, chased it with a long swallow of beer, and sat down on a couple of bar stools. Clutch said, "Jake, I had a few things I wanted to say to our brothers tonight about my visit with Diego. Since almost all of our conversation concerned you, I decided it was best to discuss those things with you ahead of time."

"Okay."

"Diego told me he believed you would be for me what he was for Viejo, only better. Better, he said, because you were even-tempered and a natural leader. He told me to prepare you to take my place in the Houston chapter, because at some point you will be the chapter president. I intend to pass his advice on to our brothers in the chapter and outline for them what our relationship will look like. He also made it very clear that he supported your relationship with Carmen and that he had actually asked you to marry her. Tonight, I will clear up all questions regarding your relationship with Carmen and I promise you this, no one will ever judge either of you again."

"Thank you, Brother, I appreciate that."

Clutch poured another shooter of Jack, and tipped his glass in salute. "Here's to the both of you."

He went to the fridge and brought back two more beers. "Jake, you have been a brother now for a little over a year and a half and in that short time you have risen quickly. Most brothers at this stage are just now figuring out what it means to be a good brother, but you have done more in your time here than some brothers ever do. Those things earned you Diego's trust. He trusted you, Brother, and so do I. Having said that, I am going to ask you to step up and take on even greater responsibility. I want to put control of our business relationships in your hands. The Los Patrons will grow in influence and profit with you in control of the business."

"Clutch, Diego told me the same exact thing. He told me to support you in everything and to press our position with the business contacts as he had done, and Brother, that is exactly what you can expect from me."

"Good! I'll announce that change in responsibility tonight at church. So how was your first night home, Jake?"

"I paid a visit to that cop yesterday afternoon."

"Alone?"

"I went alone, Brother, and I know that is a big no-no."

"Mother fucker, Jake! Here I am talking to you about trust and you go and do the one thing that could cause your brothers to distrust you by meeting with a fuckin' cop. It's fuckin' hard to trust a brother that has secret meetings with cops, Bro, it just doesn't look right. Even if your motives are good, you put yourself at high risk when you go to a meet alone and when you meet a cop, you also raise a lot of suspicion among your brothers."

"It was a spur of the moment decision and I didn't consider what anyone else might think, I just went."

"Okay, Jake, so you're telling me now. What happened?"

"The man's my brother."

"No fuckin' way!"

I nodded my head. "He's my brother, alright. The short of it is, we have the same mother but different fathers. I have no real memory of him and he lost track of me, that is, until I shipped out for Afghanistan. My mother found him and made contact."

"Well, what the fuck is his problem with you, Jake? I would think finding a long-lost brother might be a reason for celebration, not a reason for hate, even if the two of you don't necessarily live the same kind of lifestyle."

"He has a sister who was born after his father remarried, and he is very protective of her."

"Okay, Jake, so what happened? Did one of our brothers fuck her or maybe rough her up or something?"

"Clutch, his sister owns the Parrot's Cove."

Clutch got quiet and leaned forward. In a very low tone, he said, "That's a real problem, Jake. That club's been a source of issues for the Los Patrons ever since we got involved with that cock-sucker Tommy."

"I know, Carmen filled me in on what she knew."

"Did she tell you that Diego killed that mother fucker?"

"She told me that Diego said he became dog food and I took that to mean that he met with the same fate as Britt."

"That is exactly right, Jake, and I'm the one who took care of that nasty little job, just like you did with Britt."

He grinned and lifted his beer. "Here's to dog food. Okay, so what is it that your long-lost brother wants from us."

"He wants us out of his sister's business, and that's it."

"That's it, huh? He just wants us to pack up and leave? Shit man, we own twenty-five percent of that place, and it's all legal. That fuckin' Tommy came begging for money, we helped him, and he had his chance to make good on that loan before trying to have us tossed like some bag of garbage. Bro, we ain't gonna just pack our shit and run because some fuckin' Barney the Bozo cop says we can't have a business relationship with his little sister."

I leaned back in my chair, lit a cigarette and just kinda grinned at him as he took another long swallow of beer.

He slammed his beer can on the bar. "What the fuck are you grinning at?"

I poured a third shooter, leaned forward, and handed it to him. "I don't think I have ever seen you mad, Clutch. Did you know your face gets as red as your hair when you're mad?"

He swallowed that shooter, grinned back at me, and asked, "What do you want to do, Jake?"

"I told him that nothing was free here and that we would not walk away from the business without some kind of trade off. He knows we have a legal interest in the place, but he also told me the business wasn't doing well. According to him, the place will soon close unless something happens quickly."

"He told you right, Jake, we're not taking much from that place anymore. Shit, man, that bitch doesn't know squat about running a bar, and she sure as shit has no business running a place like that down on Canal Street. Okay, suppose we can work something out, how does that impact you and what's the benefit for the Los Patrons?"

"Brother, I've lived my entire life thinking I had no family and until I became part of the Los Patrons, I had no one. I found family here and I'll never betray any part of that family, but, Brother, I want to help him and her if I can."

"You know, Jake, we could just kill them both, burn the place to the ground and, as the only remaining owners of that place, collect the insurance and just move on. If we did that, we would settle all the issues once and for all."

"We could do that, Clutch, or we could buy her out and run the place ourselves. If we did that, we'd have a revenue stream that is one hundred percent legit. You know, Brother, it would be damn hard to distinguish between cash deposited from the Parrot's Cove and cash deposited from other business interests we don't want the cops knowing about."

"Jake! Are you suggesting we could use the place to launder money?"

I poured a fourth shooter and slid one to him. "Damn straight we can!"

"What about your brother?"

"I'll help his sister, which will bind our relationship, and the Los Patrons will gain another friend in law enforcement."

"I like it, Jake. Do you think he'll go for it?"

"As long as we take care of his sister in the deal, I think he'll be good with it."

"Like I said, Jake, I like it. You and Bullet work out the details, and get Carmen to look it all over. If we can do this thing the way you're describing it, I'll get behind it. You do know this thing will take a one hundred percent vote of the brothers before we can move on it."

"Yeah, as it should be."

"Okay, I want to see it all on paper before we present it at church, so no mention of any of this tonight."

Chapter Sixteen
FAMILY

he gavel fell at church at exactly eight o'clock, just as Clutch had wanted. The night was to be an extraordinary night for gathering since this would be our first meeting with the newly converted brothers from the now defunct Warriors Motorcycle Club. Bullet called roll while Whiskey noted that everyone present acknowledged their presence, save one. When it came to Buck, there was no answer, even though he was clearly standing amongst the brothers.

One more attempt was made for him to acknowledge his presence, when he walked straight up to Bullet, laid down his cut and said, "I'm not going to be a member of this fuckin' club." He turned, looked straight at me, gave me the middle finger, and walked out the door.

Whiskey started toward the door after him when Clutch said, "Let him go. In fact, if there are others here who can't find themselves capable of being a Patron, now is the time to leave and no one here will challenge your right to do so." Two more men threw down their cuts and followed Buck out the door.

After the door closed behind them, Clutch got up from his chair. "We've all risked much to ensure our club has the ability to move freely where we exist. We've no room for men who lack either the commitment or courage to stand with us, so fuck those assholes!"

The meeting went as planned with Clutch advising the brothers on my duties as vice-president. There was some discussion regarding my plans and exactly how I intended to move forward with the business contacts. I responded quickly to those concerned that my first priority was to get with Bullet and be personally introduced to each contact. I went on to say that my second priority was to send a very clear signal to each of those contacts that the Los Patrons MC would accept no less than the business arrangement already in place. Everyone seemed satisfied with my statement and Clutch moved on with his next topic for discussion. Earlier in the afternoon, Clutch had the left saddlebag removed from Diego's bike and placed in the chapel. He asked Bullet to put it on the table so that everyone present could see it.

Clutch detailed his conversation with Diego regarding the relationship between me and Carmen, saying, "I told him that every brother here would honor his request and Brothers, I expect each of us to put every hard feeling and suspicion about Jake and Carmen behind us from this night forward." He pointed at the saddlebag. "Bullet, open the lid on that bag and see if you can see a tear that's been repaired with red leather."

Bullet said, "Yeah, I see it."

By now the entire chapter, including me, was wondering what the fuck all of this staged drama was about. Clutch told Bullet to open the tear and remove what was inside. Bullet did as he was instructed and removed a sealed envelope roughly six inches long and about three inches thick.

Clutch said, "Open it."

Bullet took out his knife, opened one end of the envelope. "It's full of cash."

The entire room stood as Clutch motioned for everyone to sit down. "Count it, Bullet."

As instructed, Bullet counted out five thousand in cash and handed it to Clutch.

"The last thing Diego did before I left him was to hand me a letter that he wanted read to the chapter."

Clutch opened the letter and read, "Clutch, in my left saddlebag, you will find a tear that has been loosely repaired with red leather. Open the tear and you will find an envelope inside with five thousand dollars in it. I want that money used for a party celebrating my brother's wedding. Make sure that he and Carmen know that I paid for the party and that I wish them both a happy life together."

"Anyone who wants to read the letter can see that it is handwritten and signed by Diego."

Clutch handed the cash back to Bullet. "Keep this separate from the chapter treasury and let's plan our brother and his bride-to-be one hell of a party, *Patron Style.*"

Clutch stood, put his arms around me, and whispered, "Congratulations, Brother."

Each brother in the room followed Clutch's lead and all hugged and congratulated me. The meeting adjourned quickly after that, with some of the brothers sitting at the bar and others shooting pool. Clutch, Bullet, and I went back inside the chapel where Clutch and I laid out the plan for buying the Parrot's Cove. It was decided that Bullet would provide the Cove's profit and loss statements for the last six months so we could get an idea of how much we could afford to pay.

Starting the next day, Bullet, Whiskey, and I would begin the tour of the sixteen different bars and the three body shops in which the club owned interests. Figuring for some difficult discussions with some of the owners, we expected the visits to wrap up in a couple of days. We would meet with Sam at the Parrot's Cove first, and I had only one agenda, which was to soften the tension between the Los Patrons and her so we could have a reasonable conversation later in the month.

It was now well into the night and the brothers were all getting restless for some bar hopping and an evening run. Clutch left for home and so did I. Whiskey and Bullet left with the others, headed for the Bayside Gentlemen's Club, a fifty-six mile ride to the causeway between the mainland and Galveston. The place was built about five hundred feet off the highway on the mainland side of the bay and it being an all-nude environment made it a favorite hangout for the brothers. I got home to find Carmen wrapped up in a blanket on the couch, fast asleep. There were a couple of boxes full of old photos on the floor in front of the couch and it was easy to see she had been on a walk down memory lane just minutes before I had gotten home. I took a shower, then woke her long enough for her to find her way to bed. We must have been very tired as sleep overtook us both in only a few minutes.

I woke the next morning to find a note on my pillow saying she had left for an early massage appointment, so I got dressed, hopped on my scoot, and headed up Highway 6 to my favorite kolache shop. After a quick breakfast, I motored over to the clubhouse where I saw the entire front of the building had been spray painted with the words, "Fuck the Los Patrons." *This has to be the work of Gene Buchtel, (Buck).* I decided right then, he would get a visit from us soon and delivering a lesson in painting would not be the purpose of our visit.

As I was opening the doors, Bullet rolled up. He got off his bike, took one look at the wall and said, "Buck."

"Has to be that son of a bitch. He's the only one I know of with an axe to grind."

We went on inside and had just put the coffee on when Whiskey rode up. He walked in and said, "Looks like our ole buddy, Buck, is looking for an ass whipping. What do you say, V.P.?"

I poured a cup of coffee, and took a sip. "Under normal circumstances, I would tell you to go make it happen. Given this little incident involves a member who is 'out in bad' Clutch has to approve it. I'm pretty sure I know what he will say, but you need to call him, just to be sure."

Whiskey called Clutch and, as expected, Clutch gave the go ahead. He was very clear that an ass whipping was approved, but that he didn't want Buck permanently injured. After getting off the phone with

Clutch, Whiskey called Cappie and Patch, getting them set on their job for the day, which was painting the building.

He looked at me. "The prospects are going to paint that shit over, so while they're at it, do you want me to have them go ahead and add red trim like the old place?"

"Damn straight. That fuckin' Buck did us a big favor by forcing us to give this place a facelift."

Looking at Bullet I asked, "Do we have enough unassigned cash to repaint this place inside and out?"

"Sure. We gained about ten thousand dollars with the patch-over. As long as Clutch is good with it, we can spend whatever is needed."

I picked up the phone and dialed. Clutch answered, "What the fuck? Can't a brother take a shit without the damn phone ringing every five fuckin' minutes?"

"Wake up on the wrong side of the bed this morning, Brother?" I asked.

"What is it, Jake?"

"Are you good with spending a couple of grand to repaint the place?"

"Jake, I already said yes to that shit, do I gotta come down there and peel off enough cash for you fuckers to get it done, or maybe you want me to come paint the fuckin' place, too?"

With that he hung up the phone in my ear. I looked at Whiskey and Bullet, saying, "Be warned, he's definitely not in a good mood today. Bullet, make sure the prospects get receipts for everything they buy. I sure as shit don't want Clutch up my ass over sloppy record-keeping."

Bullet just nodded. "I'll give Cappie what he needs and then we can make our way to the Parrot's Cove."

"Does Sam know we're coming?"

"Yeah, I called her before I left the house. She asked if you were coming, so I guess her brother has already told her about you."

"I'm not surprised. It was pretty apparent to me that she was very important to him."

We finished our coffee and heard Cappie ride up on his scoot followed by Patch in his truck. Bullet gave them the needed cash and instructions and they were off to buy the supplies.

Whiskey looked at me and said, "Okay, V.P., are you ready for this?"

"It's just another day, Brother," I said as I mounted my bike and pulled out onto the road.

Highway 59 was like a parking lot and the idiots in their cages were just as dangerous as ever. It was slow going but we made the trip over to Canal coming up from Navigation. Bullet pointed out one of the body shops and two other bars we would come back to after our visit with Sam. It was going to be a busy day, and all I could think of was how badly I wanted this part of the day behind me.

We turned the corner and rode into the parking lot where I was surprised to see the Fort Bend County Sheriff's cruiser sitting.

As we got off our bikes Bullet said, "Having him here wasn't part of the arrangement."

"Don't worry about it," I said. "I'll handle him, you guys just stay back and make sure he's the only surprise we have to deal with."

We walked in and I saw Nate sitting at the bar drinking coffee. His sister, intimidated by our presence, immediately got busy wiping down the bar.

I walked up to Nate and put my hand out to him. When he took it, I pulled him close and gave him the customary hug a brother would give another. I looked at Bullet and Whiskey and said, "Brothers, let me introduce you to my brother, Nate."

Nate looked at me with a surprised look on his face as both Bullet and Whiskey shook hands with him and said, "It's a pleasure."

After a moment of stunned silence, Nate finally looked at his sister. "Sam, this is my brother, Jake."

I reached out and as she took my hand in hers. "No way, you're far too pretty to be Nate's sister."

She smiled big. "Do you know Whiskey and Bullet?"

Her smile quickly turned to a frown. "I know them."

An awkward silence followed and finally I broke it with, "That coffee sure smells good."

Sam was quick to fill me a cup and offered the same to both Bullet and Whiskey, but they politely refused. Sam said, "There is a table set up for us not far from the front door," and quickly ushered us over to a seat.

We all sat down. "I'm glad you're here," I said to Nate. "It keeps me from having to repeat the conversation and nothing gets lost in the translation." I leaned over to him and whispered, "Nate, you're going to have to place a little trust in what we're doing here. Surprises like this morning don't add to the trust factor, okay?"

"Well, let's see how the morning goes and we can talk about trust afterward."

"Fair enough."

I looked at his sister. "We all know what the business arrangement here is. The Los Patrons own twenty-five percent of the Parrot's Cove and we also know the club is failing."

Sam immediately said, "Says who?"

I looked at Bullet and motioned for him to speak up.

"Sam, I know you don't like me and I understand why. Thing is, you and I both know that you're barely keeping the place open and by the end of the week, I'll have a complete financial report put together showing exactly that."

She looked at Bullet and asked, "What's your real name?"

"What possible impact could that have on this conversation?" he asked.

"You know everything about me, including my social security number, my address, the year and make of my car - hell, you might even know the color of my favorite panties. All because of that damn contract Tommy signed. He's gone and I'm sitting here talking to someone whose name I don't even know. Now, please tell me, what's your real name?"

Bullet glanced at me and I nodded my approval. "My name is Tim O'Conner," he said.

She grinned. "I'm negotiating my future with someone named Tim O'Conner?" She blinked her eyes in a very provocative manner. "Okay, Timmy, whatcha got for me today?"

The look on Bullet's face was one of instant fury. He leaned forward and was about to speak when I put my hand up, motioning for him to relax.

I smiled wide and said, "My name is Jake Coleman and I'm the brother of your brother. We're here today because my brother asked me to help you and that's what I intend to do. So you know, it'll be me you negotiate with and my intention is to make things right for you and the Los Patrons. Now, picking a fight with my brother Bullet here shows me you have salt in your ass, but sister, salt becomes bitter when applied too heavily, so how 'bout you relax a bit."

"Brother of my brother, huh? What does that make you to me?" she asked.

I looked first at Nate, then back at her, and said, "Family."

Chapter Seventeen
THE PARROT'S COVE

S am looked at me with surprise in her eyes. It was very apparent that neither she nor Nate were prepared to hear me refer to them as family. So after a moment of silence I said, "My plan is to offer you the opportunity to sell your interest in the Parrot's Cove to the Los Patrons."

Nate spoke up. "Hey, man, we didn't discuss you buying the place, we discussed you getting out of her business."

I looked at Sam. "If we can come to an agreement that will get you out of here and away from this environment, are you willing to discuss that option with me?"

"If you make me a fair offer, I'll happily sell the Cove to you. But if you think I am going to roll over and let you steal the place, you have another thought coming."

"Sam, do you want to know what I would do if I wanted to steal the place from you?"

"I don't know, Jake, do I want to know?"

I took a stern position and looked at her closely. "I'd simply kill the both of you here today and burn the place to the ground tonight."

Nate's reaction to what I had just said was quick. He tried to rise from his chair but before he could get up from his seat, I put my .45 in the middle of his chest and motioned for him to sit back down. I spoke again to Sam. "With the two of you gone, we would simply cash in the insurance and be done with it. But, as I said earlier, we are family and I'm not willing to do that."

I looked back at Nate. "Remember what I said earlier, Brother, there's going to be a need for trust."

He answered angrily. "Yeah, and I remember telling you we'd talk about trust after we were finished here."

With that, I pulled the gun away from his chest and handed it to him, grip first. I thought Bullet and Whiskey were about to shit themselves, but they kept their composure while I finished my statement.

"Sam," I said, "Our brother now has the ability to shoot all three of us, and I am quite sure he has the skill to get the job done. Somehow, though, I'm trusting that family is just as important to him as it is to me. How important is it to you, Sam?"

"It's very important."

"Okay then, trust me. I want to do the right thing here and when this is all finished, maybe Nate here will invite us all over for a Sunday afternoon BBQ and I can enjoy some of the family I didn't know I had. Will you trust me, Sam?"

She smiled. "I'm not sure why, but yes Jake, I'm going to trust you."

"How about you, Brother?" I said to Nate.

His gaze took in Whiskey and Bullet first, and then me. "You're asking a lot."

"Yes, I am."

He took my gun, laid it on the table, slid it to me, and grinned. "So, you want to come over for Sunday afternoon BBQ, huh?"

"Hey, you provide the BBQ and I'll provide the beer. How's that?"

I stood, and Nate and I shook hands. I turned and immediately reached for Sam, hugging her tightly. "Suddenly, I find myself rich with family," I said.

She hugged me back and whispered, "Thank you."

Whiskey, Bullet, and I gathered up our things and as we were about to leave I said, "We'll have everything put together by the first part of next week. I'd like to see us get back together then."

Both Nate and Sam motioned that they were good with that and we started out the door. Bullet walked out first, followed by Whiskey, then me. After the door closed, Whiskey said, "V.P., you fuckin' scared the shit out of me when you handed that cop your gun. No disrespect, but what the fuck were you thinking about? You just told them both you could kill them, and then you hand that fucker your gun? Jeez, man, are you completely off your rocker?"

I just looked at him. "Where are we going now?"

Bullet spoke up. "You got balls, Brother, but I wouldn't suggest pulling that shit where we're going next. If you hand this mother fucker your gun, he'll fuckin' blow your head off with it."

"Okay. This is the asshole who owes us twenty heavy, right?"

Whiskey answered, "That's right, Jake, and he ain't nobody to fuck around with."

"What's his name?"

"Everest," Bullet said. "You'll understand where he got the name when you see him."

"Okay. Let's go!"

It took less than five minutes for us to motor over to the body shop called Gulf Coast Body and Wrecker Service. The place stood out like a sore thumb, all dolled up like some kind of palace. You could tell it was a place for pimps just by the way the place was laid out. Our agreement here was the Los Patrons furnished the property, the product and the buyers - Everest supplied the labor. They took the cars and bikes provided by our prospects and support clubs and would clean them up so they were capable of crossing the US border into Mexico where we had plenty of buyers and a steady flow of cash. Pretty simple deal; we steal them – they fix them – we sell them! It was the perfect set up for a chop shop and the arrangement was an even split on the deal, but lately we weren't getting our split. Today, we planned to settle up.

We got off our bikes and Whiskey said, "See that big mother fucker with the ball cap on?"

"Yeah, I see him, is that Everest?"

Bullet spoke up. "That's Everest and I'm telling you, Brother, you gotta watch your shit with this big bitch."

"Okay, I see where he gets his name – Mount Everest, huh?"

Whiskey said, "I'm telling you, V.P., be careful how you handle this big fucker. He truly is one mean son of a bitch."

I just smiled and said, "Follow my lead."

We walked in and Everest marched straight toward me and was about to speak, but I caught him in a turn and kicked his left knee out, same as I did Buck. That fucker went to the ground hard and I put my boot in his chin so hard he began to choke on his teeth and blood. Whiskey closed the bay door while Bullet quickly corralled his crew and locked them in the men's restroom. We dragged that big mother fucker over to his vise-bench, put his wrist inside the vise, and I turned the crank. It didn't take long before he was screaming. I tightened that vise until I heard bone break and then I tightened it some more. By now he was begging for me to stop and I leaned over to him and shouted, "Where's my fuckin' money, you big bag of shit?" I stood up, cranked that vise another turn, and his screams turned to whimpers.

"In the safe. The money is in the safe," he said.

"What's the combination? Tell me, you mother fucker, before I break your other arm."

By now, he was in so much pain he could only mutter. "No combo, it's a keyed safe. The key's in the top drawer of my desk."

"If any part of that office is rigged to hurt my brother, I will fuckin' kill you, man!"

"No trap, there's nothing there to hurt him. Please let go of my arm."

I looked at Bullet. "Go get our fuckin' money."

A couple of minutes went by before that big bastard passed out. Bullet came out of the office. "Brother, there is almost one hundred thousand dollars here."

I looked down at that fucking turd and cranked the vise twice more but he barely moaned. I walked over to his pipe tree and picked out a three foot section of one-inch cast. I walked back with the pipe in my hand and hit that fucker in the back of his head so hard that his head busted open like a watermelon dropped off someone's kitchen table. I looked at Whiskey. "Go bring his crew out here."

"You got it, V.P."

It took less than a minute to get them all in front of the scene and they were all shaking in their boots, that is, except for one. I walked up to him and said, "Who runs this place when Everest is gone?"

He pointed to the short, skinny, black guy at the end of the line. "That's his cousin Rafael. He's the boss anytime Everest is gone."

I turned toward Rafael, pulled out my .45 and put a round right in the middle of his chest. He fell, convulsing for only a moment, then gurgled up a bunch of blood and just quit moving. I looked at Bullet. "Count out half of that money and bring me the rest."

Within a couple of minutes Bullet brought me the money. "Forty-nine thousand dollars, Jake."

I looked at the man again. "What's your name?"

"Kavon Jones."

"Okay, Kavon, here's the deal. Those two mother fuckers got greedy and you see what it got them, right?

"I see very well, Patron."

"My deal with them was a fifty/fifty split. I'll make the same deal with you, if you want it."

"I want it."

I shoved the money into his chest. "Don't get greedy, Kavon."

"Can I borrow your gun, Patron?"

"My name is Jake and what do you want my gun for?"

"I'm gonna kill the only man here that'll get in the way of us doing business."

I took out my pistol, as did Whiskey and Bullet, and handed it to him. He quickly turned and shot the man standing next to him in the side of the head. The man fell, spewing long cords of blood over everything, including the men next to him. Each of those men froze in position for fear the same might happen to them. Kavon handed the gun back to me and I asked, "What'd he do?"

"Nothing, but now the rest of these fuckers all know who the boss is."

"Okay. Taking care of business doesn't seem to be an issue for you, so is taking care of these bodies gonna be a problem?"

"Nope, we'll handle them."

I told him that Bullet would come back in a few days and help him set up a system for recording his business, and that we would collect our cut twice a month. He said he understood, and we shook hands and walked out the door.

We stopped at my bike and Whiskey said, "Brother, I have an all new and different kind of respect for you. Believe me, I will never question your judgment again."

Bullet just looked at me and said, "Wow!"

Feeling they needed to hear me say something, I said, "Nate and Sam represent the better part of me, Brothers. That part that helps me remember I still have a soul. That fuckin' turd inside and his cronies don't mean shit to me, and I could give a glorious fuck what happens to any of them. My family, the two of you, and our brothers are the only tomorrow I have. I'll do what I have to do to make sure all of you have what you need to get along, and that includes coming back here and killing every one of those cocksuckers if they try to screw us on this deal."

Whiskey walked over to me and put his arms around me, hugging me hard. He pulled away and looked me straight in the eyes. "Whenever and wherever, I want to be at your side, Brother."

Bullet stepped up. "Tell me what you want me to do and I'll do it. Tell me where to go and I'll go. Tell me who you want dead, and Brother, I will personally go kill that mother fucker."

That night earned me not only the love and loyalty of these two brothers, but a respect that can't be bought any other way but by action. We spent the next couple of days seeing the rest of our business contacts and we only had one situation involving a tough guy at a small icehouse on Navigation who thought he was empowered somehow to change our agreements. It didn't take long for Whiskey to convince him to change his mind. All in all, my time with Bullet and Whiskey was well spent. I did exactly as Diego had recommended, which was to press our interests and it paid off, with collections totaling just under $100,000. There was no question in anyone's mind that the Los Patrons were firmly in control of their business.

The weekend came and went and Bullet produced his proposal for the purchase of Sam's portion of the Parrot's Cove. The place had not produced a profit in more than three months. There wasn't enough money in the business account to pay for another liquor delivery and barely enough to make one more payroll and cover the utilities for the month. The only thing of worth left in the place was the current stock of liquor, the furniture, and the kitchen equipment. In total, there was roughly fifty thousand dollars in assets. The only real liability was a liquor license that would have to be renewed in nine months and a lease that was now one month behind. The Los Patrons owning a legitimate and legally operated business was, without a doubt, a smart move. With a little planning and smart use of our own assets, we could infuse the place with cash and have it in the black quickly. Knowing we had nine months before we had to cough up a license fee, Bullet recommended we purchase Sam's assets for face value and give her a twenty percent split on the profit for one year. That projected out to be about $150,000, if we hit the monthly profit targets that Bullet projected. I called Clutch and suggested we get together with Carmen to discuss the deal and we agreed to meet that night at the clubhouse to look it over.

Carmen and I arrived at the clubhouse a little before seven o'clock, followed shortly by Clutch and Whiskey. Bullet arrived at seven-thirty and had all of the spreadsheets ready for us to review. He presented the numbers and Clutch said, "We give her $50,000 up front and the place is ours, right?"

Bullet said, "Yes, but we will still have to make monthly payments for the first year and those could be bigger or smaller than what I've projected. It's all dependent on how well we run the place."

"Can we use sheep to run the place and save on payroll?"

"We can do that for the bar-backs but you need a bartender and wait staff that know what they're doing or the place will fail for sure."

"Jake," Clutch asked, "will this win us a friend with your brother?"

"It will eliminate his hate for us and that will hopefully find him friendlier toward us."

"How much cash are we going to have to put into the place to get it on its feet?" Clutch asked.

Bullet said, "We'll need to put roughly fifty thousand in the business account to cover payroll and liquor deliveries and that will also cover the nine thousand for last month and this month's lease. All total, we're out a hundred grand up front."

"Clutch," I said, "That's about what we collected last week. I really can't see us losing on this deal."

"Okay," Clutch said. "I'm good with it. Carmen, how long will it take you to get this deal put to paper?"

"Since we're not buying the property, I'll need a couple of days to prepare the buy/sell agreements and then two weeks for permitting, registration with the City of Houston, and transfer of the liquor license with TABC. We could have everything up and running by the end of March."

Clutch nodded. "Get started on the paperwork, Carmen. Bullet, make sure everyone gets the message to meet here tomorrow night at seven o'clock, for church. Let's get the vote and then we'll move on it."

"Jake, you got a minute?" Whiskey asked.

"Sure, Brother, what's up?"

"I got a call earlier today from Braid, up in Dallas, They've set the benefit up for the second weekend of March. It's Antonio's birthday and they wanted to use his birthday for the event, thinking it would help with donations. Braid wanted to make sure you still wanted to be involved, so are you good with that weekend?"

"Damn straight I am. Call Braid back and tell him that we'll come the night before. I'm bringing Carmen so I can introduce her to my little brother."

"Leave it to me. I got it handled."

Carmen and I walked outside and she put her arms around my neck and said, "John from The Night's Ink is on his way to our house."

"For what?"

"I'm getting a cover up and a new tattoo."

I looked at her a little confused. "A cover up? What have you got to cover up?"

"Jake, I'm covering that 'Property of Diego' tattoo with a small pussycat and I'm getting *JC* tattooed on the high side of my left breast where everyone can see it."

"I don't want a property stamp on you, Carmen."

"It's not a property stamp, Jake. It's the initials of the man I love and it's for me. Besides, the club has seen how you treat me and they all know I'm not property."

I smiled at her, kissed her, and threw my leg over my bike. Motioning to the passenger seat I said, "Okay then, hop on, old woman."

She looked at me. "I AM NOT your old woman, thank you!" Folding her arms and acting like her feelings were hurt, she just stood there.

I grinned wide. "Okay, Carmen, hop on and I'll take my ole' lady home so she can get inked."

She straddled the back of my bike and whispered in my ear, "It's the end of February, the divorce is filed, and we will be eligible for a marriage license in the middle of May."

"Do you have a date in mind?" I asked.

"Of course I do! I want to get married on Saturday, May the thirteenth, and I want an evening wedding so we can slip away from the club and have a real wedding night before leaving for our honeymoon."

"Well, Carmen, it sounds like you have it all worked out. I'll bet you've even decided where we are going for the honeymoon, haven't you?"

"As a matter of fact, Jake, I have."

"And where would that be, Carmen?" I asked, almost laughing.

"There isn't enough time for us to get passports, so I thought we would go to Puerto Rico. I've always wanted to see the bioluminescent bay and I want to see it with you. The weather will be perfect and we'll be perfect. Please say you're okay with going there."

"Woman, I love you and if Puerto Rico is where you want to go, Puerto Rico is where I want to go."

She kissed me and giggled like a little girl as I started my scoot. I rode up next to Bullet who was now packing his paperwork from the night into his bags and I said, "Brother, you better get busy with the party plans for our wedding because we just set the date for May thirteenth."

I rode past Clutch and Whiskey who were also getting on their bikes and I know they must have thought we were crazy because Carmen was yelling, "We're going to Puerto Rico," as she waved to everyone we passed.

We all gathered at the clubhouse the next evening and presented our plan for the purchase of the Parrot's Cove. As expected, we received a unanimous vote, which gave us what we needed to move forward with the deal.

The balance of our weekend was uneventful with most of my time being spent with Carmen. For the first time in several months, we spent all of Sunday doing nothing but watching old movies, and eating ice cream. I don't think I can remember a time when I felt such a sense of peace and complete satisfaction with the way my life was going. The club had opened so many doors for me and now I had a brother – and although Sam was not my sister, I fully intended to claim her as such. Our wedding plans, complete with a honeymoon, were just around the corner and I couldn't have been happier.

As we were preparing for bed Sunday night, Carmen asked, "How do you think Nate and Sam are going to feel about me being at the meeting?"

"I hadn't given that any thought, Carmen, why do you ask?"

"Jake, I'm the one who drafted the contracts for the Los Patrons to receive twenty-five percent ownership in the Parrot's Cove, and there may be some hateful feelings when I suddenly appear on the scene again."

"Okay. So here is what I want you to do. Wear that dark skirt, you know, the one I like so much and wear a low-cut, white blouse with it. Make sure that new tattoo you're sporting is visible to the both of them. When we walk in, I'll introduce you as my fiancée, and quickly invite them both to our wedding. You be your same sweet, sexy self and just charm the shit out of both of them. They're good people and I'm betting they'll accept you just like they have me."

"What if that doesn't work, Jake? What if they're not willing to accept me being there?"

"You're worrying far too much, Carmen, things will be fine, I promise. We're meeting them tomorrow at ten in the morning and by eleven, the Los Patrons will be on our way to owning a legitimate business, and we'll have accomplished a great thing for our family."

The alarm went off at six-thirty the next morning and I was excited to get the day underway. Carmen was already in the kitchen cooking breakfast. I walked up behind her and kissed her good morning. "I was planning to take you for breakfast."

"No sir. You can take me to lunch or you can take me to dinner." She turned to face me and smiled from ear to ear. "Or, you can just take me. Breakfast, however, is something I'll do for you every morning that you and I are together."

She poured me a cup of coffee and sat it on the table as she went back to her cooking.

I watched her as she cooked and once again, I felt those same feelings of complete satisfaction, thinking, *I really don't know how I could be any happier.*

After breakfast we showered and got ready for the day. We both dressed for business, with me in my jeans, short-sleeve tee shirt, and my cut. Carmen dressed as I asked her too, wearing the dark skirt with the low-cut, white blouse, and she put on the pair of black high heel shoes I'd bought for her not long ago. I thought her ankles were simply sexy as hell and they showed off well in those shoes. Together we looked the pair – rough and tumble with a whole lot of class!

I heard the roar of pipes as Whiskey and Bullet, along with Prospects Patch and Cappie, all pulled up in front of the house. I asked Whiskey where Clutch was. "Clutch told me the V.P. was running this deal and he trusted him to take care of business."

"Alright then. Let's get moving."

I pulled into the street with Whiskey tight on my right peg. Bullet and the prospects were behind us, followed by Carmen in the car. *Another day of trying to get through downtown on 59 in Houston traffic,* I thought to myself, as I tried to keep from being run over. *I think we'll just move to Lake Livingston. Fuck this big-city bullshit and all the crazy mother fuckers trying to kill you with their cars. Man, wouldn't that be nice – just move to the lake and fish all day long.* My daydream was quickly interrupted by some jackass flying in and out of traffic in his sporty little Mazda. He almost put me into the road barrier with his antics, and for a moment I considered chasing him down and kicking the dog shit out of him. If it hadn't been for the business at hand, I might've done that very thing, but I was anxious to get this thing done, so I motored on.

It was a little before ten when we pulled into the parking lot of the Parrot's Cove. Bullet and the prospects went in and Carmen and I followed them, with Whiskey close behind. Sam's expression was one of surprise when she saw Carmen walk in. Nate was standing at the bar drinking a cup of coffee.

I decided to take advantage of the moment. I walked up to Sam and hugged her tightly. "This is going to be a good day, Sam."

I turned to Carmen. "Sweetheart, let me introduce you to my sister, Sam."

Carmen stepped forward, smiling, and extended her hand. "It's nice to see you again, Sam."

Sam responded politely, "Hello, Carmen."

I turned to Nate with a chuckle, "I know the two of you are acquainted."

Nate responded coldly, "Counselor."

I looked at him and said, "C'mon, Brother. You can do better than that. Hell, man, on May thirteenth, Carmen will become your sister-in-law."

Sam said, "The two of you are getting married?"

I said, "Yes, we are and I sincerely hope you will both be at the wedding."

Carmen walked over to Nate and said, "It's good to see you again, Nate, and I hope it is okay for me to call you that."

Nate just smiled and nodded his approval.

Carmen, still trying to break the ice, said, "I have never seen Jake as happy as he is now, and I have the two of you to thank for that."

Nate walked up to me with this serious look in his eyes. "She's awfully pretty, Jake. In fact, she is way too damn pretty for someone as ugly as you." He laughed, then hugged me tight. "Congratulations."

Turning to Carmen, Nate gave her a careful hug and smiled. "My Christmas list is growing. Welcome to the family, Carmen."

We spent the next two hours going over the details of the buy/sale agreement and with the documents signed, both Nate and Sam commented on the fairness of the deal. The business at hand concluded, the transfer of funds into Sam's bank account could take place.

Sam walked up to Carmen and said, "I find myself with a new brother and a sister, neither of which I expected. I am truly grateful for everything you did here today."

"Sam, I've never known a man quite like Jake Coleman and I've certainly never loved a man such as him. I'm glad I was able to help, but all of this was made possible because of Jake. I hope you can grow to love your brother as much as I love him. He truly is quite a man."

"You know, Carmen, he really isn't my brother. He's Nate's brother."

Carmen looked at her and smiled. "Sam, he's your brother alright. I can tell by the way he speaks of you and of Nate that he is also grateful for you. Remember, the wedding is May thirteenth and I really hope you will both be there."

"We'll both be there," she said.

Chapter Eighteen
PAYBACK

Gus McElroy was one of the brothers who patched-over from the Warriors and he was someone we thought was a solid brother. I decided tonight would be a good time to see how solid he was. He knew the way to Buck's house in West Houston, so we took him with us to settle things. Cappie and Patch were waiting in the parking lot at the job site where Buck worked and called me when he started home. They followed behind him in Cappie's old truck, keeping far enough back so Buck wouldn't spot them, but close enough so they could call me when he was near. The trailer park Buck lived in was west of the Grand Parkway on Morton Road, not far from the old city cemetery. That fucker lived at the very back of the park and his place was grown up with weeds and cluttered with trash and junk from old cars. The dumbass left the back door to his house unlocked so Whiskey, Gus, and I just walked on in. I looked at my watch seeing it was almost midnight, so we waited. We were all itching to get at this piece of shit and why not – he had it coming.

I told Whiskey and Gus, "Remember what Clutch said, he's good with an ass whipping but no permanent injuries. Let's fuck him up good and leaving him hurting, but nothing worthy of a hospital stay."

My cell phone rang and it was Cappie. "That asshole just turned into the trailer park. He'll be there any minute."

"Okay, hold back and wait until he is in the house, then pull up and come in."

I no more hung up the phone with Cappie than we heard Buck's bike pull up out front. He shut the engine down and immediately started talking on his cell phone. It was easy to hear that he had a piece of ass on the way to his house. Considering he had someone coming, we were going to have to get this done quickly and get the hell out of there. We could hear him walking up the steps as he struggled to get the key in the lock. I sat on his couch and waited. Whiskey stood in the shadow next to the closet, with Gus kneeling behind a chair just off to the right. That goofy fuck walked into the living room and froze with a blank stare on his face, just looking at me.

"Howdy, Buck," I said, "How was your day?"

Finally realizing what was about to happen, he turned and tried to get out the same way he'd come in, but he ran into Cappie and Patch, who by now were standing on his front porch. Whiskey grabbed him by his collar and pulled him back in the house. As Buck was turning to face me, Gus hit him hard in the stomach. He dropped to the floor and all four of them took turns hitting and kicking him. After about a minute of this he was just lying there, so I put up a hand, motioning for them to stop.

I went to his fridge, opened a bottle of water, and said, "Sit him up."

After a moment, he had his breath and I handed the water to him. He drank a couple of swallows but mostly used it to rinse the blood out of his mouth.

"All of this cause I don't want to be in your club?"

"You are such a fuckin' moron, Buck. You know damn good and well you handled your exit all wrong, and then you come back and paint a bunch of bullshit on our house. You're lucky I don't fuckin' kill you here and now."

"Why don't you just get on with it, Jake, if that's what you have in mind?"

"Don't fuckin' tempt me, you son of a bitch, or I might just go ahead and do that very thing."

I looked at Whiskey and said, "Get him on his feet."

Whiskey and Gus held him tight as I took out my knife. "I'm going to give you something to remember this night by." I cut the right side of his face from just above his ear to the bottom of his chin. "If I ever see you again, I will fuckin' kill you Buck!"

Using his shirt, I wiped the blood off my knife then Whiskey shoved him onto the couch. Before we left, Gus walked over and spat on him, then called him a coward. I got back in the car with Whiskey and Gus, with Cappie and Patch following in Cappie's old truck. As we were driving away, we saw his entertainment for the evening drive up and walk in.

I looked at Whiskey and said, "Next time, we finish him."

"You give the word, V.P., and it's done."

Carmen was up watching an old movie on television and drinking a glass of wine when I got home. She took one look at me and said, "You're not wearing your cut, I see. Am I to assume you may soon have need of my legal services?"

I smiled as I sat next to her. "The kind of service I want from you, woman, has nothing to do with the courts."

She sat down her glass of wine, reached for my face, and raked my cheek with her fingernails. "You come home horny after a night out with your brothers? I may have to suggest more nights out for you, Jake."

Grinning, she pulled the tassels loose that held her negligee closed, allowing her breasts to be completely exposed. I could see from the look in her eyes that she had been thinking of my return for most of the evening. It was late but her scent was so alluring and her passion was so intense that time just seemed to stand still. She pulled me down on top of her, ripping the buttons loose from my shirt as I worked feverishly to free myself from the bondage of my boots and jeans.

After a few moments, I leaned down to kiss her, but she pushed my shoulders back and said, "I want you to fuck me, Jake! Don't make love to me, just fuck me!" She moaned as I entered her, then dug her fingernails deep into my flesh and clawed from my shoulders to the cheeks of my ass. It hurt like crazy, so I pulled her hands away from my back and held them tight above her head as I began to thrust. It didn't take long before her body shuddered and she screamed with orgasm. I exploded instantly and just collapsed on top of her. We lay there for only a moment when she put her arms around me. The pain I felt from the claw marks as she touched my back was so intense, it caused me to jump up from the couch, moving away from her.

She looked at me, then covered her mouth and said, "Jake, you're bleeding!"

Jumping up from the couch, she ran to the bathroom, coming back with a wet towel and some disinfectant spray, saying, "I'm sorry Jake, I didn't mean to hurt you!"

She cleaned me up, sprayed me with the disinfectant and said, "I got carried away, Jake, I'm sorry."

"I'm not a bit sorry. That was the most intense fucking I can remember." I grinned and looked at her hands. "Look at your fingernails."

She looked at her hands and saw there were small pieces of flesh still embedded underneath a few of her nails. She just shook her head.

I laughed. "The next time you want to fuck, I'm going to put a pair of gloves on you, woman!"

The alarm woke me at eight-thirty the next morning. I got up and headed straight for the shower. The water stung the scratches on my back and I couldn't help but grin at how intense the night had been. *Getting married to this woman is going to be an adventure all of its own.* I got dressed and headed to the kitchen where Carmen was just finishing up with breakfast.

She kissed me and asked, "How's your back?"

I hugged her tight. "My back is just fine, woman." Grabbing her ass with both hands, I said, "If I had more time, we'd go back to bed and do it all over again."

She just looked at me. "You go eat your breakfast and quit teasing me, man!"

I made quick work of breakfast, put on my cut, and kissed her goodbye as I hurried out the door. I had a meeting with Clutch at ten that morning, and he'd told me not to be late because he had a whole range of subjects to discuss with me. The morning was warm for late February and I was anxious to ride. I quickly started the Heritage, pulled into the street, and motored over to the clubhouse, arriving a few minutes before ten. I was surprised by how great the place looked. I hadn't been back since Cappie and Patch had done their magic with the paint brush. The building was painted white with red trim along the roof line and all three doors had been painted red as well. The out-building was painted the same and the place looked terrific.

Clutch rode up as I was admiring the work. He got off his bike and said, "Wow, look at the place. It really looks like a Los Patrons club-house now. Nice job with the prospects, Jake."

"Thanks, Brother, but it was their work not mine. Shit, I had no idea the place could look this good."

Clutch unlocked the door and walked in. "Mother fucker, Jake. Look at this place!"

I walked in fearing the worst, but was surprised to see even the inside of our clubhouse completely transformed. The walls were painted white with the doors and trim painted red. Even the strip-per stage had been transformed with red and white tiles for the floor and the base painted white and trimmed in red. New lights had been installed above the stage and over the bar, and the place looked and smelled brand new.

Clutch asked, "How much money did you give the prospects to spend?"

"Fuck if I know, Clutch. Remember, you told me to just handle it, then slammed the phone in my ear. So I passed the job on to Bullet and told him to keep receipts."

"Well, the place looks great. So, tell me about last night."

"We left him hurting and with a very clear warning that if we ever saw or heard from him again, he would pay with his life. I don't think he'll surface again."

"How did Gus deal with it?"

"I was surprised at how Gus handled it. He was the first to throw a punch and he kicked the hell out him, same as the others. As we were leaving he walked over to Buck and spit on him. I don't think we have any reason to question his loyalty."

"Good. We need a road captain and he knows his way around. How would you feel if I appointed him to the job?"

"You know, Brother, he hates cops and as road captain he'll be the one with the most contact with them, especially when he's planning a run."

He started laughing. "Jake, you're the only one I know of in this club that has any love for the cops!"

I just gave him the finger. "I have a brother that's a cop and that doesn't make me a lover of cops."

He just kept laughing. "Yeah, yeah, yeah!"

I was getting a little irritated with his teasing. "Fuck you and the horse you rode in on."

"Okay, all joking aside. What do you think?"

"I'm good with it. We need a road captain for the trip to Dallas Saturday after next and he can take responsibility for coordinating that run. That'll take the burden off Whiskey, for sure. Are you going to Dallas?"

"Yeah, I'm coming, but I gotta cage it up there."

"How come?"

"I'm having surgery on my right foot next week and I'll be on crutches for about six weeks. I can't drive for a couple of weeks and I sure as shit can't ride my scoot for a while."

"That's not a problem, Brother, you can ride up with Carmen. She was wanting to do some shopping while there and is taking her car. She'll be happy to have the company, I'm sure."

"I appreciate it, Jake. I have a one more issue to discuss with you, Brother."

He just sort of paused as if trying to collect his thoughts and I finally said, "Something's on your mind, I can tell. What's up?"

"I got a call yesterday morning from The Bull."

"Yeah? What'd The Bull have to say?"

"He asked me to take Ringo's place on the national board."

"Really? What's up with Ringo?"

"He's retiring back to the Corpus Christi chapter. Getting too old, I guess, to be a sergeant at arms."

"That's fuckin' awesome, Brother, and quite an honor for The Bull to call you for the job. Are you interested in moving to Corpus Christi?"

"Yeah, Jake, I am. My kids live there and it gives me the chance to get closer to them. You do realize when I leave Houston you will automatically become the new Houston Chapter President."

In my excitement for him, I hadn't considered what that move would mean for me. I looked at him and said, "Clutch, I'll do whatever you trust me to do and if you decide that you want to move on to be a national sergeant at arms, I'll not let you down as the Houston Chapter President. On the other hand, if you decide to stay here as president, I'll continue to serve you as is, and happily so!"

"The decision was made yesterday, Brother. I'm going to Corpus Christi and you'll soon be president here."

I was completely taken back by what he had just said to me and I asked, "What do you think the other chapter presidents will say? I've been a patch for under two years and V.P. for only a couple of months. For some, that could be an issue."

"The Bull had a conference call with all the chapter presidents in the Houston area and he asked for honest feedback. The response was unanimously in favor of me as Ringo's replacement and of you for my replacement. The Bull wants you installed before the national meeting in June, so he is coming to the benefit in Dallas and installing you as president there."

Clutch poured two shooters of Jack and opened two bottles of Bud. Handing one of each to me, he said, "Here's to you, Brother!"

We shot the Jack and chased it down with long swallows of Bud. Then I poured two more shooters. "Here's to my friend and my brother."

We spent the next couple of hours shooting pool and just having a few laughs. It was a good day for both of us, and once more I felt a huge sense of gratitude for where my life was going and for the friends I had made along the way.

Chapter Nineteen
A CHANGING OF THE GUARD

Friday, March 12, 2013 was a cold morning. I had just put my leather on and was about to cover my face with the neoprene mask Carmen had bought me, when Clutch, standing on his crutch, started laughing. "This is gonna be a good trip to Dallas. I get to ride in a warm car with a beautiful woman that always smells so fine, and I get to do that while watching you ride the interstate in forty degree weather."

I just looked at him and said, "I'm about to kick that crutch you're leaning on out from under that smart ass of yours. Then it will be me with a grin on my face."

"Now, now, Jake. That's no way for you to talk to a brother who's about to take a long trip with your soon-to-be-wife. Man, I might decide to pull over and steal her away from you, using my manly skills."

Carmen, listening to our banter, walked over to Clutch. She put her arm over his left shoulder and said, "Hmmm, ya got a lot of manly skills to share, do ya, Clutch?"

Putting his arm around her waist and pulling her close, he looked at me and smiled. "Don't be jealous, Jake, I won't keep her...long."

I looked up at the both of them and laughed. "Well, if you do decide to stop somewhere along the way to share your manly skills I suggest you put a pair of gloves on the woman before you do."

That threw him off his stump because he didn't have a clue what I was talking about. Carmen, on the other hand, walked over to me and whispered in my ear, "You are such a naughty boy," then kissed me goodbye before helping Clutch get into her car.

Whiskey rode up as I was putting the mask over my face and said, "Brisk morning, ain't it, V.P.?"

It was ten o'clock when Carmen pulled to the side of the parking lot to give us space to ride out onto the road. As I rode up beside Whiskey I said, "After today I'm gonna need a V.P. and I am hoping you'll accept the job. So, let's enjoy this brisk ride and talk about it tonight in Dallas."

Whiskey looked as though he had just been told the world was ending, because until today, I hadn't told anyone except Carmen what was happening. The four of us were making the trip the night before the benefit so I could introduce Carmen to Antonio. I had arranged for him and his father to eat dinner with the four of us at a place called The Stockton. We were meeting there at seven o'clock, and I was feeling a real sense of excitement about the evening. I hoped Carmen would fall in love with this kid, same as me.

There would be a couple of brothers from each of the Houston chapters arriving Saturday, with Gus leading as our newly appointed road captain. There would also be brothers from chapters in and out of the state as well as support club members, and of course, the general public who were aware of Antonio's situation. We were expecting a large crowd and had secured the bar services and campgrounds offered by a place called the Shallowater Saloon. The place was only a few miles north of the clubhouse and was well known as one of the oldest operating saloons in the state of Texas. The owner was friendly with the club and really liked what we were trying to accomplish for Antonio. He helped us out by offering the grounds and pavilion free of charge, and he also offered to donate the profit from all beer sales that day to the fundraiser. There would be a 50/50 drawing, BBQ plates, and a silent auction with thirty-five items ranging from movie tickets to liquor baskets. The big draw for the benefit was the auction of a 1957

Harley Panhead, donated by a local bike-builder that sometimes did repair work for the Dallas chapter. All in all, I thought the Dallas brothers had done a great job of putting this thing together, and I hoped it would generate enough cash to make this little boy's life a little easier with what time he had left.

Tomorrow would usher in a new beginning for the Houston Chapter and although I felt I was up for the job, I'd heard it said many times that speed kills, and given the short time I'd been in the club that thought left me feeling a little uneasy. It really didn't matter if I felt uneasy, it was my responsibility to take over and I would give it my best effort. I was anxious to talk to Whiskey because he and I had developed the right kind of relationship to make this work, and I really needed him at my side. The trip took longer than normal because traffic getting out of Houston was worse than usual. After stopping for fuel in Buffalo and grabbing some lunch, we rolled into the clubhouse parking lot at straight-up four o'clock. It had been a cold ride and it felt good to get off my scoot and get inside where it was warm. Braid met us at the clubhouse and opened it up, giving both Whiskey and me a key. He told me that Diablo (the Dallas president) was on his way and should be there within the hour. It didn't take long for Carmen and me to get our things stowed in one of the two VIP bedrooms. Clutch took the other and Whiskey put his gear in the bunkroom. Carmen wanted some time to rest, which was perfect because I wanted to get Clutch and Whiskey together so we could discuss the upcoming changes. I walked to the bar, poured three shooters of Jack, and got each of us a cold beer. As I was setting them up, Clutch came gimping in on his crutch with Whiskey at his side.

They both took a seat and Whiskey was the first to speak. "Okay V.P., you want to explain that statement you made to me this morning?"

I said, "Come tomorrow, Whiskey, I will no longer be the V.P. of the Houston Chapter, but I'm sure as shit hoping that you'll agree to take that job."

I looked at Clutch and said, "If you don't mind, Brother, why don't you give Whiskey a rundown on what's going on?"

After hearing what Clutch had to say, Whiskey looked at me, stood and hugged me so hard he lifted me off the ground. "Congratulations, Brother! That is just fuckin' awesome news. Clutch, I watched the way you protected Diego when you were the sergeant at arms for the chapter and I have no doubt that you'll serve The Bull very well. I'm fuckin' happy for you too, man. Congratulations, Brother."

"Whiskey," I said. "From the beginning you and I have had a special relationship. I'm not taking anything away from any brother in the club when I say this, but I love you brother. You were with me in San Antonio and you have been at my side from that day until now. After Britt was killed you started doing double duty as road captain and after I became V.P. you started doing triple duty protecting Clutch and me, and still organizing rides like any other road captain would do. Not one fuckin' time have I heard you complain, In fact, it's been just the opposite – you just keep giving more. What about it, Brother? Will you take on a little more and be my V.P.?"

"Jake, I have never said no to anything I've been asked to do in this club. Working with you as V.P. is a bonus that I'm not sure I could've ever expected. Of course, Brother, I'll happily serve as your V.P."

I pushed one shooter his way and one to Clutch and holding the shot glass high, I said, "I Am My Brother's Keeper."

We all finished off the shots and drank down our beer as Diablo and Braid came walking in the room. Diablo immediately approached Clutch, hugging him and congratulating him on his new role in the club.

Turning to me he said, "I'm not a bit surprised to hear of your confirmation as president of the Houston Chapter. You've come far in a short period of time and I have only one thing to say. Men follow men who lead. There is no doubt in my mind that you'll do one hell of a job leading that chapter. If there is anything I or any of my crew can do to help and support you, we're only a phone call away."

He hugged me tight. "Where the fuck are the strippers? I thought we were having a fuckin' party here tonight."

As Diablo was about to say something else, Carmen walked into the room and he stopped short of whatever he was about to say. Walking up to her, he said, "I'm sorry about the baby, Carmen." Then putting his arms around her in a soft hug he added, "What's this rumor I hear, that you and Jake here are planning a trip to Puerto Rico for a honeymoon?"

"It's not a rumor. I asked Jake to marry me, he said yes and we're going to Puerto Rico for our honeymoon."

He looked at me. "She asked you and you said yes?"

"That's exactly the way it went, Brother! Good fortune seems to follow me everywhere!"

"Are we going to have a big wedding party?" he asked.

"Yes, we are. We're getting married May thirteenth and Bullet will send you the details."

"Okay then. Braid, where the fuck are the prospects? We got brothers here having to serve themselves?"

"I was told that Jake and Carmen were having dinner with Antonio and his dad tonight, so I didn't plan for a party. Sorry boss."

"Oh, okay I get it. What time is dinner?"

"We're meeting them at the Stockton at seven," I said.

"Really? You better get going if you are going to make seven in this traffic. Before you take off, the prospects will be at the Shallowater at eight-thirty tomorrow morning to set up and start cooking. I have a prospect picking up the kid and his dad at ten-thirty and we'll be ready to kick things off at straight-up eleven. I heard from Braid that the kid really enjoyed riding with you that morning, so we got about a dozen brothers ready to give him some time on two wheels."

"Yeah, he did enjoy riding, and it sounds like he'll have a big time tomorrow, too."

"Last thing – The Bull wants all the brothers here at ten o'clock tomorrow morning. He'll install both of you in your new roles and then we'll ride on over to the Shallowater as soon as we're finished."

"Sounds like a plan," Clutch said.

"Okay then," he said. "You have keys to the place, so take off and we will lock up, and see you tomorrow."

We were ten minutes late arriving at the Stockton and Antonio and his dad were sitting in the waiting area when we arrived. Whiskey and I rode into the parking lot as Carmen was parking the car. As I was backing my scoot into the space, Antonio came running out with his dad not far behind him.

I hurried to meet him in the middle of the parking lot and he was yelling, "Jake! Jake! Please take me for a ride!"

He stumbled and fell, scraping his left hand, which bled heavily as his dad quickly applied a handkerchief to the wound.

I asked, "Is he okay?"

Ignacio replied, "It's the chemo, I have to make sure the bleeding stops and his hand is clean. He is very susceptible to infection right now."

I looked at Antonio as Carmen and Whiskey stood by watching. "You need to slow down a little, Brother, we have all of tomorrow to ride. You go with your dad and clean your hand and we'll go inside and get a place for us to sit."

Ignacio and Antonio hurried off to the restroom and we went in and were seated. Once again, the people in the restaurant eye fucked the shit out of us as the hostess took us to our table. I just ignored their looks, and demonstrated for the staring table on our left that even a hardened biker could show manners and class as I pulled the chair out for Carmen and waited until she was comfortably seated before I sat down.

I think I shocked even the waiter as I ordered a bottle of St. Henry Shiraz, a pricy red wine, which was great when paired with beef, and a bottle of Chateau Montelena Chardonnay, which was Carmen's favorite and her preferred white when eating seafood.

The waiter looked at Whiskey and asked if there was anything else, and he politely replied, "No thank you."

Ignacio and Antonio were both escorted to our table by the hostess and quickly took their seats. Ignacio looked at me and said, "This is a very expensive restaurant and we have never been to a place like this. Thank you very much."

"It's our pleasure and we hope you enjoy it. How's his hand?"

"It will be fine, it was just scratched and we cleaned it well."

I looked at Antonio and said, "Little brother, say hello to Carmen."

He sheepishly waved his hand but his father said, "Antonio, your manners!"

Antonio then said, "Hi, my name is Antonio and I am Jake's little brother!"

Carmen smiled at the little boy and said, "Hello, Antonio, my name is Carmen and I will soon be Jake's wife."

Then looking at his father, she extended her hand and Ignacio stood and took her hand. "It is a pleasure to meet you and congratulations on your upcoming marriage."

"We will be married in May, and it is our hope that both you and Antonio will come."

"We will be in Houston during that time, so hopefully we can be there."

I said, "If you're going to be in Houston anyway, we can help with getting you to the wedding. Are you visiting family?"

Ignacio looked at Antonio and said, "No, we have no family in Houston but the cancer center in Dallas told us that we need to go to Houston for treatment. They can't give him what he needs here any more. The mission where we live is trying to arrange a place for us to stay near the hospital while he is being treated, so, though we both want to come, much still has to be done before we really know what our circumstances will look like."

"When are you leaving for Houston?" Carmen asked.

"We have to be at the hospital next Wednesday, but transportation is a problem. The mission has no one that can take us."

I said, "Transportation isn't a problem. You can ride with Carmen and Clutch when we leave Sunday and you can stay with us until the mission has found a suitable place for you near the hospital."

Antonio became very excited at hearing the conversation and said, "Really, Jake, we can come stay with you, really?"

"Yes, you can little brother, if that's ok with your father."

Ignacio wiped his eyes and sipped some water before speaking, then said, "My son and I have no one in this world other than the church and it has been difficult to ask for help. Antonio and I are grateful for your kindness." He looked at Antonio. "We will need to go home tonight and pack our things so we can be ready to leave with our friends on Sunday." He then looked back at me. "If possible, we would like say our prayers at Mass on Sunday before we leave. The mission offers an early morning mass and we can be ready to leave by nine thirty, if that is okay."

I said, "We can arrange that, but on one condition."

"Of course. Whatever you ask, my son and I will happily agree to."

"That's fine. Carmen and I would like to attend mass with you. Then afterward, we can leave for Houston together."

Carmen took my hand and spoke to Antonio, "Have you been baptized and received your confirmation?"

"Yes. Last year before I turned nine."

Ignacio asked, "Are you Catholic, Carmen?"

"Yes, I am and I, too, would like to pray with you."

"Of course," Ignacio said. "Mass begins at eight-fifteen in the mission. We will wait for you by the fountain in the courtyard, next to the mission entrance."

The server took our orders and for the next hour we sat and talked of things that were mostly of interest to Antonio. Shortly before we were about to leave, I excused myself and headed to the restroom. Whiskey followed me and as we turned the last corner of tables and started up the hallway toward the restrooms, an older, well-dressed man said, "Excuse me."

I turned to face him, as did Whiskey, and the man said, "My wife and I are seated at the table next to you and we could not help but overhear much of your conversation. May I ask what is wrong with the little boy?"

Whiskey moved forward and was about to step between us, but I put a hand out to him and he stopped.

I said, "He has brain cancer and is not expected to live beyond the year."

The man extended his hand. "My name is Spence Marshall and I would like to help, if I can."

I shook hands with him. "Really? Why would you want to help us, you don't know anything about us."

"May I know your name?"

"My name is Jake."

"Jake, leukemia took our only child when she was just eleven years old and though it has been twenty years from then until now, I still feel the loss. Tell me how I can help."

The man's eyes looked full of pain and I could see that he was being genuine with his words. "The boy's father has sold everything he owns trying to care for his son and they are completely penniless. We're having a benefit for him tomorrow, beginning at eleven in the morning at a place called the Shallowater Saloon. We're hoping to raise enough money to lighten the burden on him and his father, in hope that the boy's quality of life might improve a little with the time he has left."

"I see. Is the event open to the public?"

"Anyone can come and all are welcome, as long as they are coming because they want to help."

"Thank you, Jake. I will be there."

He was about to leave but stopped short, and turned once again to face me. "Jake, I do know a little about your organization, mostly from what I have read in the papers and seen on the news. It appears to me the news people don't have all the facts. It is a real pleasure to meet you, young man."

He turned and walked away and when Whiskey and I returned to the table, he and his wife were gone.

I paid our bill and we all walked to Carmen's car. I kneeled down and hugged Antonio. "Tomorrow is going to be a big day, little brother, and you need to rest well tonight. There will be some friends of mine coming to get you and your father in the morning, so get some sleep and I will see you tomorrow."

He hugged me tight. "Okay, Jake, I'll see you tomorrow." He held up a hand for a high five.

Carmen helped Clutch get in the car and Ignacio and Antonio both got into the back seat. Carmen pulled into traffic, and Whiskey and I pulled out right behind her. We followed them to the mission and they both waved as they were buzzed through the old iron gate, leading into the courtyard. Carmen once again pulled into traffic and headed for the clubhouse, which was only a few blocks away.

She pulled into the parking yard, followed closely by Whiskey and me and after shutting down the engine on his bike, Whiskey walked over, closed and locked the gate for the evening. I unlocked the back door and we all followed Clutch inside, taking a seat at the bar.

Whiskey walked behind the bar and looking at Clutch asked, "What'll you have, Prez?"

"Give me a shooter of Jack and a bud, Whiskey."

I walked in and Whiskey asked, "How about you V.P.? Can I get you something?"

"Yeah, I'll take a Jack and water, Brother."

"Carmen?" Whiskey asked.

"I'm taking a shower and going to bed." She kissed each of us good night and headed off to the bedroom.

Clutch said, "Jake, you're in deep with this kid and I sure as hell hope you know what you're doing."

"Clutch, I haven't got a fuckin' clue what I'm doing, except trying to help out a little."

It was eleven-thirty by now and Clutch said, "I got a text from The Bull while we were at the restaurant. They're checked in at the hotel and will be here between nine forty-five and ten tomorrow morning. Braid told me he'd be here with a couple of sheep and one prospect to take care of cooking breakfast and serving the brothers."

"Who all's coming with The Bull?"

"The national board, the other four Houston area presidents, vice-presidents, and their sergeants at arms."

"Okay."

I finished my drink and went to bed.

Carmen was reading the Bible when I came into the room.

I looked at her and said, "Well, here's a side of you that I didn't know existed."

"Jake, he's such a precious little boy, but he's really frail. I can tell by looking at him, he doesn't have much time."

"His condition looks to have worsened since I saw him last and it's only been a few weeks. Are you thinking your prayers might make a difference?"

"He's received his baptism and was confirmed, so he belongs to God now. It's up to him what happens, but prayers can never hurt."

After a shower, I came back to bed and found Carmen fast asleep. I crawled into bed, tired from the day, and as I lay next to her, my mind drifted back to a time when my mother took me to church, and I remembered the stories I'd learned in Sunday school. Those memories now seemed so distant that I wondered if they were actually my memories or just stories I had heard repeated through the years. It really didn't matter because I found comfort in knowing that Carmen had prayed. I added a prayer of my own for this little boy and just hoped it would do some good.

The alarm went off at seven o'clock sharp and I could smell bacon frying. I turned over to put my arms around Carmen but she wasn't there. I got dressed and headed into the kitchen and there she was, cooking.

"Carmen, Diablo told us last night that he had women coming to cook."

She brought me a cup of coffee. "You need to remember, as long as I'm here, I'll be the only woman cooking your breakfast."

I set my coffee down, kissed her and held her tightly. "I love you, woman."

She and I finished breakfast together and left the dishes in the sink. "I cooked your breakfast, but I have no problem leaving the dishes for the other women to clean." She grinned as she picked up her purse. "I'm leaving for the Shallowater," she said as she kissed me goodbye.

She hadn't been gone five minutes before Whiskey came walking in. "I smell food cooking"

"Yeah, Carmen cooked for us this morning."

"You got a good woman there, Jake."

Clutch came in the room, poured himself a cup of coffee, and was about to sit down when the quiet of the morning was interrupted by the sound of motorcycles. We walked out the back door just as The Bull, along with his board officers and the balance of the group, all came riding in. It was a clear March morning about fifty degrees and everyone came shaking hands and hugging. A car drove up with the two women that had volunteered to cook and the prospect who hurriedly ushered them in to the kitchen. Breakfast was cooked and over with by ten o'clock, and as the women were busy cleaning things up, Diablo opened the chapel and invited The Bull and his board to the table. Clutch and I, along with the rest, all followed. Braid posted the prospect outside the door, told him there were to be NO interruptions, and closed and locked the chapel doors.

The Bull opened the meeting by saying, "Clutch, you've been in the club for over ten years and you've served the Los Patrons with a great deal of honor and at a good deal of personal sacrifice. It's time for you to come home. I'm very happy to present you with this sergeant at arms patch and I am equally happy to have you at my side. I have asked each Texas chapter to furnish a prospect to assist with moving you to Corpus Christi and whatever costs you incur will be absorbed by your brothers."

With that, he stood and walked over to Clutch, hugged him tight and handed him his patch.

Looking at me he said, "Jake, in all of the years since becoming a brother of the Los Patrons, I have never seen a brother rise to the position of president so quickly. I've talked to your brothers in Houston and to other brothers of yours inside and outside of Texas and we all agree. There's no other brother better suited for the job than you."

He handed me the patch. "Who is your choice for V.P.?"

I called Whiskey to the front. "My brother Whiskey will serve as V.P."

The Bull handed him his V.P. patch. "Congratulations, Whiskey!"

All three of us spent the next thirty minutes receiving congratulations from everyone there, drinking a quick beer, and hurriedly sewing on our new patches. Finally, The Bull said, "I want to meet this young man we're raising money for."

Clutch got a ride with the prospect who had brought his car just for that very purpose, and the rest of us, on our scoots, were barreling down the highway at ninety miles an hour, peg to peg and fender to fender, headed for the Shallowater Saloon.

Chapter Twenty

A LITTLE BOY'S DAY IN THE SUN

It took about twenty minutes for us to make the trip to the Shallowater and there was quite a crowd already there. Parking had been reserved for The Bull and those riding with him, so we simply followed the instructions from the prospect who was directing traffic on where to park our scoots. There were other prospects attending to the cookers and they were churning out barbecue plates by the dozen. The local meat market had provided ten precooked briskets that had been chopped into small pieces just the right size for sandwiches and the local grocer had provided the beans and condiments along with the plates, forks, and spoons and a couple of cases of paper towels. The owner of the Shallowater was furnishing soft drinks and tea at no charge and was donating the profits from the beer sales for the day. From the looks of the crowd it appeared that today was going to be a good day for Antonio. Carmen was standing underneath the cook tent helping serve when I arrived, and as I walked toward her, the Dallas prospect escorted the two women from the clubhouse to the tent where they immediately took her place.

She walked up to me and said, "I see you have a new patch. Congratulations!"

"You know what, Carmen? I might just want to wear my cut to bed tonight and see just how presidential I can be. How do you feel about that?"

"Oh, you've heard that song, Jake!"

"Yeah? What song is that, Carmen?"

"Oh, Jake, it goes like this. Bad boy, bad boy, whatcha gonna do, whatcha gonna do when I *cum* for you." She put two fingers to her lips, then pressed them to mine, then glanced away saying, "The prospect just drove up with Antonio and his dad."

"Carmen, Antonio will need a lot of attention between the bike runs. Please keep an eye on him and make sure he doesn't get too tired. His father isn't real sure how to handle himself with all the different brothers."

"Okay, Jake. I'll keep a close eye on him."

The Bull walked up while we were talking. "Carmen, I wanted to congratulate you personally on your engagement to Jake. He's going to make a fine husband and if he doesn't, you just let me know and I'll straighten him out. When is the wedding?"

"It's May thirteenth, Bull, and we're both hoping that you and Carrie will come and help us celebrate."

Placing his hand on my shoulder he said, "Don't worry, we won't be missing that party." He gave Carmen a soft hug then looked at me. "C'mon, Jake, let's go meet your young Antonio."

Antonio and his father were standing in the shade of the Shallowater's porch when we walked up. Antonio immediately ran to me asking, "Are you going to take me for a ride, Jake?"

"I sure am, little brother, but first I want you to meet my brother, Bull Taylor."

The Bull bent to a knee and put his hand out to the little boy. Antonio immediately took his hand, shook it for all he was worth. "My name is Antonio and I am Jake's little brother. He's going to take me for lots of rides on his motorcycle today."

"Well, good morning, Antonio, my name is Bull Taylor. Jake has told me that you are nine years old and already a man."

"Yes, I am and I'm going to go back with Jake and live at his house for a while. It's going to be fun."

The Bull looked at Crewman, his national treasurer, and motioned for him to hand him the bag he was holding. He returned his attention to Antonio. "Antonio, Jake told me that you were a real brave young man and I was wondering if you would let me take you on your first motorcycle ride of the day."

Antonio looked up at me as though to ask for permission and I said, "Go ahead, little brother, it'll be fun to ride with Bull."

Antonio said, "Okay, are we going far?"

"We're going to where the road meets up with the lake and then we will get an ice cream at the store before coming back."

The offer of ice cream seamed to clinch the deal and Antonio was for sure ready to go then.

The Bull said, "Before we can leave, I need you to put this on so you can be safe."

Out of that bag The Bull pulled out a black helmet that had Antonio's name painted on it, along with the words, Los Patrons Supporter. The El Patron was painted in the center without the rockers. For Antonio, today was becoming Christmas in March.

The Bull helped that little guy get his helmet on and then said, "Okay, I have something else for you to try on and I hope it fits."

He pulled out a full-sleeved leather jacket that had been patched like every brother's there except for two things. The top rocker read, Los Patrons Supporter and the bottom rocker read, World. Antonio hurried to take his jacket off and put the leather one on and it fit perfectly.

The Bull looked at Antonio. "Now let's get our picture taken together."

By now it was about all anyone could do to keep their eyes dry. I saw brothers of mine that had earned many, many battle scars from various fights and wrecks, with their faces distorted from the emotion they were feeling observing this exchange.

Carmen had her cell phone out and had snapped a dozen or more pictures before The Bull finally said, "How about it, Antonio, are you ready to ride?"

That little boy was so happy. The Bull took him on at least a dozen rides that day and there were so many brothers lining up to take him on a ride that by three o'clock, he was completely exhausted. Carmen was preparing to take him and his father back to the mission when a stretch Cadillac pulled onto the property, and of course every person there saw it and stopped to see what was going on. Out of that car stepped the man and his wife from the night before at the restaurant.

The man walked up to me and extended his hand saying, "I would have been here sooner but my morning was very busy."

I said, "Spence, right?"

"That's right."

"Well, you're here now and thank you for coming."

I introduced him to The Bull and a few others and as Antonio was standing close by, I said, "Little brother, before you leave, come meet another friend of mine."

Antonio and his father walked over. "This is Spence and he has come to wish you a safe trip to Houston."

Spence leaned over and shook Antonio's hand. "It is my pleasure to meet you, young man." Then looking up at Ignacio, he said, "Are you Antonio's father?"

"Yes, I am. My name is Ignacio and thank you for coming."

Spence handed an envelope to Ignacio and said, "There is a credit card in the envelope that is for your use while you are staying in Houston. Also in the envelope is a hotel reservation confirmation at the Princeton Hotel across the street from the Cancer Center. Your reservation is open-ended and the credit card is for your use in settling the charges for your stay. Please use the card for whatever else you may need while you are there. When you check out of the hotel, the card will be kept at check-out and returned to me, but until that time you should not be concerned for anything."

Ignacio's emotions overtook him as he held the envelope tightly. After a moment, he looked up at Spence. "Your kindness will never be forgotten and I will remember you every day in my prayers, thank you."

Looking back at me, Spence said, "This is my wife, Lilian."

I shook her hand. "My name is Jake Coleman and it's nice to meet you. Thank you for coming. What you're doing is very kind."

"Mr. Coleman, we received an insurance settlement when our daughter passed away that Spence and I used in the creation of a trust. We have been waiting for the right opportunity to help some young person who might be in need of a miracle, and we have decided to use that trust for your Antonio." Handing me an envelope, she said, "When he is checked into the hospital, please register him using the enclosed information. The instructions in the envelope will walk you through what to do. There is a medical team assigned to that trust who will immediately take responsibility for Antonio's care and believe me, Mr. Coleman, that team is the best money can buy."

She reached up and kissed me on the cheek and then bent down and kissed Antonio on his forehead and hugged Ignacio. Then both of them disappeared back inside the stretch. Just as quickly as this couple had come, they were gone.

Shock was the only word that could be used to describe the events of the day. Carmen took Ignacio and Antonio back to the mission, returning about an hour later.

She walked up to me and said, "I want to have a baby, Jake."

I put my arms around her and I held her tightly to me.

The event went on until late in the evening and between the food, the silent auction, the 50/50 and the sale of the Harley Panhead, we raised $70,000 in cash. That didn't include the generosity of Spence and Lilian and there was no way to put a value on that. In a world so filled with extremes, it felt great to do something entirely selfless and I couldn't wait for tomorrow and the trip home.

Life for Antonio and life for me seemed to just now be getting under way.

Chapter Twenty-One

A LONG TRIP HOME

Before leaving the Shallowater the night before, we decided that Whiskey, Clutch, Cappie, and Patch would all go with Carmen and me to the mission. There was no reason for anyone else that had traveled to Dallas to wait on us. They all left en route to their various home cities while the six of us headed for the mission. We arrived at seven-thirty, and as expected, the gate to the courtyard was standing wide open. As promised, Antonio and Ignacio were waiting for us at the fountain. Antonio was not very energetic; he was pale and appeared tired. Ignacio explained that the activities of the previous day had been very taxing on him, but hopefully the trip back to Houston might give him the additional time for rest he needed. For now, we were here to attend Sunday morning mass, and although I had heard a few things about the Catholic faith, I really had no idea what to expect. Clutch and the others decided they would wait for us in the parking lot, so I left my cut and my gun with Whiskey. Ignacio and Antonio entered the old church, followed by Carmen and me. They all kneeled as they entered the pew and crossed themselves before taking a seat. We were each given a service guide that was to help us follow the order of worship, but the guide was written in Spanish and I couldn't read any of it.

Carmen whispered, "Don't worry, just follow my lead and I'll explain everything to you later. Oh, Jake, you must be Catholic to receive communion, so when we leave the pew you'll need to remain seated until we return."

I sat back, thumbed through the papers in the pew, stood when everyone else stood, knelt when they knelt, and I hummed to the music. Before I knew it, the entire church was moving to receive communion and I sat waiting in our pew. Within just a few moments, the kneeling rails were once again lowered and we were all on our knees again. I took this quiet time to say a prayer of my own that Antonio might indeed receive a miracle, and then we all stood for the benediction and dismissal.

Ignacio said, "Jake, you have done so much for Antonio and me and we can never repay you, but there is something I would like to give you. You gave my son your pendant and he never takes it off. Now, I would like to give you one in return." He took the necklace from around his neck. "This pendant represents Saint Michael, the Archangel of God. I pray that he will protect you from all the evil in the world and keep you safe." With that he put it in my hand. "Please wear it. It will protect you."

He smiled as I placed the necklace around my neck, then he helped Antonio make his way through the crowd. As we were leaving, the mission priest, Father Jose, came and blessed Antonio and Ignacio, offering his blessing to Carmen, but she said, "Father, I haven't been to confession in over a year."

"Daughter, a lifetime with us is but a moment in time with God. Take a moment to confess, then I will bless you."

She looked at me and I said, "Go, Carmen, we're not in a big hurry."

She gave me a quick kiss, then followed the priest out of sight. The rest of us made our way to the parking lot. Clutch opened the door to the car for Ignacio and Antonio and started it so they could have some heat. The rest of us waited until Carmen came running through the gate with a huge smile on her face.

I asked, "Did he bless you, Carmen?"

"Yes, he did and I love you, Jake." Getting into the car she said, "Antonio will need to eat lunch, so can we stop in Buffalo?"

"Buffalo is perfect," I said.

I looked at Whiskey and the prospects. "Being Sunday, traffic will be light, so let's keep it tight at eighty miles an hour. I want to get home."

We left the mission parking lot at ten o'clock straight up and were in Buffalo eating lunch at eleven forty-five. Antonio looked much better than he did earlier, having slept the entire way. Carmen commented on the sun coming out and the temperature warming, as it was now sixty-one degrees.

"That's right," Clutch said. "We'll have good weather until about three-thirty and if we get our asses moving, we'll be almost home by then."

"Okay," I said, "Let's gas up and go."

Carmen was just getting ready to get in the car when she closed the door and walked over to my motorcycle. She kissed me tenderly and said, "I love you and I'll see you at home."

M.C.

Returning to the car, Carmen followed Jake and the others onto Interstate - 45 South and immediately encountered road construction. Slow speed and crowded traffic conditions in a construction zone is never a good way to travel on motorcycles and Carmen felt tense as she watched Jake and the others maneuver in and out the areas where the flag men directed the traffic. It took some time for everyone to clear the work zones and she felt relieved to see traffic moving ahead at a safer speed. Looking at her watch, she saw it was already after four o'clock and Antonio was getting restless. "Who wants to play I spy?" she asked.

"I do, I do!" Antonio said with excitement.

She looked over at Clutch and asked, "Will you play?"

"Sure I will. It's been years since I've played, but I'll bet I beat you all."

Carmen said, "Okay, Antonio, you're first."

"I spy something green."

They all kept guessing wrong until they finally gave up, and he laughed, saying, "It's the grass. C'mon, you guys can do better than that."

Next he said, "I spy something black," which turned out to be Carmen's hair.

He was about to spy something else when Carmen said, "Just a minute Antonio! Clutch, look, they're slowing down and it looks like Jake is talking to someone in that truck next to him."

Carmen had no more gotten those words out of her mouth when shots were fired from the window of the truck and Jake went down. Whiskey and Cappie both swerved to miss him but Patch ran into his motorcycle as it was tumbling down the road.

"Oh my God! " Carmen yelled. "They shot him."

Antonio yelled, "Jake, Jake!" and started crying hysterically.

Ignacio tried to calm Antonio while Carmen pulled off the road. Traffic swerved in the attempt to miss the wreckage with Patch lying in the center of the highway. Jake and his bike were both off the highway and Carmen was frantic. Whiskey and Cappie attended to Patch as Carmen bailed out of the car and took off into the deepest part of the center median, which was completely overgrown with brush. Clutch hobbled over to Whiskey, and yelled, "I've got him, Whiskey, go help Carmen find Jake!"

𝔐.ℭ.

Daylight was fading and the pain was crippling. I couldn't have been there more than a couple of minutes, but the smell of blood mixed with gasoline left me wanting to puke. My right shoulder was blown to hell, my left leg was broken and it was hard to move without hurting.

I can't believe it, that mother fucker shot me! He watched me go down, and now, here I am, lying in this ditch buried in a twisted heap of spokes, chrome and blood. Oh, man, there is so much blood and I'm so light-headed. I gotta find a way to get moving or I'm going to fuckin' bleed out, right here!

My head was swimming so much, it was hard to tell if I was dreaming, but I swear, I thought I could hear Carmen yelling my name. *There it is again, I'm sure of it.* I tried to yell out, but my bike had me pinned and I couldn't manage enough air to yell anything. *Okay,* I thought, *they'll find me soon enough.*

Realizing I was close to passing out, I decided to fire a round from my gun, if I could reach it. It was lying just off to my left and appeared to be out of my reach, so I tried to stretch, but it was no good, it was just too far. There were a couple of spokes from the wheel lying close so I grabbed one, thinking I might be able to hook the gun. Sure enough, it gave me the reach I needed to drag that .45 over to me. As I picked it up, I thought, *I owe this round to you, Britt,* and removing the safety, I fired a single round straight up into the air.

Then everything went dark.

M.C.

By now, there were several cars and trucks stopped, assisting Clutch with Patch. Patch was in really bad shape and the State Troopers had just arrived. Carmen, Whiskey and Cappie were all in the center median looking for Jake when they heard the gunshot. Cappie yelled, "OVER HERE! I FOUND HIM, HE'S OVER HERE!"

Jake's bike had tumbled down the slope and was lying on top of him in a part of the median that was overgrown with bush and weeds. Whiskey was yelling, "Where are you? I can't see shit down here."

Carmen got there before Whiskey and saw Jake lying there. She started crying, and asked, "Is he dead, Cappie? Is he?"

"No, I don't think so, Carmen, but we have to get him some help fast or he will be. Stay here with him while I get to the roadside. I'll get some help and be back."

Cappie started up the side of the median and ran into Whiskey. "He's down there, Whiskey, and Carmen's with him. He's in bad shape, man, and I'm headed up for help."

"GO!" Whiskey said. "I'll go see what I can do to help him!"

Cappie reached the roadside and immediately called out to one of the DPS officers on the scene, "I have a man down in the ditch with his motorcycle on top of him. He's all broken up and bleeding badly, I need help!"

The officer ran to him. "Where is he?"

"He's down there but he's tangled up in all that brush. I have no idea how we're gonna get him out of there."

Looking around, the officer spotted a wrecker driver who had just shown up at the scene and told him to park his truck facing the median. Pointing to Cappie he said, "This man and I are headed down there to clear those bushes away from the wreck and I need your winch activated to help pull that stuff up and get it out of our way, got it?"

"I got it," he said.

"When the paramedics arrive you tell them we have a man in the median with a motorcycle on top of him and we need them down there immediately."

"What about that guy up on the road?" he asked.

"He's dead," the officer said. "Send the paramedics to me."

Cappie's heart sank as he heard those words because he and Patch had been friends for many years, but Jake was still alive and he was going to do all he could to help keep him alive.

The officer looked at Cappie. "Take the hook from that winch and follow me down." He called out to the wrecker driver, "When I give the signal, you activate that wench and don't stop unless I tell you."

The wrecker driver said, "Wait a minute."

He quickly ran to his tool box and came back with a hand axe and small bow saw. "You'll need these if you're going to clear away that brush."

The officer took the tools and started down the median, followed by Cappie pulling the winch cable. As soon as the cop reached the bottom, he saw Whiskey who was busy trying to clear away the bush entangled in the wreck. The officer handed him the hand axe. "Use this."

The officer moved forward toward Carmen who was dug in behind Jake, praying. She had taken off her blouse and was using it to stop the bleeding in Jake's shoulder. By now, she looked as though she might be injured from all the blood that was on her.

The officer asked, "Are you okay, ma'am?"

"I'm not hurt."

Looking at Jake's gun, the officer asked, "Ma'am, are you comfortable handing me that gun?"

She picked up the gun by the barrel and handed it to the officer. "Please don't let him die."

He put the gun in his back pocket and looked at her with compassion. "Ma'am, my name is Jim Mallory and I'm going to do everything I can to keep him alive, but I need your help."

"Tell me what to do."

"I can only see a part of his body from here. Aside from his shoulder, where is the rest of this blood coming from?"

"His left leg is broken. The bone has come through the skin below his knee and again just above his ankle. I used part of my blouse to make a tourniquet for his leg. He is still bleeding, but not as bad as he was."

"Okay, can you see any other places where he might be injured?"

"No."

"Okay, you're doing great. Try to cover his face and yours too as I cut some of these bushes away."

Between the bow saw and the hand axe, most of the brush was cut loose before Cappie got down with the winch. They bundled the brush using the cable and signaled for the wrecker driver to engage the winch. As the brush was moving up the hill, the Coal Hill Volunteer Fire Department and ambulance along with two more DPS units arrived. The driver told the paramedics exactly what the DPS officer had instructed and down the median they went. By now, another ambulance had arrived along with the county coroner who pronounced Patch dead at the scene. The Paramedics radioed the fire chief, who was also on the scene, requesting a life flight knowing that Jake's injuries were so severe that he would not survive transport by ambulance. The DPS officer who helped clear the brush away along with help from Whiskey assisted Carmen back to the highway.

Carmen looked at Clutch. "Can you drive?"

"I can drive, Carmen, what do you need me to do?"

"I'm going to ride with Whiskey to wherever they take Jake and I need you to take Antonio and his father to our house and get them settled in. I'll call you as soon as I know where they're taking him and then you need to bring my briefcase out of my office to me. It has the power of attorney in it, and Clutch, you're the only one who can authorize treatment, so PLEASE HURRY."

He quickly hobbled off to the car and tried to leave, but was stopped by the officers managing the scene. Carmen had to explain the situation before he was allowed to leave and after a couple of minutes, they were gone. As she watched the firemen remove Jake from the wreck, Whiskey got a shirt and his rain gear out of his saddlebag. "I know this stuff stinks, Carmen, but you're going to have to stay warm on the ride into Houston."

She looked up at him with her face a mess with tear-streaked mascara and blood. "Whiskey, if you know how to pray, please pray. I'm so afraid we'll lose him."

The blades from the helicopter chopped the air as the Life Flight approached the accident, landing on the highway about a hundred feet away. Carmen asked the paramedic where they were taking Jake and he said, "To the trauma unit at Houston Memorial, just off I-610 and Fannin."

Carmen called Clutch and told him where they were taking him then quickly handed the phone to Whiskey. By this time, Jake had been secured into the rescue basket and had been carried up the median. Carmen ran to his side, but the paramedics rushed him past her as he was placed inside the helicopter. Within only a couple of minutes, the helicopter was gone.

The officer approached Carmen. "I am sorry, ma'am, but I have to take a report. You appear to be the one closest to... I'm sorry, but I don't know his name."

"His name is Jake Coleman."

"What is your name, ma'am?"

"My name is Carmen Santiago and he is my fiancé."

"May I call you Carmen?"

"Officer Mallory, I don't mean to sound unappreciative, you've been very kind, but you can call me whatever the fuck you want to as long as we get moving. Jake is already on his way to the hospital!"

"I'm sorry ma'am, but I have to collect the required information for the report, here or there, either way, I have to collect the information. How are you getting to the hospital?"

"I'm riding on the back of his motorcycle," she said, pointing to Whiskey.

"Dressed like that? No, ma'am you're not."

He opened the back door to his car. "If you will kindly get in, please, I'll take you to the hospital." Looking at Whiskey he asked, "Do you know the way?"

"We'll follow you," Whiskey replied.

It took almost an hour to make the fifty-mile trip to the hospital. Riding in the officer's duty vehicle allowed Carmen time to call Clutch and make sure that Antonio and Ignacio were both okay and that he had found the briefcase. Once at the hospital, Mallory collected the critical information relating to Jake that was necessary for Carmen to gain access to him. HIPAA regulations governing the privacy of the patient are very strict and this officer helped gain access that would have otherwise taken half the night. Carmen went to the restroom to clean up while Whiskey went to the vending machine and purchased coffee. He returned to find the officer and Carmen talking to the surgeon called in by the emergency room doctor.

"My name is Dr. Williamson and I will be operating on Mr. Coleman. Are you his wife?" he asked Carmen.

"I'm his fiancée."

"Mr. Coleman was shot in the right shoulder and the bullet is lodged in the muscle tissue surrounding the clavicle. The clavicle itself is broken, but will be repaired using, in lay terms, a collar-bone pin. With therapy and some time, he will regain the full use of his arm. His left leg presents a different problem. Mr. Coleman suffered a previous injury to that leg and a titanium rod was used in its repair."

Whiskey said, "Yeah, his leg was broken when he was in the army and they fixed it over in Germany."

"I see. Well, that rod splintered the tibia, and in addition to the tibia, his foot was crushed in the accident. I am sorry to break this news to you, but we will not able to save the leg. It will require amputation below the knee."

Appearing faint, Carmen reached for Whiskey and the doctor quickly moved to have her seated. "Ms. Santiago, since you are not married to Mr. Coleman, we can't accept your authorization to perform such a surgery. We are giving him whole blood, which has stabilized him, but we need to move quickly to remove the leg or his condition will worsen."

Carmen stood. "There is someone on the way who holds power of attorney over Jake's very soul. He will be able to authorize whatever procedure is required."

The doctor handed her a card with an extension number on it. "As soon as that person arrives, call this number. One of the staff will meet you in the lobby to copy the document and secure the required signatures on all of the releases."

Before leaving he said, "If we don't have that authorization soon, he could lose his entire leg."

The DPS officer was becoming more insistent on gathering the required information for his report and Carmen was beginning to unravel. Whiskey approached the officer. "Look man, she was in the car and didn't see shit. I was riding on his left and saw everything."

While Carmen worked to reach Clutch, Whiskey gave the officer what information he had. "Unfortunately, it happened very quickly and I can't tell you if it was a white man or a black man driving that truck. For all I fuckin' know, it might have been some fuckin' gorilla shooting that gun. Look man, we can use your help with one thing, if you're willing."

"How can I help?"

"Jake has a brother that's a deputy for the Fort Bend County Sheriff's office. His name is Nathan Pearsall. It would be a huge help to us if you could reach out to him and let him know what's happened."

Mallory agreed to get in touch with Nate then Whiskey spent the next twenty minutes giving him all the details surrounding the shooting that he could, that is, except for one. He reserved the truth regarding the identity of the shooter and would only give that to Clutch. It would be up to Clutch what he did with the information.

Jake had been moved from the emergency room to the surgical floor and was actively being prepped when Clutch stepped off the elevator and hobbled into the waiting room.

Carmen said, "Thank God, Clutch, I've been calling you. Why haven't you answered the phone?"

"I'm sorry, Carmen, but the battery died and I didn't have a charger."

He handed her the briefcase. "It took an act of Congress to get anyone here to tell me a damn thing. I finally showed them the Power of Attorney with his name on it and they told me where you were."

Carmen looked at Clutch with tears in her eyes. "They're preparing to amputate his leg."

"Oh, fuck. Where's Whiskey?"

"He just went to the emergency room to see about Cappie. He's been down there waiting for you. I'm surprised you missed him." Walking over to the phone, she dialed the number from the card the surgeon had given her and returned to her seat.

The nurse came right out with a clipboard. "Who will be authorizing the surgery?"

"I will," Clutch said.

"I need to see your identification and the Power of Attorney."

Clutch handed her his driver's license and the Power of Attorney. She looked at the information. "I need to copy the documents. I'll be right back."

While the nurse was busy copying the documents, Carmen called Whiskey to let him know that Clutch was with her.

The nurse returned, handed Clutch his license, and had him sign the required authorizations. As he signed "Frank Cannon," to the different pages, he thought, *Wow, I haven't used that name in so long, it seems almost foreign to me.*

Taking the signed documents from Clutch, the nurse said, "The surgery will be completed in two parts. First, because of the severity of his leg injury and the risk to Mr. Coleman by waiting, the surgeon will complete the amputation first. Once the amputation has been completed, and if at that time Mr. Coleman's vitals are strong, the surgeon will repair the shoulder. You should expect that he will be in surgery between four to six hours and I will be coming out periodically to give you updates on his condition."

The nurse looked at Carmen. "I know you are all very worried and I want to assure you that Dr. Williamson is one of the most sought-after orthopedic surgeons in the country. Mr. Coleman is in very capable hands."

Whiskey walked out of the elevator as the nurse disappeared behind the surgical doors. Walking up to Clutch he said, "I don't know how we missed you, Brother, but I sure am glad you're here. What's going on?"

"I just signed off on having his leg cut off."

Carmen looked at Whiskey. "Please tell me you know who did this."

Whiskey helped Clutch take a seat next to Carmen as he pulled his chair up close. "Carmen, I saw him clearly and I promise you, that mother fucker is going to experience the absolute worst kind of pain before we let him die."

Carmen's reaction to Whiskey's statement was quick. "Tell me who the son of a bitch is."

The expression on Clutch's face when Whiskey revealed his name was one of pure fury. "I need to borrow your phone, Whiskey, it's time to call The Bull."

M.C.

The cell phone rang only a couple of times before Samantha answered. "I get a call from you on Sunday? Wow, I am feeling privileged, Nate."

"Sam, I just got a phone call from the DPS. Jake was shot on his way back from a club benefit in Dallas. He's been transported to Houston Memorial over on Fannin."

"Shot! Oh my God, Nathan. Why? What happened?"

"All I know is he was on the motorcycle at the time and there was a crash. I don't have any more details than that, except that he's in surgery. I'm on my way to pick you up and I'll be there in ten minutes."

"Ok, Nate, I'll be watching for you."

M.C.

Clutch returned and handed the phone back to Whiskey. He looked at Cappie. "Prospect, I'm sorry about Patch. I know the two of you were tight."

Carmen walked over to Cappie and said, "I liked Patch, Cappie. I'm so sorry, I should have said something earlier."

Cappie said, "Patch knew the risks and he died doing what he loved. I'm gonna miss him for sure, but right now I'm trying to keep focused on the here and now."

Carmen gave him a hug and was about to say something when Whiskey's phone started ringing. He handed it to Clutch and said, "It's The Bull."

"Bull," Clutch said into the phone. "I assume you've listened to my message."

"Yeah, I got it. How's Jake?"

"He's in surgery. The surgeon said it will be four to six hours and he's been back there now for almost two. They promised us updates, so we should be hearing something soon."

"Okay. Nomad Whistler is on his way to get the details and I'll be turning around and heading to Houston as soon as I gas up. I'm in Victoria, so it'll be about two hours before I get there."

They both knew that neither of them could say anything on their cell phones, because cell phones were often tapped. Details about the shooting would have to wait until Whistler arrived.

It took about forty-five minutes for Nate and Sam to arrive at the hospital. The DPS officer had given them the patient code and the information desk told them exactly where to go. Sam was the first to see Carmen and went straight to her and consoled her as she cried.

Nate went to Clutch and asked, "Do we know anything yet?"

"Not much," Clutch said. "A nurse came out about twenty minutes ago and told us that Jake was doing well and the surgery was progressing. I guess there really isn't much they can tell us until they're finished."

"What happened, Clutch?"

"You need to ask Whiskey. He was riding next to Jake when it happened."

"Where is he?"

"He'll be back in a few minutes, he and one of our Nomad brothers are downstairs making some phone calls, you know, making sure that Jake's brothers know what happened."

"Nomad, huh? Those guys take care of your security issues, don't they?"

Clutch just looked at him. "Look, man, you're here because Whiskey made the decision to have you notified. He did that because it's your brother having his leg chopped off. He didn't want you here, and neither do I, in any kind of official capacity. Now someone shot your brother, my brother, and a brother of the Los Patrons. We neither need nor want your help in locating the son of a bitch and what happens after we find him, is no one's business but ours."

"I get it, Clutch and you're right, he's my brother and that's why I'm here. I just wanted to say thanks for giving the DPS my phone number. I really do appreciate it."

"Give your thanks to Whiskey, he's the reason you're here."

"Okay." Nate got up from the chair and walked over and sat with Sam and Carmen.

"Whiskey," Whistler said. "You should have killed that mother fucker while you were at his house."

"I wish I had. We thought we would rough him up a bit and he would disappear. Whistler, we have seven brothers that used to fly Warrior patches in our crew and we were trying to ensure they saw our actions as being just."

"Whose decision was it to leave that fucker alive?"

"Brother, I gotta defer the answer to that question to Clutch."

By now, the surgical floor was full of patches as brothers from every Houston chapter were showing up to check on Jake. There were so many brothers there that the hospital security began limiting the numbers allowed in the waiting room.

It had been four hours when the nurse came out and spoke with Carmen. "The amputation is finished and Mr. Coleman's vitals are strong. Dr. Williamson has moved forward with the repair of his shoulder." Smiling she said, "We should be finished within the next two hours."

Carmen shuddered at the thought that Jake had lost most of his left leg. She wondered how he would react to that news. Her thoughts were interrupted as The Bull entered the room, followed by Clutch. She watched as he walked toward her and once again, her emotions rose to the surface as she stood to accept his embrace.

"Carmen," he said as he held her close, "Jake is a strong man and he needs you to be strong." He pulled back and looked at her. "So cry now and cry all you need to, but if you appear fearful when he first sees you, he'll become fearful. Be strong and he'll be strong. And remember this, we're your family and we'll be there to support you both for however long his recovery takes."

Kissing her on the forehead, he motioned to Clutch and they both got on the elevator, on their way to the first floor where Whiskey and Whistler were waiting.

It was easy to see The Bull wanted answers as he looked at Whiskey and Whistler. "Let's go outside."

They made their way to the parking lot where the bikes were parked and as The Bull lit a cigarette, he asked. "I thought we dealt with Buck. Would someone like to explain to me, how the fuck this son of a bitch was able to shoot one of my presidents, almost killing him?"

He looked at Whiskey and Clutch. "I want a mother fuckin' answer!"

Clutch said, "I instructed the brothers to beat him down but to leave him alive."

The Bull looked hard at Clutch. "You gotta be shitting me, man!"

Looking at Whistler, The Bull said, "Get what you need from Whiskey and go finish the mother fucker. I want him dead before Jake comes out of recovery."

Whiskey gave Whistler Buck's address and told him where he worked. "Take Gus with you. He and Buck were from the same Warrior chapter and he's well familiar with Buck's routine."

Within just a few minutes, Whistler and Gus along with the three other Nomads that followed The Bull back to Houston were on their bikes and gone. It took several hours for the group to locate Buck because he hadn't gone home and he hadn't gone to work. Instead, they found his truck parked in front of a strip joint located down on Montrose. Gus said that Buck went there sometimes because he had a thing for some old skank that danced there, and sure enough that's where they found him.

The plan was simple. Gus would go in the front door with the expectation that Buck would see him and run. The Nomads split ranks with two waiting at the back door and two at the truck. As expected, Buck took off as soon as he saw Gus and ran out the back door, only to find Nomad Slicer and Nomad Whistler waiting. Whistler hit Buck in the mid-section with a piece of rebar he found half-buried in the dirt, and as Buck fell to a knee, he hit him again across the back of his head. Another four or five blows left his head bloody and grossly misshaped. Slicer rolled him over onto his back and the back of his head flattened out, resembling a flat tire on some highway. His eyes were fixed and he was bleeding from his nose, ears, and mouth. He was obviously dead, so they threw his body and the rebar into the dumpster. The task of finding Buck had taken a while, but killing him hadn't. There was a problem though, Whistler was a mess, covered with Buck's blood, and there was no way they could go back to the hospital in that condition.

Gus said, "My house is thirty minutes from here. You and I are about the same size and I've got clothes you can change into. My ole' lady can wash your stuff and you can pick it up later." They made their way to Gus's house, giving Whistler the chance to clean up before returning to the hospital.

It was seven-thirty in the morning and the sun was just coming up as Whistler and the others walked back into the hospital.

Cappie was in the waiting area and stood as they came walking in.

He looked at Whistler. "The Bull and the others are in the cafeteria."

"How's Jake?" Gus asked.

"He had some difficulty with recovery, but he's okay now. They've put him in the ICU for the next few hours as a precaution, but as I understand it, he'll be moved to a private room before the end of the day."

"Were you waiting down here for us, Prospect?" Whistler asked.

"Yeah, The Bull wanted to make sure you knew where to go when you got back."

"Have you eaten?" he asked.

"Not yet," Cappie said.

Whistler put his arm around Cappie. "I'm sorry to hear about Patch, Cappie. I didn't know him but I'm told he was one hell of a good man."

"Yes, he was."

"C'mon, let's get some breakfast."

The men walked into the cafeteria and The Bull stood as Whistler approached him. The two men hugged and spoke briefly before The Bull sat back down.

Looking at Carmen and the others seated with him, The Bull took a sip of his coffee, and said, **"God Forgives, Patrons Repay."**

I am an Outlaw,
Restrained by Morals
and Conviction,
Governed by Conscience,
Motivated by Will!

Glossary Of Terms

1%er – 99% of the motorcycle community live within the law & 1% are considered lawless/outlaw

3 Piece Patch – Three patches made up of a top rocker, center patch and lower rocker, normally signifies an outlaw club

Blow – Cocaine

Cage – Car or truck

Cager – People driving a car or truck

Chapel – The private meeting room within the clubhouse where church is held

Church – Chapter meeting

Cut – Club vest with club patches (also known as colors)

DPS - Department of Public Safety

Green Lighting – Club leadership approval for a beat-down or a killing.

Hang Around – A friend of the club or known associate

Ink-Tattoo

Line – A measure of cocaine used for snorting

LPOL – Loyal Patron Ole' Lady

Nomad – A wanderer with no specific chapter to call home. Club enforcer used for internal issues and external security

Ole' Lady – Patch member's regular girlfriend or wife

Out in Bad – A member kicked out of the club

Out in Good – A retired member

Patched Brother – A patched member within a specific chapter of a club

Patch-Over – When the dominant club forces an inferior or smaller club into submission, submitting members can be allowed to patch-over their membership to the dominant club

Poser – Fake club – usually law enforcement related

Probate – Probationary club member

Prospect – Prospective club member

Property – Anything made or tattooed with the club insignia (includes ole' ladies and wives)

Punk – A club member with knowledge of club rules, protocols, names and addresses, or information about club members that provides information to club enemies

Punking – The act of betraying the club to an enemy of the club

R.I.C.O. – Racketeer Influenced and Corrupt Organizations Act

Run- Club event requiring at least 200 miles one way on the motorcycle to complete

Sheep – Women who regularly hang around the clubhouse and willingly serve the brothers' wants and/or needs

Skin Patch – Tattoo authorized by the club with club symbols (must be removed or blacked out if a member leaves or is kicked out of the club)

Scoot - Motorcycle

Snitch – A brother who provides information about club members or club activities to law enforcement (this is considered the worst kind of betrayal and can result in a death sentence for the betraying member, hence the phrase *"Snitches are a dying breed"*)

The diamond 13 Patch – Death Patch

Turned - become an informant for a law enforcement agency

Turned Out – Prostitution on demand of a brother, old man, or relative

Bowl/Weed/Smoke/Reefer/Joint/Fatty– Marijuana

About the Author

C.J. MCSHANE

An avid motorcycle enthusiast for more than thirty years, C.J. McShane has ridden as both an independent and a patched brother in a well-known motorcycle club. He brings an insider's perspective to the unsettling world of M.C. I Am My Brother's Keeper, which is based upon his knowledge of the motorcycle club way of life and personal experience. McShane lives with his wife in Houston. This is his first novel.

The Two Sides of the Pass

Dà Thaobh a' Bhealaich

Maoilios Caimbeul (Myles Campbell)
and Mark O. Goodwin
Drawings by Eòghann Mac Colla

TWO RAVENS
PRESS

Published by Two Ravens Press Ltd
Green Willow Croft
Rhiroy
Lochbroom
Ullapool
Ross-shire IV23 2SF

www.tworavenspress.com

The right of Maoilios Caimbeul (Myles Campbell) and Mark O. Goodwin
to be identified as authors of this work and the right of Eòghann Mac
Colla to be identified as illustrator of this work has been asserted by them
in accordance with the Copyright, Designs and Patent Act, 1988.
© Maoilios Caimbeul (Myles Campbell), Mark O. Goodwin and
Eòghann Mac Colla, 2009.

ISBN: 978-1-906120-47-4

British Library Cataloguing in Publication Data. A CIP record for this
book can be obtained from the British Library.

Designed and typeset in Sabon and Zapf Humanist
by Two Ravens Press.
Drawings and cover artwork © Eòghann Mac Colla.
Cover design by David Knowles and Sharon Blackie.
Back cover photograph by Steven McKenzie, Cànan Ltd.

Printed on Forest Stewardship Council-accredited paper
by CPI (Antony Rowe), Chippenham.

FSC
Mixed Sources
Product group from well-managed
forests and other controlled sources
Cert no. SGS-COC-2953
www.fsc.org
© 1996 Forest Stewardship Council

Chuidich Comhairle nan Leabhraichean am foillsichear
le cosgaisean an leabhair seo.

About the Authors

Maoilios Caimbeul (Myles Campbell) is a Gaelic poet who lives on Skye, where he was born in 1944. After graduation from Edinburgh University, where his Gaelic tutor was the legendary William Matheson, Myles became a Gaelic teacher in Mull and later in Gairloch. Since retiring from teaching in 2004, he has been busy writing for schools, editing and doing residencies – including a period as writer-in-residence at Sabhal Mòr Ostaig in 2008, where he is currently working as a creative writing tutor. He has published five poetry collections, his work has been widely anthologised in bilingual editions, and is well represented in *An Tuil,* the definitive anthology of twentieth-century Gaelic poetry. His work has won many awards, the last being the Wigtown Gaelic prize in 2008.

Mark O. Goodwin was born in Devon in 1960 and studied at the University College of Wales, Aberystwyth, and City University, in the Department of Arts Policy and Management. After a brief spell doing a variety of jobs in London, he left to live in Scotland. He has lived for fourteen years on the Isle of Skye, where he worked for the Arts Centre *An Tuireann,* and was appointed as the gallery's Literature Development Officer shortly before its closure.

About the Artist

Eòghann Mac Colla was born in Inverness in 1970. He gained a degree in Fine Art from Duncan of Jordanstone College of Art and Design, Dundee, before embarking on a full-time career as a visual artist. He studied and exhibited in Barcelona before returning to live in Ayrshire. He was Artist in Residence at Sabhal Mòr Ostaig in 2008, and has been short-listed for the Aspect Painting Prize 2007 as well as the Sovereign European Art Prize in 2008.

Acknowledgments – Buidheachas

Thanks to the following publications and media where some of the poems by Maoilios Caimbeul (Myles Campbell) in this collection first appeared: *Northwords Now*; *New Writing Scotland*; *Poetry Scotland*; *Gath*; *An Guth*; BBC Ràdio nan Gàidheal.

Thanks to the following publications where some of the poems by Mark O. Goodwin first appeared: *The Eildon Tree Magazine*; *Northwords Now*; *Scrap*, co-produced with Robert Arnold; *Baile Beag Gun Chrìochan – A Little Borderless Village*.

Publisher's Note

The work of the two poets in this collection forms an alternating dialogue. The work of Maoilios Caimbeul (Myles Campbell) has been typeset in Zapf Humanist, a sans serif typeface, while that of Mark O. Goodwin is in Sabon, a serif typeface. The authors' initials are displayed on each page of their work, in line with the page number.

Introduction

Mark O. Goodwin and Maoilios Caimbeul (Myles Campbell) live on the Isle of Skye, roughly twelve miles apart, separated by the Trotternish Ridge. There is a single-track road which physically connects the two writers but, of course, the pass of the title is also figurative: it is a reaching out for understanding between two cultures. Mark was born in South Devon and has lived on Skye for fourteen years; Myles is a Gaelic speaker and a native of the island.

Mark and Myles have created a poetic dialogue which explores their circumstances and different backgrounds. For Myles, a sense and love of place is of vital importance in today's world, a love of one's locale in opposition to the abstract values of globalisation. Kinship ties – always an important feature of Gaelic society – are also a vital part of this *weltanschauung*.

For Mark, who has rarely experienced this strong sense of place, the poems, and the mingling of voices, have given him the chance to discover new sensibilities: the idea of *dùthchas,* the place of one's birth, and the links that exist between universal and localised themes.

Myles originally wrote his poems in Gaelic and Mark wrote his in English. Myles made transpositions of his poems into English for Mark and also translated Mark's poems into Gaelic. The result is a book where the first part is in English: Mark's original poems and translations of Myles' poems. The second section of the book is in Gaelic and contains Myles' poems and translations of Mark's.

The artist Eòghann Mac Colla has worked alongside the poets to create drawings which reflect individual poems and the collection as a whole.

Myles Campbell & Mark O. Goodwin
February, 2009

Ro-ràdh

Tha Mark O. Goodwin agus Maoilios Caimbeul a' fuireach san Eilean Sgitheanach, mu dhà mhìle dheug bho chèile, air gach taobh de Dhruim Thròndairnis. Tha rathad carbaid singilte ann eadar far a bheil iad a' fuireach, ach cuideachd tha am bealach ann an tiotal an leabhair samhlachail: tha e a' riochdhadh na strì a th' ann a thighinn gu tuigse air dà dhualchas. Rugadh Mark ann an Devon a Deas agus tha e air a bhith a' fuireach san Eilean Sgitheanach airson ceithir bliadhna deug; bha Gàidhlig aig Maoilios bhon ghlùin agus buinidh e don Eilean.

Tha Mark' s Maoilios air conaltradh bàrdachail a chruthachadh a tha a' cladhach a-steach dha na suidheachaidhean anns a bheil iad. Do Mhaoilios, tha a dhùthchas agus gaol do dh'àite air leth cudromach ann an saoghal an latha an-diugh, gaol don àite anns a bheil thu, an aghaidh nan luachan eanchainneil a tha an lùib cruinneadalais. Tha ceanglaichean teaghlaich – a bha riamh cudromach do na Gàidheil – cuideachd nam pàirt air leth cudromach den *weltanschauung* seo.

Dha Mark, nach do dh'fhairich cha mhòr riamh leithid de dhùrachd làidir do dh'àite, tha a' bhàrdachd, agus na guthan a' measgachadh, air cothrom a thoirt dha mothachasan eile a lorg: mar a tha dùthchas, àite do bhreith, agus na ceanglaichean eadar cuspairean cruinneadail agus ionadail.

Sgrìobh Maoilios na dàin aige ann an Gàidhlig agus sgrìobh Mark ann am Beurla. Rinn Maoilios tionndaidhean gu Beurla dha Mark agus dh'eadar-theangaich e cuideachd na dàin aig Mark gu Gàidhlig. 'S e a' bhuil leabhar a tha sa Bheurla anns a' chiad leth: a' bhàrdachd aig Mark agus dàin Mhaoilis air an eadar-theangachadh. Tha an dàrna leth den leabhar ann an Gàidhlig leis na dàin aig Maoilios, agus na dàin aig Mark air an eadar-theangachadh.

Bha an dealbhadair Eòghann Mac Colla ag obair còmhla ris na bàird, a' dèanamh dhealbhan peansail a tha nan sgàthan do chuid de na dàin agus don chruinneachadh air fad.

Maoilios Caimbeul & Mark O. Goodwin
An Gearran, 2009

Contents

Clàr-Innse

The Two Sides of the Pass

Rathad a' Bhealaich — The Pass Road

Welcome

Welcome, friends,
to the navel of the world,
views in abundance,
hearing replete,
the soft touch of moss.

Stay, listen, see
fifty miles of mountains
before you, rising
unforgettable. Footpaths to travel
to loch and stream,
to shores and surge,
to steep hills, tall, pinnacled,
and to remote escarpments.

Come through the circle
and see,
feel the kindness of the moor,
the gentle moss of this East Side.

Glenhinnisdal

Glenhinnisdal cups and echoes
the sounds of our lives here,
amplifies our homecoming
with a cattle-grid drum roll,
and broadcasts our leaving with the antenna
of the thin peat road
that chatters towards its end:
an estuary of mud and pebble and grit,
the tidal mark of our coming and going.

The river never looks back; gestates,
keeps its distance beneath the clouds
which choreograph the sky,
while the grasses glint and wire
the winds rush from the ridge,
forecasting rain and the rush and swell of water.
In spate, the river will slither to the sea,
give birth in the breaking waters, and trail
a placenta of white foam along the coast.

Abhainn Hinneasdail — Hinnisdal River

The Journey

Good to hear you're gravid there
and that the waters are breaking
in the glen river.
We often hear them breaking here
on the shore –

at the foot of the croft
where the crops used to be so plentiful,
hay and corn in grandfather's time,
and where the bay horse pulled
the coils and stacks to the stack-yard,
the very spot where our house is today –

and from the house, from the old stack-yard,
we hear the waves breaking at the foot of the croft
as they always did
beneath the secret jagged stars;
and on the horizon to the north-east
the Rubha Rèidh lighthouse
blinks its warning to the sea roads,
for the occasional vessel passing.

Looking Over the Nahe

The river threads history through high clefts of land.
It has washed away the blood of battle.
Guilt sparkles in the sunshine off the water.

It turns a bend in its history
curving towards the Rhine
with the railway line and the road.

The winter sun burnishes a halo of oak leaves
as red as the blush of porphyry.
Between the pinnacles, shadows slip and snake
smoothly down the sides of the Rotenfels.

Below, the winter vines are staked in rows.
Grapes fill with icy promise,
and through the haze, buildings
square the land with urban settlement.

❖ ❖ ❖

Here the path is less certain,
a wavering single track,
and beneath these needles of rock
is bog and the soft ground
which has ripened the leather of your boots
with the long years of walking;
creasing the memory with the laughter,
the songs and the weeping –
the continual craic of the mind.

Cleat — The Pass

The Pass

There's a pass to which we move,
always over there
the other country,
the unknown land.
What's happening over there
on the other side of the Pass?

The East Side
is full of little townships:
Garrafad, Stenscholl, Brogaig,
and under Ben Edra's shadow
Maligar, Marishader, Garros,
seawards Gairloch, Torridon and Rona:
today Ben Eighe is misted.
From our house I see them on the horizon
through the yellow and green leaves.
But to the West is the Pass
and Glenhinnisdal,
between the Maoladh Mòr and Loch Leum na Luirginn,
and Tobar na Slàinte –
the Health-giving Well – isn't far away.

Cutting Peat

With a half-empty back-pack
and spade in my hand,
I went in search of the black peat,
walking up the hillside in Earlish
with an untutored gait.

The air had the clarity
of a blank white page,
and there were inkwells
of water. Sepia droplets
stained my boots;
in places they sank into the ground
and the mud slid off them
like hot wax, sealing
the steps I had taken.

I climbed nearer to the loch
to reach a spine of piled rock,
the vertebrae visible
through the flesh of grazed grass,
a carcass picked clean by a ravenous wind.

Reaching the skull of land
with its bleached basalt, pools
and tusky grass clumps,
I found the old peat banks,
and Loch Mor:
an eye of water
staring at the sky.

The cutlery of tools
I carried rattled
tunes of improvisation
for the task I had set myself.

Raking through earth and roots
I searched for clumps of peat,
translating as I heaved my spade
with the rhythm of my work:

a flaughter,
to flay the skin of the earth,
a rutter,
to cut into it even deeper,
a toirsgeir,
to sink into the soft black peat
and turf out the words:
scalp, scrape, dig;
slitting knife,
turf iron,
budding iron…

while my thoughts were held in a pale blue flame
of pluffy peat that burned into the dusk and sunset.

Translating the Peat

1

It's difficult to accept
that everything
is a translation

that the word
can only give a corrupted idea
of the peat-bank.

My favourite walk
goes past Loch Langaig,
on the road to the Quiraing.

I went there yesterday again,
the green bracken browned,
smooth, upwards from the edge of the loch

and a little way past up the brae
is my grandfather's peat-bank,
a faint image only under the moor grass,

where they would insert the peat-spade
into the black or brown peat –
their only aim to get a life.

I wonder how they translated the peat
rising in little stacks on the turf?
Symbol of a winter by the hearth,

or like filthy work that had to be done,
the poor streaming peat hunks of sweat
and the son of the big house asleep in his feather bed?

2

And so I went up the path to Loch Hasco
and Leathad na Caillich rising before me
and above them the grey pinnacles of the Quiraing.

Somewhere among those pinnacles
there is The Old Lady, and I wish I knew,
but those who knew are gone.

Ancient basalt of the Quiraing, like a black and green and
grey kilt.
Ah, rocks! if you could but speak!
You'd have many a story to tell me

about primeval Laurasia,
and the dinosaurs which roamed
the slopes of ancient lands.

Ah, rocks! if you could tell –
but we have our own translations
and we'll make our story from the rock.

Beinn Edra

I have exchanged English footsteps
for Scottish ones,
although the distinction is hard to tell
on this track up to Beinn Edra.
The blanched line of the grass to the top
shimmers furtively in the sunshine, shadows
full of Gaelic reticence pool their songs,
sobbing bogs give way to the hard-edged irony
of ruined crofts. Stony outcrops,
blotched by lichen,
soak up the inked oozings
of mosses and their musings –

I am a stranger here, will always be a stranger, wrapped
and shod in a globalised context of gore-texed
weather-proofed gear.
Es ist sehr schön hier.
To the north *Bealach Ùige* and the eyes
of two lochs stare back at the sky; to the south
Bealach a' Mhorghain and the blood vessels
of burns that hurry to bury themselves.
But history has a habit
of seeping through the seams.

As the weather turns at the top of the climb,
sweat condenses inside my jacket
and scents my presence here.

Incomer

From this side, Ben Edra is high and pointed
with ridges of heather between us
and its base, stubborn roots
reciting their origination.

Not your fault, my friend,
where you were born; we all
have come into a world
sometime, without a choice in the matter.

The rocks of our rearing keep us
whole, if whole it is, much
of the rock a scattered scree, a piece
perhaps polished in the bed of a stream

and tossed by the elements
far from the mother rock.
Ruins, a trace of people
who disappeared. They came

in, in another place
where there was neither heather nor runrig,
they, and their progeny, obtained possession
far from the bitterness of departure.

Here the rocks fall,
the stream of language flows away
and the blood of the arterial streams perishes,
new arterial streams arise.

The world is mixed
and churned, the passes have opened out;
now is a straight smooth line,
and we have all come in.

[MC]   18

Skye

Skye: I'm back again;
couldn't resist your wide horizon smiles
and the jewellery of your whitewashed houses
gummed to the summer-green glens and your sensuous
coastal fringes.
Skye, I'm talking to you, can you hear me?
Only, you seem to be turning your back on me.
Sometimes you stare at me with your compound thistle eyes,
like some deadly insect, which scares me silly like leaning
over a cliff edge.

Skye, are we falling out, or is it that we are spending
too long in each other's company ...
tha thu gam chur às mo chiall. You're driving me nuts.
Skye, are you clouding over again?
It cost me £14.70 to get here
and I seem to have had this conversation some place
else before.
Will it rain again? Will it keep on raining? Will it ever stop?
Are the midges coming?
Will we ever get home together again?

Skye, I feel you have a single-track mind with no
place to reverse:
we're a battleground of passing places.
You see, I try and make sense of you, understand your
cultural sensitivities,
but forgive me, I'm a slow learner.
Eh! I was brought up in England,
fed on greed and nostalgic spoonfuls of Empire,
and now my feet keep sinking into your bogs.

[MG]   19

God, you have so many bogs. All that water stored up there
for years, lacking minerals, and then what do you do?
Release the lot in a gush and guilt of waterfalls...
Skye – you obliterate me with your long nights
you turn my head with your sunsets
you make me dizzy with your giddy winds;
you know, sometimes they go on and on and on:
it's the only conversation we have for days,
and it drives me crazy.
And your bog myrtle perfume is making me ill.
I need a drink. More whisky. I haven't drunk enough
                                            of you yet.

Skye, let's put our relationship in some sort of order.
I know about the clan warfare, the Clearances,
the painful baggage of a previous marriage;
but can't we now tie our own individual Celtic knot with
                                            a little more hope?
Skye, you are not East Timor; Portree is not Dili.
I know, I know, it's not going to be easy:
crofting daughter is in trouble again;
she's being flattered with riches.
You've come over all postmodernist in Portree,
and Urban Nightmare, he stalks the shadows in the square
with the latest in mobile phone technology.

Locals are being barred from hotels in case we embarrass
                                            the guests.
Hey, where can I get a clootie dumpling this time of night?
Huh! Kilt Rock tilts, it's laughing at me. You bastard!
                                            You looking at me?
Ha, aye: I know what you're up to, standing there, pissing
                                            in the wind;

and those lochans so full of water, glassy eyes staring
                                          into the night.
The fossils are moving again, I can hear dinosaurs grazing,
I can hear the primordial howl. The lava's flowing.
I'm feeling sick. I am feeling very sick. Sorry.
Tha mi duilich, tha mi air chall. I am lost.

Skye, I am not going to worry about us any more. I love
                                          you. Will always.
You know I really mean it, don't you? Please say you'll
                                          forgive me.
It's been a long night. We are both tired. I understand.

You're still having a rough time with your sons and daughters,
trying to sort out what's best for them;
keeping the Gaelic going. The best part of you.
Tha mi duilich. Can we just lie down here together, quietly?
I'm going to keep on singing your praises, I promise.
Listen to the psalms that silt the wind. Dè nì mi? Dè nì mi?
What will I do before the next war plunges us
into darkness, leaving only the starlight to hover over
                                          Rubha Hunish?
I will swallow my tears and drain my glass and reach for
                                          your softness
and put one hiking boot in front of another –
tapadh leat, tapadh leat, tapadh leat.

Labelling

'Gâteau', it says,
and you can see sponge and cream and fruit,
but hidden from sight
are sugar, eggs, margarine and flour,
salt, baking soda, lemon juice and whatever...

'Scotland', we say,
and you see Glasgow's and Edinburgh's buildings,
splendid, Victorian, sculpted,
and some bare, high, cold, unwelcoming
places where you wouldn't put your dog...
and also there are cool glens
with bog-cotton and heather and lochans edged with reeds
and trout hidden beneath ledges.
Faces also of every kind,
genetic gleams from stone age,
from the Norse and from the Picts,
and from every tribe on earth
and we place the 'Scotland' label on it.

'England', we say,
and see a man from southern England with a toff accent
or a female ignorant of Scotland,
or a Scouser crying in the Kop,
or great London of the thousand tribes,
the black man with slave ancestry
now at the head of a business,
Cambridge's meadows, Cumbria's moors,
and we give it the label 'England'.

[MC]   22

God save me from labelling you,
my friend, ignorant of what you truly are.
As if I should say 'world'
thinking just because I said the word
that I understand it to some extent
while under the label there are a million things
I have never seen nor ever will see.

À la Prufrock

The sky is grey – I almost said liath,
but it's in Uist they say that,
liath instead of gorm, as we say –
but today the sky is grey
and not the sky but the head as well.

The sky is grey and the stream runs briskly
and the pools like clouds in the middle of the croft,
and the world itself so grey and strange
like sheep
like knots of sheep here and there.

Herself said to me, 'Won't we go visiting the MacDonalds
tonight? They'll be sitting there alone,
watching *Emmerdale* and *Coronation Street*.'

As I remember it, the sky was blue
and the deck red with rust, the sun skinning us,
shuddering with the electric drills
going phut, phut, phut, phut,
crossing the Indian Ocean,
crossing the equator
blinded by dust,
where the hell is the port!

'We sit here on our own
watching the news and *Emmerdale*;
they would think it unusual for us to go near them.'

Unusual?

The streams white-ringleted
leap and dash impetuously;
Aeolus, 'god of the storm', combs the long hairs back.

'Think it unusual?'

'You see I'm grey
and long since seen the world.
They know everything I've ever done.'

'While we think about it,
would you like a cup of tea?
A cup of tea would be good,
as long as we keep an ear for the wind.'

'That would be as well while we wait...
one spoon of sugar and a little milk.'

The autumn on the St Lawrence was fine,
the yellows, reds and browns
while Presley and the Beatles sang,
making for Quebec and Three Rivers,
and the great river so wide, calm and smooth
and while Finlay's sheep were on the hill
where the streams would sing –
and Bishop Robinson writes Honest to God *–*
where the wethers would weep.

It's getting wet again and the wind is roaring.

'Were you speaking? Did I hear your voice?'

'No, my dear, it was the rain.

[MC]   25

Don't you hear the wind rising,
don't you hear the gusts approaching?'

Right enough the globe is warming
and the rain forests are being cut down,
there will be no food for the little birds.

'You're right, it's wild outside,
I think we'll stay in.'

Isn't it a pity the flock's on the hill
on a fierce night like this
and the MacDonalds by themselves by the fire
and another death in Iraq
and the hair growing grey.

'Will you draw the curtains, Donald?'

Tomorrow I'll see how the flock is.
I'll perhaps put on the black bonnet...
will I put on the trousers with the holes...
will I put on the trousers?

'Will you draw the curtains, Donald?'

'Yes, my dear, I'll do that.'

'Did you give the cat milk?'

A Page Torn from a Naturalist's Diary, May 16th 2007

I've heard it said that storks are flying into southern England.

Here birds migrate, once again, in other directions:
feathered, they take flight from their westerly nests
plump with ambition, to roost in cities
to fly by neon rather than the moon
and take their chances with the urban fox

leaving the crows to pick at the carcasses of old crofts...
memorials that slump like graveyards,
the lichen licking at the words inscribed
on stone; their words preserved in speech, but
blown by the wind as soon as they are spoken...

And then, the strangest sight of all:
a house is wheeled into the glen,
rumbles over the cattle-grid to its temporary destination.
The net curtains are drawn, the front door shut,
the chimney yet to puff its smoke of new allegiance.

There are fewer songbirds to sing this lay of the lie
of the land.

To Crofts

Loosely after To Meddowes, *with apologies to Robert Herrick*

You have woven orchids and flowers,
staged dances at the shielings
where blushes bloomed in summer hours,
or faded to nights of tears and weeping.

You have witnessed the back-break
of bone-hard labour, and the toil
to cut and stack the peat, the ache
of hours, raising runrig from the soil.

You have heard the women sing,
bare hands waulking cloth, crotal red,
heard the blether of burns, rising,
lacing the lands with silver thread.

Now, white houses fruit indisciplined,
among the stones decrofted.
Hardly fit for a westerly wind
they strut and swagger, aloft.

Like trader's stock your slopes are spent,
the heather blackened by desire,
and you are left improvident
your heritage fuel for the pyre.

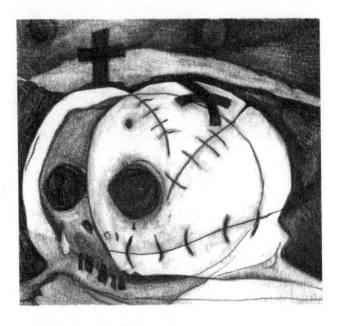

Òran a' Chlaiginn — The Song of the Skull

The Song of the Skull
or – The State of the Gaelic-speaking Community

Sitting by the grave,
looking at its edge,
I saw an ashen skull on the ground ...

Dugald Buchanan (1716-1768)

White and hard on Scotland's edge,
I've been routed to the grave;
where there was an amiable, quicksilver tongue,
there is only a formless, soundless hole.

Once I could move trunk and feet
from Cape Wrath to the banks of Clyde;
now, good grief, all I am
is a thin worthless shell.

In Rothesay there would be conversation and joy,
old ladies gossiping kindly.
There would be a feast of songs from Lochaber
and a flood of banter in Bowmore.

When artery and sinew kindled me,
and with healthy laugh on my face,
I would take a trip to the Long Island,
or I would have a chat in Letterewe.

Today the earth knows another discourse
and the heath whistles in my ear;
the old skulls are my friends.
Like myself, they are hard bone.

Fresh skulls in a heap beside me,
little they heed the dead or living;
whatever language they rejoiced in,
they have neither word nor breath.

Quite

Although dead,
we're still
not quite dead quite;

while there's sap in the leaf
and seed for sowing in the earth
(and pleasure in the tune)
and eyes in the seed
we have not quite perished
or perished quite.

When the crop surfaces,
we'll live
in hope
of breath in death
and great growth from the seed.

Note on the transposition: It is not possible to translate all aspects of this poem adequately as it plays so much with the multiple meanings of words, e.g. buileach: quite, complete, absolutely, fully; fonn: earth, land, delight, humour, tune; bàrr: top, cream, crop, harvest.

A House in Flodigarry

A thought begins a journey:
it brushes through rooms,
it moves between familiar chairs and tables,
eyes the history of a group of photographs
taken in the 1920s,
sees the cloche hats and the stockings,
the faces charmed by excitement,
the dare of modernity,
bright against the sunlight on Princes Street.
It watches the watch-chain swing from the waistcoat
of an uncle who used to live nearby
and it slowly refocuses
to the glaze and gauze of the here and now.
It floats over the rug by the fireplace,
it hovers like a flame
where the kitchen range
used to be, and it flies to find
a curve of space to cradle in,
near the thick wall of a window
as the front door opens...
Shadows silhouette in the hall,
seep all the way
to the bedroom door
as if to wake a pair of dreamers.
A breeze follows,
freshening the rooms with whispers.
With nowhere else to go,
thought stirs and treads the air, circles,
embraces the smell of grass and bracken,
and vanishes from the mind of this place.

[MG]   34

The Thought Continues

The thought continues on its journey
and sees the people sitting
where they were, once, around the bare
wooden table, Mary and Roddy and Peter

and Gran and Grandfather and Flora
with the cod and dry tasty potatoes
they planted themselves and lifted, eating them
with the milk they milked that morning.

The place has changed, the house
has been renovated, but the thought continues,
seeing the shadows of memory, the stove
which isn't there rising before it,

the scullery with the enamel basins, filled
with milk waiting for the cream to rise
to the surface, and the dresser where
the jam jars and butter and sugar were kept,

and the bench by the window, the dog under it,
its nose peeping out, an eye for the table, ready
for the titbits. The thought remembers
when it belonged to the boy; it runs off

out past the entrance hall
where the coats would hang
and out the front door to the side of the house,
to the gravel of the pathway, where the shed stood

with its gear, fishing equipment and the rest, green
and transparent buoys, the long
and the small nets with hooks of all kinds;
for the lads were fishermen.

The thought continues on its journey,
the thought the boy had, its shadows
on the land, where the stable and byre
and hen-house and stack-yard were, now

there is only memory, a faint map
of what was once, where the cows
would stand in the stalls
in the smell of their dung, there is the garden

of the new house and flowers growing
and the boy's thought becomes fainter
like the moss's hue on the surface of stone
like the lisping of the sea hardly heard.

Iuchair dhan Chrait — Key to the Croft

Key to the Croft

Over the gate, just before your foot treads
on the early purple orchid
and your hand catches on a rusting nail;
just before the rush of wind slices
across your face, scrubbing the stubble of the field opposite,
you see it glinting in the grass
on the verge of the single track road:
a key, glittering, precious,
like a raindrop, opal in the evening light,
while the sky plays with its veils.

Pick it up and feel the roundness of it melt
between the rough edges
and its two smooth sides; along the top
a ridge that's been blunted,
Trotternish in miniature,
trails its braille of peaks and troughs
in the palm of your hand.
You can cut yourself with your own grip,
or hold out your arms with the impression
that any lock will open from now on.

The Auction

The speckled snake lies coiled
On the plains where once flourished
The great men I witnessed there;
Take this message to the poet.
William Livingstone (1808-70)

After the charming words
falls the hard hammer of truth;
all that will be left will be the songs.
   Take this message to the poet.

The auction goes splendidly,
home after home is lost to us
and the language of the stranger takes possession of us.
   Take this message to the poet.

The tinkling of the coins rules
and Gaelic goes to hell
and the community is blanched.
   Take this message to the poet.

If our language is withering,
it's well-deserved, it's well-deserved,
the market in everything we do.
   Take this message to the poet.

Furiously the auction goes,
the coin is blind that sells our all;
heritage, soul and language to the dump.
   Take this message to the poet.

[MC]   40

Don't blame cunning strangers
for sending our ways and tongue to the seabed:
the frailty is in ourselves.
    Take this message to the poet.

Soay

This man's home is a ruin, a hollow space of grass,
nettles and scattered pegs of sheep's bone.
Brushing aside the wind, we wander in
to graze on memories of his life on Soay;
conversation fills in gaps, rebuilds walls,
and thatches the open roof with its laughter.
Between two stones a lintel, pale and scarred,
sketches a doorway, a hint of two rooms,
and the past as it used to be. But now this island
drowns in cloud, in drizzle, in a rain of foreign words.

Sòaigh — Soay

Twelve Verses for a House

Cement blocks, windows
and red roof tiles –
an elegant stub in the ground.

Keeper of secrets,
sacred magnet
to which regard returns.

Amused night joy,
who keeps laughter
stored under rafters.

You welcome the sun
enchain the light;
yellow flowers in the window.

Or place of shadow;
grief and extremity
soil the walls.

Soul symbol – under the joists
id; ego itself on a high
superego in bed.

Out and out drunk, throws things,
your slates shake,
cans blow.

Eaves harvester of birds,
yearly they return;
protector of brood.

[MC]   45

A ship tears the sky,
white clouds nibble
the chimney masts.

A boat under sail,
four yellow masts
stretch the red sails.

A door to quietness
after rose fades:
listen to the ebb sough.

The soft sound distils
short of the cold street;
comfort – listen.

Loch na h-Ìghne — The Loch of the Girl

Reeds

scratching the surface, reeds arrow
points of departure
which dissolve and film the water

Flodigarry Well

the well
tourmaline disc
calm, balancing the breeze
it scoops our splashes like prayers
last words

At Sacred Loch Well

Dedicated to Keiko Mukaide, a Japanese artist living in Scotland who visited the well at Loch Shianta in 2006. She has an interest in sacred wells. The locals pronounce the name as 'iana'. It appears to come from the word sianta/seunta, *meaning enchanted, defended by enchantments, sacred. This well in Trotternish was renowned in the old days as a healing well and people came to it from near and far.*

A cold showery day,
the loch itself restless,
with a brisk northerly wind

but the well is calm
under shelter of fuchsias
and a streamlet runs

from the sacred loch –
we a threesome at the well
guided by its virtue

as it flows quietly,
communicating peace –
a shy, half-hidden diva.

We raise water to our lips
without the analytic word
stopping its wholeness:

if there is a word it is prayer,
remembering the *hado*
between mind and water.

[MC]   49

The water comes from the table
upwards from far beneath the wood,
from the kind earth we see:

the transient, lasting water,
today in Flodigarry
and tomorrow above some ocean.

East and west come together
at the well in this moment:
the word is simpatico.

Our Love

our love is like a pebble
worn smooth
by the tide –
and when the next wave
sweeps us up
we will be washed from ourselves

Glenbrittle

and I remember turning from the sea,
crossing the beach of Glenbrittle,
marbled like some antique book cover,
trying to read your thoughts,
scuffing sand with my footsteps
while looking at those paced out
with such precision moments before
you turned your back …

but you waited for me to return,
standing on a ridge of pebble,
and watched with a slow smile,
knowing that I would be able to read
the sketch of your walk,
without having to retrace
my own scribbles on the pale grey sand.

My Pure Love

1.

I will remember tonight, the bright one of my love,
where you would walk
long happy days ago,
beside the Sacred Loch and to the Big Wood,
or by Dunans Loch
walking to Kilmuir,
for there was no other means.

2.

When you were old
in Achmore in Lewis
you would speak about Voilteir
and Flodigarry. Among the plates
on the wall, in your blindness,
there were the banks and hollows and lochs
and the kind people deceased.
The one thing you could see clearly
in the end was the moon
and you would stand at the window
looking at it in its fullness.

3.

And here where you would run and jump
when a little girl,
memory is a shadow under the land.
Here is where the byre was
and where you would milk the cows
and where the barn and stable were
and the stance of the lean-to shed

with the nets and fishing tackle
and where the fish would dry against the wall.

4.

I see you in photos in the Twenties
on a street in Edinburgh with a friend,
with a long dress and bonnet,
and another photo in front of the hotel in Kyle,
slim and pretty, just married,
yourself and my father
and another photo in Borve, Lewis,
surrounded by your brood,
and in every photo you are gentle and kind
and affable, as was natural to you.

5.

Even though you were blind,
you would be knitting. At last
only stockings, and after your death
I sat looking at them, the heap
of stockings on the shelf. That's how you were,
always doing for others
and the Bible and Christ
a stocking on your heart.

6.

Today, all that is left of you
on earth is in the ground in Crossbost.
Peace be with you, pure mother,
and with him by your side.

[MC]   53

Staffin Bay

An teid mi dh'ionnsaigh na mara
a shireadh cala dom smuain ...?

Shall I make for the sea
to seek refuge for my thought...?

Derick Thomson

Standing outside your door tonight
you can hear

your childhood mingling
with the sea spray

and your language lapping
the shore of Flodigarry Island

it's like the sparrows
that sing their lyrics to the wind

or the stamp of feet
dancing trysts on an earthen floor

or the smell of memory
rising from a ganglia of seaweed knots

that conjures up
the love of this place

like when the bagpipe was played –
the notes of pibroch pungent and plangent

noting with precision
your love of this place

and the revelation that, in Staffin Bay,
waves were rolling verses.

The Moon is the Lamp of the Poor

With how sad steps, o moon, thou climbs't the skies
Sir Philip Sidney, *Astrophil & Stella*, Sonnet 31

Poor pale light
how you wither on this road through the glen
how you shiver in the gloam of early evening
how you tiptoe from puddle to puddle
shaking your lamplight with delight
before the fear of daylight takes hold
before the sun strikes
and the rain comes down
and the winds stir the world…

how you shudder when dawn opens its lips
devouring the modesty of your light
the evenness of your demeanour
the delicate balance of your beams,
those beams that are swallowed whole…

and day breaks to sheep that graze the thin grass,
to the fences that stake their claim
to the wind farms that spin their charms
for signs of hope and redemption.

Can these islands ever unfurl their cloaks
of crooked coastlines of basalt and gneiss,
to expose the assassins of the day
and the assassins of the night, smooth out
the warp and weft of angst and anxiety, unpick
the needlework of hate, patched with a darn
of an old story, an old yarn
and the keening of an old song?

[MG]   56

Pale light of the moon,
the light of everyone who dares to dream,
your light is still strong in these parts,
your starlight still thick with promise in this night sky.

As the Moon Said

You are a white and blue ball
in my vision for eternal aeons
like a jewel on a black sheet, so far
away and yet so near me.

O world, you have
drained me, left me dumb, silent
in the emptiness, so far
out amongst the remote stars.

I am tied to you by
an umbilical cord, like
a child that can never be
free to get his life.

What happens on your surface?
You are like a living thing in space,
are you as beautiful
as your colours imply?

My heart will break, earthly
mother, thinking of you
in this time without end; love,
is that what moves you?

Musing on you every night
my heart will break, asking
what moves the far-off one
birthed from the stars, from her womb

did other infants come
moving in cold isolated
skies as I do
or are they in the warm embrace

of her bosom? Tell me, world,
what on earth is your state tonight?
What red cloud sometimes
sweeps across your face?

What are we doing, what
do we mean to each other
in the dark emptiness?
Answer me, answer me, world.

Creag na Cuthaige
Rock of the cuckoo

Here you are in a gallery.
A constellation of white space surrounds you,
it is like being in the moon's womb.
And there! Already, some framed idea stands proudly
from the wall, issuing colour and confusion:

a sketch from the cuckoo's crag
graphite and mixed media

you want to spit at it,
shake your tiny fists and hit out...

but then you look at it again with older eyes,
and see the world
shining blue, back at the white moon's walls,
an igneous red streaking through rock and water.

'Can you hear me,' says the world,
can you hear the noise of grass growing,
the calf and cow calling in the glen,
a car going past, chewing its cud of petrol,
and the cuckoo, always the cuckoo, recalling Spring?
And the shadows that shape eternity
birthing the memory of these moments.

It is a late May evening in the Hebrides.
A neighbour taps quietly
to the tune of new thoughts,
and an island embraces the pattern of itself.

[MG]   60

Holy Week

1

It is the eyes at first, and then perhaps
the arch of the brow, or the skin, unblemished,
pale as the moon, unlike the leathered landscaped
faces, with barancos etched into foreheads,
cheeks swallowing the years in shadows.
And then, there, faintly, hope expressed:
you can see its smile from the rope of light, coiled
over the stones of these crumbling walls.
The Virgin Mary returns the stare of the world
with our own, imprisoned behind the masque
of a white metal frame that is chipped and curled;
her gaze never changes, even when a pane of glass
is covered in algae and grime, as in a Florentine street,
or here, veiled with the faded paper wrapper of sweet.

2

And with the night, your expression never changes,
or blushes, carried as you are like a doll
through narrow streets, past pastel flaking walls,
beneath electric wires, above our heads for all to see.
Your hips sway, you lilt through passages of time
as the bells ring and ring again. You float in midair,
while women with black mantillas chant your prayers,
and we wait to catch the cadence of a rhyme
that catches at the heart like a Gaelic psalm.
And a drumbeat melts slowly like candle wax,
serpentine, down the length of a candlestick,
while we stand together, massed in a moment of calm,
like foolish lovers, discovering the cracks,
the pain, and the burn to the stump of the wick.

[MG]   61

The Just Feather

The shudder of horse, they come
from the bounds of the kingdom
with a thrum on the earth,
nearer they come,
pandemonium of hooves
thunder and rumble
as in a dream,
humanity's dream,
as would come in a vision,
a nether god making
from remote depths,
from the ravenous heart.

(Herod sits in his chamber,
his turbid mind perturbed,
disturbed by the power of Rome.)

But not the stern power of horse
with hazard of hosts,
as in the vision,
threatening terror and fear;
not the pound of their trampling
tearing the earth
will triumph in the end ...

but another dream,
the nails,
the nails through the palms,
the feeble, holy thing yielding
from pity to the cruel;
Rome and the Innocent,

[MC]   62

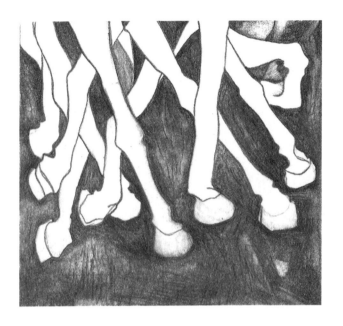

An Ite Bheusach — The Just Feather

and in the end,
the just feather will fell the horse,
as love is the ground,
love and justice –

and the clamour will cease.

Hitchhiker

I gave time a lift the other day. He appeared
out of the glen, lichen sticking to his coat;
patched by the sun, he walked towards me dragging
                                        shadows.
A backpack bent his back – you could see how weary he was,
I guessed it was the weight of years –
he put it on the back seat, and we set off for Portree.

We talked about how things had changed
in the last few years...
most of what he had to say was nostalgic,
like the way commerce looks boarded up,
but he had an eye for the future too.

We reached the harbour. 'I hope there's someone to
                                        meet you,'
I said, just as the door was closing.
'No one you'd know,' he said.

I watched him looking at the boats rocking the
                                        water sideways,
this way and that, as water always does, never taking sides.
He walked to a fish-and-chip shop
scattering seagulls hassling for chips:
greed was thick with salt and vinegar and the smell of grease.

[MG]   66

He seemed to be talking to himself as he reached

                                the end of the pier.

Memories sprang like herring caught in nets,

flipping and rolling in the catch:

ambitions gutted, packed and shelved...

I turned the key in the ignition to get away

but the car wouldn't start.

Wanting a Lift

He's the bane of my life as well,
standing on the verge, knife in hand,
with an appeal in his eyes
as if I had the power to help him,
knowing damn well that I'm in his hands
today and every other;
the tyres and the head grow bald,
ruler of everything
from Orion to the little tormentil of the Bealach,
from the glow of the great galactic wall
to rusting starting on the side.

Go and get knotted, I said to him in the passing,
knowing I would pay for it
as the words came out of my mouth.

Grianan nam Maighdean agus Cnoc Hàsgo —
The Sun Bower of the Maidens and Hasco Hill

A Stone by the Way

Not gneiss but a great lump of basalt
which fell thousands of years ago
from Grianan nam Maighdean and down Leathad na Caillich,
and now lies by the edge of the path above Loch Hasco
scrubbed by the elements' untold years.
Like something living, bright and shining,
covered by a multi-coloured film of life,
brown and yellow and red moss,
and algae of all kinds gripping you like a skin.
And though we all know you're dead,
of the dust of the earth, you support what's alive,
the film of life that surrounds you,
and draw me to you like a magnet
every day I pass, renewing the whims of memory
that come with age, a symbol and sign
by the way, inspiring thought and thoughts
all like a transitory layer of moss
on the surface of stone,
a stone anciently from the stars
and which will long outlast us
carrying the colour of life.

St Columba

There, ahead, this figure giddy,
dressed in a cloak of clothes, face hidden,
hovering between one foot and another.

He is throwing stones by the shoreline
one by one, each an arch,
a promise of a plunge into water.

Then a pause, a shift of feet, steady
as ripples of afterthoughts engrave the waves.
He bends to pick and sift the beach, until

loaded, staggering, he lurches
towards a recess of rock and crouches
to stare the devils out, perhaps, and welcome angels in.

Behind his back a sheep gut lies,
stretched and stiff, with the first delicate traces
of promises to be read.

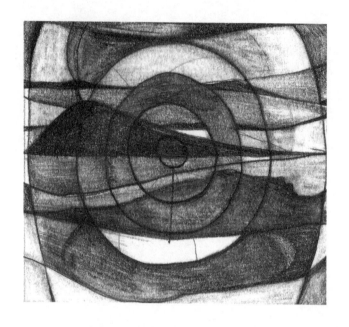

Eilean Dòrais (an t-Eilean) —
Doras's Island (the Island)

Doras's Island

About a mile to the North lies the Isle Altvig, it has a high rock facing the East, is near two miles in circumference, and is reputed fruitful in corn and grass, there is a little chapel in it, dedicated to St Turos.
From *A Description of the Western Islands of Scotland* by Martin Martin, 1703

1. The Island

Island of the three names,
Altavaig, Isle of the Big Headland
and Flodigarry Island

where Dòras lived
all these long years ago
before the Norsemen came from the north

with targets and bloody work,
but it's his name that's still remembered,
Cill Dòras on Flodigarry shore,

Poll Dòras between the shore and the island,
an ancient fallow island, with nothing to be seen
but streaks of lazybeds and stones;

but Dòras was there once upon a time
and left his blessing for us in his name
left it like a prayer on sea and land

like fragrant mist blessing
the old earth
as the breeze blows over.

[MC]   75

2. Saint Turos
Once upon a time

On this island nothingness surrounds me
like a garment, in my cell I pray,
supplicating the Almighty
as the wind shakes my cloak
and the renunciation shivers my flesh –
sic transit gloria mundi.

I fall on my knees
at sunrise,
the lark rises to the heavens,
we both praise the Lord
with the sound of the sea in our ears –
sic transit gloria mundi.

When the dear Sabbath comes
I will put my coracle to the waves
and go to the church by the shore
where the flock will be gathered;
we will read from the holy Book,
we will say mass,
we will praise Your name,
we will remember the dead –
sic transit gloria mundi.

I shall return to my island
where I will imbibe nothingness
which the Son will fill with beauty.
I shall tread down the flesh,
to you, O God, will be the glory –
sic transit gloria mundi.

[MC]   76

Dà Thaobh a' Bhealaich

An Naomh Dòras — Saint Doras

Fàilte

Fàilte oirbh, a chàirdean,
gu imleag na cruinne,
farsaingeachd sùla,
iom-chlaisneachd cluaise,
suathadh caomh na còinnich.

Fuirichibh, èistibh, faicibh
leth-cheud mìle de bheanntan
mu ur coinneimh, gu greannmhor
ag èirigh. Ceumannan
air am faod sibh a dhol
gu lochan is uillt
gu cladaichean is tuinn
gu stùcan àrda bideanach
's gu bearraidhean iomallach.

Thigibh tron chearcall
is faicibh,
fairichibh coibhneas na mòintich,
còinneach chaoin an Taobh Sear.

[MC]   79

Gleann Hinneasdail

Cuachan Ghleann Hinneasdail, mic-talla
fuaimean ar beatha an seo,
a' glaodhaich ar teachd gu baile
le torghanaich cliath a' chruidh,
agus iadhairean rathad fada na mòine
a' craoladh ar dol a-mach,
's a' cabadaich nuair a thig thu gu a cheann:
inbhir de pholl 's de mholaig 's de ghrinneal,
comharra tràighe ar teachd 's ar falbh.

Cha sheall an abhainn air a cùlaibh; bidh i torrach,
pìos air falbh bhuainn fo na sgòthan
a tha a' dèanamh dealbh-dhannsa san adhar,
fhad 's a tha am feur le gath is guth,
tha a' ghaoth na deann bhon druim,
a' ro-aithris uisge is fors is at an t-srutha.
Na lighe, sleamhnaichidh an abhainn gu muir,
a' breith ann am briseadh nan uisgeachan, a' triall
a plaiseanta de chop geal sìos ris an oirthir.

Air Turas

Nach math gu bheil sibh air turas thall an sin
agus gu bheil na h-uisgeachan a' briseadh
an abhainn a' ghlinne.
Cluinnidh sinn iad tric
a' briseadh air a' chladach an seo –

aig bonn na craite
far am b' àbhaist am bàrr a bhith cho pailt,
feur is arbhar, ri linn an t-seanar,
agus far an slaodadh an t-each ruadh
na cùirn agus na cruachan chun na h-iodhlainn;
an dearbh spot
sa bheil an taigh againn an-diugh –

agus bhon taigh, bhon t-seann iodhlainn,
cluinnidh sinn na tuinn a' briseadh
aig bonn na craite
mar a bha iad bho chian
fo na rionnagan dìomhair biorach,
agus air fàire chun an ear-thuath
taigh-solais Rubha Rèidh,
a' priobadh a rabhadh dha ròidean a' chuain,
dhan chorra eathar a thèid seachad.

Sùil Thairis air an Nahe

Tha an abhainn a' snìomh eachdraidh tro sgàinidh
                           àrda an fhearainn.
Tha i air fuil a' chatha a ghlanadh air falbh.
An cionta deàlrach ann an lainnir grèin san uisge.

I toirt leatha lùb de a h-eachdraidh
a' tionndadh chun na Rhine
leis an loidhne rèile agus an rathad.

Tha grian a' gheamhraidh a' losgadh fàinne dhuilleagan
                               daraich
cho dearg ri rudhadh porphyry.
Eadar na binneanan, sgàilean sleamhainn a' toinneamh
gu mìn sìos cliathaichean na Rotenfels.

Gu h-ìosal tha fionain a' gheamhraidh nan sreathan dìreach.
Geallaidhean reòthte a' lìonadh fhìon-dhearcan
agus tron cheò, nì togalaichean
an tìr ceàrnagach le tuineachadh bhailtean.

              ❖ ❖ ❖

An seo chan eil an ceum cho cinnteach,
rathad critheanach singilte,
agus fo na binneanan seo
tha boglach is mòinteach
a tha air leathar do bhrògan abachadh
le bliadhnaichean fada na coiseachd;
filleadh na cuimhne air los na gàire,
nan òran agus na caoidh –
crac leantainneach na h-inntinn.

[MG]   82

Am Bealach

Am bealach dha bheil sinn a' gluasad,
an-còmhnaidh thall an sin
tha dùthaich eile,
dùthaich nach aithne dhuinn.
Dè tha tachairt thall an sin
air taobh eile a' Bhealaich?

Tha An Taobh Sear
làn bhailtean beaga:
An Gàrradh Fada, Steinnseal, Brògaig,
agus fo sgàile Bheinn Eadra
Màileagear, Mairiseadar, Geàrros;
thar na mara
Geàrrloch is Toirbheartan is Eilean Rònaigh:
an-diugh tha Beinn Eighe fo cheò.
Bhon taigh againn chì mi iad air fàire
tro na duilleagan buidhe is uaine.
Ach chun an iar tha am Bealach
agus Gleann Hìnnneasdail,
eadar am Maoladh Mòr agus Loch Leum na Luirginn,
's chan eil Tobar na Slàinte fada air falbh.

A' Gearradh na Mòna

Le pocan leth-fhalamh air mo dhruim
agus spaid na mo làimh,
chaidh mi air lorg na mòna duibh,
suas a' bhruthach ann an Eàrlais
le ceum neo-ionnsaichte.

Bha an àile soilleir
mar dhuilleig bhàin ghil
's bha meurain uisge
mar inc ann, boinnean sepia
a' salach mo bhrògan;
an àiteachan, chaidh iad sìos dhan ghrunnd,
's thuit am poll dhiubh
mar chèir theth, a' dùnadh
suas nan ceumannan a ghabh mi.

Dhìrich mi nas fhaisge air an loch
airson druim de chàrn chlachan a ruighinn,
's na cnàmhan-droma a' stobadh an-àirde
tro fheòil an fheòir luim air gach taobh,
mar chlosaich air a criomadh lom le gaoith chìocraich.

'S aig mullach a' chlaiginn fhearainn seo,
le a chreagan gealaichte, lochain,
agus cnapan stobach feòir,
fhuair mi na seann phuill-mhòna,
agus Loch Mòr:
mar shùil uisge
a' spleuchdadh ris an adhar.

[MG]   84

Bha na h-innealan
a bha mi a' giùlan
a' glagadaich seòrsa de dh'fhonn
airson na h-obrach a chuir mi romham.

A' ràcadh tron ùir 's tro fhreumhan,
choimhead mi airson fàdan,
ag eadar-theangachadh mar a ghluaisinn an spaid
ann an ruitheam na h-obrach:

flaughter
airson an riasg a rùsgadh
rutter
airson gearradh eadhon nas doimhne,
toirsgeir
airson bogadh a-staigh dhan mhòine dhuibh thais
's na faclan a thilgeil a-mach:
a' sgalpadh, a' sgrìobadh, a' cladhach;
sgian sgoltaidh,
toirsgeir,
iarann cartaidh...

fhad 's a bha mo smaointean air an cumail ann an lasair liath
de mhòine bhrìoghmhor a loisg a-steach dhan eadar-sholas
                                    agus dol fodha na grèine.

[MG]   85

Ag Eadar-theangachadh na Mòna

1
Tha e doirbh gabhail ris
gur e eadar-theangachadh
a tha sa h-uile nì

's nach urrainn am facal
ach gleus truaillidh a chur
air a' pholl-mhòna.

Tha a' chuairt as fheàrr leam
a' dol seachad air Loch Langaig,
air an rathad dhan Chuith-raing.

Chaidh mi ann an-dè a-rithist,
am fraineach a bha uaine air donnadh,
rèidh suas bho oir an locha

agus pìos seachad suas a' bhruthach
tha am poll-mòna a bh' aig mo sheanair,
gun ann ach fiamh-shamhla fo fheur a' mhonaidh,

far an cuireadh iad an toirsgeir
dhan mhòine dhuibh no ruaidh –
bith-beò aon amas a seilbhe.

Saoil ciamar a dh'eadar-theangaich iad a' mhòine
a bha ag èirigh na rùdhain air an riasg?
Na samhla air geamhradh taobh na cagailt'

no mar obair shalach a dh'fheumt' a dhèanamh,
am bochd a' sileadh nam fàdan fallais
is mac an tùir air leabaidh it' na chadal?

2
'S mach a chaidh mi suas an ceum gu Loch Hàsgo
is Leathad na Caillich ag èirigh romham
's os an cionn stùcan liath-ghlas Chuith-raing.

An àiteigin am measg nan stùcan sin
tha A' Chailleach, agus dh'iarrainn gum biodh fios agam,
ach tha an fheadhainn aig an robh fios air falbh.

Basalt àrsaidh Chuith-raing mar èileadh dubh is uaine is glas.
À, a chreagan! nam b' urrainn dhuibh bruidhinn!
Nach iomadh sgeul a bhiodh agaibh dhomh

mu Laurasia fad' o chian,
mu na dìneasairean a bha triall
air bruthaichean nan cian-thìrean.

À, a chreagan! nam b' urrainn dhuibh innse,
ach tha ar n-eadar-theangachadh fhìn againn
is nì sinn ar sgeulachd às a' chreig.

[MC]   87

Beinn Eadra

Gabhaidh mi ceumannan Albannach
an àite feadhainn Shasannach,
ged a tha e doirbh an diofar a dhèanamh a-mach
air an t-slighe seo suas gu Beinn Eadra.
Tha an loidhne bhàn de dh'fheur chun a' mhullaich
le crith-sholas fàilidh sa ghrèin, faileasan
làn Gàidhlig dhiùid, a' toirt nan òran còmhla,
's boglaichean nan glug-caoinidh a' gèilleadh do dh'ìoranas
faobharach nan craitean millte; teangannan creagach
le tuthagan còinnich,
a' sùghadh a-steach inc aoidionach
nan còinneach 's am meòrachaidhean –

'S e coigreach a th' annam an seo, gu bràth nam
                                    choigreach, suainte
's air mo chrùidheadh ann an saoghal cruinneil
de dh'aodach dìonach a' ghore-tex.
Es ist sehr schön hier.
Bealach Ùige mu thuath agus sùilean
dà loch a' spleuchdadh air ais ris an adhar; mu dheas
tha Bealach a' Mhorghain agus cuislean
nan allt a tha greasad gus iad fhein a thiodhlacadh.
Ach tha dòigh aig eachdraidh
a bhith sìoladh tro na beàrnan.

Mar a thiondaidheas an t-sìde aig mullach na streap,
tha am fallas a' taiseachadh broinn mo sheacaid
's a' dèanamh mo làthaireachd cùbhraidh.

Air an Druim (Bealach a' Mhorghain) —
On the Ridge (The Morghan Pass)

Air Tighinn a-staigh

Bhon taobh seo, tha Beinn Eadra àrd
agus biorach, le iomairean
fraoich eadarainn 's a bonn, freumhan
righinn ag aithris am prìomh ghin.

Chan e do choire, a charaid,
far an do rugadh tu; thàinig
sinn uile a-staigh do shaoghal
uaireigin, gun rogha sa chùis;

creagan ar n-àraich gar gleidheadh
slàn, mas e slàn a th' ann, mòran
dhen chreig na sgàirneach sgapte, bloigh,
math dh'fhaodte, lìomhte am bonn lòin

's air a thulgadh le siantan
fada a-mach on mhàthair-chreige.
Tobhtaichean, lorgan nan daoine
a chaidh à sealladh, thàinig iad

a-staigh an àiteigin eile
far nach robh fraoch no roinn ruith,
iadsan 's an sliochd a' sealbhachadh
fada bho shearbhachd an imrich.

An seo na creagan a' tuiteam,
sruthan na cainnt a' sìoladh às,
fuil nan allt-chuislean a' traoghadh,
uillt-chuislean ùra ag èirigh.

[MC]   91

An saoghal air a mheasgachadh
's air a mhaistreadh, na bealaich 's iad
air tuiteam; loidhne rèidh dhìreach
's sinn uile air tighinn a-staigh.

Dùn Cana bho Lùib — Dun Caan from Luib

An t-Eilean Sgitheanach

An t-Eilean Sgitheanach: tha mi air ais a-rithist;
cha b' urrainn dhomh do chraos-ghàire àicheadh
agus do thaighean geala mar sheudan
air an glaodhadh ri glinn uaine an t-samhraidh 's ri oirean
                 brìoghmhor a' chladaich.
Eilein, tha mi a' bruidhinn riut, a bheil thu gam chluinntinn?
Ach, tha thu mar gum biodh tu a' cur cùl rium.
Uaireannan spleuchdaidh tu orm led shùilean
                 ioma-chluaranach,
mar bhiastaig mharbhtaich, a tha gam chur à cochall
                 mo chridhe
mar gum bithinn a' lùbadh thairis air oir na creige seo.

Eilein, a bheil sinn a' dol a-mach air a chèile, no an e gu
                 bheil sinn ro fhada an cuideachd a chèile…
Tha thu gam chur às mo chiall. You're driving me nuts.
Eilein, a bheil thu a' fàs gruamach a-rithist?
Chosg e £14.70 faighinn an seo
agus tha e mar gum biodh an còmhradh seo air a bhith
                 againn am badeigin roimhe.
Am bi an t-uisge ann a-rithist? An cùm e air a' sileadh? An
                 dèan e turadh idir?
A bheil a' mheanbh-chuileag a' tighinn?
Am faigh sinn dhachaigh còmhla gu bràth a-rithist?

Eilein, tha mi faireachdainn gu bheil d' inntinn
                 aon-shligheach 's gun àite ann dhut dol air ais:
's e th' annainn blàr de dh'àiteachan-seachnaidh.
Bheil thu faicinn, tha mi feuchainn ri do thuigsinn,

cùram do dhualchais a thoirt fa-near:
ach thoir dhomh mathanas, tha mi mall gu ionnsachadh:
Eh! Chaidh mo thogail ann an Sasainn,
air mo bhiathadh air sannt agus spàintean cianalais
na h-ìmpireachd,
's a-nis tha mo chasan a' dol fodha nad bhoglaichean.

A Dhia, 's ann agaibh a tha na boglaichean. A h-uile
boinne uisge a tha sin air a stòradh,
airson bliadhnaichean, a dhìth mhèinnearan, 's an uair sin
dè a nì thu?
Leigidh tu às e ann am spùt is ciont de dh'easan...
Eilein – tha thu gam sgùradh às led oidhcheannan fada
ga mo chur tuathal led iomadh dol fodha grèine
gam fhàgail luaireanach le tuainealaich do ghaothan;
a bheil fhios agad, uaireannan leanaidh tu ort is ort is ort:
's e an aon chòmhradh a th' againn fad làithean,
's tha e gam chur às mo chiall.
'S tha cùbhrachd do roid gam dhèanamh tinn.
Feumaidh mi deoch. Tuilleadh uisge-beatha. Cha do dh'òl
mi mo leòr dhìot fhathast.

Eilein Sgitheanaich: dèanamaid seòrsa de dhealbh shlàn de
ar càirdeas:
tha fios a'm mu chogaidhean cinnidh, na Fuadaichean,
an trom-uallach a ghiùlain thu bho phòsadh eile;
ach nach urrainn dhuinn a-nis ar snaidhm Ceilteach fhìn a
cheangal le beagan a bharrachd dòchais?
Eilein Sgitheanaich: cha tusa Tìmor an Ear; chan e Port
Rìgh Dili.
Tha fhios a'm, tha fhios a'm, cha bhi e furasta:

tha nighean na craite ann an càs a-rithist
ri linn brosgal a' bheairteis.
Tha Port Rìgh air fàs cho thar-ùr-nodha
agus Trom-laighe a' Bhaile-mhòir, e ag èaladh ann am
faileasan na ceàrnaig leis an teicneòlas fòn-làimhe as ùire.

Muinntir an àite toirmisgte bho thaighean-òsta air eagal
nàire a chur air na h-aoighean.
Haoi, càit am faigh mi clootie dumpling aig an àm seo a
dh'oidhche?
Huh! Creag an Fhèilidh a' dol cam, a' magadh orm.
A dhonais! Bheil thu coimhead ormsa?
Ha, aidh: tha fhios a'm dè tha thu ris, nad sheasamh an
sin, a' mùn an aghaidh na gaoithe;
agus na lochain cho làn de dh'uisge, sùilean glainne
stàrr-shùileach ris an oidhche.
Tha na fosailean air ghluasad a-rithist, cluinnidh mi na
dìneasairean ag ionaltradh,
cluinnidh mi an ulfhart àrsaidh. Tha an làbha a' sruthadh.
Tha mi faireachdainn tinn. Uabhasach tinn. Duilich.
Tha mi duilich, tha mi air chall. I am lost.

Eilein, chan eil dragh gu bhith orm tuilleadh mu ar deidhinn.
Tha gaol agam ort. Bithidh gu bràth.
Tha fhios agad gu bheil mi ga chiallachadh, nach eil?
Siuthad, can rium gun toir thu mathanas dhomh.
Tha an oidhche air a bhith fada. Tha an dithis againn
sgìth. Tha mi a' tuigsinn.

Tha do nigheanan 's do mhic a' toirt dùbhlan dhut fhathast,
feuchainn ris an rud as fheàrr a dhèanamh dhaibh;

a' Ghàidhlig a chumail a' dol. A' chuid as fheàrr dhìot.
I'm sorry. Am faod sinn dìreach laighe sìos an seo
                                       le chèile, gu socair?
Cumaidh mi orm gad luaidh, tha mi 'gealltainn.
Èist ris na sailm a tha nan dust anns a' ghaoith.
                                       Dè nì mi? Dè nì mi?
Dè a nì mi mus sguab an ath chogadh sinn
dhan dorchadas, a' fàgail dìreach soillse reul os cionn
                                       Rubha Hùnais?
Sluigidh mi mo dheòir 's traoghaidh mi a' ghlainne 's
                                       ruigidh mi airson do thaobh caoin
's cuiridh mi bròg coiseachd air beulaibh na tèile –
tapadh leat, tapadh leat, tapadh leat.

A' Cur Bileag air …

'Gâteau', tha e ag ràdh,
is chì thu spuinnse is bàrr is measan,
ach falaichte bhon t-sùil
tha siùcar, uighean, margarain is flùr,
salann, sòda, sùgh liomaid agus eile …

'Alba', canaidh sinn
is chì thu togalaichean Ghlaschu is Dhùn Èideann,
greannmhor, Bhictòrianach, snaighte,
's cuid lom, àrd, fuar, neo-fhàilteach,
àiteachan anns nach cuireadh tu do chù …
agus tha cuideachd glinn fhionnar ann
le canach is fraoch is lochan le cuilc ris na h-oirean
agus bric a' falach fo na leacan.
Aodainn cuideachd de gach seòrsa,
deàlraidhean ginteil bho linn na cloich'
bho na Lochlannaich, bho na Cruithnich,
agus bhon a h-uile treubh air thalamh
agus cuiridh sinn 'Alba' mar bhileig air.

'Sasannach', canaidh sinn,
is chì sinn fear à tòn Shasainn le amaideas na ghuth
no tè le aineolas mu Alba,
no Scouser a' sileadh dheur anns a' Chop,
no Lunnainn mòr nam mìle cinneach,
an duine dubh le sinnsirean nan tràillean
a tha a-nise air ceann gnothaich,
cluaintean Chambridge, monaidhean Chumbria,
agus cuiridh sinn 'Sasainn' mar bhileig air.

[MC]   99

A Dhè, glèidh mi gun a bhith a' cur bileag ort,
a charaid, 's mi cho aineolach air d' fhìor ghnè.
Mar gun canainn 'saoghal'
's mi smaoineachadh seach gun tuirt mi am facal
gu bheil mi ga thuigsinn an ìre bhig no mhòir
's am millean nì fon bhileig nach fhaca mi a-riamh.

À la Prufrock

À la Prufrock

Tha an t-adhar glas – cha mhòr nach tuirt mi liath,
ach 's ann an Uibhist a chanas iad sin,
liath an àite gorm, mar a chanas sinne –
ach an-diugh tha an t-adhar glas
agus chan e an t-adhar ach an ceann a tha liath.

Tha an t-adhar glas 's an lòn a' ruith gu bras
's na lòin mar sgòthan ann am meadhan na crait,
's an saoghal fhèin cho liath 's cho ait
mar chaoraich
mar shnaidhmeannan chaorach an siud 's an seo.

Thuirt i fhèin rium, 'Nach tèid sinn a chèilidh a-nochd
air na Dòmhnallaich? Bidh iad nan suidhe an siud leotha fhèin,
a' coimhead *Emmerdale* is *Coronation Street*.'

Rim chuimhne, bha an t-adhar gorm
's an deic ruadh le meirg, 's a' ghrian gar feannadh,
sinn air chrith leis na drileachan dealain
dol phut, phut, phut, phut,
dol tarsainn air a' Chuan Innseanach,
dol tarsainn Crios na Cruinne
's an dust gar dalladh,
càit an diabhal a bheil an cala!

'Tha sinne nar suidhe an seo leinn fhìn
a' coimhead nan naidheachdan is *Emmerdale*;
chuireadh iad uibhreachd oirnn tighinn faisg.'

Uibhreachd?

Tha na h-uillt nan cuaileanan geala
a' leum 's a' ruith gu bras
's Aeòlus, 'dia na stoirm', a' cìreadh nam fuilteanan air ais.

'Uibhreachd oirnn?'

'Tha thu a' faicinn gu bheil mi liath
's gum faca mi an saoghal o chian.
Tha fios aca gach nì a rinn mi riamh.'

'Fhad 's a smaoinicheas sinn mu dheidhinn,
a bheil thu 'g iarraidh cupa tì?
Bhiodh e math an cupa tì,
fhad 's a chumas sinn cluas ri claisneachd 'son na gaoith?'

'Bhiodh sin cho math fhad 's tha sinn feitheamh…
aon spàin siùcair is rud beag bainne.'

Bha am foghar air an St Lawrence grinn,
na dathan buidhe is dearg is ruadh
fhad 's a bha Presley is na Beatles a' seinn,
a' dèanamh air Quebec is Three Rivers
's an abhainn mhòr cho leathann, ciùin is rèidh
's fad' air falbh caoraich Fhionnlaigh anns a' bheinn
far am biodh na lòin a' seinn –
's an t-Easbaig Robinson a' sgrìobhadh Honest to God –
far am biodh na muilt a' caoidh.

Tha i a' fàs fliuch a-rithist 's a' ghaoth a' bòilich.

[MC]   104

'An robh thu a' bruidhinn? An cuala mi do ghuth?'

'Cha robh, a ghràidh, 's e bh' ann ach an t-uisge.
Nach cluinn thu gu bheil a' ghaoth ag èirigh,
nach cluinn thu na sgalan a' tighinn nas fhaisge?'

Tha an cruinne a' blàthachadh gun teagamh
's na coilltean mòra gan leagail,
cha bhi biadh ann dha na h-eòin bheaga.

'Tha thu ceart, tha i robach a-muigh,
cha chreid mi nach fuirich sinn a-staigh'.

Nach mòr am beud gu bheil an treud sa bheinn
air oidhche cho robach seo
's na Dòmhnallaich leotha fhèin aig an teine
's naidheachd bàis eile bho Iorag
's am falt a' fàs liath.

'An tarraing thu na cùirtearan, a Dhòmhnaill?'

A-màireach chì mi ciamar a tha an treud.
Cuiridh mi orm a' bhonaid dhubh, 's dòcha...
an cuir mi orm a' bhriogais leis na tuill...
saoil an cuir mi orm a' bhriogais?

'An tarraing thu na cùirtearan, a Dhòmhnaill?'

'Seadh, a ghràidh, nì, nì mi sin.'

'An tug thu bainne dhan a' chat?'

[MC]   105

Duilleag air a Sracadh à Leabhar-latha Neach-eòlais-nàdair, 16mh an Cèitean 2007

Chuala mi gu bheil corrachan-bàna ag itealaich gu
                         ceann-a-deas Shasainn.

Ann an seo nì eòin imrich, aon uair eile, bho àirdean eile:
iteagach, thèid iad air sgèith à neadan san iar
reamhar le miann, gu spiris sna bailtean-mòra
a dh'itealaich le neon 's chan ann leis a' ghealaich
a' gabhail a' chothruim am measg sionnaich a' bhaile

a' fàgail nam feannag airson closaichean seann chraitean
                            a spioladh…
cuimhneachain, sleuchdte mar chladhan
an crotal ag imleachadh nam facal
snaighte sa chloich; an cuid fhacal
air an gleidheadh ann an còmhradh, ach
air an sèideadh leis a' ghaoith mar a thig iad a-mach…

An uair sin, an sealladh as iongantaiche buileach:
taigh air chuibhlichean a-steach dhan ghleann,
le torran air a' chliath-chruidh gu a cheann-uidhe sealach.
Na lìon-chùirtearan air an tarraing, an doras-aghaidh
                            air a dhruideadh,
an similear fhathast gun cheò ag innse cò dha a bhuineas e.

Tha nas lugha de dh'eòin ceilearaidh ann airson fonn air
                            an fhonn a sheinn.

[MG]   106

Na Faingean, Ceann Ghleann Hinneasdail —
The Fanks, Top of Glenhinnisdal

Do Chroitean

le leth-shùil air To Meddowes *agus leisgeulan do*
Robert Herrick

Dh'fhigh thu ùrachan ballach 's flùraichean,
chùm thu dannsaichean aig àirighean
far na thàrmaich rudhadh-gruaidh' fad uairean
                     as t-samhradh:
no a chiaraich iad gu oidhcheannan dheòir agus caoidh.

Chunnaic thu briseadh-cridhe
agus an dubh-chosnadh, saothair
gearradh agus cruachadh mòna, spàirn
nan uairean, a' togail fheannagan on ghrunnd.

Chual' thu am bannal a' seinn,
làmhan a' luadhadh aodach le deirge a' chrotail,
chual' thu bleadraich nan allt, ag èirigh,
a' sìneadh an lìon airgid air an fhearann.

Ach a-nis spreadhaidh taighean geala,
am measg nan clachan, gun chrait –
gann freagarrach airson gaoth an iar,
le àrd-cheum stràiceil, gu h-àrd;

Mar stoc neach-malairt, tha do bhruthaichean lom,
do fhraoch air a dhubhadh le sannt,
air d' fhàgail gun chuid gun chòir,
do dhualchas na connadh dhan bhraidseal.

[MG]   109

Òran a' Chlaiginn
no – Cor nan Coimhearsnachdan Gàidhlig

'S mi 'm shuidh' aig an uaigh,
ag amharc mu bruaich,
feuch claiginn gun snuadh air làr...

Dùghall Bochanan (1716-1768)

Geal is cruaidh air bruaich na h-Alba,
Chaidh mo ruagadh dhan an uaigh;
Far 'n robh teang' bha ceanalt' ealamh,
Chan eil ach toll gun chruth gun fhuaim.

Bha uair ghluaisinn com is casan
Bhon a' Pharbh gu bruachan Chluaidh;
A-nis, mo thruaighe, chan eil annam
Ach slige thana air bheag buaidh.

Am Baile Bhòid bhiodh còmhradh 's caithream,
Cailleachan le cagar còir.
Bha brod de dh'òrain à Loch Abar
'S tuil seanchais am Bogha Mòr.

Nuair bhiodh cuisle 's fèith gam lasadh,
'S gàire fhallain air mo ghnùis,
Bheirinn cuairt san Eilean Fhada,
No dhèanainn crac an Leitir Iù.

'N-diugh còmhradh eile aig an talamh
Is fead an aonaich na mo chluais;
Na seann chlaiginn 's iad mo charaid,
Iad mar mi fhìn nan cnàmhan cruaidh.

Claiginn ùr' nan tiùrr fam chomhair,
'S beag an diù dhaibh marbh no beò;
Às bith dè 'n cànan a bha mòr ac',
Chan eil facal ac' no deò.

Buileach

Ged a tha sinn marbh,
chan eil sinn
buileach marbh buileach;

fhad 's tha sùgh san duilleig
agus sìol-chur san fhonn
(agus fonn sa phort)
agus sùilean san t-sìol
cha deach sinn buileach a dholaidh
no a dholaidh buileach.

Nuair a thig am bàrr am bàrr,
bidh sinn beò
an dòchas
gum bi anail sa bhàs
's an sìol fhathast le brod fàis.

Taigh ann am Flòdaigearraidh

Tòisichidh turas le smaoin:
sguabaidh i tro rumannan,
gluaisidh i eadar bùird is sèithrichean eòlach,
chì i eachdraidh grunn dhealbhan
a thogadh sna Ficheadan,
chì i na curracan 'cloche' 's na stocainnean,
na h-aodainn air am beò-ghlacadh
le dànachd an nuadhachais,
soilleir fo ghrian Sràid a' Phrionnsa.
Bheir i sùil air sèinichean uaireadair ri siùdan
bho shiosacot bràthair-màthar a dh'fhuirich an seo uair
's gu slaodach bheir i fa-near
loinn 's brèid-lìn an-dràsta seo fhèin.
Seòlaidh i os cionn brat-làir an teallaich,
crochaidh i mar lasair
far an robh stòbh a' chidsin,
agus thèid i air iteal a lorg
còs dhen àile airson lùb-fhoistinn,
ri taobh balla tiugh uinneige
's an doras-aghaidh a' fosgladh…
Faileasan san fhor-thalla,
a' sìoladh fad na slighe
gu doras an t-seòmair-chadail
mar gum biodh a' dol a dhùsgadh dithis luchd-bhruadar.
Thig oiteag,
ag ùrachadh nan rumannan le cagarsaich.
Gun àite eile dhan tèid i, dùisgidh smaoin
's nì i ceumannan san àile, cuairtichidh i,
gabhaidh i thuice fàileadh feòir agus rainich,
agus thèid i à sealladh à aigne an àite seo.

An Smaoin a' Leantainn oirre

Tha an smaoin a' leantainn air a turas
's i a' faicinn nan daoine nan suidhe
far an robh iad uair mun bhòrd
lom fhiodha, Màiri is Ruaraidh is Pàdraig

is Seanair is Seanmhair is Flòraidh
le trosg is buntàta tioram blasta,
a chuir is a bhuain iad fhèin, ga ithe
leis a' bhainne a bhleoghain iad sa mhadainn.

Tha an t-àite air atharrachadh, an taigh
air ùrachadh, ach leanaidh an smaoin oirre,
a' faicinn fhaileasan na cuimhne, an stòbha
nach eil ann ag èirigh fa comhair,

a' chùlaist leis na mìosan cruan, am bainne
annta a' feitheamh gus an èireadh an t-uachdar
chun a' mhullaich, 's an dreasair far an robh
na crogain silidh, an t-ìm 's an siùcar air an cumail,

's an t-sèise fhiodha ris an uinneig, an cù foidhpe
a shròin a-mach 's a shùil ris a' bhòrd, deiseil
airson nan corran. Tha an smaoin a' cuimhneachadh
nuair a bha i leis a' ghille, 's thèid i na deann

a-mach seachad air an fhor-thalla
far am biodh na còtaichean an crochadh
's a-mach air an doras-aghaidh gu cliathaich an taighe,
far a bheil grinneal an starain, sin far an robh an seada

[MC]   114

le uidheam is acfhainn iasgaich is eile, putan
glainne uaine is trìd-shoilleir, na lìn-mhòra
is na lìn-bheaga is dubhain de gach seòrsa,
oir b' e iasgairean a bh' anns na gillean.

'S tha an smaoin a' leantainn air a turas,
an smaoin a bh' aig a' ghille, faileasan dhith
air an tìr, far an robh an stàball is a' bhàthach
is taigh nan cearc is an iodhlainn, a-nise

chan eil ann ach cuimhne, mapa fann
dhe na bh' ann, far an robh an crodh
nan seasamh anns na stàilichean
ann am fàileadh an todhair, tha gàrradh

an taighe ùir agus flùraichean a' fàs
's an smaoin a bh' aig a' ghille a' fàs fann
mar lì na còinnich air uachdar na cloiche,
mar liotachas na mara 's gann a chluinnear.

Iuchair an Taighe

Seachad an geata, dìreach mus cuir thu cas
air ciad flùr purpaidh nam bochd
's mus steig do làmh air tarraig mheirgich;
dìreach mus reub oiteag gaoithe
tarsainn d' aodann, a' sgùradh asbhuain an
achaidh mud choinneamh,
chì thu aiteal bhuaipe san fheur
aig fàl an rathaid shingilte,
iuchair, lainnireach, prìseil,
mar bhoinne uisge, opal sa chiaradh,
fhad 's a chluicheas an t-adhar le a sgàilean.

Tog i 's fairich a cruinnead a' leaghadh
eadar na h-oirean corrach
agus a dà thaobh mìn; ri a mullach
druim air a mhaoladh,
mion-ìomhaigh Thròndairnis,
a' slaodadh braille 'àirdean 's ìsleachdan
ann am bois do làimhe.
Dh'fhaodadh tu thu fhèin a ghearradh leis a' ghrèim
a th' agad,
no do ghàirdeanan a chur mu sgaoil, a' cur an cèill
gum fosgail glas sam bith a-nis.

[MG] 116

An Rup — The Auction

An Rup

Tha an nathair bhreac na lùban
Air an ùrlair far na dh'fhàs
Na fir mhòr a chunnaic mise;
Thoir am fios seo chun a' bhàird.

Uilleam MacDhùnlèibhe (1808-70)

Às dèidh briathrachas bòidheach
Thig òrd cruaidh na fìrinn;
Cha bhi air fhàgail ach na h-òrain.
    Thoir am fios seo chun a' bhàird.

Tha an rup a' dol gu h-òrdail,
Taigh is taigh a' dol a dhìth oirnn,
Is teang' a' choigrich gabhail còir oirnn.
    Thoir am fios seo chun a' bhàird.

Gliongarsaich nam bonn a' riaghladh
'S a' Ghàidhlig a' dol a thaigh na galla,
'S a' choimhearsnachd air a blianadh.
    Thoir am fios seo chun a' bhàird.

Ma tha ar cànan a' crìonadh,
'S math an airidh, 's math an airidh,
A' mhargaid anns gach nì a nì sinn.
    Thoir am fios seo chun a' bhàird.

An rup a' dol aig astar gòrach,
Dall am bonn tha reic na th' againn,
Dualchas, anam 's cainnt dhan òtrach.
    Thoir am fios seo chun a' bhàird.

[MC]   119

Na cuiribh coire air coigrich sheòlta
Bhith cur ar dòighean 's cainnt dhan aiginn:
'S ann annainn fhìn a tha a' bhreòiteachd.
    Thoir am fios seo chun a' bhàird.

Sòaigh

Tha dachaigh an duine seo na tobhta, lag feòir,
deanntagan is bloighean chnàmhan caorach.
A' cur na gaoith gu aon taobh, gabhaidh sinn cuairt a-steach
a dh'ionaltradh air cuimhneachain a bheatha ann an Sòaigh;
lìonaidh facail beàrnan, ag ath-thogail bhallachan,
is tughaidh iad am mullach fosgailte le an gàire.
Eadar dà chloich tha àrd-doras, bàn is sgròbte,
a' dèanamh sgeidse air far an robh doras, sanas air dà rùm,
mar a bha e o shean. Ach a-nis tha an t-eilean seo
a' dol fodha ann an sgòthan, ciùthran, ann an tuil de
                                  dh'fhacail choimheach.

Dusan Earrann do Thaigh

Blocaichean saimeant, uinneagan
's leacagan-mullaich dearg –
stob loinneil san talamh.

'S tu buachaille rùintean,
clach-iùil sheunta
gu 'm bi spèis a' tilleadh.

Èibhinn, ait air an oidhche,
gleidhidh tu gàireachdaich
taisgte fod sparran.

Fàiltiche na grèine
a chuireas sèine air solas;
flùraichean buidhe san uinneig.

No àite an dorchadais;
dubh-bhròn is èiginn
a' grèidheadh a' bhalla.

Samhla anam – fo na sailthean
eadh; fèin fhèin shuas gu h-àrd
agus sàr-fhèin san leabaidh.

Air mhisg, a' tilgeil rudan,
do sglèat air chrith,
na canaichean a' sèideadh.

Taisgire eun san anainn
dhan till iad gach bliadhna;
dìonaire beatha nan àl.

Long a' reubadh an adhair,
sgòthan geala a' criomadh
nan crann shimilear.

Eathar fo sheòl,
ceithir croinn bhuidhe
a' sìneadh nan seòl ruadha.

Doras gu sàmhchair
às dèidh fannachadh an ròis:
èist an osna a' traoghadh.

Ionad fannachaidh fuaim
nach ruig air fuar-shràid;
cofhurtachd – èistibh.

Cuilcean

a' sgrìobadh an uachdair, tha cuilcean nan saigheadean
a' comharrachadh àiteachan triall
a tha leaghadh 's a' fàgail meamran air an uisge.

Tobar Loch Shianta

an tobar
truinnsear 'tourmaline'
ciùin, a' cothromachadh na h-oiteig
taomaidh i na steallan a nì sinn mar ùrnaighean
facail dheireannach

Aig Tobar Loch Shianta

Dha Keiko Mukaide, neach-ealain à Iapan a tha a' fuireach
ann an Alba agus a thadhail air Tobar Loch Shianta. 'iana'
– 's ann mar seo a tha muinntir an àite ga fhuaimneachadh.
A rèir choltais, 's ann bho sianta/seunta *a tha an t-ainm a'*
tighinn. Bha an tobar seo, ann an Tròndairnis, ainmeil mar
thobar slànachaidh sna seann làithean.

Latha fuar frasach,
an loch fhèin luasganach
le gaoth tuath rapach

ach tha an tobar sìochail
fo fhasgadh chraobh fiùise
agus caochan a' sruthadh

bhon loch sheunta –
's sinne nar triùir aig an tobar
a' gabhail stiùir a brìgh

's i a' sruthadh gu ciùin,
a' samhlachadh sìth –
diva mhàlda, leth-fhalaichte.

Togaidh sinn uisge gu ar bilean
gun mhìr-mhìneachadh an fhacail
a' cur casg air a shlàinte:

chan eil facal ga ràdh,
a' cuimhneachadh a' *hado*
eadar aigne is uisge.

[MC] 125

Thig an t-uisge bhon ghrunnd
a-nìos, fada shìos fon choille,
bhon talamh choibhneil:

an t-uisge diombuan is buan,
an-diugh ann am Flòdaigearraidh
's a-màireach os cionn cuan.

Ear is iar a' tighinn còmhla
aig an tobar san tiotan seo:
's e am facal simpatico.

Ar Gaol

tha ar gaol mar mholaig
air a dèanamh mìn
leis an làn –
agus nuair a sguabas an ath thonn
sinn suas
bidh sinn air ar n-ionnlaid bhuainn fhìn

Gleann Breadail

agus tha cuimhn' a'm a' tionndadh air falbh bhon mhuir,
a' dol tarsainn air tràigh Ghlinn Bhreadail,
a bha breacte mar sheann chòmhdach leabhair,
a' feuchainn ri do smaointean a leughadh,
a' sguabadh gainmheach le mo cheuman
fhad 's a choimheadas mi air an fheadhainn eagarra
a chaidh a choiseachd tiotan no dhà
mus do thionndaidh thu do chùlaibh…

ach dh'fhan thu rium gus an tillinn,
nad sheasamh air bruaich mholagan,
a' coimhead orm le mall-ghàire,
's fios agad gun deigheadh agam
air sgeidse do ghluasaid a leughadh,
gun agam ri dhol air ais thairis air
mo sgròbail fhìn air a' ghainmhich liath-ghlas.

Tè Gheal mo Rùin

1.

Cuimhnichidh mi a-nochd, a thè gheal mo rùin,
far am biodh tu a' coiseachd
làithean fada geal air ais,
ri taobh Loch Shianta is suas dhan Choille Mhòir
's a-null ri taobh Loch nan Dùnanan,
a' coiseachd a Chille Mhoire,
oir b' ann a' coiseachd a bhitheadh sibh.

2.

Nuair a bha thu nad sheann aois
air an Acha Mhòr ann an Leòdhas
bhiodh tu bruidhinn mu Bhoilltir
is Flòdaigearraidh. Am measg nan truinnsearan
a bha air a' bhalla, 's tu air fàs dall,
bha na bruaichean 's na glaicean 's na lochan
's na daoine còire a bha air chall.
An aon rud a chitheadh tu ceart
mu dheireadh, b' e a' ghealach
agus sheasadh tu aig an uinneig
ga coimhead agus i làn.

3.

'S ann an seo far am biodh tu a' ruith 's a' leum
's tu nad nighinn bhig,
tha cuimhne mar sgàile fo uachdar na tìre.
Seo far an robh a' bhàthach
's far am biodh sibh a' bleoghan na bà
's far an robh an sabhal is stàball
's far an robh an seada an tacsa an taighe

leis na lìn is uidheam iasgaich
's far am biodh an t-iasg a' tiormachadh ris a' bhalla.

4.

Chì mi thu sna dealbhan anns na Ficheadan
air sràid an Dùn Èideann còmhla ri banacharaid,
dreasa fhada ort agus currac,
agus dealbh eile, air beulaibh an taigh-òsta sa Chaol,
tana is bòidheach is sibh air pòsadh,
thu fhèin is m' athair,
agus dealbh eile ann am Borgh Leòdhais,
thu cuartaichte led àl
agus anns gach dealbh tha thu caoin is caomh
is suairce, mar bu dual dhut.

5.

Ged a bha thu dall fhèin,
bhiodh tu a' fighe. Mu dheireadh
dìreach stocainnean, agus às dèidh do bhàis
shuidh mi a' coimhead orra, an tiùrr
stocainnean air an sgeilp. Sin mar a bha thu,
an-còmhnaidh a' dèanamh do chàch
agus am Bìoball agus Crìosd
mar stocainn air do chridhe.

6.

An-diugh, tha na tha air fhàgail
air talamh dhìot anns an ùir ann an Crosbost.
Sìth gum biodh leat, a mhàthair gheal,
agus leis an fhear a tha rid thaobh.

Eilean Fhlòdaigearraidh — Flodigarry Island

Bàgh Stafainn

An teid mi dh'ionnsaigh na mara
a shireadh cala dom smuain …?
Ruaraidh MacThòmais

A' seasamh aig do dhoras a-nochd
cluinnidh tu

do leanabachd a' measgachadh
le cathadh na mara

agus do chànan a' slapail
air cladach Eilean Fhlòdaigearraidh

e mar na gealbhuinn
a' seinn an ceilearaidh ris a' ghaoith

no casan a' stampadh
ris an dannsa air talamh cruaidh

no fàileadh na cuimhne
ag èirigh à snaidhmeannan feamann

a tha gu draoidheil a' toirt am bàrr
gaol dhan àite seo

mar nuair a sheinn a' phìob
a pìobaireachd gheur agus shoillseach

a' toirt an aire gu pongail
do ghaol dhan àite seo

agus an sùileachan gun robh, ann am Bàgh Stafainn,
na tuinn a' cur car air char de rainn.

[MG]   133

Lòchran Àigh nam Bochd

With how sad steps, o moon, thou climbs't the skies
Sir Philip Sidney, *Astrophil & Stella,* sonnet 31

A sholais thruaigh bhàin
mar a sheargas tu air an rathad seo tron ghleann
mar a tha thu air chrith ann an ciaradh an tràth-fheasgair seo
mar a tha thu air chorra-biod bho lochan gu lochan
thu crathadh do ghathan le aoibhneas
mus gabh eagal solas an latha grèim ort
mus buail a' ghrian
agus mus tig an t-uisge a-nuas
agus mus crath na gaothan an saoghal...

mar a thèid gaoir tromhad nuair a dh'fhosglas
                                    bilean na maidne
a' slugadh màldachd do sholais
socair do ghiùlain
agus co-chothrom meanbh do ghathan,
na gathan sin a thèid a shlugadh slàn...

brisidh latha air caoraich a' cnàmh an fheòir ghann
air feansaichean ag agairt an còraichean
air tuathan-gaoithe le an caran seunta
a' sireadh aiteal dòchais no saoraidh.

Am fosgail na h-eileanan seo gu bràth an cleòcaichean
de dh'oirthirean lùbach basalt agus gneiss,
a shealltainn mhurtairean an latha
agus murtairean na h-oidhche, an lìomh iad

cur is dlùth na h-imcheist 's na h-iomagain, an rèitich iad
obair-ghrèis an fhuatha, air a càradh le seann fhuaigheal
seann sgeulachd, seann sgeul
agus turadh seann òrain?

Solas bàn na gealaich
solas gach duine a tha dàna gu aisling,
ann an seo tha do sholas fhathast làidir,
do reul-shoillse fhathast làn geallaidh ann an
speur na h-oidhche seo.

Mar a Thuirt a' Ghealach

Thu nad bhall geal agus gorm
nam lèirsinn fad linntean sìorraidh
mar sheud air brat dubh, cho fad'
air falbh 's an dèidh sin cho faisg orm.

À, a shaoghail tha thu air
mo chlaoidh, air m' fhàgail balbh, nam thost
anns an fhalamhachd, cho fad'
a-mach am measg nan reultan cian.

Tha mi air mo cheangal riut
mar le caolan imleagach, mi
mar leanabh nach fhaigh gu bràth
saor airson a bheatha fhaotainn.

Dè tha tachairt air d' uachdar?
Thu mar nì beò anns an iarmailt,
a bheil thu cho brèagha 's a
tha do dhathan a' cur an cèill?

Brisidh mo chridhe, 'mhàthair
thalmhaidh, a' smaoineachadh ort
anns an tìm seo gun chrìch; gaol,
an e sin a tha gad ghluasad?

Gad mheòrachadh gach oidhche
brisidh mo chridhe, a' faighneachd
dè tha gluasad na tè ud
a ghin na reultan, às a broinn

Mar a Thuirt a' Ghealach — As the Moon Said

an tàinig naoidhein eile
a' gluasad ann an speuran fuar
iomallach mar tha mise
no a bheil iad ann an glaic bhlàth

a h-uchd? Inns dhomh, a shaoghail,
ciod e idir do chor a-nochd?
Dè an sgòth dhearg tha sguabadh
uaireannan thairis air d' ìomhaigh?

Dè tha sinn a' dèanamh, dè
anns an dubh-fhalamhachd a tha
sinn ciallachadh dha chèile?
Freagair mi, freagair a shaoghail.

Creag na Cuthaige

Tha thu an seo ann an gailearaidh,
grìoglachan fànais mun cuairt ort,
e mar gum biodh tu ann am machlag na gealaich.
Seall a-nis! Mu thràth, beachd ann am frèam na
                            sheasamh gu pròiseil
air a' bhalla, dathan agus breisleach a' sruthadh às:

sgeidse bho Chreag na Cuthaige
grafait agus meadhanan measgte

tha thu ag iarraidh smugaid a thilgeil air,
do dhùirn bhìodach a chrathadh ris agus slaic a thoirt ...

ach an uair sin coimheadaidh tu a-rithist air le sùil nas sine,
agus chì thu an saoghal,
gorm a' deàrrsadh, air ais gu ballaichean geala na gealaich,
strìochan dearg teinnteach a' dol tro chreig is uisge.

'An cluinn thu mi,' their an saoghal
an cluinn thu fuaim an fheòir 's e fàs,
laogh is bò a' geumnaich sa ghleann,
càr a' dol seachad, a' cnàmh a chìre de pheatrail,
agus a' chuthag, an-còmhnaidh a' chuthag, a'
                            cuimhneachadh an earraich?
Agus na faileasan a tha a' cumadh na sìorraidheachd,
ag aiseid nan tiotan sin chun na cuimhne.

Fadalach air feasgar sa Chèitean, ann an Innse Gall.
Nàbaidh a' gnogadh gu socair
ri fonn a smaointean ùra,
agus glacaidh eilean gu uchd a phàtran fhèin.

[MG]   140

An t-Seachdain Naomh

1

'S e na sùilean an toiseach 's an uair sin 's dòcha
bogha na mala, no an craiceann, gun smal,
cho bàn ris a' ghealaich, eu-coltach ri cruth-tìre leathair
nan aodannan, le barancothan snaighte sna malaidhean,
gruaidhean a' slugadh nam bliadhaichean fo fhaileasan;
's an uair sin, an sin, thig fiamh an dòchais;
chì thu a ghàire bhon ròpa sholais a' dèanamh cuairteig
thairis air clachan nam bloighean bhallaichean seo.
An Òigh Muire a' toirt sùil an t-saoghail air ais
le ar sùil-ne, dùinte air cùl na h-ealain
a th' air frèam meatailt geal le mìrean às agus lùbte;
's cha tig caochladh air a sìor-amharc, eadhon nuair a
                                 tha leòsan glainne
làn còinnich is salchair, mar a th' ann an sràid ann a' Florence,
no an seo, còmhdaichte le ablach de phàipear suiteis.

2

'S nuair a thig an oidhche, cha tig caochladh air d' fhiamh,
no air do rudhadh-gruaidh, air do ghiùlan, mar a bhios
                                 tu, mar dhoile
tro shràidean cumhang, seachad ballaichean bleideagach
                                 pastel,
fo uèirichean dealain, follaiseach dha na h-uile os cionn
                                 ar cinn.
Do chruachain a' luasgadh, thu tonn-ghluasad tro
                          thrannsaichean tìm
's na cluig a' seirm agus a' seirm. Thu air bhog san adhar,

fhad 's a sheinneas boireannaich ann an mantillathan
dubha d' ùrnaighean,
agus feithidh sinn ri fonn de chomhardadh
a nì grèim air a' chridhe mar shalm Gàidhlig.
Agus leaghaidh buille an druma mar chèir coinnle,
mar nathair, sìos faid na coinnle,
agus sinne nar seasamh còmhla, cruinn còmhla ann an
tiotan ciùine,
mar leannanan gòrach, a' lorg nan sgàinidhean,
am pian, agus an dathadh ri bun na siobhaig.

An Ite Bheusach

Criothnachadh nan each, thig iad
bho chrìochan na rìoghachd
le torman air talamh
a' tighinn nas fhaisge,
na cruidhean a' gleadhraich
le tàirneanaich 's tartar
mar ann an aisling,
aisling na daonnachd,
mar a thigeadh am bruadar,
dia-chruthachadh ìochdarach
bho dhoimhneachdan iomallach,
às na cridheachan cìocrach.

(Herod na shuidhe na sheòmar,
an inntinn ruaimleach far a dòigh,
cumhachd na Ròimh ga bhuaireadh.)

Ach chan e neart cruaidh eachraidh
le maoidheadh mòr fheachdan,
mar anns a' bhruadar,
a' bagairt oillt agus geilt;
chan e faram an saltairt
a' reubadh na talmhainn
a bheir buaidh aig an deireadh …

ach aisling eile,
na tàirngean,
na tàirngean sna deàrnaibh,
an nì anfhann, naomh a' gèilleadh
le truas do an-iochd,
An Ròimh agus an t-Ionracan,

agus aig a' cheann thall,
leagaidh an ite bheusach an t-each,
seach gur e gràdh an grunnd,
gràdh agus ceartas –
's bidh an tartar na thost.

Am Fear a Bha ag Iarraidh Lioft

Thug mi dha lioft an latha roimhe. Dh'èirich e
a-mach às a' ghleann, còinneach steigte ri chòta,
brèidean grèine air, choisich e thugam a' draghadh
                    fhaileasan.
Bha a dhruim crom le poca-droma – chitheadh tu cho
                    sgìth 's a bha e,
shaoil mi gur e eallach nam bliadhnaichean a bh' ann –
chuir e san t-suidheachan cùil e, 's thog sinn oirnn
                    a Phort Rìgh.

Rinn sinn crac air mar a bha cùisean air atharrachadh
anns a' bhliadhna no dhà a dh'fhalbh…
cha robh ach cianalas anns a' mhòr-chuid a thubhairt e,
mar a bha malairt leis na bùird air,
ach bha cuideachd sùil aige ris an àm ri teachd.

Ràinig sinn am port. 'Tha mi an dòchas gu bheil cuideigin
                    gad choinneachadh,'
thuirt mi, dìreach mar a bha an doras a' dùnadh.
'Chan eil duine a dh'aithnicheadh tusa,' thuirt e.

Choimhead mi air a' toirt sùil air na bàtaichean a' dubadh
                    an uisge gu aon taobh,
an taobh seo 's an taobh seo eile, mar a nì uisge
                    an-còmhnaidh, cho cothromach.
Choisich e chun an chipper:
a' sgapadh fhaoileagan air bhoile airson shliseagan;
sannt tiugh le salann 's fìon geur agus fàileadh crèis.

[MG]   145

Bha e mar gum biodh a' bruidhinn ris fhèin 's e tighinn
                              gu ceann a' chidhe.
Leum na cuimhneachain mar sgadain glacte ann an lìn,
leumannan roid is cur char san tarraing:

glòir-mhiann air a cutadh, pacaidean air sgeilp…

Chuir mi an iuchair san adhnadh airson falbh
ach cha tigeadh srad às a' chàr.

Ag Iarraidh Lioft — The Hitchhiker

Ag Iarraidh Lioft

Tha e na chrois dhòmhsa cuideachd,
na sheasamh ri oir an rathaid, sgian na làimh,
's le guidhe na shùilean
mar gum biodh cumhachd agamsa a chuideachadh
's fios deamhnaidh math aige gu bheil mi na làmhan
a h-uile latha a chì 's nach fhaic;
na taidhrichean agus an ceann a' maoladh,
e na riaghladair air gach nì
bho Orion gu cairt làir bheag a' Bhealaich,
bho dheàrrsadh Balla Mòr nan galagsaidh
chun a' mheirgidh a' tòiseachadh air a' chliathaich.

Fhalbh 's tarraing, arsa mise ris san dol seachad,
's fhios agam gum pàighinn air a shon
mar a bha na facail a' tighinn a-mach às mo bheul.

Clach ris a' Cheum

Chan e gneiss a th' annad ach cnap mòr basalt
a thuit na mìltean bhliadhnaichean air ais
bho Ghrianan nam Maighdean 's sìos Leathad na Caillich,
thu nis nad laighe ri oir a' cheum' os cionn Loch Hàsgo
air do sguabadh le bliadhnaichean nan sian.
Thu mar nì beò, soilleir, soillseach,
le lìon bheatha ioma-dhathte gad chòmhdach,
còinneach dhonn is bhuidhe is dhearg,
is algae de gach seòrsa cho dlùth riut ri craiceann.
'S ged tha fhios againn uile gu bheil thu marbh,
's de dhust na talmhainn, tha thu nad thaic dhan nì tha beò,
dhan lìonraidh bheatha tha gad chuartachadh,
's thu gam tharraing thugad gach latha thèid mi seachad ort
mar mhagnait, ag ùrachadh mhagaidean na cuimhne
a thig leis an aois, nad shamhla 's nad shoidhne
ris an t-slighe, 's a' brosnachadh smaoin is smaointean,
a tha mar sgannan còinnich diombuam
air uachdar cloiche, a' chlach a thàinig o chian
às na reultan, 's a mhaireas fada às ar dèidh
a' giùlan fiamh na beatha.

Colum Cille

Ann an sin, air thoiseach, an creutair tuainealach seo,
air èideadh ann an cleòc, aodann falaichte,
le foluaimean bho chois gu cois.

Tha e a' tilgeil chlachan ris a' chladach
aon às dèidh aon, gach tè na bogha,
i gealltainn tumadh san uisge.

A' gabhail anail, gluasad chasan, daingeann
fhad 's a ghràbhaileas iar-smuaintean na tuinn.
Lùbaidh e gus an tràigh a ghlanadh 's a chriathradh, gus

luchdaichte, air thurraban, 's le siaradh
thèid e gu lag sa chreig, na chrùban
a dhùr-amharc nan deamhan, no 's dòcha, a
dh'fhàilteachadh ainglean a-staigh.

Air a chùlaibh, tha caolan caorach na laighe,
sgaoilte agus rag, 's na ciad shanasan finealta
de gheallaidhean rin leughadh.

Eilean Dòrais

About a mile to the North, lies the Isle Altvig, it has a high rock facing the East, is near two miles in circumference, and is reputed fruitful in corn and grass, there is a little chapel in it, dedicated to St Turos.

Bho *A Description of the Western Islands of Scotland* le Màrtainn Màrtainn, 1703

1. An t-Eilean

Eilean nan trì ainmean,
Altavaig, Eilean a' Chinn Mhòir
agus Eilean Fhlòdaigearraidh

far an robh Dòras a' còmhnaidh
na bliadhnaichean mòra ud air ais
mus tàinig na Lochlannaich bho thuath

le targaidean is obair fala,
ach 's e ainm-san fhathast a tha air chuimhne,
Cill Dòrais air Cladach Fhlòdaigearraidh,

Poll Dòrais eadar an cladach is an t-eilean,
eilean aosmhor bàn, gun ri fhaicinn
ach strìochan fheannag is chlachan;

ach bha Dòras ann uair air choreigin
's dh'fhàg e a bheannachd againn na ainm
's dh'fhàg e ainm mar ùrnaigh air muir is fearann

mar cheathach cùbhraidh a' cur beannachd
air an t-seann fhonn
mar a ghabhas an oiteag thairis.

2. An Naomh Dòras

Uaireigin dhen robh an saoghal

Air an eilean seo tha aonarachd umam
mar èideadh, nam chill nì mi ùrnaigh,
ag aslachadh an Tì as àirde,
a' ghaoth a' cur crith nam chleòca
agus crith fèin-àicheidh nam fheòil –
sic transit gloria mundi.

Sleuchdaidh mi air mo ghlùinean
aig àm èirigh na grèine,
èiridh an uiseag chun nan nèamhan,
molaidh sinn le chèile an Tighearna
fuaim na fairge nar cluasan –
sic transit gloria mundi.

Nuair a thig an t-Sàbaid chaomh
cuiridh mi an curach dha na tuinn,
thèid mi chun chill ris an tràigh
far am bi an treud cruinn;
leughaidh sinn an Leabhar naomh,
abraidh sinn aifreann,
molaidh sinn d' Ainm,
cuimhnichidh sinn na mairbh –
sic transit gloria mundi.

Thèid mi air ais dham eilean
far am faigh mi eòlas air neonitheachd
a bhios am Mac a' lìonadh le a mhaise.
Saltraidh mi air an fheòil,
's ann dhutsa Dhè a bhios a' ghlòir –
sic transit gloria mundi.

Notaichean — Notes

An Turas (The Journey): Rubha Rèidh means 'the smooth point or promontory'.

Looking over the Nahe: The Nahe river is in the Rhineland Palatinate of Germany.

The Rotenfels are part of the Nahe heights, and have pinnacles of rock similar in shape to The Storr, which is part of the Trotternish Ridge, Skye.

Am Bealach (The Pass): Garrafad, Stenscholl, Brogaig, Maligar, Marishader and Garros are townships in the Staffin area.

Rona is a small island visible from Staffin.

Beinn Eighe, Britain's first National Nature Reserve, is in Wester Ross. The meaning is 'file peak'.

Maoladh Mòr – 'the great rounded hill'.

Loch Leum na Luirginn – appears to mean 'the loch of the leap of the ridges'. (Lurgann literally means shaft, shin or leg.)

Tobar na Slàinte – 'the well of health'.

Cutting Peat: 'Slitting knife', 'turf iron' or 'ire', 'budding iron' or 'spending ire' are Devonshire and Dartmoor terms for the implements used for cutting and raising the peat. 'Pluffy peat' is a term used to describe the best burning peat.

Ag Eadar-theangachadh na Mòna (Translating the Peat): 'the slope of the old woman'. This refers to a rock column on the slope.

Beinn Eadra: Bealach Ùige and Bealach a' Mhorghain are two passes down the steep sides of the Trotternish ridge.

Skye: Ginsberg's *America* was the starting point for this poem.

Dili is the capital of East Timor.

The Kilt Rock and its waterfall are well-known landmarks on the coast of Skye, near Staffin. There have been significant fossil discoveries of dinosaur bones and footprints in the area.

Rubha Hunish is the most northerly point of Skye.

Òran a' Chlaiginn (The Song of the Skull): Dùghall Bochanan (Dugald Buchanan 1716-68) was born in Strathyre, Perthshire and is one of the few outstanding Gaelic religious poets.

An Rup (The Auction): Uilleam MacDhùn-lèibhe (William Livingstone 1808-70) was born in Islay. An autodidact and ardent nationalist. The lines are taken from 'Fios thun a' Bhàird' ('A Message for the Poet'), a poem condemning the evictions.

Tè Gheal mo Rùin (My Pure Love): Voilteir is part of the Flodigarry township in Staffin. The meaning is unclear.

Creag na Cuthaige: The Rock or Crag of the Cuckoo.

A Stone by the Way: Grianan nam Maighdean means 'the sun-bower or palace of the maidens'.

Two Ravens Press is the most northerly literary publisher in the UK, operating from a six-acre working croft on a sea-loch in the north-west Highlands of Scotland. Two Ravens Press is run by two writers with a passion for language and for books that are non-formulaic and that take risks. We publish cutting-edge and innovative contemporary fiction, non-fiction and poetry.

Visit our website for comprehensive information on all of our books and authors – and for much more:

- browse all Two Ravens Press books by category or by author, and purchase them online, post & packing-free (in the UK, and for a small fee overseas)

- there is a separate page for each book, including summaries, extracts and reviews, and author interviews, biographies and photographs

- read our daily blog about life as a small literary publisher in the middle of nowhere – or the centre of the universe, depending on your perspective – with a few anecdotes about life down on the croft thrown in. Includes regular and irregular columns by guest writers – Two Ravens Press authors and others.

www.tworavenspress.com

Hedgehogs

James Lowen

B L O O M S B U R Y   W I L D L I F E

LONDON • OXFORD • NEW YORK • NEW DELHI • SYDNEY

BLOOMSBURY WILDLIFE
Bloomsbury Publishing Plc
50 Bedford Square, London, WC1B 3DP, UK
29 Earlsfort Terrace, Dublin 2, Ireland

A catalogue record for this book is available from the British Library

Library of Congress Cataloguing-in-Publication data has been applied for

ISBN: PB: 978-1-4729-5008-6; ePub: 978-1-4729-5007-9; ePDF: 978-1-4729-5006-2

6 8 10 9 7

Design by Susan McIntyre
Printed and bound in China by RR Donnelley Asia Printing Solutions Limited

MIX
Paper from
responsible sources
FSC® C144853

To find out more about our authors and books visit www.bloomsbury.com and sign up for
our newsletters

giving
nature
a home

Published under licence from RSPB Sales Limited to raise awareness of the RSPB (charity registration
in England and Wales no 207076 and Scotland no SC037654).

For all licensed products sold by Bloomsbury Publishing, Bloomsbury Publishing will donate a minimum
of 2% from all sales to RSPB Sales Ltd, which gives all its distributable prots through
Gift Aid to the RSPB.

Contents

Meet the Hedgehogs

The star of Beatrix Potter's *The Tale of Mrs Tiggy-Winkle* has worked its way into the hearts of successive generations of children and has long been coveted by gardeners for munching slugs. It is little surprise then that the Hedgehog routinely tops polls of favourite UK animals. Yet behind the Hedgehog's appealing front lies a little-known, scarcely seen and ever-rarer mammal with which humans have a contradictory and complex relationship that encompasses reverence and persecution, humour and hope, death and resurrection.

There may be no more immediately recognisable European mammal than the Hedgehog *Erinaceus europaeus*. Packed with prickles, this is not a species that one can mistake. Yet many of us – *too* many of us – know the Hedgehog only by image or by icon. Just one-fifth of UK residents claim to have seen a live Hedgehog in the wild – far fewer than are familiar with fictional characters such as Mrs Tiggy-Winkle or Sonic.

Opposite: Cute face and spiny body: who can fail to be charmed by the Hedgehog?

Below: A welcome garden visitor.

This is ironic, for Hedgehogs live among us – manoeuvring between our gardens, trotting along our pavements and crossing our roads. They are often our closest wild-mammal neighbour, yet we understand so little about them. We have long been fascinated by their resurrection in spring, yet their waking months largely pass us by. Many people devote chunks of their life to caring for Hedgehogs, yet our recent ancestors treated them as vermin. This book seeks to redress the balance, to celebrate Hedgehogs and what they have meant to us across several millennia.

Hedgehogs' family tree

Above: Carl Linnaeus, the godfather of taxonomy.

Below: A pointed snout is one clue that shrews (left: Pygmy Shrew) and hedgehogs are close relatives.

If there is one thing that biologists truly delight in arguing about, it is taxonomy – the science of classifying species. In the mid-18th century, a Swedish naturalist named Carl Linnaeus produced a ground-breaking attempt to classify and name all life forms. Many of his decisions have stood the test of time. But with the rise of DNA technology, in particular, scientists are increasingly changing how they group animals (and plants and fungi, and so on). Hedgehogs bear witness to this.

Until the early 21st century, hedgehogs were associated with moles, shrews and other small mammals within the order 'Insectivora' (literally 'insect-eaters'). Biologists were aware that this grouping was a bit of a dumping ground for mammalian miscellanea – not least because many of its members feasted on things other than insects. So there was comparatively little disgruntlement when various components of the Insectivora were spun off into separate groupings. Hedgehogs were granted their very own order, Erinaceomorpha, an accolade that suggested they had no particularly close relatives.

Many biologists think this classification makes sense and have stopped the taxonomic wheel here; however,

Current classification within the order Eulipotyphla

Order			Eulipotyphla		
Family	Erinaceidae		Soricidae	Talpidae	Solenodontidae
Subfamily	Erinaceinae (spiny hedgehogs)	Hylomyinae (hairy hedgehogs)	Soricinae	Talpinae	
Example genus	*Erinaceus*	*Echinosorex*	*Sorex*	*Talpa*	*Solenodon*
Example species	*Erinaceus europaeus* West European Hedgehog	*Echinosorex gymnura* Gymnure	*Sorex minutus* Eurasian Pygmy Shrew	*Talpa europaea* European Mole	*Solenodon paradoxos* Hispaniolan Solenodon

others consider it too radical. The alternative view is that hedgehogs form Erinaceidae, one of four living families making up the order Eulipotyphla (which means 'truly fat and blind'). The rest of the quartet of families comprises those that house familiar species such as shrews and moles, but also lesser-known mammals such as desmans (bizarre aquatic mammals from Eurasia) and solenodons (odd burrowing animals from Caribbean islands). The 'family tree' above adopts this second approach.

Whichever approach is correct, what does this mean for other conspicuously spiny mammals, such as porcupines, spiny rats, echidnas (spiny anteaters from Australia) and tenrecs (prickly insectivores from Madagascar that are nearly dead ringers for hedgehogs)? Given that spines are a particularly peculiar physical characteristic, you might be forgiven for thinking that all mammals possessing them might be closely related to hedgehogs. But they are not. Porcupines, for example, are part of the rodent family, which contains rats and squirrels. It transpires that all these spiny mammals evolved their unusual outer layer independently – a phenomenon that biologists call 'convergent evolution'. The connection between these lookalikes is barely skin-deep.

Echidnas (**above**) and porcupines (**below**) are both spiny mammals, but neither are related to hedgehogs.

Hedgehog evolution

The direct ancestors of hedgehogs probably first appeared in Asia during what is known as the Eocene period, 34–56 million years ago – although there is some recorded evidence of hedgehog-like animals 70 million years ago (when dinosaurs still ruled the Earth!). The first recognisably modern-day hedgehog trotted across the ground around 15 million years ago (and trot they did, dispersing through Africa, Europe and North America). This makes hedgehogs far older than famous, long-extinct mammals such as sabre-toothed cats and woolly mammoths.

Even more remarkably, the inaugural design of the hedgehog has survived largely intact, without need for modifications. Hedgehogs have been pretty much fit for purpose since the outset.

Evolution within the genus *Erinaceus* has been relatively recent. Scientists have used DNA 'footprinting' to unravel the role of ice ages in creating new species of hedgehogs. When ice sheets moved southwards across Europe, animals were trapped in three principal regions: Iberia, Italy and the Balkans. Isolated from one another, populations developed slightly different characteristics. As the ice retreated, the hedgehogs spread out – but by now they were distinct species, incapable of breeding with one another.

Fascinatingly, it appears that humans have been aware of the existence of hedgehogs for many thousands of years. This conclusion is based on the astonishing discovery from the Swabian Jura (present-day Baden-Württemberg, Germany) of more than 50 figurines carved from mammoth ivory. These were found in six caves that were occupied by humans 43,000 to 35,000 years ago. One of the ancient sculptures is a representation of what appears to be a hedgehog, approximately 3cm (1in) long, with incisions representing the spines (see below). In 2017, the caves – and their ice-age art – were added to UNESCO's World Heritage List.

A world of hedgehogs

As we have seen, working out where hedgehogs slot into the mammalian world order has proved tricky. At least there is no dispute about what constitutes a 'hedgehog'. Following extinctions in North America 5–20 million years ago, the hedgehog family (Erinaceidae) is now wholly restricted to the Old World, occurring across Europe, Africa and Asia.

The family is divided into two subfamilies: 'spiny hedgehogs' (the subfamily Erinaceinae) and 'hairy hedgehogs' (the Hylomyinae, sometimes known as the Galericinae). The latter comprises the moonrats and gymnures of South East Asia. These eight or so species are split between five genera. Somewhat shrew-like in appearance, Hylomyinae are furry rather than spiny and possess long, rather hairless, rat-like tails. It takes imagination to think of them as 'hedgehogs' (and indeed, these two subfamilies last shared a common ancestor 26–38 million years ago), but exchange an elongated tail for prickles and you might manage it.

Left: The hedgehog family (Erinaceidae) encompasses 'spiny hedgehogs' (above) and 'hairy hedgehogs' such as this Lesser Gymnure (below).

Current classification within the spiny hedgehog subfamily Erinaceinae

Order				Eulipotyphla			
Family				Erinaceidae			
Subfamily				Erinaceinae			
Genus	*Atelerix*		*Erinaceus*	*Hemiechinus*	*Mesechinus**		*Paraechinus*
Example species	*Atelerix albiventris* Four-toed Hedgehog		*Erinaceus amurensis* Amur Hedgehog	*Hemiechinus auritus* Long-eared Hedgehog	*Mesechinus dauuricus* Daurian Hedgehog		*Paraechinus micropus* Indian Hedgehog

*Not all biologists think that *Mesechinus* is a valid genus.

Top row (left to right): Four-toed Hedgehog (*Atelerix albiventris*), Amur Hedgehog (*Erinaceus amurensis*).
Centre row (left to right): Long-eared Hedgehog (*Hemiechinus auritus*), Daurian Hedgehog (*Mesechinus dauuricus*).
Right: Indian Hedgehog (*Paraechinus micropus*).

The spiny group is what we immediately think of when we hear or see the word 'hedgehog'. Biologists' views of how the Erinaceinae is composed have evolved over time. Even now, there are different perspectives on how many species the group includes and how many genera they are split between. Current approaches cut the subfamily into either fourteen species across four genera (*Atelerix, Erinaceus, Hemiechinus* and *Paraechinus*) or sixteen species across five (additionally *Mesechinus*, see figure opposite).

Whichever approach is correct, obvious physical differences between the genera are typically slight, and are more than outweighed by shared features such as largely concealed legs, a long muzzle and spiny coat. Compare this with, say, the much more obvious variance within the cat family (Felidae), which includes members with spotted, striped and plain fur, short and long tails, and physiques built for speed or for strength.

All four species of *Atelerix* hedgehogs are African, although one – the Algerian or North African Hedgehog *Atelerix algirus* – has been introduced to the Mediterranean coasts of Spain and France, and to islands such as the Canaries. Uniquely among hedgehogs, all members of this genus have a distinctive pale band of fur across their foreheads. *Atelerix* also differ from *Erinaceus* hedgehogs (see overleaf) in being lighter-bodied and more agile, with poorly developed claws that make them less suited to climbing. One species – variously called the White-bellied, African Pygmy or Four-toed Hedgehog (although always known as *Atelerix albiventris*, the hedgehog most frequently kept as a pet) – lacks a fifth toe.

Aside from these differences, the genera *Atelerix* and *Erinaceus* are very similar; they even share a noteworthy physical characteristic, a parting in the spines on the forehead, that is absent in other hedgehog genera. Accordingly, scientists continue to ponder the evolutionary relationship between *Atelerix* and *Erinaceus*. One line of thought is that an *Erinaceus* hedgehog (or a similar ancestor) wandered from Europe into Africa, 'founding' that continent's stock of hedgehogs.

Above: Algerian or North African Hedgehog (*Atelerix algirus*).

Above: Collared or Hardwicke's Hedgehog (*Hemiechinus collaris*).

Above: Ethiopian or Desert Hedgehog (*Paraechinus aethiopicus*).

Above: White-breasted or Eastern European Hedgehog (*Erinaceus concolor*).

The taxonomic uncertainty continues with the genus *Hemiechinus*. It contains at least two species: the Long-eared Hedgehog *Hemiechinus auritus*, which ranges from the eastern Mediterranean to China and Pakistan; and the Collared or Hardwicke's Hedgehog *Hemiechinus collaris*, which occurs exclusively in India and Pakistan. Both exhibit the long ears enshrined in the name of the former but lack the central parting of spines on the forehead shown by *Atelerix* and *Erinaceus* hedgehogs and have no facial mask.

The jury is out on whether two poorly known species from central China – the Daurian Hedgehog '*Hemiechinus*' *dauuricus* and Hugh's Hedgehog '*Hemiechinus*' *hughi* – sit in the genus *Hemiechinus* or in the controversial genus *Mesechinus*. Both species have shorter ears than the two long-eared *Hemiechinus*, which implies they might be ecologically distinct.

Uncertainty also prevails over the number of species of 'desert hedgehog' in the genus *Paraechinus*, which collectively ranges from North Africa through the Middle East to India. There are certainly three species: the Ethiopian or Desert Hedgehog *Paraechinus aethiopicus*, the Brandt's Hedgehog *Paraechinus hypomelas* and the Pale or Indian Hedgehog *Paraechinus micropus*. Some authorities maintain that the Indian Hedgehog in fact 'conceals' a fourth species, known as the Madras or Bare-bellied Hedgehog *Paraechinus nudiventris*. All three (or four) species possess a white forehead, long ears projecting beyond their spines (a boon for their nocturnal lifestyle) and a central parting to spines on the crown. They are also all small, around roughly half the weight of *Erinaceus* hedgehogs.

That brings us again to the most familiar genus of spiny hedgehogs, *Erinaceus*. It's also the most widely distributed of the hedgehog genera, with constituent species collectively ranging from Ireland and Spain east into China and Korea. *Erinaceus* hedgehogs have a faint central parting to spines on the forehead, short ears and a very well-developed big toe on the hind foot. Even this genus is subject to uncertainties about the number of species it includes and their names. As with the genus *Paraechinus*, there are certainly three species in *Erinaceus*, and possibly four. Some biologists think that the White-breasted or Eastern European Hedgehog *Erinaceus concolor* ranges from eastern Europe into Russia and south to the Middle East. Others believe that those restricted to the Middle East are Southern White-breasted Hedgehog (the 'true' *Erinaceus concolor*), with the remaining population comprising a separate species, the Eastern or Northern White-breasted Hedgehog *Erinaceus roumanicus*. There is no such doubt with the Amur or Manchurian Hedgehog *Erinaceus amurensis*, which occurs in China and Korea.

The final hedgehog species in the *Erinaceus* genus is the one we all know and love, and which will be the focus for this book. In yet another example of experts being reluctant to adopt consensus, this species is variously called the European, West European, Brown-breasted, Western or Common Hedgehog. The scientific name, however, is invariably *Erinaceus europaeus*. Of all the hedgehog species, *Erinaceus europaeus* is most similar to the White-breasted Hedgehog (either of them!), but it differs by having a slightly shorter snout, darker chest fur and more prominent face mask.

To avoid confusion and unnecessary mouthfuls, I will call *Erinaceus europaeus* simply 'Hedgehog' (upper case) when referring to this particular species. When I use 'hedgehog' (lower case), I am referring to hedgehogs more widely.

Below: The star of this book goes by many names: the European, West European, Brown-breasted, Western or Common Hedgehog (*Erinaceus europaeus*). In the UK, of course, we just call them Hedgehogs.

Closest British relatives

While debate may still rage about exactly how the taxonomy of shrews, moles and hedgehogs fits together, what is not in doubt, in the context of the British Isles, is that these small mammals are each other's closest relatives. A superficial resemblance is obvious. All have short legs relative to body size, long snouts and cylindrical bodies, and all eat copious quantities of invertebrates that live on or below ground. Including the Hedgehog, seven different species are involved. Here are the other six:

Common Shrew A voracious, active predator of small invertebrates that needs to munch up to 90 per cent of its body weight every day just to stay alive. Like other shrews, it has a long, pointed snout, small eyes and short legs. It is very common but hard to see in thick ground vegetation.

Greater White-toothed Shrew This shrew was not known to occur in the British Isles until skulls were found in Barn Owl and Kestrel pellets in Ireland as recently as 2007. Most likely introduced by humans accidentally, it is spreading across southern Ireland.

Pygmy Shrew The smallest mammal living in Great Britain and Ireland, it is hardier than the Common Shrew, readily inhabiting boggy and montane areas.

Water Shrew As its name suggests, this shrew is as adept at hunting in water as it is on land. It swims buoyantly and dives rapidly in search of prey as large as frogs and newts.

Lesser White-toothed Shrew Within the British Isles, this noticeably pale and large-eared shrew occurs solely on the Isles of Scilly. Like its larger relative, it probably didn't reach the Cornish archipelago of its own volition, but was introduced several centuries ago.

Mole As any gardener or lawn-keeper knows, conical piles of earth are a clear sign that one or more Moles reside underground. With its cylindrical body, dense fur, spade-like forelimbs and tiny eyes, this mammal is wonderfully adapted to a subterranean lifestyle. Seeing one in the wild is very tricky!

European relatives

Across Europe as a whole, there are ten additional shrews in the same genus as Pygmy and Common Shrews. Their collective distribution extends from the Arctic to the Mediterranean and even up into the Alps. Europe also hosts a further six species of shrew, plus the remarkable Pyrenean Desman (below), which inhabits mountain streams in northern Spain. Southern Europe also hosts four species of mole, as well as the widespread animal that inhabits Great Britain.

Hedgehogs across Europe

Above: Hedgehogs occur from southern Spain north to Sweden (as pictured on the sign) and beyond, almost to the Arctic Circle.

Below: The northern limit of Hedgehog distribution roughly matches the frontier of deciduous woodland.

It is for good reason that the Hedgehog is familiar to people across Europe, in particular. Its distribution in the region is wide and the species is generally common. Hedgehogs occur throughout western and central Europe, from the southern tip of Spain to just shy of the Arctic Circle in Finland, and from Ireland to eastern Italy and western Poland, with a spur heading east from the Baltic states into Russia. There are also isolated enclaves on islands big and small – from Corsica and Sardinia to parts of the Scottish Hebrides and the Azores. Human introduction has contributed to such insular presence, as it has for an outlying population at the other end of the world, in New Zealand.

Most Hedgehogs live between sea level and 600m (2,000ft) altitude (roughly the maximum height of Dartmoor in Devon, UK); however, some are veritable mountaineers (or at least hill-climbers), inhabiting land at 1,500–2,000m (5,000–6,500ft) in the Alps. The northern limit of Hedgehog occurrence roughly follows the frontier of deciduous woodland. Any further north and the harsher winters mean less food. Despite such constraints, Hedgehogs are pushing boundaries. In the last few decades, hardy souls have pressed the species' range northwards through Finland and Sweden. While largely due to human interventions (from introductions to artificial feeding), this expansion may partly reflect a warming climate. If this continues, might we see Hedgehogs in the Arctic by 2100?

There are two caveats to this general thesis of the Hedgehog being common and widespread. The first is that it tends to be rare at high altitude and latitude. The second is that scientists and conservationists know little about Hedgehog population numbers – there are no estimates at all for most countries – and there are signs of a decline in several nations. Will we still be able to describe the Hedgehog as 'common' come 2100?

British Hedgehogs

Although fossil evidence does not shed light on exactly how long Hedgehogs have inhabited the British Isles, we know that they became established at least 9,500 years ago when sea levels rose, cutting off the British Isles from mainland Europe. Hedgehogs are widely distributed throughout Great Britain, ranging pretty much from Land's End to John o'Groats, and on the island of Ireland, from Brow Head to Malin Head.

Such a broad distribution includes smaller islands as well as the mainland: only a handful of the land masses in Orkney and the Hebrides are bereft. Although Hedgehogs can swim, they are unlikely to have made it across channels and seas by paddling (doing the 'hoggy paddle'?). Instead, their presence on the Isles of Scilly, the Isle of Man and even Ireland is most likely due to intentional or inadvertent introduction by humans. Some deliberate translocations have been in the name of pest control – gardeners 'importing' them to control slugs – while unwitting movements have probably comprised slumbering, invisible Hedgehogs bundled up in hay or other vegetation.

Hedgehogs have been better studied in Great Britain than anywhere else in their range. Nevertheless, we have little solid feel for how many there are. In the 1950s, the

Below: Hedgehogs have been introduced (unwittingly or intentionally) to islands such as the Isles of Scilly.

Above: Hedgehogs appear to be more common in sheltered, untidy suburban gardens than they are in the wider British countryside.

Opposite: Road-casualty counts are one means of estimating Hedgehog populations.

British population was thought to be around 30 million. The most reliable recent estimate, published in *The State of Britain's Hedgehogs 2018* (see page 121), suggests a much smaller population of around 1.5 million. Given that in the early 1990s around 1.55 million Hedgehogs were thought to live in Britain (split roughly 70/20/10 between England, Scotland and Wales), this indicates that, in recent years at least, overall numbers may have begun to stabilise. But however many (or however few) Hedgehogs are left, they seem to be unevenly distributed. Since the turn of the millennium, rural populations have apparently declined faster than their urban counterparts.

If the estimates are correct (and if the 1950s population estimate was accurate), they imply that for every 100 Hedgehogs living in Britain 60 years ago, just 5 remain today. Certainly the decrease is precipitous: one interpretation of road-casualty counts broadly suggests that the population halved during 1990–2001 then halved again in 2002–2017.

But the 2018 report offers some good news too. There are hints of a very recent improvement in urban areas. Hedgehogs are not disappearing from sites as rapidly as they were 15 years ago, and might even be returning. Where they are found, numbers appear to be growing, perhaps because of conservation initiatives involving the public (see page 90).

When Hedgehogs become Kiwis

Probably the world's healthiest population of 'European' Hedgehog lives precisely where it shouldn't – in New Zealand. With the exception of a few species of bat, no mammals occur naturally in New Zealand. But ever since people arrived in the 13th century, a raft of non-native, warm-blooded and furry animals have colonised and frequently imperilled New Zealand's indigenous species, which had adapted to a ground-dwelling existence free of mammalian predators.

In terms of Hedgehogs, New Zealand's 1861 Animal Acclimatisation Act was the country's undoing. It allowed 'acclimatisation societies' to ease the pain of living so far from 'home' by importing familiar animals from the British Isles. The Hedgehog was one. The first pair arrived in 1870 aboard a ship called the *Hydaspes* and many more followed over the next two decades. The arrivals were particularly welcomed for their proficiency in controlling pests in gardens and pastures. New Zealand gardeners rejoiced.

As the population exploded, however, perspectives have changed. Short, mild winters suppressed winter mortality, and possibly allowed females to raise two litters per year (although this has never been proven). Hedgehogs spread rapidly across suitable habitat, with a typical population density of 2–4 animals per hectare (2.47 acres) (compared with roughly one per hectare in the British Isles). They have become a major predator of native and rare ground-nesting birds such as Black-fronted Tern, scarce lizards and weta (large cricket-like insects, see below). Such is conservationists' concern that Hedgehogs are now formally considered pests, and are subject to eradication measures. If only they hadn't been introduced to New Zealand in the first place!

Bodywork

On even the briefest of glimpses, there is no mistaking the Hedgehog. Its spiny coat and ability to curl into a protective ball both betray its identity and convey much about its approach to life. But there's much more to a Hedgehog's body than prickles. Its squat, tubular physique is perfect for life trundling through the undergrowth. Unexpectedly long legs enable it to trot at surprising speed. Its nose, teeth and toes are perfectly designed for Hedgehog life. Even the famous spiny coat itself has hidden secrets.

Prickles are the Hedgehog's defining – and most remarkable – characteristic. The animal's back and sides are covered with up to 7,000 individual spines, each up to 3cm (1in) long and about one-tenth that in diameter. Examined closely, a spine follicle looks like a modified hair and that is exactly what it is. Spines are made of the same material as hairs – keratin – but are thicker, tougher and harder. Each follicle is embedded in the skin and kept in place with a swollen base. As the spine exits the skin, it narrows and angles, then broadens out before tapering to a sharp tip.

The purpose of the spine's tip is obvious: to inflict pain (or at least surprise) on any would-be predator that touches the Hedgehog. The spine's slender, angled neck is a subtler, but more impressive, adaptation. Should the Hedgehog suffer a blow (from a predator or a fall), the spine absorbs the force by flexing. Even cleverer, the spine's slightly

Opposite: The spiny sphere of a nervous Hedgehog.

Below: Hedgehogs can walk surprisingly quickly.

Hedgehog spines (**above**) are banded and have a narrow base and a sharp tip. Their bands of colour give the animal's flanks a grizzled appearance (**right**).

The Hedgehog's underside is furry and free of spines (**above**), as is its face (**below**).

Opposite: Below the Hedgehog's spines is a 'skirt' of muscle covered by shaggy hairs.

bulbous base prevents it from being pressed into the animal's internal organs. Best of all, if examined in cross section, each spine is hollow with strongly ridged inner 'walls', which provides maximum strength for minimum weight. This combination of smart features enables the Hedgehog to withstand a force 200 times greater than that which would otherwise suffice to snap its spine.

Particularly when seen in daylight, Hedgehogs have a distinctly grizzled appearance. This impression derives from the banded pattern on each individual spine. The tip is typically white, ceding abruptly to a broad, dark brown band. The middle section of the spine is cream, browning again towards the base.

Prickles do not cover the Hedgehog's entire body: if they did, it couldn't roll up into a ball. Instead, the face, breast, throat, belly and legs are covered with long, pleasantly coarse, greyish fur. The belly covering is intriguingly sparse – probably an adaptation to avoid the covering being clogged up with mud and water while the animal is on the move through soggy undergrowth. In contrast, the hairs are particularly shaggy along the Hedgehog's flanks, and this too is for good reason. These hairs cover a 'skirt' of muscle that the Hedgehog can either contract to provide extra defensive cover when it feels threatened or that it can hitch up when it needs to walk quickly – something that makes me imagine a Victorian girl lifting her voluminous dress and underlying petticoats before skipping along.

Variations on a theme

Hedgehogs look largely buff and brown – with a flecked appearance courtesy of coloured bands across each spine – and have a contrastingly darker face, muzzle and legs. Some individuals differ slightly, possessing yellower fur or patches of wholly white spines; however, genetic abnormalities may create marked exceptions to the rule. Although no melanistic (all-black) Hedgehogs have ever been found, three other variants are well known, if rare.

The first is an all-cream version, with wholly white or pale yellow spines. These 'leucistic' animals are a particular phenomenon on Alderney in the Channel Islands. Here the oddities muster roughly two-thirds of the population. Such a remarkably high proportion is thought to be due to in-breeding among the original artificially introduced (and thus small) population. However, it could also possibly be due to light-coloured individuals being easier for a vehicle-driver to spot and thus avoid. This would mean more pale hedgehogs surviving to breed for longer, so their genes get passed on. Is this evolution in action? If so, it begs the question as to why we don't see more pale animals elsewhere.

The second variation on the theme comprises true albinos: entirely white animals with pink eyes and a pink nose. Don't be surprised if you haven't seen one: an estimate suggests that there is just one such anomaly in every 10,000 Hedgehogs.

The final anomaly is baldness. Such 'naked' Hedgehogs suffer a genetic abnormality that prevents them from producing keratin. They therefore entirely lack fur and spines.

Leucistic Hedgehogs are comparatively common on Alderney, Channel Islands.

True albino Hedgehogs are extreme rarities.

Naked Hedgehogs suffer from a rare genetic abnormality.

Roll up! Roll up!

Above: To a curious dog, the Hedgehog's spiny sphere is impregnable.

Above: Like Hedgehogs, woodlice are also able to roll into a ball.

Above: The 'frowning' forehead that enables a Hedgehog to compress into a sphere is most obvious in newborns.

It is pleasing that the Hedgehog's best-known physical characteristic (its spines) is integral to its most remarkable and enchanting behaviour: rolling up into a bristling ball. Such a defence mechanism is not unique in the animal kingdom, but it is certainly very rare. Two 'armour-plated' mammals, the pangolins of Africa and Asia and the three-banded armadillos of South America, also recoil into an impenetrable sphere. Among invertebrates, some species of woodlice and centipedes do something similar, reducing the surface area susceptible to attack and presenting a predator with an infuriating ball game rather than a meal.

The Hedgehog works its particular magic by contracting special muscles under the skin. First a pair of muscles pulls the skin over the forehead, working like an extravagant frown. Another pair does something similar at the animal's rear end. A third muscle, large and circular, runs beneath the skirt of spines. When flinched, this muscle pulls the spiny skin inwards, pressing head, legs and tail inside and tucking them up against one another. Hedgehogs can stay like this for hours, safe and relaxed. If they need to make a predator's life even more difficult, Hedgehogs can contract tiny muscles at the base of each spine, shunting erect prickles

in all manner of directions, like a ball of barbed wire. For almost all predators (see page 75), there is simply no way in.

Much as we associate Hedgehogs with rolling into balls and love them for it, this is far from their first line of defence. Should it sense potential danger, a Hedgehog typically freezes, erects its spines and becomes alert. If the threat persists, running for cover is one response. Another is to crouch and pull the spiny skin down to conceal its vulnerable soft parts. By employing this defensive method, the animal remains cylindrical and ready to move rather than becoming spherical and immobile.

Above: In a relaxed Hedgehog (top left), the spines point in roughly the same direction (bottom left), whereas they bristle in a nervous Hedgehog (top right), pointing in all directions (bottom right).

Below: The Hedgehog can still protect most of its soft parts without rolling up completely.

The body beautiful

Above: Low-slung and cylindrical, the Hedgehog is well suited to life in tangled undergrowth.

The ability to form a spiny ball is far from the Hedgehog's only characteristic facilitating life in the undergrowth. From its typically shuffling gait and low-slung posture, you would be forgiven for thinking that Hedgehogs have stumpy legs. Not at all. From hip to toe, these limbs extend up to 10cm (4in) – one-third of the animal's body length – and are surprisingly lithe.

The legs are also dual-purpose. In addition to powering an unexpectedly elegant turn of foot, they enable the Hedgehog to groom. Given the mammal's reputation for being a fleabag (see page 79), this is just as well. Five toes with long, strong claws help too: perfect for having a good scratch – and also for digging and climbing – even if the claws lack the sharpness needed to rip apart tough prey.

Below: Hedgehogs have surprisingly long legs and an equally impressive turn of speed.

Left: Close examination of Hedgehog feet reveals long claws and a pronounced heel on the hind foot, which help digging and momentum respectively.

Close examination of the Hedgehog's feet reveals one particular secret of its success. The hind feet are longer and narrower than the forefeet and they have a pronounced heel. Although the hind feet differ so markedly as to appear to belong to an entirely different animal, the elongated heel is actually an adaptation: it increases stride length, powers forward momentum and also provides leverage when the animal squeezes through small gaps in the undergrowth.

At the business end of the Hedgehog, the jaw houses 36 teeth of varied size and shape. The combination enables the animal to munch on a wide range of food without any pretence of giving a serious bite (so no bone-breaking). There are incisors for clasping prey and pointed molars for crushing hard-shelled insects.

The Hedgehog nose, sited at the tip of a moderately long snout, is relatively large, shiny and black. It is perpetually wet, an adaptation that helps it detect prey.

Below: The Hedgehog's nose is constantly moist.

Above: Hedgehog ear size varies between genera: those of the Long-eared Hedgehog (*Hemiechinus auritus*) are longer (left), while those of 'our' Hedgehog (*Erinaceus europaeus*) are short and largely concealed (right).

Hedgehog eyes are relatively small and black, while the ears – at least those of the genus *Erinaceus*, including 'our' Hedgehog – are short and largely hidden by fur. Other hedgehog genera have more prominent ears. This adaptation reaches its extreme in the Long-eared Hedgehog of arid North Africa and the Middle East. The presumption is that the genus *Hemiechinus* relies on hearing to detect prey more than *Erinaceus* does, although long ears may conceivably also play a role in regulating body temperature in hot deserts.

One ostensible mystery is the Hedgehog's tail. This is hard to spot, being at most 2cm (¾in) long and largely hidden by spines. That's not long enough to serve any useful purpose – so why invest energy in creating one? The explanation is that it is an evolutionary relict. The shared ancestor of hedgehogs and shrews possessed a tail, and the lifestyle of shrews meant that theirs was worth retaining. Hedgehogs had no use for a tail however, so across millions of generations, it evolved to become shorter. In a million years' time, perhaps hedgehogs will be entirely tailless.

Hair today, gone tomorrow

Our old hair falls out on a continual basis and new hair grows to replace it. Other mammals are no different and moult regularly. Shrews and moles – hedgehogs' closest relatives, remember – replace their fur twice each year. In autumn, they lose their fine summer coat, replacing it with longer, warmer winter fur. They reverse the process in spring. Hedgehogs do things rather differently. A comprehensive, no-holds-barred moult twice a year would be not only inconvenient but also kamikaze: a spine-free Hedgehog would be too vulnerable to survive an attack from a predator. Therefore, Hedgehogs follow a similar approach to humans: losing and replacing spines gradually over time, so that the overall prickly ball remains intact.

Do the locomotion

Above: Although hard to spot, the tail is definitely there. This is an evolutionary legacy from an ancestor of both hedgehogs and (long-tailed) shrews!

If you bump into a Hedgehog at night, it may well remind you of a remote-controlled car. With legs hidden beneath spines and a skirt of muscle, it appears to glide steadily as if on wheels. Wandering around, nose to the ground and snuffling away, you might think that there is no particular sense of urgency in this mammal's world.

The Hedgehog's sudden turn of speed, whether in response to threat or an interesting scent, thus comes as a surprise. With legs extended, propelling the animal forward, it can easily beetle across ground, covering 100 times its body length in under a minute. That's the equivalent of us walking at about 3 metres per second (m/s) (10ft/s). Hedgehogs can even sprint for short distances, scarpering 2m/s (7ft/s). For humans, that would mean covering 15m/s (50ft/s) – a feat well beyond even Olympic athlete Usain Bolt!

Below: A Hedgehog trotting for cover.

Above: A slow amble is the Hedgehog's preferred rate of movement.

This athleticism notwithstanding, a slow (if alert) meander is the Hedgehog's preferred gait while foraging. Pauses to sniff the air are interspersed with short dashes to grab an unsuspecting victim. The overall impression is of a bustling – rather than bumbling – animal, with males travelling faster than females. Unsurprisingly, short grass helps both sexes trundle quicker than dense vegetation.

For such a chunky animal, the Hedgehog is also remarkably adept at squeezing through tight spaces – small holes, cracks under gates, gaps between wires and so on. This is because much of a Hedgehog's apparent bulk is actually due to loose-fitting skin. By flattening its spines, a Hedgehog can squeeze itself into places that might seem inaccessible for a mammal the dimensions of a small football. Such flexibility is perfect for life in the undergrowth.

We think of Hedgehogs as purely terrestrial (ground-dwelling) animals. Yet again, they can surprise us. All

Right: The Hedgehog's skin lies loosely on its body, enabling the animal to squeeze through tight gaps easily.

hedgehog species – even those inhabiting arid regions in Africa and the Middle East – are strong swimmers. Although Hedgehogs are occasionally found drowned in ponds, this is because they are unable to climb out rather than because they are unable to swim.

Hedgehogs are also deft climbers, readily ascending lofty obstacles ranging from wire netting to ivy-clad walls. This is an aptitude of which I have personal experience. A friend was caring for two young male Hedgehogs over the winter, having found them in late autumn and judging they were too small to survive unaided. While she was travelling, I offered to look after them. We transported my friend's outside wire enclosure and installed it, and the animals, in my garden. I covered the 'cage' with rigid plastic … but clearly not well enough. Come the morning, only one Hedgehog remained. The other had shinned up the chain link, pushed aside the cover and absconded. I named him Houdini.

Above: Adult Hedgehogs are somewhere between the size of a football and (as here) a pétanque ball.

Below left: Hedgehogs are surprisingly capable swimmers, even those species inhabiting deserts.

Below right: Climbing is another skill in Hedgehogs' repertoire. They can ascend wire fences and even loftier obstacles.

Making sense of the world

Above: Principally an animal of the night, the Hedgehog learns about the world mainly through its ears and nose.

As befits a primarily nocturnal mammal that lives in the undergrowth, the Hedgehog gets most of its information about the world via its ears and nose. Its acute hearing is particularly attuned to high frequencies, enabling it to pinpoint the source of rustling amid the leaf litter. That said, given the racket a Hedgehog makes through its own movement, it is somewhat surprising that it can hear anything!

Although not possessing a particularly large brain, the section of the organ responsible for interpreting smells is remarkably well developed. The Hedgehog's long snout ends in a perpetually sniffing, wet nose: the moistness helps the nostrils gather scent. This enables Hedgehogs to detect prey (even if it's buried 3cm/1in below ground), predators and potential mates alike, and to recognise locations and offspring.

Many nocturnal mammals use long, sensitive whiskers to detect prey by touch. The Hedgehog doesn't. Although it has a few such hairs on its muzzle, touch appears to be an inconsequential sense. A Hedgehog's eyes are understandably small: big eyes would be a hindrance in the undergrowth. Nevertheless, their eyes

Left: Although the Hedgehog possesses a few whiskers, it doesn't use these to detect prey by touch.

are comparatively and absolutely larger than those of their near relatives, shrews and moles. This suggests that Hedgehogs can probably see well enough in moonlight to distinguish shapes and movement – something to bear in mind when watching them by night.

Below: A foraging Hedgehog sniffs its environment, gathering scented information through moist nostrils.

Breeding and Growth

Pretty much all animals engage in a race against time. The fundamental principle is to breed as efficiently and effectively as possible, thereby ensuring the continuity of their species. Hedgehogs are little different. They have just a few short months in which to replenish energy levels after hibernation, mate, give birth and raise young to independence, with those youngsters then racing against time themselves to build up sufficient fat reserves to survive the winter.

As soon as Hedgehogs emerge from hibernation, it is all systems go. Having lost weight after eating little all winter, the first task is to replenish energy levels. That done, hormonal surges turn Hedgehog attention to the business of procreation.

Both sexes are able to breed from their first spring and remain fertile throughout their life (typically two years). In Great Britain, Hedgehogs emerge from hibernation in April and the breeding season lasts from late April (when the female uterus doubles in size) to October. Theoretically, females could cram two litters in before autumn – particularly in central and southern Europe and in New Zealand, where autumns are milder and longer – but there is no firm evidence that this has occurred. Most second litters are likely to be responses to the early loss of a first litter.

The breeding season is shorter where the climate demands longer hibernation (in more northerly regions, for example) and longer where clement conditions enable a shorter period of torpor. In Sweden, mating does not occur after July (and second litters are unknown), whereas in England, males remain sexually virulent into late September. Indeed, one study of English animals found that females actually had a greater chance of becoming pregnant in September than during the main breeding period of May–July. But the issue then becomes one of ensuring infant survival before winter kicks in.

Opposite: A typical Hedgehog litter numbers four or five hoglets.

Below: British Hedgehogs begin breeding from late April.

Courtship

There's an old joke among mammalogists about how hedgehogs mate. 'With great care' is the time-honoured answer. Copulation is a prickly affair indeed.

Although scientists are not entirely sure what the smell is or how it is produced, a male picks up the scent of a fertile female and tracks her down. Fertile does not, however, necessarily imply immediately receptive. So an energetic circular dance occurs, delightfully known as a hedgehog carousel.

Huffing and puffing, the male tries to position himself behind the female; however, she is far from certain that this is a good thing, so turns to face him – forehead lowered aggressively, prickles bristling – and seeks to deter the male with snorts, sneezes and even occasional lunges. Should other males arrive, attracted by sound or scent, the incumbent male will badger them away. Then the waltz resumes, sometimes continuing for hours, until either the female is persuaded of the suitability of her mate (stamina indicating robust genes, presumably) or the male abandons hope. In one study, just seven per cent of carousels culminated in coupling.

And in instances of successful courtship, there's the small matter of pain-inducing spines to consider. The willing female exposes her genitalia by lifting her tail, flattening her belly to the ground and pointing her muzzle skywards. Still snorting away, the male carefully noses the spines on her back, then mounts from behind, trying to balance his

Below: The male and female engage in a circular courtship dance, known as the hedgehog carousel, which may (or may not) lead to mating.

forefeet on her dorsal spines, and gripping prickles on her shoulders with his teeth. He then inserts what is a relatively (and unsurprisingly, in the circumstances) long, retractable penis and copulation ensues.

Males further increase the chance of successful mating by generating comparatively huge quantities of sperm. Relative to body size, the organs responsible for producing and storing sperm are thought to be larger in Hedgehogs than in any other mammal. Part of the male's secretion may serve as a 'vaginal plug', which – in theory, at least – should physically prevent rival males from copulating with the same female.

Once mating is over – after a matter of a few minutes – the two Hedgehogs part company. The male's contribution to his offspring is over. He neither guards his mate nor provides for her, and takes no part in rearing the young. Instead, the male's attention turns to the next available female. (Sex) life goes on for the female as well as the male. Both sexes are highly promiscuous, with no concept of pair bonds. Studies across a single breeding season have shown one male to court (if not copulate with) up to ten females, and for one female to have a dozen suitors (which, should they converge simultaneously, typically engage in skirmishes to develop a pecking order). Other research has revealed that a single litter of Hedgehogs may have more than one father. This all sounds worthy of a soap opera…

Pregnancy and birth

Above: A female Hedgehog with offspring in her maternal nest.

Given the palaver involved in getting in 'the family way', it is doubtless a relief to Hedgehogs that almost all pregnancies result in birth. Gestation normally lasts just under five weeks but sometimes takes longer. The reasons for this are unclear, but one possible explanation is that, like bats, female Hedgehogs have the ability to press the pause button should a cold snap force them into temporary hibernation.

Once pregnant, a female sets about constructing a special maternal nest (see page 65). This is larger than the winter nest and is made of leaves and grass. A typical litter numbers four or five. The average number

Below: Newborn Hedgehogs' spines are concealed by fluid-filled skin.

of offspring seems to be slightly higher in northern and eastern Europe than in Great Britain, with up to seven or eight hoglets sometimes born. Why such a difference exists is unclear.

In Great Britain, most births occur in June or July, but – given their tardier emergence from hibernation – northern Hedgehogs mate and give birth later than their southern counterparts. Bringing several spiny animals into the world is potentially a perilous undertaking. Fortunately for the female, the process is made easier by the newborns' prickles being concealed by fluid-filled skin. Upon birth, the liquid is rapidly reabsorbed and the spines pop out.

Left: In its first few days of life, the Hedgehog does little more than suckle.

The early weeks

Right: A baby Hedgehog's eyes open when it is two weeks old.

For the first day or so, the mother does not let the newborns out of her sight; the whole family remains in the maternal nest. Thereafter, the female forages at night, returning to the nest by day to feed her offspring and sleep. The first five days or so are a dicey period. If the female feels threatened, she may abandon the nest or even eat her babies. Later, however, disturbance is more likely to result in the female moving her youngsters to a new nest.

A newborn Hedgehog greets the world pink, hairless and blunt-nosed, with its eyes sealed tight. Although perhaps one-quarter the length of its mother, the newborn hoglet is barely two per cent of her weight. The birth spines are sparsely distributed and wholly white; a second generation of prickles emerges after a couple of days and completely cloaks the initial set within 2–3 weeks.

For the first few days, a baby Hedgehog is capable of little more than hauling itself around the nest and suckling its mother's milk. Should a hoglet stray too far and realise it has lost contact, it calls plaintively until its mother retrieves it. If disturbed by an intruder, it jerks its body upwards, puffing and thrusting spines towards the aggressor. Such a response may startle a would-be predator, if not ultimately force its retreat.

By the time it is two weeks old, a baby hoglet's defence mechanism has improved: it can roll up rather effectively.

Around this time, the youngster's eyes open and it becomes more mobile and coordinated. Siblings may jostle with one another. Their fur grows rapidly and by 3–4 weeks old, hoglets start to look less like an alien, morphing into bonsai versions of their mother. Horizons rapidly broaden and infants willingly explore outside the nest and investigate solid food. At 5–6 weeks old, the mini-Hedgehogs are weaned, have increased their birth weight tenfold and accompany their mother as she forages. A glorious mid-summer sight is of a too-cute-to-be-true 'caravan' of hogs, with Mum leading her troop out into the night.

Above: It takes a few weeks until a young Hedgehog is able to roll fully into a ball.

Below: At 5–6 weeks old, young Hedgehogs are able to accompany their mother on foraging missions.

Striking out

Independence strikes before offspring are 50 days old. The race is now on for them to accumulate sufficient fat reserves to survive hibernation. By the time they retire for the winter, youngsters need to double their weight at weaning. In Great Britain this means reaching a minimum of 450g (1lb), although scientists think the bar may be much higher in continental Europe, at around 700g (1½lb). To do this, young Hedgehogs must disperse to a new area (so they are not competing for food with their mother or siblings) and learn to feed proficiently.

These are testing times. Many immature Hedgehogs, particularly those born in late litters, die due to starvation or thirst, accident or illness, exhaustion or predation. Premature cold snaps also pose threats: youngsters' fur and spines provide poor insulation so they lose heat readily. Unhealthy individuals may be found wandering about, often by day and typically stumbling or otherwise poorly coordinated. If left to their own devices, their prospects are not good.

Below: At seven weeks old, Hedgehogs are entirely independent and ready to leave the nest and start accumulating weight before their first hibernation.

On average, roughly one in five siblings will not survive its early weeks, dying in the nest. In Great Britain, more than half of all hoglets born fail to make it through a full year of life; the proportion is three-quarters in Germany. For those that do survive, fortunately, things get easier. Roughly two in three adult Hedgehogs will live another year. The average life expectancy in Great Britain and Sweden is two years. Many Hedgehogs (particularly in New Zealand) live to be three years old, four in a thousand may reach seven, and the occasional fortunate, resilient individual (estimated to be 1 in 10,000) may enter its second decade.

Above: Sadly, this small and probably sick Hedgehog curled up in the autumn sun may not survive its first winter.

In praise of mother

Let's take a moment to recognise the achievements of a female Hedgehog. She is a single parent, solely responsible for all aspects of raising a family – from building a nest to producing independent hoglets. (The male's only contribution is over within a few short minutes.) If she weans just four youngsters to the typical weight of 250g (½lb), she has produced and shared her own body weight (roughly 1kg/2lb) in milk. Dogged, dutiful and diligent, a female Hedgehog is one impressive animal. I salute her.

Home, Habits and Food

There are relatively few constraints on where a Hedgehog can live. As long as the landscape provides adequate food, water and shelter, Hedgehogs can usually make a viable home. Having a wide taste in prey helps. But suitable places in which to make a nest are often at a premium, and are vital if a Hedgehog is to use its famous strategy of hibernation to survive the vagaries of winter. Through decades of research, scientists have unravelled many of the secrets of Hedgehog life. But even the most experienced biologists are perplexed by some of the Hedgehog's more peculiar behaviours.

Hedgehogs make a home both in semi-natural habitats and those substantially altered by humans. They reside in woodlands and grasslands, on arable land and within orchards and, of course, in gardens, parks and other shrubbery-rich manifestations of human settlement.

A few themes run through the collective habitat preferences of Hedgehogs. Lowlands are preferred over montane areas. Access to water sources is important: there needs to be enough water, but not too much. So, damp pasture is good, but dry sandy heaths and saturated marshes are bad. Coniferous woodland attracts fewer Hedgehogs than deciduous, as the former's spartan undergrowth offers less concealment for nests than the generous ground layer of the latter.

Moorland and intensively farmed, hedgerow-free, pesticide-sprayed arable fields are largely shunned – being too bare and insect-poor – but meadows are spot on. Finally, a mosaic of vegetation, with gradations between habitats – forest edge, encroaching scrub, field margins, hedgerows bordering grazed fields and so on – entices Hedgehogs more than a uniform landscape. Such 'edge habitats' seem to attract the greatest diversity of prey, which suits the Hedgehog's wide-ranging diet down to the ground.

Opposite: Invertebrate-rich habitat is essential for foraging Hedgehogs.

Suitable habitats for Hedgehogs include parks (**above**) and meadows (**below**).

Ideal home show

Have you ever watched a Hedgehog cross a lawn or other grassy area, only for it to vanish into thin air (or, rather, under bushes, through a fence or into a nearby park)? Have you ever wondered where it is going – and how far it wanders? And have you ever mused as to whether it is the same Hedgehog visiting the bowl of food you leave out each summer night – or a succession of them?

If the answer to any of these questions is 'yes', you are in good company. Even biologists studying Hedgehogs (see page 120) have problems keeping track of their subjects. It is only with the advent of technologies such as radiotracking and GPS backpacks that scientists have begun to unravel the secrets of this unrepentantly furtive mammal.

Once a Hedgehog has established a home range – the area over which it normally travels to do its everyday (or every-night) business – it tends to spend its entire life in that vicinity. In Great Britain at least, males seem to range over three times as wide an area as do females (around 30ha/75 acres compared with 10ha/25 acres, but sometimes up to 50ha/125 acres). To put this in context, a typical football club pitch is about two-thirds of a hectare. One Spanish study revealed that the heavier a male (but not female) Hedgehog is, the larger its home range. Big boys need more space.

Right: Biologists have radiotracked Hedgehogs to reveal the secrets of their travels.

On an average night, British males also travel between half and three-quarters as far again as females (1.2km/¾ mile, but occasionally up to 3–4km/2–2½ miles), particularly when searching for mates. Both sexes range less widely in wooded areas than they do in open terrain, presumably because invertebrate food is easier to find in the former habitat. In a similar vein, a study in Switzerland found that Hedgehogs travelled further when food was scarce (such as early spring and late autumn). In periods of abundant prey (such as summer), Hedgehogs have no need to hunt widely, so they don't.

Wherever Hedgehogs occur, home ranges of individuals overlap; there seems to be no pretence of territoriality (defending one's patch to the exclusion of others). Other than during courtship, animals appear to pass each other like ships in the night. How this happens is unclear. One line of thought is that Hedgehogs use cues such as scent trails to avoid one another (see page 70).

Why this happens is easier to surmise. If there is plenty of food around, why waste energy (and possibly risk limb or even life) defending a territory? This strategy – needing personal space but not sole ownership of an estate – means that several Hedgehogs can reside within a single patch of habitat. In turn, this means each may visit your garden during the course of a single night; 'your' Hedgehog is likely to be Hedgehogs plural. One study discovered that an amazing 11 different individuals visited a single garden over 17 nights.

Above: You may think that the same Hedgehog visits your garden each night, but in fact you're likely to be visited by several individuals.

Above: Garden lawns offer excellent foraging opportunities.

Above and below: Providing they have entry and exit points, a network of suburban gardens can provide very good Hedgehog habitat.

Is suburbia Hedgehog nirvana? Think about it. Here is a large area of potentially well-connected habitat (provided animals can move between properties). It contains ample areas of short grass – we humans call them lawns – giving access to earthworms and slugs. Trees, hedges, bushes and shrubs each have their own stash of invertebrate prey. Some of the two-legged, upright inhabitants of suburbia add to the bounty by providing saucers of food and water. Buildings, fences and garden borders provide shelter. There are log piles, tangled undergrowth and compost heaps in which to make a nest. There are fewer predators such as, depending on location, Badgers and Eagle Owls. And it's warmer too; cities are 'heat islands'.

Little wonder then that urban populations of Hedgehogs across several northern and western European countries are faring better than (or, strictly speaking, not quite as poorly as) their rural counterparts. In France, one study found the population density of Hedgehogs in the town of Sedan to be nine times higher than in the surrounding countryside. Urban hedgehogs aren't quite out of the woods yet, but there is enough evidence to suggest that well-managed urban green spaces can be a boon for the species.

Eat seasonal, eat local

Although professionals who have cared for injured or weak Hedgehogs well know that individual animals can have very different tastes, the species as a whole is amenably catholic in its diet. Strictly speaking, Hedgehogs are omnivorous, consuming a wide variety of food, but they are predominately very carnivorous. They are also opportunistic, taking whatever is available at that moment. They need to eat a lot too. A daily requirement for a normal-sized Hedgehog of 500–700g (1lb 2oz–1lb 9oz) is 90–140 calories. This means eating perhaps 90g (3oz) of prey per night (equivalent to a few hundred caterpillars), which in turn requires the Hedgehog to fill its belly two or three times before it retires for the day.

Large invertebrates make up most of the diet. Earthworms, ground beetles and caterpillars top the list, forming at least three-quarters of a typical Hedgehog's calorific intake. Second-tier foodstuffs include slugs, millipedes, earwigs and (presumably slumbering) grasshoppers/crickets. Towards the bottom of the invertebrate list come ants and spiders. Hedgehogs are also partial to the odd vertebrate meal, should Lady Luck bless them. A Hedgehog won't hesitate if it encounters a catchable or freshly dead small mammal. Other recorded prey items include mice and, somewhat disconcertingly, Hedgehogs' near relatives: shrews and moles. The same applies to amphibians (small frogs, toads and newts),

Left: The Hedgehog diet is varied and can include vertebrates such as frogs.

Hedgehogs typically avoid eating butterflies or moths (**above**), but they will snaffle up Common Cockchafers (**below**) with relish.

Below: Hungry young Hedgehogs will attempt to eat snails, usually without success.

which, contrary to popular belief, spend most of their life out of water, and reptiles such as lizards.

Across such dietary breadth, there are a few surprising omissions. Despite being readily available, flies, woodlice and bugs such as aphids are shunned. Why is unclear: perhaps Hedgehogs' dentition makes them tricky to catch? Another mystery is why caterpillars are eaten commonly but the winged adults only occasionally (whether butterflies or moths), despite many species roosting close to the ground. Similarly unclear is why centipedes are avoided yet millipedes devoured – particularly given that the latter produce foul-tasting chemicals that deter many predators. More explicable is the Hedgehog's avoidance of snails. Hedgehog teeth are not up to task of cracking snail shells, although that doesn't appear to stop naïve youngsters trying. Live and learn…

What an individual Hedgehog consumes on a particular night depends on what is out and about. In spring, for example, Common Cockchafers (also known as May Bugs) are snapped up. Bird eggs are another seasonal classic, usually being available for a few short weeks each year. Earthworms feature on mild, humid nights, but not when the soil is dried hard, trapping the moisture-loving wigglers underground. Adult beetles are mainly eaten in summer, and their larvae in autumn.

A taste for snake

One surprising food source for Hedgehogs is snakes,
specifically the Adder. It is unexpected for two reasons.
First, Adders (aka Common Vipers) are largely diurnal
and should be underground on all but the warmest night.
Second, Adders are venomous, so a Hedgehog would
seem to be courageous, skilful or daft to take one on.
Agility is certainly part of the Hedgehog's secret, but only
part. The mammal's spines are longer than the Adder's
fangs, meaning that the snake will strike
in vain if the Hedgehog is protecting
its soft parts. The amazing element
is that some Hedgehogs have
evolved considerable resistance
(if not complete immunity) to viper
venom. This means that, for many
Hedgehogs, the risk of being attacked
is outweighed by the reward of a
substantial meal.

Above: Hedgehogs also help
themselves to bird eggs, should
they encounter them.

Below: Hedgehogs can eat snakes
if the opportunity arises.

Above: Caterpillars (here, that of a Striped Lychnis moth) are a staple prey item of Hedgehogs.

The perfect meal

Given this emphasis on consuming what is seasonally available, researchers have conducted investigations to work out what an ideal dinner table would look like for a Hedgehog. If their entire menu were available on any particular night, Hedgehogs would favour prey that is slow-moving and soft-bodied, easily digestible and rich in calories. Slugs, caterpillars and earthworms fit the bill. Studies also revealed food items only grudgingly consumed when nothing better was available. Carabid beetles – such as Stag Beetles – were a key group. These insects have hard, indigestible exoskeletons and chemical defence mechanisms, and can put on a sudden turn of speed, making them a pain for Hedgehogs to catch and energetically unrewarding to eat: a lot of effort for not much gain.

The accidental omnivore?

Although almost exclusively carnivores, Hedgehogs do eat plant material – but not, it appears, intentionally. Grass, pine needles, straw and the like are accidentally ingested when munching invertebrates (indeed, the plant matter may be *inside* the stomach of prey). Intriguingly, suburban Hedgehogs consume more plant material than their rural brethren – perhaps because they chomp on pesky bits of grass from newly mown lawns. Windfall fruit and berries

Bird-eating hogs

One particular taste has got Hedgehogs into trouble with different land managers: birds. Some Hedgehogs eat eggs, chicks and even adults of certain ground-nesting bird species. This has incensed gamekeepers (see page 85), who blame Hedgehogs, among other animals they consider to be 'vermin', for the loss of captive-reared Red-legged Partridges (right) and Pheasants (though not Red Grouse, given that Hedgehogs occur only rarely on moorland). Poultry farmers have objected to Hedgehogs munching their chicks or eggs. Separately, conservationists have faced dilemmas when dealing with evidence that some Hedgehogs eat eggs of waders, gulls and terns, an issue that has become synonymous with a few Scottish islands (see page 93).

are sometimes found inside the gut of a dead Hedgehog; at least benefit from calories provides a more logical case for deliberate consumption than with grass and straw.

Plants have also been suggested, albeit unconvincingly, as a source of water for Hedgehogs. More persuasive cases have been made that Hedgehogs obtain water from prey (some insects they eat can comprise nearly two-thirds water!) and from droplets of dew lapped up while foraging. Standing sources of water such as puddles are a boon to a thirsty Hedgehog. This is one reason why well-meaning householders should always pair food offered to hogs with a bowl of water and refresh both daily (see page 103).

Above: Hedgehogs seem to ingest plant material accidentally while foraging for invertebrates.

Below: Thirsty Hedgehogs welcome natural water sources (left) and will also readily make use of artificial water sources in gardens (right).

The lies of lore

The Hedgehog diet is well known to be wide-ranging but, even so, there are also several distinctly exaggerated or wildly fanciful claims about Hedgehog foodstuffs. One is that Hedgehogs have such a taste for milk that they suckle at dairy cow udders. At best, there is some evidence that Hedgehogs may occasionally grab a teat and either lick leaking milk or chew at it (perhaps mistaking it for a worm or similar). Either way, the once-held fear that Hedgehogs may be responsible for reducing milk yields looks like fantasy.

The same holds for a story doing the rounds since it was shared by the Roman natural philosopher Pliny the Elder. The account suggests that Hedgehogs gather fruit such as an apple, grape or fig by rolling on it, impaling it on their spines and trotting away with it. While it is just about conceivable that an apple could drop from a tree at the precise moment a spine-bristling Hedgehog walks underneath, the odds may be akin to winning the lottery. Needless to say, no scientist has ever observed such behaviour, and any association between Hedgehogs and fallen fruit is more likely to relate to searching for the slugs that often congregate around the decomposing matter.

Above: The setting sun provides a wake-up call for hungry Hedgehogs.

A night in the life

Given the prickly defence strategy evolved by Hedgehogs, one question often asked is why they are not more active by day. After all, they should be safe from almost all diurnal predators. The answer is threefold. First, activity under the cover of darkness is the norm for mammals: it's actually a wonder that we see any mammals during daylight hours. Second, and critically, Hedgehogs' prey is more active or easier to catch by night. If they are to eat, Hedgehogs must be largely nocturnal. Finally, there are times when even healthy Hedgehogs are out and about by day. The short nights of midsummer are a case in point. With limited darkness, it is unsurprising that Hedgehogs may start foraging before sunset and continue after dawn. Autumn also sees periods of Hedgehog activity after sunrise: the season is a race against time to put on enough weight to survive hibernation.

These exceptions to the rule notwithstanding, Hedgehogs are all about nightlife. They are active throughout the hours of darkness, with slight peaks in the three hours before midnight and at around 3.00 a.m. Such intensive foraging is also draining, so Hedgehogs often pause for short rests or naps throughout the night.

Opposite: Although nocturnal, Hedgehogs are sometimes seen by day, particularly during summer.

Above: Much of the Hedgehog's night is spent foraging.

Foraging strategy

A typical Hedgehog searches for food for roughly half to two-thirds of the night (more in the case of females, presumably because they are foraging to feed their litter). The Hedgehog meanders steadily in areas anticipated to harbour prey (particularly 'edge habitats' where the menu may be wide), with pauses to sniff the air and dashes to grab the next meal, which is rapidly dispatched. Hedgehogs trot quickly across prey-poor areas; why waste time in unsuitable spots? Males proceed faster than females, and both sexes forage more quickly in short grass than in dense undergrowth.

The Hedgehog varies its hunting technique to suit its prey. Its sharp claws aid digging into ground, but the holes produced are shallow. Beetles and earthworms are grabbed from behind and eaten forwards. In the case of the former, this avoids the Hedgehog being bitten or sprayed with noxious liquids. Hedgehogs use their paws to wipe slime from slugs before eating them. Lacking the teeth and jaw muscles to clinically dispatch a small mammal or reptile, a Hedgehog gnaws at live prey until it succumbs: a lingering, painful death indeed.

Above: A Hedgehog preparing to tackle its prey. **Below:** Tree bases make for perfect hunting grounds.

Getting through winter

Right: The arrival of November cues warnings about checking bonfires for hibernating Hedgehogs before you set fire to them.

There are three things that pretty much everyone knows about Hedgehogs: they have spines, roll into a ball and hibernate. In the UK, each Bonfire Night (5 November, in memory of Guy Fawkes's failed Gunpowder Plot to blow up London's Houses of Parliament in 1605) comes with warnings about checking bonfires for hibernating hogs before setting them on fire.

Despite widespread familiarity with the concept of hibernating Hedgehogs, there are common misunderstandings about the process. Let's take two examples. First, hibernation is not sleep, but is in fact a mechanism to conserve energy. Second, once entering hibernation, Hedgehogs are not inactive until spring, but wake regularly and move about if the weather is clement. So, let's examine the what, why, how, when and where of hibernation a little more closely.

First up, the 'what'. Unlike reptiles and amphibians, mammals use energy they generate themselves to keep warm. While this is more flexible than relying on the sun, it's an 'expensive' way to use energy. Many mammals rectify the imbalance by insulating themselves with fat and fur and keeping cosy in shelters such as nests and burrows. A complementary technique is to 'shut up shop' when it

Left: Hedgehogs hibernate to survive extended periods when food is scarce.

doesn't pay to stay active. Hedgehogs (and many other mammals, such as Hazel Dormice and bats) conserve energy by turning down their internal thermostat during cold periods of the year. This is hibernation.

But it begs the question: 'why?' Hedgehogs have evolved to make a trade-off between defence and warmth. Spines help deter predators, but fail miserably to keep

Below: Garden Hedgehogs may use artificially constructed hibernation chambers.

Above: Bats like this Daubenton's Bat (left) are well known for hibernating; Swallows (right) prefer to migrate away from the UK to escape winter's impoverished food supplies.

out the winter cold. In order to keep warm in this season, Hedgehogs would need to eat copiously. Another reason is that their predominantly invertebrate prey is rare at this time, as it doesn't deal well with cold either. With no chance of eating their way through winter (nor any chance of migrating south, as insect-eating birds such as swallows and warblers do), Hedgehogs have no option but to hibernate.

So to the 'how?' Fundamentally, Hedgehogs drastically reduce their metabolic rate. This lessens their body temperature to as low as possible (1–5°C/34–41°F, from a norm of around 35°C/95°F) without freezing. By following this strategy the Hedgehog also decreases its oxygen consumption, lowers its breathing rate (often to once every hour) and slashes its heart rate by an astonishing 90 per cent or more, resulting in a torpor that is very different to sleep.

The 'when' depends on location (and thus climate). Unlike sleep, hibernation is optional and its duration a

Good fats and better fats

As dieticians and other health professionals regularly tell us, our diet includes good fats (unsaturates such as fatty acids) and bad fats (everything else). In a Hedgehog's body, however, there are good fats (which are white) and even better fats (which are brown). Ordinary white fat keeps the body ticking over during hibernation. Brown fat is used to rapidly raise body temperature if so needed, jump-starting the Hedgehog's metabolism during arousal or saving the animal from freezing. Brown fat may constitute just 3g (⅒oz) of every 100g (3½oz) of Hedgehog, but the mammal cannot survive without it.

Left: Cold temperatures in Great Britain induce Hedgehogs to hibernate for up to six months of the year.

matter of strategy. If the air temperature was sufficiently warm all year and enough food was available, there would be no need to hibernate at all. In Great Britain, however, these factors mean that for Hedgehogs hibernation starts during October/November and ends in March/April. A five- or six-month torpor might be a rule of thumb. Further north, in Scandinavia, persistent cold means that hibernation may exceed 220 days. In southern Europe (and in New Zealand, where Hedgehogs have been introduced – see page 19), gentler winters mean early springs and prolonged autumns, which means more invertebrates early and late in the year, and therefore less need to hibernate for as long.

One twist in the duration and timing of hibernation is that males start and end hibernation earlier than females. This is because it pays for the males to be on the prowl as soon as there is a chance of encountering fertile females and because there is no chance of successful procreation in the autumn.

Right: An undisturbed area of the garden can provide a secluded location for a hibernation nest.

Last but not least, the 'where' of hibernation. For a Hedgehog, this means the nature and location of its winter hibernation nest (see page 64). This nest needs to be weatherproof to keep out the rain and wind, and to serve as a buffer against fluctuations in outside temperature. The more constant the temperature inside the nest – and this means avoiding frosty dips as well as warm spikes – the more efficiently a Hedgehog can spend its energy budget. The ideal nest keeps the ambient temperature at 1–5°C (34–41°F), whether the air outside in the 'real world' is -10°C (14°F) or +10°C (50°F).

Managing hibernation

How a Hedgehog decides when the time has come to hibernate is far from clear. Logically it is some combination of them observing daylight reducing (earlier and longer nights), temperatures cooling and food supplies dwindling. It follows that the opposite cues in spring bring the Hedgehog around from hibernation; lengthening daylight is known to reduce the production of melatonin (the hormone that regulates sleep and wakefulness) and stimulate the generation of testosterone (which is essential for the race to breed). Timings vary with geography and from year to year. In Great Britain, for example, the cold spring of 2013 meant that Hedgehogs emerged late from hibernation, whereas the mild autumn we had in 2016 delayed the start of their winter retreat.

Once hibernating, the Hedgehog is far from free of peril. In Sweden, one-third of Hedgehogs die during hibernation; in milder New Zealand, the figure is one-fifth. Both really cold snaps and unseasonably warm spells rapidly burn fat reserves, hence the ideal hibernation nest provides an unchanging temperature. Should the temperature dip as low as -5°C (23°F), Hedgehogs have to consume more than 20 times as much oxygen as they do at the ideal rest temperature of 4°C (39°F). However, a mild spell will wake the Hedgehog, and waking also means using up energy: fine for the end of winter, but not when February's worst is yet to come. Up to nine-tenths of the energy consumed during a Hedgehog's entire hibernation is gobbled up during these brief awakenings. Moreover, even lightly touching a hibernating Hedgehog doubles its heart rate, so resist the temptation to search for them during winter.

In Great Britain, a typical Hedgehog emerges from hibernation one-quarter lighter than when it entered that state. Further north, where colder winters burn more fat, Hedgehogs may lose 40 per cent of their weight. To survive its first hibernation, scientists have calculated that a British Hedgehog must weigh at least 450g (1lb); in colder Denmark it must weigh at least 510g (1lb 2oz). The heavier the hog, the better its chances of surviving the winter.

Above: A Hedgehog needs to weigh at least 450g (1lb) to survive hibernation in Great Britain, and even more further north.

Aestivation

For species of hedgehog living in hot, dry climates, surviving the winter is less of an ordeal than enduring the summer. During such scorching conditions, the hedgehogs' invertebrate prey may hide to avoid overheating, so starvation becomes a real risk. To survive, hedgehogs adopt a similar strategy to hibernation: they 'aestivate' (from the Latin *aestivare*, which means 'to spend the summer'), conserving energy by shutting down their body for a few critical weeks.

The nesting instinct

Above: Well-constructed hibernation nests keep Hedgehogs warm and dry throughout the winter months.

It's a little-appreciated fact that Hedgehogs are master builders. We think of birds or, at a pinch, Harvest Mice or Hazel Dormice, as building the best nests in the British Isles. But the Hedgehog is also a contender.

We have learned of the supreme importance of the winter nest if a Hedgehog is to hibernate successfully. But we have not explained the magic of the construct. Winter nests are spheres 50cm (20in) in diameter and with condensed leaf-walls 10cm (4in) thick. These walls encase a hollow bed chamber – the inside of which has been smoothed by the repeated rotations of its owner – that leads directly to an exit tunnel. Nests are sited to afford optimum protection from the elements, whether that's tucked against fallen trees, beneath bramble tangles or in underground burrows (created by Rabbits or dug by the Hedgehog itself). So sturdy is the winter nest that it can last intact until the following winter – although the builder prefers to construct a new hibernation home rather than make do with a second-hand property.

In contrast, summer nests (also called day nests) are flimsy, temporary affairs: think of a tent rather than a house. Building materials for these nests include leaves and grass, but no great effort is put into shaping the shelter. Some, indeed, are barely more than a scattering of vegetation. This makes perfect sense. The objective of a summer nest is concealment from predators, not temperature regulation. Moreover, if a Hedgehog has a large home range, it makes little sense to expend energy walking back to the same nest each night. Far better to have a selection of retreats from which to choose the nearest.

Male Hedgehogs are particularly fastidious, usually building a new nest every summer day, whereas females may stick to the same abode for a week or so. In fact, *owning* (and defending) a nest does not appear to be a concept in the Hedgehog world. Instead, give-and-take seems to be the guiding principle. In summer, one animal may use a nest built by another should they find it unoccupied, in acceptable condition and in a convenient

Above: As well as winter and summer nests, Hedgehogs build maternal or breeding nests for female and hoglet tenants.

location. This never happens in winter, however: nests used then are too important to place one's survival in the paws of another.

A different form of nest-sharing has been recorded during the coldest months – one that is quite surprising for a notably unsociable animal (see page 69). Scientists have sometimes found Hedgehog winter nests that contain two chambers (and that presumably had two occupants). There are three plausible explanations for such behaviour. The occupants could be siblings. The residents could be a mother and her offspring. Or perhaps energy conservation came into play: Hedgehogs huddling together in very cold periods might be a literal lifeline.

As well as winter and summer nests, a third type of abode is a breeding (also known as maternal) nest. As its name suggests, this is for the exclusive use of a female and her litter. As this nest is the infants' home until they are independent, it needs to be fairly large and reasonably robust. The growing family is very vulnerable to disturbance. Should a mother feel threatened, and provided she neither abandons nor kills her young (see page 40), she will move and quickly build a new nest in which to install her offspring.

Two mysterious behaviours

Those who study or care for Hedgehogs are sometimes privy to two remarkable, apparently unique and currently inexplicable behaviours exhibited by the spiny animals. The first is known as self-anointing; the second involves running in circles.

Scientists sometimes do themselves no favours. 'Self-anointing' is hardly the most user-friendly of names for what transpires to be a quite fascinating and bizarre practice.

Every so often, an otherwise apparently 'normal' hedgehog breaks off from its day-to-day (or night-to-night) business to produce great quantities of white, foaming saliva from its mouth. In some other mammals, you might initially suspect an outbreak of rabies but that particular malady is unknown in hedgehogs. It soon becomes apparent that the frothy liquid is being deliberately produced, as the animal smacks its lips and then uses its flickering tongue to smear the substance thickly over its flanks and rear.

The process may continue for just a minute or two, or may last for an hour. It ends with the mammal looking like it has been through a soapy carwash – but what *starts* it remains a mystery. The trigger appears to be a strong smell or taste from incongruous sources as varied as cigarette butts, dog poo, human sweat, fish, tar and old shoes. Yet other smelly substances, such as olive oil and whisky, produce no such reaction. A study from Belgium suggested that while all ages and both sexes of West European Hedgehogs self-anoint, males do so twice as frequently as females, and youngsters do it more often than adults.

The practice evidently has a purpose, given that it occurs in several genera of hedgehog and that reaching hard-to-access parts of its anatomy requires some quite physical contortions. But what that point is continues to puzzle biologists. In the absence of certainty, scientists conjecture. Disappointingly, none of the ideas seem particularly convincing.

Below: Quite why hedgehogs lick white, foaming saliva over their bodies is a mystery. This process is known as self-anointing.

One theory is that the odd-smelling saliva might disguise the hedgehog's own odour, thereby concealing it from some predators. Alternatively, might the saliva be imbued with a substance poisonous to predators? Another hypothesis is that self-anointing rids the hedgehog of fleas or other parasites; if that's the case, it isn't very effective. Perhaps it has a sexual function, helping distribute reproductive odours – but, if so, why do hoglets do it? The closest specialists come to a conclusion is that it is some form of scent-marking behaviour, announcing the individual's presence to other hedgehogs – but the reason for it remains obscure. How little we know about even some of our most familiar species!

Meanwhile, since the 1960s, some people studying West European Hedgehogs have reported watching them run round and round on a circular track some 10–15m (33–50ft) in diameter. Some animals would continue their laps for an hour or more, and even repeat the process on successive nights. What they are doing and why is utterly baffling. The individuals involved were always alone, so this isn't anything to do with courtship or communication. Indeed, there seems to be no benefit to the Hedgehog in expending energy in such an odd fashion. The best guess is that the circuit-trainers are suffering from an infection (perhaps in one ear) or perhaps – given that the behaviour has coincided with accelerating use of agrochemicals – from pesticide poisoning. Another mystery for aspiring scientists to seek to resolve!

Below: Running in circles for apparently no reason is another puzzling Hedgehog behaviour.

(Anti)social Life

Like their near-relatives the shrews and moles, Hedgehogs appear to be unsociable mammals. It 'takes two to tango', of course, so courtship necessarily demands that two individuals do meet up, if only briefly. But other than procreation and family life (a female and her offspring, or siblings together), Hedgehogs have little urge for social interaction. Such unsociability demands an explanation.

Hedgehogs are clearly likely to encounter one another when wandering around each night. This is particularly the case when at notably good foraging areas such as a garden that offers tasty morsels each night. Yet when Hedgehogs 'meet', their air appears to be one of studious indifference. Granted, fights occasionally break out between rivals for a particular food source or female, but squabbles are otherwise rare, and there is no sense of territoriality (see page 47).

So how does an animal signal its presence in a way that enables another animal to avoid it? How do those 'ships in the night' know to pass each other rather than crash? And how does a male Hedgehog know where to find a female and surmise that she is fertile and thus worth courting? Hedgehogs may be solitary animals, but they must still communicate. How?

Opposite: Hedgehogs are stand-offish animals and will typically ignore each other if they meet while foraging.

Below: Courtship, however, elicits more sociable behaviour.

How Hedgehogs communicate

To be honest, scientists don't know for sure. Given that Hedgehogs' most acute sense is smell, body odour is the most likely explanation for how these animals manage to give one another personal space. When two Hedgehogs approach within a few metres of each other, both pause, sniff the air (and presumably detect one another), then change direction. The odours could come from a number of sources, including glands in the bottom and mouth. The smells may also come from urine and faeces, although there is no evidence that Hedgehogs (unlike Badgers, say), use their waste matter to mark out territories.

In terms of courtship, males may be able to investigate a female's urine to determine whether she is sexually receptive. Vaginal secretions may also help. Before mating, a male often marks the ground with scent from his penis. Given that the female often checks out this scent, it likely communicates information about the male's suitability as a mate.

As we have already learned (see page 36), mating can be a noisy business. This means that, in courtship at least, sounds may be an important Hedgehog communication tool. Quacking and snorting can be audible from up to 50m (55yd) away. Antagonistic encounters may be accompanied by snorting or puffing. Hedgehogs routinely snuffle as they forage, but this serves no communication purpose. Other sounds produced by Hedgehogs relate to contact between mother and offspring. These include high-pitched twittering, shrill whistles and clucking.

Above: Hedgehogs are not thought to use excretions to mark any kind of territory.

Below: The smell from faeces may signal to a Hedgehog that another individual is nearby.

Left: We don't know for sure, but having such an acute sense of smell must play an important role in Hedgehog communication.

And that, in terms of Hedgehog sociality, is that. Hedgehogs are unsociable animals, avoiding each other wherever possible. There is no concept of territoriality, and occasional fights break out only over mating rights or access to particularly prized foodstuffs. In as much as they need to do so, Hedgehogs communicate by scent and, if push comes to shove, by voice.

Below: Mating can be especially audible.

The Hedgehog year

For a Hedgehog living in Great Britain, this is what a typical year looks like:

January Should the month remain consistently cold, the Hedgehog hibernates throughout. It is snug inside a leaf-rich nest, which is concealed from intruders and elements alike by a bush, log or similar.

February Although still hibernating, the Hedgehog wakes periodically. In mild weather, it may leave the nest, wandering around or perhaps foraging.

March At the start of the month, the Hedgehog is at its lightest, its fat reserves are depleted and it may be exhausted. Most animals (particularly males) emerge from hibernation this month and start replenishing energy levels, although they may return to seasonal torpor should nights be markedly cold.

April Both sexes are now out and about. Their priority is to take on board as many calories as possible, and to do so as quickly as possible. This is key to entering peak breeding condition. Some early starters will mate by the end of the month.

May Courtship and copulation are top priority this month. Hedgehogs are so promiscuous, and their affairs so noisy, that there is a good chance of you encountering prickly love on a nocturnal walk in suitable habitat.

June The peak month for births across southern Great Britain, and the start of the year's most intensive period for the female. Four or five young is typical, and they are cared for exclusively by their mother. The hoglets' future is in her paws.

July Most fertile females that have not yet given birth do so this month – particularly in northern Great Britain. Babies already born develop rapidly and accompany their mother on foraging excursions; many will become independent by the month end.

August Hedgehogs born in June get to grips with fending for themselves. Those that greeted the world in July take their first steps away from mother and siblings.

September All Hedgehogs, young and old, face a race against time to build sufficient fat reserves to get them through winter hibernation. Late litters remain dependent on their mother; the chances of them reaching spring are slight.

October The onset of autumn sees a flurry of Hedgehog activity. Every minute is vital in these final weeks before hibernation. The more fat-rich food a Hedgehog can consume, the better its chance of survival. Nest building is also on this month's agenda.

November Any Hedgehogs you encounter out and about this month are likely to be young animals or those in poor health, engaged in a last-ditch attempt to avoid admitting defeat. Other Hedgehogs should already be hibernating.

December Almost all is quiet in the Hedgehog world. Hibernation is the order of the day, week and month, with only occasional sallies into consciousness.

Threats and Conservation

Throughout western Europe, you hear the same story. Middle-aged people fondly remember Hedgehogs mooching around their childhood gardens, yet haven't seen a live one for many years. Their children know Hedgehogs only in theory or in representation – Mrs Tiggy-Winkle, say, or Sonic – but have never clapped eyes on the real thing, except as an occasional spiky pancake littering the gutter. But how bad are the threats that Hedgehogs face? Who is doing what to save them? And, more controversially, are Hedgehogs ever the 'bad guys' in conservation terms?

Across a broad swathe of its range, the decline in Hedgehog populations is real, rapid and disconcerting. Some threats to the species' existence are natural – predators and parasites, for example – but the principal finger points unreservedly at human actions, from traffic to habitat fragmentation, from industrial agriculture to persecution. We profess to love the Hedgehog, yet also appear to be driving it towards the unthinkable: extinction.

Opposite: This Hedgehog was spotted in time. Sadly, most of our encounters with hogs are of flattened animals killed by vehicles.

Below: American Mink will prey on Hedgehogs.

Predators

The Hedgehog's principal defence mechanisms – spines and an ability to roll into a near-impenetrable ball – mean that its natural predators are few. Indeed, no animal specialises in a diet of Hedgehogs. Nevertheless, Hedgehogs feature in the diet of one nocturnal aerial carnivore, the Eagle Owl, which has the strong talons needed to get past the spines. The prickly ones occasionally succumb to a Fox, which probably dispatches them with a swift bite to the head before they can fully curl up. There is evidence that mustelids such as American Mink,

Above and below: Hedgehogs are occasionally on the menu for Foxes and Eagle Owls, but Badgers are Hedgehogs' biggest nemesis.

Polecats and Pine Martens are able to catch and consume Hedgehogs. But the biggest predatory threat Hedgehogs face is that of another much- (if not universally) loved mammal, the Badger.

With its strong forelimbs, the Badger has no problem in flipping a Hedgehog onto its back. Long, sharp claws prise apart the Hedgehog's defences and 'unzip' flesh from spine-coated skin. The Badger makes a formidable predator, and one against which the Hedgehog's defences are limited. The best a Hedgehog can hope for is not to run into a Badger. Unfortunately, because the species overlap in both habitat and diet, and thus compete for the same resources (see page 78), Hedgehogs and Badgers frequently encounter one another. When this happens, there is only one victor.

Left: Badgers are both a competitor and predator of the Hedgehog, although in areas of abundant food, such as gardens, the two species may peacefully coexist.

There is some evidence to suggest that predation by Badgers may have a population-level impact on Hedgehogs. Research in parts of Great Britain has shown that Hedgehog abundance varies in direct relation to the density of Badger setts. In Oxfordshire, Hedgehogs were absent from areas where there were more than 2.27 Badger setts (or 13 individuals) per 10km² (4 square miles). Hedgehogs are known to avoid or move faster through areas where they detect the odour of Badgers. In agricultural areas inhabited by Badgers, Hedgehogs avoid predation by sticking closer to cover such as hedgerows (where that landscape feature remains!); in Badger-free zones, they forage more freely. The Hedgehog's rarity in western England is thought to be partly due to the local abundance of Badgers. In north-east France, the further a female Hedgehog lives from a Badger sett, the more young she raises.

Hedgehogs vs Badgers

There are two dimensions to the Hedgehog's problem with Badgers. The first is predation. The second is competition. The two mammals live in much the same habitat and have an overlapping diet (primarily worms and beetles). The same food can only be eaten once. Moreover, a Badger eats roughly five to seven times as much as a Hedgehog. If food availability remains constant, then every additional Badger means an area of land can support five to seven fewer Hedgehogs. If food availability decreases (which appears to be the case in Great Britain, at least, as a result of human actions; see page 83), the relationship changes from being primarily competitive (where the Badger wins) to being predatory (ditto).

Moreover, as Hedgehogs avoid otherwise suitable habitat where Badgers are present, the latter species essentially 'fragments' Hedgehog habitat. As Badgers spread, so they effectively trap Hedgehogs. In the Netherlands, one study showed that Hedgehogs now mainly inhabit urban areas and mooted that this might be due to displacement by Badgers.

Above: The diets of Badgers and Hedgehogs overlap markedly.

Evidence suggests that Badgers may be displacing Hedgehogs from rural areas (**left**) into towns (**right**).

Diseases and parasites

Snuffling along with its nose to the ground and belly brushing through the undergrowth, it is unsurprising that a Hedgehog picks up its fair share of unsolicited parasites and unwanted maladies. External examples of the former comprise fleas, mites and ticks, but never lice. While an irritant, such hangers-on are not fatal. Internal parasites such as nematode worms, however, infect lungs (particularly of male Hedgehogs, judging from a study in the Republic of Ireland) and frequently cause death.

Fleas are the Hedgehog's most notorious infestation, with a hundred or more being a typical collection, although one unfortunate young Hedgehog was reported to have 932. In an inspiring example of evolution, the flea species involved is uniquely associated with Hedgehogs: *Archaeopsylla erinacei* frequents no other host. So although in theory a flea may transfer to you or a pet, it cannot breed, and therefore the species cannot survive in your home. Why Hedgehogs are such fleabags is unclear. With long limbs and strong claws, they are physically able to groom their spines … they just clearly don't do it very successfully. If, indeed, they bother at all. The prevailing Hedgehog attitude to fleas is to simply ignore them, even when they are within easy reach. Such a minimalist approach to personal hygiene also makes life easy for ticks. A study in Iran found that two-thirds of Hedgehogs hosted these blood-sucking arachnids. Some individual animals are particularly badly affected: a survey of Belgian hogs found that around 10 per cent collectively harboured more than half the ticks counted.

Hedgehogs host a variety of infections, whether fungal, viral or bacterial. Around a quarter of Hedgehogs suffer from ringworm, and viruses such as foot-and-mouth disease have been found in Hedgehogs (although the species is not a significant carrier for this or bacterial illnesses such as bovine tuberculosis). None of these infections appears to be a major cause of Hedgehog death. We must look elsewhere for the principal threats to Hedgehog existence.

Above: As its scientific name suggests, the flea *Archaeopsylla erinacei* specialises in infesting Hedgehogs.

The road to hell

How many more Hedgehogs, I wonder, have we each seen squashed on the road than trotting around full of life? It is surely a sorry state of affairs when our addiction to motorised transport and the clamour for ever more asphalt results in so many thousands dying each and every year.

In truth, although it is clear that rolling up into a ball serves the Hedgehog no protection against speeding vehicles, we do not know how many die on roads in the British Isles. A survey in 1985 suggested that 1.3 million Hedgehogs might die annually in Great Britain; although oft-cited since, most scientists now pooh-pooh this claim as a vast overestimate. Fairly old surveys in Denmark, which is roughly one-fifth the size of Britain, suggest 70,000–100,000 road deaths per year. A more recent study in the Netherlands suggested 113,000–340,000 deaths per year, equating to 3–20 per cent of the national population there.

Since 2001, the People's Trust for Endangered Species (PTES) has engaged the British public in its Mammals on Roads survey, where drivers count and identify each mammal they see along a vehicular journey of defined length. From 2011–2014, counts ranged from 0.8–1.4 dead hogs per 100km (62 miles) of road. The instigator of this study,

Right: Road traffic is a major cause of Hedgehog mortality.

Above: As well as causing death by vehicle-strike, roads can also prevent Hedgehogs from accessing feeding areas.

Pat Morris, is a renowned Hedgehog expert. Extrapolating from the survey, he initially reckoned that perhaps 12,000–15,000 Hedgehogs are killed annually on British roads. In the context of a population that is thought to be around 1.5 million (according to *The State of Britain's Hedgehogs 2018* report), 15,000 deaths per year represents a sizeable mortality.

Other studies suggest that road traffic is actually an even bigger killer. In surveys of marked animals, road-traffic accidents (RTAs) variously accounted for the deaths of 2.5 per cent (at one of Morris's sites in England), 4 per cent (New Zealand, Sweden), 12 per cent (Netherlands) or 24 per cent (Poland) of the population. In a study by another British Hedgehog expert, Nigel Reeve, just shy of one-fifth of Hedgehog deaths were due to vehicles. The equivalent proportion in an urban Finnish survey was around 70 per cent. In 2016, Pat Morris joined colleagues led by David Wembridge, Mammal Surveys Coordinator at PTES, in revisiting four surveys conducted from 1952 to 2004. This led to an estimate of 167,000–335,000 deaths per year – an order of magnitude higher than Morris's initial calculation. Given the most recent population estimate of around 1.5 million, the researchers calculate that this suggests an annual mortality rate of 10–20 per cent. This may not be far off: the equivalent figure for Badgers is at the top end of that range.

Right: New roads can fragment habitat and have a dramatic impact on Hedgehog populations.

What is certain, however, is that the PTES study demonstrates a long-term decline in Hedgehog RTAs – and that this represents an equivalent decline in the species' population (rather than suggesting that Hedgehogs are getting better at avoiding cars!). Another interesting finding from the PTES survey is that in spring, two-thirds of RTA Hedgehogs are male – but in autumn, three-quarters are female. This is explained by differences in activity patterns between the sexes. Males emerge from hibernation earlier than females and travel further in spring as they search for mates; but they also hibernate earlier, meaning more females are active (near roads and elsewhere) in autumn.

There are other worrying implications to this story. The more roads we build (in particular, dual carriageways, given their width), the more obstacles we place in the way of Hedgehog movement. If Hedgehogs cannot successfully disperse, populations become isolated. In fragmenting Hedgehog habitat, road building places them at greater risk of one-off incidents (such as fire or disease), inbreeding and low nesting success, and also limits access to feeding grounds. A study from the Netherlands calculated that the overall impact of roads was to reduce Hedgehog density by 30 per cent, which puts it well within the realm of local extinctions.

Habitat change

Building roads is just one way that humans inadvertently change Hedgehog habitat for the worse. As well as fragmenting and destroying their living quarters, we also degrade what habitat we deign to leave *and* reduce the amount of food it offers. All in all, we could hardly do a better job of making life difficult for Hedgehogs if we tried.

So what do we do that is so bad – and how does it hinder hogs? We make habitats unsuitable for Hedgehogs by 'tidying up' parks and gardens, infilling developments, paving over gardens and intensifying farming. In turn, these actions reduce the number of Hedgehogs that an area can support, remove nesting locations, expose animals to predation (or disturbance by pets), disrupt dispersal routes and diminish foraging opportunities.

Intensive farming (or gardening) methods, such as liberal application of pesticides, kill off invertebrates on which Hedgehogs feed. Their food, simply, has gone. (Half of natural deaths in one Finnish study were attributable to starvation.) Reduction of permanent grasslands and ploughing of field margins have similar impacts. So too poor management (or outright removal) of hedgerows, among a panoply of harmful impacts.

Above: Excessively tidy parks are not Hedgehog-friendly.

Above: Prime Hedgehog habitat can disappear under new housing estates.

Above: Pesticide-sprayed fields hold no prey for Hedgehogs.

Left: Urbanisation also increases disturbance from pets such as this dog.

They aren't called Hedgehogs for nothing: a 'token' hedge (**above**) may enable hogs to move through farmed landscapes but is no match for a thick, bushy hedge (**below**) that offers ample protection and food.

Hedgehogs – the clue is in the name – spend 55–60 per cent of their time within 5m (16ft) of a hedge or woodland edge. Hedges provide hibernation sites (for half of Dutch Hedgehogs in one survey) and breeding nests (75 per cent in the same study). They also offer concealment from predators (particularly Badgers), a linear restaurant, and a thoroughfare for safe movement through the landscape. Remove, hack away at or undermanage hedgerows, and hogs suffer markedly. During the 1990s, England and Wales lost 18,000km (11,180 miles) of hedgerows annually. That is a lot of missing Hedgehog habitat.

Quite aside from destruction of Hedgehog habitat, some of our other activities also unwittingly expose Hedgehogs to direct hazards, which collectively can cause local extinctions. Hogs fall into cattle grids, are chopped by garden strimmers or lawnmowers (as immortalised by Philip Larkin in his 1979 poem *The Mower*), are burnt in bonfires, die from poisoning (including by ingesting slug pellets scattered by gardeners), drown in garden ponds, and get caught up in elastic bands that bundle together our post. The garden chemical issue is particularly ironic. Hedgehogs are a natural pest-eradicator; by weakening Hedgehogs through poisoning, invertebrates will benefit – and gardeners end up with a bigger problem than they started with.

Right: This Hedgehog has burnt spines and was probably caught in a bonfire.

Direct persecution

All the previously mentioned anthropogenic pressures on Hedgehogs are inadvertent and indirect – borne out of ignorance or disregard. But some people also choose, or have chosen, to wreak deliberate, direct havoc on hogs. For more than 300 years until the mid-18th century, Hedgehogs were designated a pest species in the UK on the grounds that they munched eggs and allegedly slurped cow's milk. A bounty was placed on their heads, with parish church wardens authorised to make payment. In his 2007 book *Silent Fields: the long decline of a nation's wildlife*, Roger Lovegrove calculates that – across 140 years in just 10 English counties – this resulted in the death of 500,000 Hedgehogs.

The rise of country (shooting) estates during the 19th and 20th centuries gave rise to further direct persecution. British gamekeepers killed a minimum of 10,000 Hedgehogs (considered to be 'vermin') a year until at least the 1960s. Those responsible for protecting their masters' Pheasant population had a modest leg on which to stand, as Hedgehogs certainly did predate nests. However, in one assessment, the prickly ones were responsible for just 10 per cent of game bird failures (and, in another, just 1.3 per cent) – fewer than feral cats and dogs, whose antics did not prompt their grisly demise. Fortunately, Hedgehogs can no longer be deliberately trapped, as a result of protection afforded by the Wildlife and Countryside Act 1981 (see page 87).

Finally, Hedgehogs also suffer the occasional attentions of mindless, sadistic hooligans – although at least there is none of the systematic torture that befalls other British mammals such as Brown Hares (coursing) and Badgers (baiting). Nevertheless, in 2016 two brothers were jailed for six weeks for playing football with a Hedgehog. Other press reports over the past decade include a gang of teenagers who sprayed a Hedgehog with deodorant, then set fire to it, and a live hog placed on a barbecue. I defy any reader of this book to provide a rational explanation for such barbarity.

Above: During the 19th and 20th centuries, Hedgehogs were persecuted by gamekeepers.

Going down

Throughout western Europe, the picture is the same: Hedgehog numbers are in freefall. Great Britain's hogs may have declined by 95 per cent in 60 years, and three out of four citizen-science surveys have shown statistically significant annual population declines of 3.1–13.7 per cent since 2000. In the Netherlands too, Hedgehog distribution has shrunk, and the species seems to have retreated (or been driven) into urban areas.

These changes are noticeable to the layperson and to the conservationist. 'I don't see Hedgehogs as much as I used to' is a common refrain across Europe. In Sweden, people interviewed in 2010 had seen a Hedgehog less recently than those questioned in 1993. Almost half of British citizens participating in the 2006 Hogwatch survey felt that Hedgehog numbers had declined over the previous five years. Surveys of 2,600 gardeners by *BBC Gardeners' World* magazine found that 51 per cent did not see a Hedgehog at all during 2016, compared with 48 per cent a year earlier. Just 12 per cent – less than one gardener in eight – saw a Hedgehog regularly.

Below: Despite overall declines, Hedgehogs seem to be doing better in cities than in rural areas.

Saving Hedgehogs

From pest to imperilled within 150 years is quite a terrifying trajectory for British Hedgehogs. Fortunately, conservationists have not been sitting on their hands. Far from it. The scarier the news on the Hedgehog's status, the more conservationists and citizens alike have been galvanised to take action.

Hedgehogs and the law

In the UK, the first official notice of conservation concern was given when the Hedgehog was added to the list of species covered by Schedule 6 of the Wildlife and Countryside Act 1981. This makes it illegal to kill, trap or collect Hedgehogs without a licence (which may be granted for scientific purposes, for example). In theory, the Act stops gamekeepers (or anyone else) from dispatching hogs as vermin – although animals are still caught unintentionally in traps set legitimately for other species. There are similar laws in place across much of Europe, including those implementing the Bern Convention on the Conservation of European Wildlife and Natural Habitats.

Below: An unfortunate Hedgehog trapped in a cage that was intended to catch rats.

Right: Current UK legislation does little to spare Hedgehogs from threats such as habitat destruction.

Since 1996 in the UK, the Wild Mammals (Protection) Act has made it illegal to treat wild Hedgehogs with cruelty. It was under this law that the brothers who treated a Hedgehog like a football were imprisoned. In 2006, the Hedgehog became one of the 943 'species of principal importance' under the Natural Environment and Rural Communities Act (2006). This requires local authorities to factor Hedgehogs into their decision-making and action. Well and good though this body of legislation is, none of the laws do anything substantive to directly counter the raft of significant threats that Hedgehogs face, from vehicular traffic to hedgerow destruction.

Hedgehogs as a biodiversity indicator

Not only is the Hedgehog a much-loved and increasingly rare animal – two robust reasons for dedicating conservation effort towards it – it is an *important* one too. This is because biologists have determined that the presence of Hedgehogs in an area indicates that the local environment is unfragmented, has varied habitat and is rich in invertebrates. In contrast, an absence of Hedgehogs (a generalist carnivore, remember) in otherwise suitable habitat suggests that all is not well locally.

Strategies and plans

In 2007, the Hedgehog was added as a 'priority species' to the respective Biodiversity Action Plans of England, Scotland, Wales and Northern Ireland. Such priority species (1,149 in total at the time of writing, double the number of the inaugural plan in 1997) are those considered to be the most threatened and that require conservation action. The Welsh action plan, for example, sets a target to halt the decline of the country's Hedgehogs and maintain their current range.

Committed wildlife charities have subsequently taken up the gauntlet and developed a national conservation strategy for UK hedgehogs. The initial document was produced by Hedgehog expert and journalist Hugh Warwick in 2010, on commission from the PTES and British Hedgehog Preservation Society (BHPS). An updated, ten-year blueprint was published by the same organisations in 2015.

The strategy sets two primary aims: to stabilise urban Hedgehog populations by 2025 and to understand what Hedgehogs need for populations to be sustainable in a farmed landscape. These aims are underpinned by a suite of objectives that cover monitoring (because it is worrying how little we actually know about this supposedly familiar mammal), habitats (how best to manage them for Hedgehogs), mortality (understanding the impacts of diseases and traffic, in particular) and public engagement and training (see overleaf). The strategy also proposes lobbying the Government to move Hedgehogs from Schedule 6 of the Wildlife and Countryside Act to Schedule 5. Among other things, this would make it illegal to disturb a Hedgehog in its nest or to damage or destroy its nesting area.

Above: Conservationists are seeking to determine the fundamental requirements for viable Hedgehog populations on farmland.

Hedgehog Street

The encouraging news about the conservation strategy is that it is packed with real actions, rather than empty words. National and county-level organisations alike have inspired initiatives and individuals that seek to make a tangible, positive difference to the UK's Hedgehogs.

Funded by the BHPS, Warwickshire Wildlife Trust created the UK's first 'Hedgehog Improvement Area' in Solihull in the West Midlands in 2015. At the heart of the area sit 90ha (222 acres) of green space – the equivalent of two 18-hole golf courses – encompassing a Trust reserve and a municipal park. This provides a green hub from which Hedgehogs can disperse. Such a large area is critical because researchers have determined that the minimum number of Hedgehogs for a population to be viable is 32, and the smallest possible area they need is 90ha. Within the wider landscape, the project helps communities to make improvements for Hedgehogs and to monitor their distribution throughout the area.

Burton Fleming, a village in east Yorkshire, has not let its diminutive size curb lofty aspirations. In 2016, its residents declared the village a Hedgehog-friendly zone – with ample suitable habitat welcoming the arrival of several rehabilitated Hedgehogs. Other villages are expected to follow suit.

These various initiatives lie under the umbrella of a national campaign, 'Hedgehog Street', which is led jointly by the PTES and BHPS (see page 125). This aims to ensure

Right: Hedgehog Officers from Warwickshire Wildlife Trust conducting a torchlight survey of an open green space.

that Hedgehogs remain a common and familiar part of British life by getting people to garden in a Hedgehog-friendly way and to cooperate in allowing the species free movement throughout each neighbourhood.

Within six years of the campaign's launch, 45,000 people have pledged to become 'Hedgehog Champions' – ambassadors for the initiative and role models for urban gardeners. By 2015, tangible benefits for Hedgehogs included linking 10,000 gardens via Hedgehog highways, installing 3,929 Hedgehog houses, removing 4,776 hazards and raising awareness at 252 events. In April 2017, the campaign even opened a showcase Hedgehog-friendly garden at the Royal Horticultural Society's Yorkshire venue, Harlow Carr. Best of all, Hedgehog Street shows no sign of losing momentum towards its target of 100,000 Hedgehog Champions by 2025.

Each year, the BHPS organises a Hedgehog Awareness Week to complement the work of Hedgehog Street. The initiative runs in spring, when Hedgehogs are freshly emerged from hibernation. A media campaign and associated events highlight the problems that Hedgehogs face, and how people can help them. Each year has a different focus: in 2017, the BHPS guided people on the safe use of garden strimmers; stickers were sent to people in organisations involved in habitat maintenance – from councils to tool-hire companies – prompting operatives to check for Hedgehogs before cutting vegetation.

Above: The key to opening up urban habitat is to create gaps in boundaries to allow the safe passage of Hedgehogs.

Above: The Hedgehog Street campaign is hugely inspiring.

Become a Hedgehog Champion

Hedgehog Champions are the individual people who make the Hedgehog Street campaign work. A Champion's role is all about their local neighbourhood. They make simple changes to their garden – such as putting a hole in their fence – that make life easier for Hedgehogs. They put up posters or give talks about Hedgehogs to raise local awareness. They distribute flyers to recruit neighbours to the hoggy cause. The Champions' community shares stories and experiences, and helps itself with all manner of Hedgehog-related issues. Joining takes seconds: just visit www.hedgehogstreet.org/register

A Hedgehog-friendly town

Like Warwickshire Wildlife Trust, Suffolk Wildlife Trust has a dedicated Hedgehog Officer, Ali North, who is charged with reversing the species' fortunes in the county.

'I have been the Suffolk Wildlife Trust's "Ipswich Hedgehog Officer" since September 2016. My goal is to make Ipswich the UK's most Hedgehog-friendly town (see page 125).

(see page 125)

I have always been intrigued by how unusual and distinctive Hedgehogs are and I applied for the job because it sounded like an exciting project to promote and record conservation action for this well-loved spiny mammal. It's an amazing opportunity to see the difference that is being made for wild Hedgehog populations across Ipswich, to contribute wider knowledge about the species and to enthuse a wide audience in wildlife conservation.

Suffolk Wildlife Trust set up this new role, funded by the Heritage Lottery Fund and the BHPS, against a backdrop of worrying declines in Hedgehog populations in town and country alike. In urban areas, Hedgehogs face a number of problems. Impermeable boundaries such as fences and walls make access into and between gardens difficult. Tidy gardens limit feeding and nesting opportunities. The use of chemicals limits the numbers of invertebrates on which Hedgehogs rely. If these threats can be tackled, however, towns have the opportunity to become havens for Hedgehogs.

My job is incredibly varied. I organise community and school events, run courses for land managers, approach businesses to encourage Hedgehog-friendly fencing, enthuse and recruit Hedgehog Champions, train volunteers in Hedgehog survey methods and help coordinate research to better understand the species' ecology.

The main focus of the project is to create a network of Hedgehog-friendly streets across Ipswich. This means linking each garden by a Hedgehog highway (ground-level fence hole or gate gap) and connecting Hedgehog-suitable green spaces across the town. My favourite experience with a wild Hedgehog was probably when I found its poo in my garden for the first time this year! I proceeded to take photos of the droppings – and then showed everyone I came across, forgetting that perhaps not everyone appreciates seeing animal poo as much as I did.'

Are Hedgehogs a conservation problem?

Amid all this positive news about the efforts organisations and individuals are putting in to saving Hedgehogs, there is a problematic undertone to the conservation story. Hedgehogs can cause problems too, namely their predation of the eggs of ground-nesting birds such as terns, gulls and waders.

Nowhere has the conflict between hogs and conservationists been more intense than on particular Scottish islands: the Uists (Outer Hebrides) and North Ronaldsay (Orkney). In 1972, a postman brought two Hedgehogs to the latter island, releasing them in an attempt to control slugs. By 1986, surveys by Hugh Warwick suggested that the population on this three-mile-long island might be as many as 400–600 animals.

Hedgehogs predate ground-nesting birds such as terns, gulls and waders on the Scottish islands of North Ronaldsay, Orkney (**above**), and North Uist, Outer Hebrides (**below**).

Ground-nesting birds that may have suffered from Hedgehog predation on Scottish islands include Redshank and Ringed Plover (**above**), and Arctic Tern (**below**).

Warwick was brought in because Hedgehogs were suspected of causing the failure of the island's colony of Arctic Terns, a migratory marvel of a seabird, and Ringed Plovers, a short-billed, beach-nesting shorebird. A decision was taken by the island's residents to capture the island's Hedgehogs and move them to the mainland. Over a few years, around 180 animals were translocated.

Although the Hedgehogs were certainly implicated in munching birds' eggs, were they actually the cause of the decline? Warwick's eventual conclusion was that other factors, including a dramatic shortage of sandeels in the case of the terns, were primarily responsible. So, while the effect of the Hedgehogs may not have been negligible, it was, in Warwick's view, secondary.

Within two decades, a similar – but bigger – story hit the headlines. In 1974, a local resident quietly introduced Hedgehogs to South Uist to help control garden pests. With little use of pesticides to curtail their food supply, light traffic and no Badgers, Hedgehog numbers rapidly expanded and their range spread to the neighbouring islands of Benbecula and North Uist. Within 20 years, the Hedgehog population was variously estimated at between 3,000 and 5,000.

Many Hedgehogs moved onto the machair, the wildflower-rich, sandy grassland that hems the islands' Atlantic coast. Here they found easy pickings, including the eggs of ground-nesting waders such as Redshanks, Dunlins, Oystercatchers and Ringed Plovers. Conservationists were understandably worried: in the early

1980s, an internationally important 17,000 pairs of waders bred on the Uists, including a quarter of the UK's Dunlins and Ringed Plovers. When wader populations began to drop rapidly, marauding Hedgehogs were soon labelled as the culprits. And justly so, to an extent, as experiments to remove Hedgehogs from small areas resulted in improved bird breeding success.

Scottish Natural Heritage (SNH) was obliged by EU law to prioritise protecting the waders. In 2003, it decided that Hedgehogs must be culled. Over four years, 650 were killed. Succeeding in eradicating only a small proportion of the population – and at considerable cost to the taxpayer – brought criticism from some quarters; local residents and animal-welfare organisations deemed the project ineffective and expensive.

The issue really flared up when local residents vented their fury that Hedgehogs were being killed rather than (as on North Ronaldsay) translocated. A coalition of wildlife and animal-welfare organisations formed Uist Hedgehog Rescue and started trapping and relocating Hedgehogs to the mainland. Within four years, the groups had moved 750 individuals (for a fraction of the cost). Roughly three-quarters of the relocated Hedgehogs survived and, judging by the weight they put on, thrived in their new homes. By 2007, SNH had looked and learned. It called time on the cull and began funding the translocation programme instead. So far, more than 1,600 animals have been moved.

SNH is also sponsoring research to more thoroughly investigate the extent to which Hedgehogs are responsible for the waders' decline. At first sight, evidence seems compelling: more than twice as many wader nests fail where Hedgehog densities are high, and Hedgehogs are responsible for more than half of all predated nests. But not everyone is completely convinced. Hugh Warwick, for example, wonders why waders have declined on islands that are free of Hedgehogs. He muses whether climate change or changing agricultural practices may be holding sway. Is it right to make the Hedgehog the fall guy? At least everyone can agree on one thing: introducing Hedgehogs to islands where the species does not occur naturally is an unequivocally bad idea.

Below: Scottish Natural Heritage scientist preparing to translocate a Hedgehog from the Hebrides to mainland Scotland.

Hedgehogs and People

For thousands of years, people have been fascinated by hedgehogs' ability to come back from apparent death. For hundreds of years, people have persecuted hedgehogs, treating them as vermin, resources or playthings. It is only in the past few decades that people have openly loved hedgehogs. Our relationship with hedgehogs is as contradictory as it is complex.

In the UK, the Hedgehog has often been rated our favourite mammal, yet disturbingly few of us have ever observed a live one. We instantly recognise the Hedgehog, yet our understanding of the animal is barely (prickly) skin-deep. We admire the Hedgehog's focus on defence rather than attack and we gawp at its unique appearance. We adore Hedgehogs' inquisitive nature, yet reluctantly acknowledge that they are ultimately untameable. We care for troubled individuals as if they were our own offspring, then feel bereft when they forsake us. We recognise that a Hedgehog's spines indicate its desire to be left alone, but nevertheless wish to handle and comfort it. The Hedgehog is the gardener's friend, yet many of us are blithely unaware that it lives right beside our homes. The Hedgehog has ample meaning for us, yet we often misrepresent and misunderstand it.

Opposite: The relationship between hogs and humans is a complicated one.

Left: Slug-munching hogs are a gardener's ally.

What hedgehogs mean to humans

Above: Evidence from beneath Stonehenge suggests that humans had an affinity with hogs at least 3,000 years ago.

Below: A marble sculpture of Artemis, the Greek goddess, whose 'epiphany' took the form of a hedgehog.

As common, widespread, immediately recognisable mammals, it is unsurprising that hedgehogs have a long and rich human history. What is surprising, however – given the widespread love for all things hoggy – is how piecemeal their cultural significance is.

In the British Isles, Hedgehogs unlike Badgers, say, are not architects of our countryside; they do not construct citadels that assume prominence in the landscape, but live solitarily in secluded transient nests. This might explain why in Great Britain Badgers (colloquially known as Brock) feature commonly in place names (think Brockenhurst, Brockley and Broxbourne), yet Hedgehogs do not. Granted, there are a few British pubs with 'hedgehog' in their name. One such establishment is The Hedgehog in Welwyn Garden City (Hertfordshire), so named perhaps because residents of the county's small towns are known locally as 'hedgehogs' (reputedly because, like the antisocial animals, they made for bad neighbours).

Reassuringly, somewhat more sacred consideration has also been given to hedgehogs. Archaeologists excavating a burial mound below Stonehenge, the UK's world-famous Neolithic monument, uncovered the skeleton of a young girl who died 3,000 years ago. She was apparently buried clutching a chalk carving of an animal thought by some to be a Hedgehog. If the identification is correct, it begs the question as to why. Perhaps (but unlikely) the girl had a pet Hedgehog? Perhaps those left behind thought an unthreatening nocturnal animal would guide her eternal night? Or perhaps she would, like the Hedgehog, awake from apparent death (hibernation) and return to life?

Support for the reincarnation theory comes from the early Greeks' use of hedgehog-shaped urns for infant burials. Artemis – the Hellenic goddess of the hunt, wild animals and wilderness – is also associated with regeneration. Greeks considered the hedgehog to be her representative on Earth. Indeed, archaeological evidence from the 5th

Left: Soldiers with a 'Czech hedgehog', an iron defence placed along the German border in the late 1930s.

century suggests that her 'epiphany' came in the form of a hedgehog. Cultures as diverse as ancient Egyptians, the Mongols and Austrians have imbued hedgehog-shaped or hedgehog-derived objects with reincarnatory significance.

Aside from hibernation, hedgehogs' other principal claim to fame is their spiny defence mechanism. This defensive technique has also breached the mammalian divide and entered human iconography, notably in the military sphere. At the Battle of Bannockburn in 1314, Robert the Bruce formed his men into a 'hedgehog' of spears. More recently, as the Second World War approached, 'Czech hedgehogs' lined the German border: these twisting iron structures could withstand (and even ensnare) a tank. *Armatus ad defendum* ('armed to defend') was the motto of HMS *Urchin*, a Royal Navy ship that saw action in the same conflict ('urchin' is an old name for hedgehog; see page 100). Rather less military in nature, there is even a strategic formation in chess called a hedgehog defence, an impenetrable formation of pawns designed to prevent the ingression of the rival 'army'.

We sometimes ascribe character to animals. We think of a fox as cunning ('as sly as a fox'), an owl as wise and a badger as dependable to the point of belligerence. However, when it comes to describing a hedgehog, we stutter to a halt. No such problem befell the Greek poet Archilochus, who wrote pearls of wisdom during the 7th century BC. One such maxim was that 'The fox knows many things, but the hedgehog knows one important thing'. Archilochus's message was that while the hedgehog may not know much, what it does know is worth knowing – and serves it well.

Some 2,600 years later, the British philosopher Isaiah Berlin reinvigorated the adage by purloining *The Hedgehog and the Fox* as the title for an essay on Leo Tolstoy's view of history, in which Berlin divided thinkers and writers into those who view the world through the lens of a single defining idea (hedgehogs, such as Plato) and those who are perpetually collecting experiences and espousing varied ideas (foxes, such as William Shakespeare).

A rather different philosophical take on what it means to be a hedgehog was proposed by German philosopher Arthur Schopenhauer in the mid-19th century. He envisaged human experience of love as a 'hedgehog's dilemma': we have an overwhelming need to get as close as possible to the one we love – yet doing so spikes us with pain.

What's in a name?

There are different ideas about the origin of the name 'Hedgehog'. The word could simply be combined references to the animal's preferred habitat (hedge) and its snuffling, somewhat porcine demeanour (hog). In informal parlance, 'hog' can of course mean 'greedy', which comedian Dan Antopolski used to his advantage with his winning joke at the 2009 Edinburgh Fringe festival. 'Hedgehogs,' he pondered, 'why can't they just share the hedge?'

The current spelling has been in existence since the 19th century, before which *hedghogge* and *heyghoge* were used. 'Hedge' is partly derived from Middle High German (spoken in southern Germany somewhere between the 11th and 15th centuries), where the word *hagen* meant 'thorn' – a potentially neat connection to the Hedgehog's spiny coat. These are not the only ideas in circulation. Some people consider that 'hog' may relate to the pork-like taste of the animal's flesh. Others profess that a newborn Hedgehog – bald and pink – looks

remarkably like a baby Wild Boar, from which domestic hogs are descended.

The name domain is textured further by monikers in former use. An antiquated word for Hedgehog is 'urchin'. Think of a spiny sea urchin and the name makes sense. Its origin is thought to lie in an old French word from Normandy, *herichon*, which has evolved into the present-day *hérisson*. Meanwhile, the Anglo Saxon name *il* or *igil* dates from the 9th century or earlier, and connects to the Dutch, German and Swedish sobriquets of (respectively) *egel*, *igel* and *igelkott*.

Local names also add colour. In Great Britain, the most common are 'furzepig' and 'hedgepig', but in East Anglia, Hedgehogs are called 'hodmedods' (meaning something that curls up). Celtic names – *crainneag* (Scottish Gaelic), *draenog* (Welsh) and *grainneog* (Irish), meaning 'horrible one' – collectively hint at yesteryear's pervading antipathy towards Hedgehogs (see page 85).

Below: Bald and pink, a newborn Hedgehog (left) recalls a baby Wild Boar (right); perhaps the reason for the word 'Hedgehog'?

Hedgehogs as friends

In 2007, to celebrate its 10th anniversary, the Environment Agency (a public body in England and Wales) polled the public on their best-loved environmental icon. The Hedgehog shuffled to the top, prompting an EA spokesperson to laud its aptness as an environmental icon, since it appears impregnable but in reality is 'vulnerable and fragile'.

Six years later, *BBC Wildlife* magazine invited its readers to adjudicate which wildlife icon deserved the title of the UK's 'national species'. Each of the 10 candidates – ranging from oaks to ladybirds – was championed by a relevant wildlife charity. It seems that the BHPS marshalled its troops effectively, as the Hedgehog gathered almost double the support of the second-placed Badger, collecting more than 42 per cent of votes cast. The magazine's features editor, Ben Hoare, sought to explain the Hedgehog's victory. He mused about the species' 'unique appearance, fascinating lifestyle and unthreatening nature' and – consciously succumbing to the temptation to anthropomorphise – also judged that the mammal's 'friendly' character was significant.

Finally – in case anyone remained in doubt as to the Hedgehog's pre-eminence in the public eye – the animal also scooped the title of 'favourite UK mammal' in a 2016 Royal Society of Biology vote. It could not be any more official: the UK loves Hedgehogs.

Below: The Hedgehog is an irrefutably popular species in the UK.

Caring for Hedgehogs

So great is our fondness for Hedgehogs that we willingly care for them when we sense they are suffering. In 2016, statistics published in the professional journal *Veterinary Record* suggested that the UK public takes an astonishing 31,000 Hedgehogs to vets every year. Even more remarkably, this figure excludes animals brought to the UK's 800 or so wildlife hospitals, the most famous of which is the Wildlife Hospital Trust, aka – a name that says it all – Tiggywinkles (see page 125). To this we can add those Hedgehogs cared for personally by a growing band of sympathetic volunteers.

The common aim of all these altruistic folk is to release fitter, more robust Hedgehogs back into the wild at the earliest sensible moment. But does all this rehabilitation effort work? The answer is unclear, as there have only been small-scale studies tracking released Hedgehogs. But the news seems quietly positive: in one study, around one-third of youngsters released after 'overwintering' survived at least 75 days after being set free. Although this may not seem a compelling success rate, had they not been cared for, none of those Hedgehogs would have survived.

Above: This Hedgehog with a broken leg is being bandaged by a veterinary nurse.

Right: A carer constructing an enclosure for an 'overwintering' Hedgehog.

Helping Hedgehogs in the wild

As well as caring for injured or weakened Hedgehogs, there is an army of individuals across the UK who help make the animals' lives easier. Thousands are 'Hedgehog Champions', whose achievements we have already lauded (see page 91). But there are also many more householders who do their bit out of sight by leaving out food and drink for 'their' Hedgehogs. Bread and cow's milk used to be the fare of choice, but experts such as the RSPB now advise against this, as Hedgehogs cannot digest these foods and end up with upset stomachs. A recent trend of offering mealworms is also counselled against, as it has been associated with physical deformities and bone weaknesses (known as metabolic bone disease). Current advice (see Resources, page 125) favours providing carefully balanced offerings, particularly formulated meals (such as those produced by Spike's World and Ark Wildlife), good-quality cat biscuits or 'wet' cat or dog food, and to accompany these with water. Other important recommendations are to remove uneaten food each morning (to avoid attracting other animals such as Foxes, rats and cats) and to refresh both food and water every evening.

Below: Hedgehogs benefit from supplementary feeding.

A Hedgehog carer's story

'The Hedgehog Street campaign inspired me to do what I can to help. In late October last year, I found a tiny young male Hedgehog, just 15cm (6in) long. I knew he was too small to make it through the winter without help, so I took him in. Meanwhile I had also regularly been providing a saucer of water for another youngster in a churchyard. When the first frost came, he was still too small to survive hibernation, so I took him home as well.

To keep the Hedgehogs "wild", I kept them outside in a safe "run", where they were protected from the elements, had ample food and water and, of course, a Hedgehog house in which to hibernate. Both animals weighed under 400g (14oz) when I started looking after them. By February, they were between 600g and 700g (21–25oz), a healthy size, and by the end of March, the duo were back in nature.'

Irina Scales

Above: In this garden, the shallow pond with sloping sides enables animals to climb in and out for a drink, and there are also plenty of opportunities for Hedgehogs to forage and take cover.

The gardener's friend

Quite distinct from all the kind folk who care for Hedgehogs, there is one group of people for whom Hedgehogs provide direct benefit: gardeners. By eating innumerable invertebrate 'pests' that might otherwise try a gardener's patience, the Hedgehog is unequivocally an ally for those who tend plants in their small fiefdom. For the gardener to profit, however, they need to do a few things to make life better for the spiny one. Leaving a part of the plot to go wild (not necessarily something that appeals to the garden-proud!) provides potential nesting habitat. Knocking a hog-sized hole in the fence enables unfettered entry and exit. Dangling chicken wire over any steep sides of a pond serves as a ladder to help bedraggled Hedgehogs clamber out. And not using pesticides ensures an ample supply of the invertebrate meals that attract Hedgehogs to the garden in the first place.

Right: A gardener enjoying a moment with a prickly visitor.

Making use of hedgehogs

As you might expect for a much-loved mammal, there are plenty of feel-good interactions between hedgehogs and humans. But there is also an unequivocally darker side to our relationship – and an ample grey area too.

Consuming hedgehogs

The dark side ends up with the hedgehog's demise. The most direct cause is consumption: eating hedgehog is common to several societies. In 16th-century Britain and France, West European Hedgehogs featured in feasts – and Roma Gypsies eat them even today (as British boxer Tyson Fury claimed, to widespread disgust, in 2016). Algerian Hedgehogs have been eaten in Mallorca since the 18th century, and White-breasted Hedgehogs and Desert Hedgehogs are consumed in Africa.

Above: The skin of a Madras Hedgehog (*Paraechinus nudiventris*) in Tamil Nadu, India, where hedgehog skins are hung up to ward off evil spirits.

Various species of hedgehog are said to have medicinal uses, although the effectiveness of these has not been exposed to rigorous scientific testing. Nevertheless, hedgehog fat and urine have been considered cures for rheumatism, ash from burnt spines has been judged to heal wounds, and the smoke from the burning to cure colds. In China, hedgehog skin is reputedly roasted and then ground into a powder that helps counter diarrhoea. The skin and spines of White-breasted Hedgehogs have been considered to boost fertility in Africa (move over, Viagra?). Somewhat more prosaically, the Romans used the dried prickly skins to comb and clean wool.

Selling hedgehogs

Or, should I say, using hedgehogs to sell things. Numerous advertisers have played on our fascination with hedgehogs to encourage us to buy their products. Some such goods are hedgehog-branded. Across the world, there are hedgehog crisps, wine, biscuits and beer. Hobsons Brewery in Shropshire produces a pale ale from which they 'make a donation of £50 for every brew to the British Hedgehog Preservation Society'; they have donated more than £40,000 since 2012. Admittedly, only the crisps

Above: Old Prickly 'hedge grog'.

Right: More cuddly than prickly, this little hog was given away to new junior RSPB members.

Above: Hedgehogs often feature on greetings cards, even if seasonally inappropriate.

manufacturer toyed with having a hoggy flavour (a claim that elicited a minor uproar and, indeed, a prosecution by trading standards authorities).

Stuffed hedgehog toys are a common feature of many a nursery, my daughter's included. The RSPB has given away such toys with junior memberships (see above), while the Wildlife Trusts (see page 125) reward children completing wildlife activities with a 'Wildlife Watch Hedgehog Award'. For adults as well as children, there are innumerable greeting cards featuring hedgehogs. Sadly these often pay little heed to natural history (such as evidently hibernation-shy hedgehogs on Christmas cards) or, less objectionably, involve wordplay (fancy 'hedgehugging', anyone?).

Other products simply play on behaviour we associate with hedgehogs. Two bleakly ironic television commercials played on the often-fatal relationship between hedgehogs and motor vehicles. Drivers of cars fitting Goodyear and Continental tyres managed to stop just before squashing a hedgehog. The cheekiest commercial, advertising cider, is a standout memory from my late teens and it flips the typical relationship between hedgehogs and vehicles on its head. An enormous hedgehog chuckles as it squashes cars flat as it speeds along a road. 'That makes a refreshing change,' quips the drinker.

Then there is the frankly bizarre. Outdoor-clothing manufacturer North Face offers a pair of mountain-worthy hiking shoes called Hedgehog, designed for trail running on tricky terrain. Exactly the type of habitat and behaviour that you wouldn't expect from a hedgehog. Meanwhile, an advert for an Icelandic bank featured a curled-up hedgehog. Again the message is unclear: might a charitable explanation be that the investor may sleep easy while the bank grows his or her investment?

Less demanding of interpretation is Black & Decker's hedge trimmer, called – you guessed it – the Hedge Hog. There is something disturbingly contradictory here too: a tool used to flail the nesting habitat of the animal that lends it its name. Considering the principal cause of hedgehog mortality is death by vehicle, there has been an even darker occasion of hedgehogs being used in advertising: in the 1990s, the British Government deployed cartoon hedgehogs to teach children how to cross the road.

Hedgehogs as pets

Although the hedgehog species that's the principal focus of this book (the West European Hedgehog) isn't subject to the pet trade, Four-toed and Algerian Hedgehogs have not been so fortunate. In the early 1990s, there was a craze for sharing one's home with these admittedly cute animals. Perhaps as many as 80,000 were shipped from Africa, almost entirely to the United States. Concern about foot-and-mouth disease ended the trade within a few years, but the fad had caught hold so breeders began creating their own hedgehog lineages to supply the burgeoning demand. To this day, there remain hedgehog shows in the US, with prickly competitors vying for supremacy in a series of categories. There are even hoggy 'Olympic Games', now rebranded as the International Hedgehog Olympic Gymboree, lest there be any confusion with the real Olympic Games! More recently, there has been increased demand within Europe (including the UK) for Four-toed Hedgehogs as pets. None of this is my cup of tea – nor, I suspect, yours.

THE TALE OF
MRS. TIGGY-WINKLE

BY
BEATRIX POTTER

F. WARNE & CO.

Hedgehogs in Culture

For centuries, people often treated hedgehogs with disdain, or worse. But universal attitudes began to change in the early 20th century. We now see hedgehog characters portrayed positively (or, at least, excitingly) in books and films, on stage and even on our computer screens. Fictional representations of hedgehogs now bring joy to our lives.

An influential hedgehog

It was the arrival of one particular literary character that overhauled the way we viewed the species. Step (or trundle) forwards, our most famous hedgehog.

The Tale of Mrs Tiggy-Winkle is a children's book published in 1905, written and illustrated by Beatrix Potter, a British writer of children's fiction who had a not-insubstantial sideline as a scientist and conservationist. Living in a tiny secluded cottage on a Lake District fell, Mrs Tiggy-Winkle – a hedgehog in a pinny – is a washerwoman who accepts help from a girl called Lucie to launder clothing for animals in the neighbourhood.

Lucie has such fun that it takes until the end of the day before she realises that Mrs Tiggy-Winkle is hedgehog rather than human. Had Lucie correctly identified the mammal at the outset, who knows where her prejudice might have taken her? Depicted as caring, industrious and sociable, Mrs Tiggy-Winkle single-handedly overhauled the way in which 20th-century Britain thought of hedgehogs. Hedgehog fans have a lot to thank Beatrix Potter for – something that the Royal Mint recognised when honouring the author and her fictional character by including Mrs Tiggy-Winkle's image on a 50 pence coin, issued in 2016.

Opposite: The most famous fictional hedgehog.

Below: One of a series of coins released by the Royal Mint to celebrate Beatrix Potter.

Above: Hedgehog from the waist up, Hans is the main character in a Brothers Grimm fairy tale.

Above: Hedgehogs are used as croquet balls in Lewis Carroll's *Alice's Adventures in Wonderland*.

Other fictional hedgehogs

While she is an undeniably influential character, Mrs Tiggy-Winkle was far from the first fictional hedgehog. *Hans My Hedgehog* is the name of a Brothers Grimm fairy tale published in 1819 about a baby boy who is a hedgehog from the waist up. He came into the world after his parents had problems conceiving, resulting in the father saying that he would be happy with a hedgehog for a child. Poor Hans could not sleep in a normal bed nor suckle milk from his mother on account of his prickles, and his father was glad when Hans eventually left home to seek his fortune. Hans' luck improved when a princess agreed to marry him. Her love enabled him to shed his hedgehog skin, leaving him fully human. This, in turn, prompted Hans – a form of prodigal son, it transpires – to return to his childhood home and resume contact with his father.

Fifty years later, Lewis Carroll wrote *Alice's Adventures in Wonderland*. This story features a famous game of croquet where flamingos serve as mallets and (unnamed and perhaps unloved) live hedgehogs as balls. Alice is amused that each time she comes to strike them, the hedgehogs regard her with a puzzled expression. As she bursts out laughing, the hedgehogs seize their opportunity and move away.

The following century, two young hedgehogs had a cameo in Kenneth Grahame's *The Wind in the Willows*, published in 1908. Disoriented in the snow, they chance upon the sett of Mr Badger, who invites them inside and serves them oatmeal porridge. Such kindness on the host's part could not be more different to real-world encounters between the two species (see page 78).

Over recent decades (and in contrast to their actual population status), hedgehogs appear to have become more common in children's fiction. In Colin Dann's *The Animals of Farthing Wood* series, several hedgehogs travel in a larger group of animals from the eponymous forest to White Deer Park. Sadly, two fail to cross a motorway successfully before reaching their destination. The remainder arrive safely, hibernate successfully and emerge, healthy, the following spring.

Left: Frances Broomfield's illustration for the cover of *Farthing Wood: The Adventure Begins*.

Celebrating ingenuity, individuality and courage, Dick King-Smith picks up on the theme of hedgehogs and roads in *The Hodgeheg*. Young hedgehog Victor Maximilian St George ('Max' for short) lives opposite a park where there are plenty of juicy slugs, worms and snails. Determined to make his way across the road to the park, Max's first attempt results in a nasty bump on the head, which muddles his speech (hence 'hodgeheg'). He perseveres though, and eventually reaches his bounty. Having solved a problem that has afflicted his family for generations, Max is fêted as a hero by hedgehogs the world over.

John Waddington-Feather was, like Dick King-Smith, a teacher-turned-author who enjoyed including hedgehogs in his books. He concocted an entire series that featured Quill Hedgehog and his gang of 'goodies', seeking to thwart the dastardly intentions of an alley cat called Mungo and his armies of rats. Their battles are a metaphor for the fight against environmental degradation, a theme inspired by the downside of rapid industrialisation during the 19th century in the author's home county of Yorkshire.

More recently, Rosie Wellesley has published *The Very Helpful Hedgehog*, a tale about a stubborn hedgehog called Isaac who likes living on his own. One day an apple falls from a tree and sticks onto the spines on his back (an old fable; see page 54). Try as he might, Isaac cannot remove it. Unexpectedly, a donkey comes to Isaac's assistance and the hedgehog learns that having friends is better than being on your own.

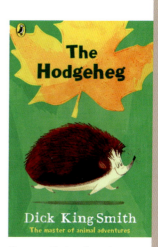

Above and below: Several children's books feature a hedgehog as their protagonist.

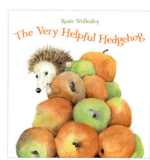

Above: Iain Webb as Mrs Tiggy-Winkle in the stage adaptation of the Royal Ballet film *The Tales of Beatrix Potter*.

Above: Mr Pricklepants, the thespian hog from *Toy Story 3*.

Hog stars of screen and stage

Mrs Tiggy-Winkle isn't confined to the pages of a book. In 1971, she was a character performed by British dancer and choreographer Frederick Ashton in the Royal Ballet film *The Tales of Beatrix Potter*. Anthony Dowell adapted the ballet for the stage two decades later. Mrs Tiggy-Winkle also starred in one of the stories in an animated BBC TV series called *The World of Peter Rabbit and Friends*, a collection of Beatrix Potter stories that was first aired in 1993.

Nor is Mrs Tiggy-Winkle the sole hedgehog to star on screen. Mr Pricklepants is an animated stuffed toy from the Disney/Pixar film *Toy Story 3*. Imbued with a considerable sense of self-worth, Mr Pricklepants – clad in Tyrolean hat and lederhosen – considers himself an actor, and treats his role as a child's toy as an art form. British actor (and former James Bond) Timothy Dalton voices him in the film.

Once Upon a Forest, a 1993 animation from 20th Century Fox, was less successful at the box office. It features a quartet of furry friends including Russell, a hedgehog. This is a film about friendship; one of the foursome – the badger – has been poisoned by people and the other three animals risk their lives (running the gauntlet of road traffic in the hedgehog's case) to find a cure for their companion.

The long-running Internet comic strip *Kevin and Kell* features a hedgehog as a significant character. In the comic strip's animal world known as Domain, hedgehog Lindesfarne Dewclaw is the adopted daughter of the protagonist, a rabbit named Kevin. Lindesfarne is initially unaware of her heritage and is pleased when she discovers that she is a hedgehog, as this means she can switch her 'schedule' to become nocturnal and therefore spend more time with her boyfriend Fenton, a bat.

Right: Lindesfarne Dewclaw, the hoggy star of comic strip *Kevin and Kell*, who is in love with a bat named Fenton.

So far, these fictional representations of hedgehogs have been positive (or, at worst, slightly comical) characters. However, a Polish creation – *Jez Jerzy* (George the Hedgehog) – heads in a different direction. A swearing, skateboarding anti-hero, Jez has a series of vices – from drink and drugs to promiscuity. His enemies include politicians and the police. Initially a satirical comic strip, a full-length feature film was released in 2011. Not one for children.

Cyber hedgehogs

Challenging the docile image of Mrs Tiggy-Winkle still further are three more hedgehogs with attitude. *Spikez* is a 2012 novel written by Richard Mayers and illustrated by John Burton. Clad in wraparound sunglasses, Spikez is half hedgehog, half machine. Inhabiting Greenacres, a world described by the author as '*Animal Farm* meets *The Matrix*', where technology has fused the human and natural worlds, Spikez's mission is to save the future of human- and animal-kind from malfunctional prototype cyborgs.

Better known worldwide is Sonic the Hedgehog. Originally a computer game released by Sega in 1991, the Sonic brand has evolved into comics, films, music and a TV series. Barely recognisable as a hedgehog, the blue-coloured Sonic speeds around the screen freeing other animals from the evil Dr Robotnik. Sonic's arch-rival is another hedgehog, this one clad in black and red, called Shadow. Is that Beatrix Potter I hear turning in her grave?

Above: Half hedgehog, half machine, Spikez is the protagonist of Richard Mayers' eponymous novel.

Below: Sega's famous mascot, Sonic the Hedgehog.

Left: The spiky mammal to which Sonic and Spikez owe a considerable vote of thanks.

How to See Hedgehogs

In many places, seeing a Hedgehog is worryingly straightforward. Drive for any length of time through the suburbs or countryside during spring, and you will surely see a spiky, tyre-flattened corpse or three. Seeing a live Hedgehog, however, is more difficult, and there is no doubt that Hedgehog numbers have plummeted. Nevertheless, seeing them need not be impossible, if you know when and where to look – and are prepared to forego a few hours' sleep.

Unlike for Badgers or Foxes, there's no easy solution to seeing Hedgehogs – nothing akin to waiting by a sett or den for the occupants to emerge. Nor are there any organised Hedgehog-watching excursions, as there are for Red Deer and Badgers. Hogs' unpredictable nightly perambulations don't help. So you're on your own. To up your chances, doing your research is worthwhile.

'Location, location, location' is as crucial for Hedgehogs as it is for people buying or selling houses. Your chances of seeing one will be far higher if you scour a leafy suburb or the scrubby fringe of a wood than if you take a nocturnal walk up a boggy mountain or through a concrete jungle. So first, refresh your memory of Hedgehogs' preferred habitat characteristics (see page 45). Second, as the word 'nocturnal' suggests, go out at night. There is little point in starting your search until daylight is but a memory. Third, the choice of month is critical. On balance, the best periods are shortly after Hedgehogs have emerged from hibernation, as they fatten up and seek mates (so April–May, in most of Great Britain) and the six or so weeks before they retire for the winter (August–September).

Opposite: A little detective work can be rewarded with a prime view of a Hedgehog.

Right: Most Hedgehog
encounters are at night, as befits
a nocturnal animal.

Above: Discovering a poo like this
is a sure sign that Hedgehogs live
in the vicinity.

Hedgehog hints

To check whether Hedgehogs are in the area you have
identified, look for clues that betray their presence.
While these are not as obvious as they are, say, for a
Badger (whose setts and 'badgerway' thoroughfares are
typically prominent in the landscape) or a Fox (with their
ostentatiously located poos), the hoggy hints that follow
will be handy in focusing your search.

Sad to say it, but the primary clue is a squashed
Hedgehog on the roadside. Where there lies a corpse,
there are likely to be live animals nearby. Next, look for
Hedgehog droppings. These are often in open areas, and
particularly stand out on the cropped grass of lawns, parks
and road verges. A typical poo (and there usually is only
one) is black, dry and wrinkled, about the length of your
little finger, and typically tapers to one end. Close up, you
may be able to discern fragments of chitin, which makes up
the hard external skeleton of beetles and the like. Unlike Fox
faeces, the Hedgehog's waste doesn't smell. As Hedgehogs
don't use it as a territorial marker, it's unlikely to crest a rock
or other 'landmark'.

In muddy ground, particularly after rain, you may
chance upon Hedgehog footprints. Both sets of feet have
five toes, although often only four toes are visible. The front
feet are wider than they are long, with the tracks looking
surprisingly like a child's hands. The back feet are slimmer
and longer, and leave correspondingly narrower tracks.

Left: Checking muddy ground for telltale footprints is a good way to determine whether hogs are around.

A final indication of the presence of a Hedgehog is its nest (see page 64). Given how frequently Hedgehogs build new temporary lairs, hedgerows and thickets should be thronged with them. Careful searching of suitable locations may reveal a suspiciously compact dome of grass, secreted below tangled vegetation.

Time for a (night)walk

Once you've used your understanding of Hedgehog ecology to pinpoint a suitable area and have confirmed this with direct evidence that they reside nearby, it's time to search for the real live animal. Wait until dusk has turned the visibility smoky, then head out. Take a modest torch with you; there's no need for one boasting a thousand lumens and, in any case, you don't want to blind any hedgehog that you do find. (A torch fitted with a red filter neatly gets around this problem.) Walk suitable areas, particularly at the boundary between habitats: woodland edges, a hedgerow next to a weedy field or a scrubby part of a meadow. And, every so often, stop to listen.

Hedgehogs are noisy animals, rustling as they move through vegetation and continuously snuffling as they forage. In the otherwise quiet of the night, they make quite a racket. Once you hear them, the best thing to do is to wait quietly at the edge of cover. At some point, the Hedgehog is likely to emerge and scuttle across to its next feeding area – giving you views at point-blank range. Brilliant!

Below: Using a torch with a red filter minimises disturbance to nocturnal wildlife.

Above: Providing suitable food may enable you to watch Hedgehogs without the need to leave home.

Letting Hedgehogs find you

There is an alternative to actively searching, of course: encourage the Hedgehogs to come to you. If you live in a suitable area for Hedgehogs or know someone who does, you can put out appropriate food and water (see page 103) for the animals each evening. It may take a few days (or longer) for the local Hedgehogs to sniff their way towards your offerings, but once they understand that they're a nightly occurrence, they will be back. If the food you provide each night disappears, stay up and watch (or rig up an inexpensive trail camera to do the work for you).

You can increase your chances of seeing a Hedgehog close to home by gardening in a Hedgehog-friendly fashion; or, rather, by *not* gardening. The less kempt your plot, the better it is for Hedgehogs, because there will be more places for them to rest up and more invertebrates to munch.

Leaving clumps of leaves to decay will attract slugs, and slugs will entice hogs. Similarly, piles of logs and stones are the perfect habitat for a rummaging hog. Choosing not to use chemicals will increase invertebrate numbers and variety. An unkempt hedge is more likely to provide a Hedgehog with shelter than one that's trimmed to within an inch of its life to keep up with the Joneses. Choose native plant species that are attractive to a range of insects. Let one area grow entirely wild – and add to it with prunings. Mulch borders with garden compost

Above: The 'messier' your garden, the more likely it is to be attractive to Hedgehogs.

to encourage earthworms. A purpose-built 'Hedgehog house' is no bad addition either (see below). Gaps in your fences serve as Hedgehog entry and exit points: the more gardens that have them in your neighbourhood, the greater the area that Hedgehogs can roam. And the more householders can delight. Given that Hedgehogs change their nest regularly, particularly in summer, you might wonder whether it's worth building and installing a Hedgehog house in your garden. According to those behind the Hedgehog Street campaign, the answer is unequivocally 'yes'. The best way, they say, to get a resident Hedgehog on your property is to offer a robust, weather-proof shelter that lasts indefinitely. The Hedgehog may change the internal bedding but is likely to use the house for extended periods, particularly over winter.

Left: Adding a purpose-built Hedgehog house to your garden increases the chances of the animals staying around.

The study of Hedgehogs

Hedgehogs are quite the paradox: reassuringly familiar yet rarely seen. So spare a thought for Hedgehog researchers whose working life depends on doing much more than merely glimpsing the animal: they need to observe it, survey it and understand it. Their success over recent decades is manifest throughout this book: pretty much every fact presented I garnered from biologists' labours of love. But how do you go about studying an elusive, nocturnal, unsociable mammal that has neither fixed abode nor a predictable nightly routine?

Pat Morris is one of the pioneers of Hedgehog research. Before the 1960s, he recalls, next to nobody was working on the wild animals. The body of knowledge about the species' natural (as opposed to captive) behaviour was scant. Morris's work set the ball rolling, with the mantle subsequently taken up by Nigel Reeve, Hugh Warwick, Amy Haigh and a growing band of researchers spread across several European countries.

Below: Scientists such as Nigel Reeve use individual identification marks, like those visible on the Hedgehog below, as one of several methods of studying Hedgehogs.

Unravelling Hedgehog secrets has demanded that scientists studying the animals use increasingly inventive survey techniques. At the outset, animals were caught and sploshed or sprayed with coloured paint on a small area of their spines. This method enabled individual recognition for as long as the colour lasted (up to six months), so the movements of known animals could be plotted and their respective behaviours recorded. But it didn't make encountering the marked animals any more straightforward: they either had to be found by torchlight in the field or temporarily caught in baited traps.

When technology advanced, radio-tracking became the method of choice. Once individuals were fitted with a radio transmitter (glued to the spines, as collars are impractical due to Hedgehogs' cylindrical form), they could be followed without needing to be seen. One step up the tech spectrum is a GPS backpack, which pinpoints the wearer's whereabouts 24 hours a day.

Lower-tech, but much more accessible to the masses, are footprint tunnels. These are long, plastic triangles that contain a removable 'tracking plate', which includes two 'ink' strips, an area for bait and sheets of paper to record footprints. Researchers place the structures along a hedgerow or other suitable 'Hedgehog alley'. Bait attracts the Hedgehog, which leaves witness of its presence through its prints.

Footprint tunnels are commercially available, but they are also easy to make at home (see Resources, page 125), which means that anyone, should they wish, can become a Hedgehog scientist. Even without access to a footprint tunnel, you can help conservationists understand what's going on with Hedgehogs. In Great Britain, several citizen-science initiatives are contributing immensely valuable data that has formed the bedrock of the regular reports on *The State of Britain's Hedgehogs* (commissioned by the BHPS and PTES). Take part in the Breeding Bird Survey (run by the British Trust for Ornithology), the Big Garden Birdwatch (run each January by the RSPB), Hedgehog Watch (The Mammal Society) or the Mammals on Roads and Living with Mammals surveys (both organised by the PTES) and you can help unravel what is happening to our beloved hogs – and what we can do to help.

Above and left: Footprint tunnels are a cheap, convenient way to confirm the presence of Hedgehogs.

An evening in the company of Hedgehogs

As I walk through the churchyard at the segue between day and night, Blackbirds bicker before bedtime, and small bats emerge from nooks and crannies. I cross the road to the park – an expanse of rolling grassland hemmed by a chalk stream, with copses, hedgerows, shrubbery and skeletons of ancient oaks. Above this habitat mosaic sits a university campus, a source of orange lights pockmarking the thickening obscurity.

The evening is warm. A Noctule Bat careers across a blushing sky. Rabbits flee at my approach. A Jackdaw hurries, late for bed. A Little Owl yelps close by but remains unseen. So too a shrieking shrew, deep in the undergrowth. Moles give notice of their presence solely through earthy pimples. A young Tawny Owl makes hoarse demands for a meal.

The light fades. I am now reliant on squinting through the corners of my retinas, where rod cells predominate, to make visual sense of this world still. Just as night passes the point of no return, my ears direct me towards scuffling in the undergrowth. Somewhere beneath the crossfire of brambles, a mammal is moving. Too large for a shrew, too clumsy for a Rabbit, not tank-like enough for a Badger.

I quieten and wait. And wait some more. Then my patience is rewarded. Grass stems part, and a twitching nose pokes out. Bimbling forwards, the Hedgehog emerges, sniffs some more, then trots past me – apparently oblivious to my presence. I stay still, stay quiet. Thirty seconds later, undergrowth bedlam resumes. A second Hedgehog emerges in the same place, sniffs and scuttles past me in the direction of the first, but with seemingly more intent.

I follow the second Hedgehog until it catches up with the first. Much huffing and puffing and snorting and sneezing ensues. I realise that I have chanced upon an encounter between a male and female. The first animal – the female, I assume – seems irritated by the other's attention. She canters ahead of him, never allowing him to approach to within a foot. They weave through long grass and over short turf, snuffling and chuckling away.

I follow them for 20 minutes until the male gives up. The female goes one way, he another. Both disappear into the nocturnal ink. Gone.

I return to my car, smiling, and drive home, through the suburbs. Just shy of my driveway, a familiar form bristles along the pavement. It's the first time I have seen 'my' neighbourhood Hedgehog this year. I park the car, open the garden gate and smile some more.

Glossary

aestivation   The summer equivalent of 'hibernation' (see below), in which animals conserve energy by shutting their bodies down in hot weather.

carnivore   An animal that feeds on other animals.

chitin   The tough, main component of the hard external skeleton ('exoskeleton') of some invertebrates, such as beetles.

competition   The interaction between two animal species (such as Hedgehog and Badger) for the same environmental resource (such as food).

dispersal   The movement of animals away from the site of their birthplace to become established elsewhere.

genus   The taxonomic level above species and below family and subfamily; the genus forms the first word in a species' scientific name, for example *Erinaceus* europaeus.

hibernation   A state of inactivity characterised by low body temperature, heart rate, breathing and metabolic rate.

insectivore   An animal that feeds on insects, worms and other invertebrates.

invertebrate   An animal lacking a backbone, such as an insect or mollusc.

moult   The process of an animal shedding its external body covering – feathers, hair or skin – to make way for new growth.

nocturnal   Done, occurring or active at night.

omnivore   An animal that eats a variety of food of both plant and animal origin.

predation   The killing and consumption of one animal by another.

predator   An animal that naturally preys on other animals.

prey   Living animals that predators catch, kill and eat.

self-anointing   An unusual hedgehog behaviour that involves the animal licking a foamy substance over its spines.

territory   An area defended by an animal or group of animals against others of the same sex or species.

torpor   A state of reduced activity during which animals save energy.

vermin   Species that are believed to be harmful to crops, farm animals or game, or which carry disease, and which are therefore sometimes legally allowed to be killed.

Acknowledgements

At Bloomsbury Wildlife, Julie Bailey kindly encouraged me to propose this book for the Spotlight series, Katy Roper managed the editorial process, Molly Arnold coordinated picture research, and Louise Morris was the copy editor. Dave Andrews, Mike Hoit, Dougal McNeill, Rich Moores, Ian Robinson and Will Soar helped me observe Hedgehogs in Norfolk. Irina Scales introduced me to the two Hedgehogs that she cared for one winter and permitted me to interview her. Ali North of Suffolk Wildlife Trust kindly talked to me about her role as Ipswich Hedgehog Officer. Henry Johnson of the People's Trust for Endangered Species updated me on the Hedgehog Street campaign. Simon Thompson clarified how Warwickshire Wildlife Trust had created the UK's first Hedgehog Improvement Area. Ben Hoare advised on the *BBC Wildlife* magazine survey. Mark Davison and Joe Tobias kindly tipped me off about specific issues. Emma Brookman (RSPB) commented on the text and Lisa Morris was the proofreader. My wife Sharon and hoglet Maya supported and inspired me throughout the period I spent writing this book.

Further Reading

Couzens, Dominic, Swash, Andy, Still, Robert and Dunn, Jon. 2017. *Britain's Mammals: a Field Guide to the Mammals of Britain and Ireland*. Princeton University Press, Woodstock.

Harris, Stephen and Yalden, Derek. eds. 2008. *Mammals of the British Isles: Handbook, 4th edition*. The Mammal Society, Southampton.

Johnson, Henry. 2015. *Conservation Strategy for West-European Hedgehog (*Erinaceus europaeus*) in the United Kingdom (2015–2025)*. People's Trust for Endangered Species and British Hedgehog Preservation Society, www.ptes.org/wp-content/uploads/2015/11/ Conservation-strategy-for-the-hedgehog-in-the-UK-2015-2025.pdf

Morris, Pat. 2014. *Hedgehogs*. Whittet Books, Stansted.

Reeve, Nigel. 1994. *Hedgehogs*. T & A D Poyser, London.

Warwick, Hugh. 2010. *A Prickly Affair: the Charm of the Hedgehog*. Penguin, London.

Warwick, Hugh. 2014. *Hedgehog*. Reaktion Books Ltd, London.

Wilson, Emily and Wembridge, David. 2018. *The State of Britain's Hedgehogs 2018*. People's Trust for Endangered Species and British Hedgehog Preservation Society, https:// www.hedgehogstreet.org/wp-content/uploads/2018/02/SoBH-2018_final.pdf

Resources

Hedgehog Street www.hedgehogstreet.org
The website of the Hedgehog Champion campaign; has advice on including Hedgehog-friendly garden features, making Hedgehog houses, creating Hedgehog highways and feeding Hedgehogs.

Ipswich Hedgehog Project www.suffolkwildlifetrust.org/node/16935
How a network of Hedgehog-friendly streets is being created in the Suffolk town.

People's Trust for Endangered Species (PTES) www.ptes.org
The place for information on the status of Hedgehogs in the UK, and how to use a footprint tunnel to monitor presence/absence in your area.

The British Hedgehog Preservation Society (BHPS) www.britishhedgehogs.org.uk
Advice on what to do if you find a Hedgehog, as well as various leaflets and posters with information about helping Hedgehogs.

The Mammal Society www.mammal.org.uk
How to get involved in the annual Hedgehog Watch survey.

The RSPB www.rspb.org.uk
Advice on how to 'give a hog a home' in your garden. Food and houses suitable for Hedgehogs can be bought online from the RSPB shop.

The Wildlife Trusts www.wildlifetrusts.org/hedgehogs
How Wildlife Trusts are supporting Hedgehogs, and what you can to do help.

Tiggywinkles www.sttiggywinkles.org.uk
Advice on all aspects of helping Hedgehogs from the famous wildlife hospital.

Image Credits

Bloomsbury Publishing would like to thank the following for providing images and for permission to reproduce copyright material. While every effort has been made to trace and acknowledge all copyright holders, we would like to apologise for any errors or omissions and invite readers to inform us so that corrections can be made in any future editions of the book.

Key t = top; l = left; r = right; tl = top left; tc = top centre; tr = top right; cl = centre left; c = centre; cr = centre right; b = bottom; bl = bottom left; br = bottom right

AL = Alamy Stock Photo; FL = FLPA; G = Getty Images; NPL = Nature Picture Library; RS = RSPB Images; SH = Shutterstock

Front cover t Ben Andrew/RS, b Ullstein Bild/G; **spine** Ben Andrew/RS; **back cover** t David Tipling/birdphoto.co.uk, b Andrew Mason/RS; **1** Laurie Campbell; **3** Rob Kemp/SH; **4** Erni/SH; **5** FL/Andrew Mason/G; **6** t Georgios Kollidas/SH, bl Rudmer Zwerver/SH, br Mirko Graul/SH; **7** t Jarrod Calati/SH, b Teekayu/SH; **8** J. Lipták/University of Tübingen (source: Conard, N.J., Malina, M. and Verrept, T. 2009. Weitere Belege für eiszeitliche Kunst und Musik aus den Nachgrabungen 2008 am Vogelherd bei Niederstotzingen-Stetten ob Lontal, Kreis Heidenheim. *Archäologische Ausgrabungen in Baden-Württemberg* 2008: 23–26); **9** t Mirko Graul/SH, b Sainam51/SH, tl IrinaK/SH, tr, cl, br Neil Bowman, cr Richard Reading; **11** Luis Casiano/Biosphoto/FL; **12** t Ashish & Shanthi Chandola/NPL, c Nigel Reeve, b Neil Bowman; **13** D. Pimborough/SH; **14** tl Barrie Watts/G, tr, bl Rudmer Zwerver/SH, br Erni/SH; **15** tl Erhard Nerger/G, tr Carmen Rieb/SH, b Daniel Heuclin/NPL; **16** t Imfoto/SH, b Colin Robert Varndell/SH; **17** Neil Duggan/SH; **18** Jack Perks/RS; **19** t Photo-SD/SH, b Akaraya/SH; **20** Ben Andrew/RS; **21** Cieciera Pawel/SH; **22** tl James Lowen, tr Colin Robert Varndell/SH, c Olga Vasilyeva/SH, b IriskaV/SH; **23** tr Alderney Wildlife Trust, cr Coatesy/SH, br Les Stocker/AL, b James Lowen; **24** t James Lowen, c Ian Redding/SH, b Eric Isselee/SH; **25** tl Steve Simmons/SH, tr Colin Robert Varndell/SH, cl, b James Lowen, cr Ben Andrew/RS; **26** t James Lowen, b Alick Simmons; **27** t James Lowen, b Mark Bridger/SH; **28** l Kefca/SH, r James Lowen; **29** t Tim Melling, b Victoria Hillman/SH; **30** t Sandra Standbridge/SH, b Ben Andrew/RS; **31** t James Lowen, bl Klein & Hubert/NPL, br Tchara/SH; **32** Ben Andrew/RS; **33** t Ben Andrew/RS, b Colin Robert Varndell/SH; **34** Nature Photographers Ltd/AL; **35** Mike Lane/RS; **36** Jane Burton/NPL; **37** Sandor Gora/SH; **38** t Yuri Shibnev/NPL, b Les Stocker/G; **39** t Vladimir Medvedev/NPL, b tbkmedia.de/AL; **40** Andrew Cooper/NPL; **41** t Mark Taylor/NPL, b Nature Photographers Ltd/AL; **42** Rob Kemp/SH; **43** t Kay Roxby/SH, b Roland Seitre/NPL; **44** Colin Robert Varndell/SH; **45** t Dmitry Naumov/SH, b Meirion Matthias/SH; **46** Nigel Reeve; **47** Erni/SH; **48** t Erni/SH, c Imran's Photography/SH, b CreativeMedia.org.uk/SH; **49** Oxford Scientific/G; **50** t Martin Fowler/SH, c Ian Redding/SH, b Mark Hamblin/G; **51** t BSIP/G, b Rich Astbury/SH; **52** t James Lowen, b Erni/SH; **53** t Garmoncheg/SH, bl Photos/iStock, br Nick Upton/RS; **54** tl smereka/SH, tr LianeM/SH, b Paul Hobson/NPL; **55** Ben Andrew/RS; **56** Gertjan Hooijer/SH; **57** t Jane Burton/NPL, b Dan Bagur/SH; **58** Oksana Golubeva/SH; **59** t Ann & Steve Toon/NPL, b James Lowen; **60** l James Lowen, r Andrew M. Allport/SH; **61** Helen Hotson/SH; **62** David T. Grewcock/FL; **63** t Photo-SD/SH, b Sergei Proshchenko/SH; **64** Coatesy/SH; **65** Dieter Hopf/G; **66** Paul Hobson/FL; **67** Alick Simmons; **68** Vasiliy Vishnevskiy/AL; **69** Andrew Thomas/G; **70** t Ben Andrew/RS, b James Lowen; **71** t Roma Chayka/SH, b Andrew Thomas/G; **72** t Arterra/G, c Les Stocker/G, b Deborah Cardinal/G; **73** t Jane Burton/NPL, c Erni/SH, b Ben Andrew/RS; **74** Oxford Scientific/Photolibrary/G; **75** Erni/SH; **76** t Frederic Desmette/Biosphoto/FL, b Imran Ashraf/SH; **77** t Colin Robert Varndell/SH, b Angie Davidson/Hedgehog Street; **78** t Pauline and John Grimshaw/Flickr, bl Rob Kemp/SH, br BSIP/G; **79** Alex Hyde/NPL; **80** James Lowen; **81** Martin Woike, NiS/Minden Pictures/FL; **82** Neil Mitchell/SH; **83** tr Monkey Business Images/SH, cr Jax10289/SH, bl Christian Mueller/SH, br Sebastien Coell/SH; **84** t Christopher Elwell/SH, c Dan Bagur/SH, b Les Stocker/G; **85** Popperfoto/G; **86** Nigel Voaden/Flickr; **87** Coatesy/SH; **88** t Art Konovalov/SH, b Kevin Sawford/RS; **89** Matthew Dixon/SH; **90** Deborah Wright; **91** t Pam Lovesay/Hedgehog Street, b Hedgehog Street; **92** John Ferguson/Suffolk Wildlife Trust; **93** t Orkney.com, b Martin Fowler/SH; **94** t Martin Fowler/SH, b Sandra Standbridge/SH; **95** David Woodfall/RS; **96** Les Stocker/G; **97** Erni/SH; **98** t shootmybusiness/SH, b SuperStock/G; **99** Pen and Sword Books/G; **100** l Les Stocker/G, r Thorsten Grohse/SH; **101** Ben Andrew/RS; **102** l Les Stocker/G, r James Lowen; **103** t Jenny Hibbert/RS, b James Lowen; **104** t Eleanor Bentall/RS, b James Lowen; **105** t Brawin Kuman and Vincent Nijman (source: Kumar, B. and Nijman, V. 2016. Medicinal uses and trade of Madras Hedgehogs *Paraechinus nudiventris* in Tamil Nadu, India. *Traffic Bulletin* 28: 7–10), b Hobsons Brewery; **106** t RS, b ©cupofsnowflakes/G; **107** Erich Schmidt/G; **108** Paul Fearn/AL; **109** Charles Dawson/Flickr; **110** t Chronicle/AL, b Culture Club/G; **111** t Frances Broomfield, from *Farthing Wood: The Adventure Begins* by Colin Dann, published by Hutchinson (RHCP). Reproduced by permission of The Random House Group Ltd. © 1994, c from *The Hodgeheg* by Dick King-Smith, published by Hamish Hamilton. Reproduced by permission of Penguin Books Ltd. © 1987, b from *The Very Helpful Hedgehog* by Rosie Wellesley. Reproduced by permission of Pavilion Children's Books © 2012; **112** t Robbie Jack/G, c Nicescene/SH, b Bill Holbrook; **113** t John Burton, from *Spikez* by Richard Anthony Mayers. Reproduced by permission of Burton Mayers Books © 2012, c Betto Rodrigues/SH, b Ben Andrew/RS; **114** James Lowen; **116** t Ben Andrew/RS, b James Lowen; **117** t Tony Hamblin/FL, b James Lowen; **118** Les Stocker/G; **119** t Rob Kemp/SH, b RS; **120** Nigel Reeve; **121** l E. Thomas, r Richard Yarnell/Nottingham Trent University; **122** Les Stocker/G; **123** Ben Andrew/RS.

Index